"Miss Campbell—"

"Christy," she whispered, and trembled with nerves at her audacity. "I'm doing this for your own protection, you know. *Someone* needs to stay with you tonight. Just to make sure you're safe, of course."

In spite of himself, his lips twitched. "And who's to make sure I'm safe from you?"

"Do you really want to be?"

For a long moment he remained silent, gazing at her. At last, he said: "What I want and what is right are vastly different things."

"James, it's not like this at *all* where I come from. I haven't been brought up with these ridiculous constraints. The rules of your time just don't apply to me, so don't judge me—or us—by them."

His fingers brushed across her curls. "You are under my protection. I cannot take advantage of you."

"I'm over the age of consent and capable of making my own decisions."

"And apparently mine, as well." A gleam lit the depths of his dark eyes, and he pulled her to him.

His mouth brushed across her cheek, then found her lips . . .

A Christmas Keepsake

Janice Bennett

ZEBRA BOOKS
KENSINGTON PUBLISHING CORP.

For Rob and Matt

ZEBRA BOOKS

are published by

Kensington Publishing Corp.
475 Park Avenue South
New York, NY 10016

Second printing: November, 1991

Printed in the United States of America

Chapter One

The typeset letters on the book's page blurred. Their lines paled, then twisted as their shapes shifted to form new words and sentences. After a moment, they phased back to their original position.

Christina Campbell's knees buckled. She sank onto the edge of the hotel's bed and with a shaking hand shoved the thick dark mass of curls from her face. She glared at the yellowed page before her, blue eyes unblinking. "All right, I *dare* you to try that again," she said.

The text did, repeating its weird metamorphosis.

"You didn't have to take me up on it!" She closed her eyes for a moment, then with deliberation, she took off her reading glasses, rubbed the lenses with a tissue, then settled the round tortoise shell frames once more on her upturned nose. Her eyesight wasn't *that* bad. As she watched, the letters began their unsettling transformation again.

"Right," she muttered. Using a finger to mark her place, she flipped back to the title page. *Life in London: A Different Perspective* she read, then the second part shimmered, and *An Account of the Recent Riots and the Events Leading to Them* appeared, only to fade again.

She dropped the book as if it burned her and scooted toward the pillows, as far from that crazy volume as she could get. She kept her wide-eyed gaze locked on it. Slowly, she drew her stockinged legs under her and hugged herself. If it moved . . .

It didn't. After a long minute, she forced herself to pick it up once more. The title shimmered, and she looked away, focusing instead on the next line which detailed the author and date. James Edward Holborn, 1811. For that, at least, the typeface remained solid.

She eased her way back through the book, glaring at each page in challenge, waiting for the print to do anything strange. It didn't. The passages remained just as they had been written, almost two hundred years before.

She turned another page and stopped; the lines near the bottom shimmered. *"House party"* she read one moment, *"bloody rioting"* the next. Other words shifted about them, refusing to come into focus.

Christy laid the book on the bedspread, propped the pillows behind her, and leaned back against them. Her glasses were fine. The hotel room provided sufficient steady light. That meant the problem lay with her. Jet lag, she supposed. An eight-hour difference stood between San Francisco and London time. It was no wonder she was going cross-eyed.

Absently, she scooped a couple of chocolate chips from their pile on the nightstand and popped them into her mouth. If her eyes were tired, why didn't *all* the words shift?

They should. An eerie, prickling sensation crept up her spine and danced along her flesh. She sat up and studied the book again. No, the beginning didn't change, only the last forty pages. In her seven years as a rare book dealer, this was the rarest book she'd ever come across. Lines blurred by age and foxing she had encountered before. Lines that blurred themselves were a new one on her.

She leaned over the edge of the bed and sorted through the box of books and printed documents she had purchased as a lot that morning at Sotheby's. Plastic sheets encased the regent's letter, which she had flown halfway around the world to buy. The rest which had been thrown in she had thought a bonus—until now.

That letter! Her heart lurched, and she rummaged through her collection again, frantic. She'd paid a fortune for it. If something was wrong with *everything* in this box, damage to the ink, perhaps . . .

The spidery hand of Prince George remained firm and clear. Just to be sure, she deciphered the contents, written to a Sir Dominic Kaye, requesting the man's assistance in passing the regency bill. Everything all right. She breathed a heartfelt sigh of relief, and picked up another letter. It, too, appeared unharmed. Nor did any of the other books display this weird phenomenon. She turned once more to the latter half of *Life in London,* and shivered as the words transformed before her eyes.

The line *"Several highly placed members of government circles"* shimmered, then took new shape as ". . . *inhabitants of the rookeries and back alleys, long denied* . . ." The next moment, the original words returned. Christy's fingers tightened, and her gaze settled on the next line. The phrase ". . . *unspeakable horrors, after the manner of their brethren in France,"* hovered briefly on the page, then faded to ". . . *dining upon the delights of this festive season."*

Her hands trembling, Christy turned the page. For one moment, the words *"blood bath"* stood out with startling clarity, then faded into a hopeless blur.

She closed the thin volume, and her hands clenched the aged leather cover. She'd seen those "choose-your-own-ending" books, but this was ridiculous. In those, it was a simple matter of turning to the correct page number for an alternate version. The ending didn't rewrite itself while the reader watched! Either she'd stumbled across the strangest case of disappearing ink imaginable, or . . .

Or what?

She rolled across the large bed and grabbed the phone, then punched the number for the hotel desk. Four more chocolate chips disappeared one at a time from the oak nightstand before the operator's voice came over the line.

"Is there a Mrs. Amanda Trent staying here?" Christy asked, and relief flooded through her at the affirmative. "Could you connect me with her room?"

Again the wait, then a brisk, welcomingly familiar voice said: "Hello?"

"Amanda? It's Christy Campbell."

"Calling to gloat over the Regent's letter, are you? Well, at least you got it instead of old Wumpus Face. Did you see him turn purple when you topped his last bid?"

"I did. Look—"

"Then when I got the *Ivanhoe,* I thought he'd have a stroke. Hot damn, what a morning. Haven't had so much fun in weeks. So what's up with you?"

"I've got a problem, I was hoping you could help me."

"Not the letter!"

"No, a book, a social commentary of about the same period. It came in the lot with it. Look, would you mind if I bring it by? I'd like you to take a look at it."

"Love to. But I warn you, I won't be impressed by anything less than a juicy scandal."

"Oh, I think you'll find this one fascinating."

"Good. I'll pull out a couple of beers and be waiting for you."

"Better not." Christy glanced at the book in her hands. "There're enough pink elephants dancing around, already."

A hearty chuckle came over the line. "Sounds like you've been celebrating. Well, don't keep me in suspense."

Christy hung up, straightened her navy wool skirt, shoved her feet into her pumps and picked up the book with care. If anyone could get to the bottom of this, it would be Amanda Trent.

Five minutes later, she got off the elevator three floors up and strode down the cream-carpeted hall, past the dieffenbachia trees and pothos in brass pots which filled every alcove. She turned the corner and found Mrs. Trent's room.

The door flung wide as soon as she knocked, and Amanda Trent, her considerable bulk enveloped in a purple paisley muumuu, waved her inside. She leaned out into the hall, peering over her thick black-rimmed glasses, and ran a hand through her blunt-cut grizzled hair. "Aw, where're the elephants? I thought you'd bring them with you."

"In here." Christy held up the book. She entered the elegant room, a mirror-image of her own.

Amanda chuckled again. "Well, don't look so solemn. I'm in the mood for a spot of pink game hunting. What's the problem?"

"I'm hoping you can tell me." Christy hesitated. "Look, you've got more experience in this business than anyone I know. Will you read Chapter Ten, then tell me what it says?"

Amanda's grin never faded, but the gleam in her gray eyes sharpened. She took the leather-bound volume and studied the cover. "Holborn. Never heard of him. A social commentary, you said?"

Christy nodded, then clasped her hands behind her back and paced to the window overlooking Piccadilly. "I was glancing through it earlier to check its condition, then started reading. It's really good, for what it is. Entertaining, not the usual sort of preaching you get from that kind of book at that time."

"Chapter Ten?" Amanda eased her bulk into a padded wing-back chair and deposited her bare feet on the footstool. After switching on the light on the occasional table at her side, she went to work.

Silence reigned behind Christy, and she stared hard at the traffic wending its slow way past, so many stories below. Maybe she just needed sleep. Maybe she'd been studying too many manuscripts and damaged editions. Maybe she needed a break from her work. She'd been going at it hard since Ryan found a new interest in life. That the interest had been a six-foot Nordic blonde, while Christy was a mere five-foot brunette, had done little for her self-esteem. At least she learned her lesson. Never again would she get involved in more than a business relationship with a client. Rare books were far more dependable than men—or so she'd thought until a few minutes ago.

A hoot of laughter escaped Amanda, and Christy spun about to face her. "Did you find something?"

"Just a turn of phrase. God, I love it! Is the whole book this good?"

Christy chose her words with care. "The parts I could read were well done."

"Why haven't I ever heard of him before? Hot damn, I love finding a funny writer. I wonder what else he wrote?"

Christy searched the older woman's face for any trace of concern, her hopes rising. Amanda had a strong streak of common sense. Maybe she already had the explanation. "Have you noticed anything odd about it?"

"Only the way Holborn mixes with the government stuffed shirts and still keeps his perspective." She pulled off her glasses and rubbed the reddened bridge of her nose. "God, I hate crusading bores. I wish more of them took this approach."

Christy crossed to a chair opposite Amanda and perched on its edge. "What is that chapter about?"

"A Christmas house party. Each of the guests is out to further his own interests instead of celebrating the season. Does that sum it up?"

"I don't know." Christy bit her lip, then raised worried eyes to her friend. "I can't read it. Aren't you having trouble with the print shifting?"

Amanda Trent stared at her blankly, then studied the pages. "Nope. Need a new glasses prescription?"

"I'm not having the problem with anything else. Only this book, from Chapter Ten, on."

"Uh-huh." Amanda nodded wisely. "Was that when you started celebrating?"

"I haven't had a drink. And no, I don't do any of that funny stuff, so stop looking at me like that. Don't you see anything in there about a revolution? Or a blood bath?"

"Could be in another chapter. I only read Ten, you know."

"No, it was right here, on the first couple of pages." Christy took the volume back from her. "There, it's doing it again, can't you see the words changing? Now it says something about riots, it's so clear—no, it's fading. It's back to the house party. Did you see?" She looked up to find Amanda regarding her with a frown.

"Someone's been slipping you Mickey Finns, girl." Amanda

10

waggled a finger under her nose. "You go back to your room and sleep it off."

Christy shook her head. "I'm stone sober."

"Then it'll be jet lag. San Francisco to London is too damned long a time to be cooped up on a plane. Florida was bad enough. You should've come over a day or two early, like I did. Go get a decent dinner and go to bed. You'll feel better in the morning."

"I'm seeing things?" Christy asked bluntly.

"I'm not."

Christy nodded. "That's what I thought. But it was only this one book. It crossed my mind there might be something peculiar about the printer's ink."

Amanda crossed her ankles, pursing her lips. After a minute, she said: "Nope. Never heard of anything that could make type change. Blur, maybe, but not become other words entirely."

Christy drew a deep breath and stared at the volume in her hand. "No, it does seem impossible, doesn't it? You're probably right about that night's sleep. And the dinner. I've been living on airline food."

Amanda rolled her eyes heavenward. "God, it's no wonder you're hallucinating. I'm surprised you're not in the hospital. Well, have we slain your elephants?"

"I think so." Christy rose. "Thanks for bearing with me."

"No problem. I owed you one for giving old Wumpus Face his comeuppance. Take care of that letter." She swung her feet to the floor and heaved herself from the chair. "I'm going to a few book shops tomorrow. Want to come?"

"What, bring your competition? I'd love to." She gave Amanda a quick hug. "I'll see you in the morning. Breakfast at nine?"

That settled, Christy took her leave, feeling somewhat better. Still, why only Holborn's book, and why only from Chapter Ten on? If her eyes played tricks on her, why didn't they do it on everything? She'd put it to the test on a restaurant menu. She wouldn't mind seeing what one of those said. She'd put away *Life in London* and not look at it again until after breakfast the next morning.

11

* * *

"It's hallucinatory," Christy breathed. She stared at the page. This time, Holborn's relating of Christmas Eve dinner blurred into an account of a mob storming the mansions of the aristocrats on Grosvenor Square. Elegant ladies, their dinner gowns stained with their own blood, screaming in anguish while angry hordes garbed in rags looted their houses and dragged gentlemen into the street where they were beaten and stabbed. . . .

The type shimmered, and the tale of the dinner party returned.

Christy closed her eyes. *Why didn't anyone else see this? What was it about this book? And why only her?*

She glanced at the clock. Eight; still an hour before she had to meet Amanda Trent for breakfast. She'd spend the time gathering a few more opinions.

With the book firmly tucked under her arm, she took the elevator to the lobby. The first person she encountered was a bellhop, and she handed him the volume.

"Is there anything odd about the type?" she demanded.

The young man looked at her in bewilderment, then glanced at the page. "No, miss. Should there be?"

She clenched her teeth. "Do the words blur?"

"No, miss." Of that, at least, he sounded certain. "If you need the direction of a good optometrist, the desk clerk can help you, miss."

"Thank you." She closed the book and walked on. That made two votes for it being all right. A few more, and she'd be convinced the problem lay with her.

She got them, one right after the other. A second bellhop, the desk clerk, two waiters and a chambermaid all agreed with Amanda Trent. Not one single thing was the matter with the type in the book. Which meant there was something whopping wrong with her.

Or did it? She wasn't one to suffer from pink elephants. She prided herself on her logical approach to life and business. Well, all right, she was a bit too impulsive, but that couldn't have anything to do with *this*. Nor had her breakup with Ryan unsettled her that much. She'd been more angry than hurt, and finally just glad to be rid of the rat.

She turned the volume over, studying the spine, then the back cover. This was creepy. Apparently, whatever the problem, it was between her and this book.

Or the writer.

James Edward Holborn. She weighed the name in her mind, searching her memory. No, it meant nothing to her. She'd never heard of him before. If this was his only book . . .

It might not be, though. *Life in London* was no amateur bit of social propaganda. The man knew his way around the written word, and how to use it for the best effect. He must have written others.

She opened the volume, this time to the eleventh chapter, and the words shifted before her eyes. Almost, the book smiled at her, as if challenging her to solve its mystery.

For one moment, a prickle of fear danced through her. A prudent person would sell the thing at the earliest opportunity, get rid of it and forget all about it. Her saner self whispered that would be the wisest — and safest — course.

But she wouldn't.

She would call the book's bluff and investigate it.

Chapter Two

At a lobby phone, Christy dialed Amanda's room. "Look," she said as soon as her friend came on the line, "would you mind if I meet you somewhere for lunch, instead? I've got some research I need to do this morning."

Dead silence indicated Amanda considered this statement. "You've still got a pink elephant dancing around?"

"Whole herds of them, and they're rehearsing Swan Lake. Amanda, the type is *still* changing on me, and no one else can see it! If it was *everything* I read, I might think I was going crazy, but it's just that one book, just that one section!"

Amanda caroled out the "Twilight Zone" theme.

"Very funny. But *why* is it happening? And why to me? And why just this book? I've got to find out who this James Edward Holborn is."

For a moment, Amanda said nothing. Then: "Sure you aren't just stressed out?"

"Who *couldn't* use a vacation?"

"Well, take a break, then. I'm staying here until after Christmas. Have BritRail pass, will travel, that's me. Going to take up brass rubbing and learn to play darts in some old pub."

Christy smiled. *"And* check out book stores."

"Of course. Think of it, three whole weeks to play. Want to come along? I've got a spare pass."

"That's right, Karen was supposed to come with you this time. What happened?"

"She went and got herself pregnant. The poor kid's sick all the time, but her husband's thrilled. God, can you see me as a grandmother?"

"No," came Christy's blunt response. "More like an Auntie Mame."

Amanda chuckled. "Well, what about it? Want to go for a train ride?"

"Sounds like heaven, but I'm going home for Christmas. I haven't seen my mom or the rest of them for eighteen months."

Amanda laughed. "Kids. You're all alike. Mine only call when they need money for something."

"Oh, no." Christy grinned. "I call. My phone bill is horrendous every month. But with them in Connecticut and New York, and me in San Francisco, we just never seem to *see* each other anymore. So I'm going directly there when I leave London and staying there until Twelfth Night, which gives us four whole weeks. After that, they'll probably be glad to kick me out for another eighteen months. At least I bet my sisters will."

"Undoubtedly. Now, if I know you and your research—*and* I do, remember—you'll never quit by lunch. How about later, say three-thirty? Remember that funky old pub across the street from the map shop in Bloomsbury?"

Christy did. With reassurances she would be there on time, or at least no more than a quarter hour late, she rang off.

Good old Amanda, she thought as she turned away from the phones. A couple of weeks gallivanting around England with her would be exhausting—but fun. She missed the warmth of her family, though. And she missed making snowmen and snow forts and going for sleigh rides and caroling and decorating the eight-foot tree her father—and now her brother Jon—always cut. No, she wanted to go *home* for Christmas, and Jon's wedding, so soon after. Nothing would make her miss that.

A quick walk through the chill morning air brought her to the Green Park Underground Station, and from there, the rail swept her through dark tunnels to the familiar stop for the British Library. The icy wind whipped about her as she emerged onto the street, and she hurried, half running, to reach her destination.

She at last pushed through the doorway, and warmth and shelter wrapped about her like a well-loved blanket. She knew the Reference Division well; she haunted it every time she managed to come to London. She drew a deep breath, and the mustiness of aged leather filled her lungs: a comfortable, soothing smell. She could never grow tired of books.

A search through the card catalogue proved her suspicions correct; the mysterious Mr. Holborn *had* written another, earlier, book on social reform. Armed with its number, she searched the stacks.

She found it easily, amid the towering shelves crammed with their aging volumes — then stood with her hand on it, mustering her courage to pull it from the shelf. What if it, too, shifted its words, said things it should not? She swallowed. There was only one way to find out.

Eyes closed, she opened it quickly, at random, then forced herself to study the page. The section described squalid living conditions for a family of seven sharing a single room. The print didn't shift.

From that she gathered a measure of encouragement, and turned the page. His words horrified her — but only their meaning, not their behavior. They remained just as they ought, firmly printed in black ink on the sheet yellowed with age.

Slowly, she leafed through the remaining pages. Not a single change, not so much as the slightest blur interrupted her scanning. She found herself reading long passages, caught up into the power of his writing, appalled by his vivid accounts of deprivation. But there were no alterations, no shifting letters.

At last, frowning, she replaced the book on the shelf. From her pocket, she brought forth *Life in London*. It opened to Chapter Ten, and at once the letters danced before her eyes, blurring, beginning their metamorphosis. . . .

She slammed it shut and gripped it tightly, afraid to open it again, as if the words might fly from the page and wing their way about the library to infect the other volumes with their peculiar madness. It still did it! Yet James Holborn's other book did not.

She shoved *Life in London* back into the pocket of her down jacket. Her fingers encountered the plastic sack of chocolate chips, and she slipped a couple into her mouth. What was different about his two books? They both advocated social reform. Yet one dealt with the poor, while the other addressed the rich and their callous attitude. . . .

No, from Chapter Ten onward in *Life in London,* Mr. Holborn wrote about a specific event, a Christmas house party, not conditions in general.

She leaned back, and the metal rim of the shelf pressed through her coat into her spine. A specific event, something that actually happened—at least in one version. In the other, something else entirely happened. Mob riots—possibly even a revolution.

She shivered, feeling as if her fingers had turned to icicles. She was getting too fanciful! What did she think, that something happened at that house party that had the potential to change history—in effect, bring about a social revolution. . . .

" *. . . unspeakable horrors, after the manner of their brethren in France."* The words, glimpsed so briefly as they shifted across the page, returned to haunt her. Dear God, a revolution, in London, in 1810. . . .

This was ridiculous. Twilight Zone time, just like Amanda suggested. Something pretty darn peculiar was going on, with that she couldn't argue. What she needed was more information about the time. Christmas, 1810, to be exact. If other books behaved strangely, altering their accounts of this particular period, she would know she was onto something. If they didn't, she'd take the book to an optometrist and find out if anything was wrong with her eyes that might pick up some unstable quality in the printer's ink. Perhaps the page had been bleached, erasing earlier

17

words, then the new ones printed over the top.

If that were the case, then she should see both versions at the same time, not the later changing into the earlier, and back again.

She ran her fingers along the shelf, and pulled out another volume on the social history of England. It covered a longer period, several hundred years, and spoke in general terms rather than specifics. The Luddites rioted in fear of losing their mill jobs to the new industrialization, but that was far from London, though they did begin in 1811. The words remained crisp and clear, easy to read.

Maybe she needed a book written at the time, as Mr. Holborn's was. She studied the shelves once more, and this time selected five different volumes. Surely, if something indeed happened over that Christmas, one of these must mention it. She carried them to a long table, seated herself in one of the slat-backed wooden chairs, and set to work.

Some three hours later, the words began to dance once again, but this time she found nothing peculiar in it. She took off her reading glasses, massaged her forehead where it began to ache, and stretched her stiff back. With a slight frown creasing her brow, she contemplated the volumes before her. From the plastic bag in her coat pocket she drew out another chocolate chip.

All five books mentioned the Christmas period of 1810. Parliament met in long sessions during that season, and finally passed the long-awaited regency bill in February 1811. Yet the populace seemed to have greeted this with indifference. The new regent made no sweeping changes in the Tory government, despite his Whiggish friends, and for some time the old king actually appeared to be in better health. Not one of the volumes mentioned so much as a single riot or protest.

Christy drew a dark curl from behind her ear and chewed the end, lost in thought. That regency bill had been the subject of the letter she'd come over here to buy, too. It must have been a major issue at the time. It might, in fact, have been the subject of discussion at the house party chronicled by Mr. Holborn.

But why should that make the type change in that damned

book? She rubbed weary eyes, knowing herself too tired to make sense out of any of this.

She glanced at her watch. One o'clock. She had two and a half hours before she was to meet Amanda in Bloomsbury. She could do with some lunch, though.

She reshelved the books, then paused, looking back at the rows of aged volumes. Maybe she needed to learn more about the man, not just the time. Maybe it all had something to do with *him*.

A consultation with the librarian set that obliging gentleman searching records. At last, he shook his balding head, and reported that nothing whatsoever seemed to be known of the mysterious Mr. Holborn. Christy thanked him and turned away.

"Holborn is the family name of the earls Saint Ives, miss," the man added. He offered his most helpful smile. "But whether or not our James Edward belonged to that branch, I'm afraid I can't say. You might try Somerset House."

Christy rocked back on her high-heeled boots, considering. She *might* find something among the records there. She thanked him again and left the building.

She shivered as the icy wind slammed into her face, but trudged on, lost in thought, mulling over the disturbing lack of progress she'd made. Should she go to Somerset House at once? And if she did, what should she look up? Maybe she should get in touch with the Holborn family and ask to see old records. And just what would she tell them? Excuse me, one of your ancestors wrote a peculiar book, and only I have trouble reading it?

A chill gust whipped her thick, unruly curls about her face and she shoved her hands into her pockets. She'd come out without her gloves and hat. A scarf wouldn't come amiss, either. The clouds that darkened the sky hovered low. A feathery white flake drifted past her cheek, followed by another, then several more.

Snow. She raised her face toward the sky. She loved December, she loved Christmas. The special time spent with her family, the decorated shops, the colored lights, the carolers, that general feeling of goodwill which existed among stran-

19

gers like at no other time of year. . . .

Oh, it was cold. She huddled deeper into her coat. She'd buy gloves at the first shop that sold woolen goods. She glanced at the frosted window panes, then up and down the street. She had no idea where she was. She must have been wandering, lost in thought. She was lucky she hadn't crossed a street looking in the wrong direction. Ah, the joys of British traffic, with their driving on the "wrong" side of the road.

She continued along the sidewalk, growing colder by the minute. White flakes gathered on her hair and shoulders, not melting. A light blanket now covered the cars parked along the road. Only early December, and already the promise of a picture-book Christmas.

Across from her, beyond a hedge, she glimpsed the knit-capped heads of children gliding in small circles. There must be a tiny pond — or at least a surface covered with ice — in the little park. Smiling, she continued her search for woolen wear.

Apparently, she had wandered into an area of antique and art shops. A number of etchings, with holly draped over their frames, greeted her at one window. In the next, a display of small statuettes and —

She stopped, delighted. Before her, on a round wooden base, stood a glass ball about six inches in diameter, filled with liquid. Within, someone had created a beautiful scene from a Regency-era Christmas, cast in silver and enameled — a man and woman ice skating, with a horse and carriage on sleigh runners behind them. At their feet lay tiny flakes of ivory "snow."

As she stared at it, the figures moved. First the man pushed forward in a sliding motion, then the woman joined him, skating through the steps of what must be a country dance. Enthralled, Christy watched until the mechanical couple completed their circuit.

On impulse, she entered the shop, then stopped, bemused by the array of objects that met her fascinated gaze. Antiques of every description lined the walls and filled tables and display cases, taking up every available inch of space in the crowded room. At the far end, behind a counter, an elderly man in a heavy overcoat and cap tinkered in the back of a clock with a long, slender instrument. Over his eyes he wore magnifying glasses.

"Excuse me?" Christy advanced with care through the clutter. "Could I see the music box in the window?"

"Music box?" The man raised his visor and peered at her. "In the window? I don't believe there is one."

"It's the snowdome. Maybe it hasn't got music, but the figures dance."

He sat back on his stool and regarded her with a frown. "There's a snowdome there, but the figures don't dance." He set down his tools, wiped his hands on a cloth, and came around the edge of the counter. With care, he wended his way to the window. "Is this the one you mean?"

He leaned over several displayed plates and picked up the glass ball. Christy caught her breath, watching as he lifted it between two Meissen statuettes. The next moment, he held it out to her.

"Is there a switch—" she began, then broke off. Again, the figurine of the gentleman took the lady's hand and skated forward. "Oh, they're doing it again. Are you certain there isn't music to go with it?"

"Doing what?" He squinted at her, then at the ball he held. "They're dancing!"

The man studied the ball, then turned his dubious regard on her. "Are they?"

Blood flooded Christy's face, flashing heat through her; then it drained away, leaving her clammy. "They—they aren't moving, are they?"

"They never have before. I don't see why they'd want to start now." The man smiled at her. "Been a long day shopping, has it, miss?"

She reached out a tentative hand to touch the glass, and the man tightened his grip on it. "What—what can you tell me about it?" she managed.

"Well, now, it's an unusual piece, I'll grant you that. Must be one of the first ever made. The date on it looks like Eighteen-Ten, but that's a good sixty years too early. Must be Eighteen-Seventy." He turned the ball over, and the tiny ivory chips floated through the liquid, so

21

that it "snowed" on the scene.

Christy's gaze riveted on the bottom of the wooden base. The number in question certainly looked like a one, not a seven. The piece was signed, too, in neat, flowing copperplate. She swallowed, and felt her throat sinking into her stomach. Even if the date were in question, there could be no mistaking the name. The letters didn't change before her eyes, they remained clear. James Edward Holborn.

"It's *his*," she breathed.

"Who's, miss?"

"James Holborn's. *He* made it."

The proprietor turned the base so he could read the neat lettering. "So he did, miss. Have you heard of him before?"

"Yes, I bought one of his books." Excitement filled her. "Do *you* know anything about him?"

The man shook his head, dashing her hopes. "Sorry, miss. Can't say I ever came across him before. A writer, was he? Maybe that's why he didn't make more of these."

Christy's gaze returned to the scene. As she watched, the enameled silver figure of the horse stamped his foot and swished his tail against the flakes that drifted over his back. The couple continued their ice dance. "They—they don't move," she repeated.

The man turned once more to the window and started to replace the ball.

"Wait!" She caught his arm. "How much is it?"

He checked the tag. "Ninety-five pounds, miss. Quite a bargain, even if nothing does move."

She managed a shaky smile. "Do you take credit cards?"

He did. Christy trembled internally, hoped it didn't show on the outside. While she watched, he swathed the glass ball in tissue paper, then nested it in a box which he placed in a shopping bag. Christy handed over the plastic, signed the slip, then took her purchase, clasping it to her as if she feared it might evaporate.

Numb, she went out into the afternoon snow. *What did it mean?* Why did the figures dance for only *her*? Why did the words in his book change for only her? Was she going quietly insane?

It all had to do with this James Edward Holborn. *His* book. *His* snowdome. And *her* nightmare.

The flakes continued to drift down from the gray skies. Blindly, she crossed to the park and followed the footpath through the shrubs until she came to the frozen pond. She stared at the skating children, not really seeing them. *Who was this James Holborn?*

With shaking hands she drew the ball from its box and unwrapped it. As she watched, the figurines once more began to move, skating in time to an unheard melody.

She fought her rising panic back under control, and forced herself to study the ball. Mr. Holborn had done a creditable job of carving the figures. They appeared quite lifelike. Too much so, the way they moved with a graceful ease. Even the horse, though not quite in perfect proportion, seemed uncannily real.

She tightened her grip as the animal once more swished its enameled tail. She wasn't going crazy. There would be a logical explanation for all this. She just had to find it. Perhaps there *was* a switch somewhere.

If one existed, it defied her endeavors to find it. Temporarily stymied, she returned her attention to the figurines. The man was tall compared to the lady, his features regular. A shock of dark red hair protruded from beneath his low-crowned hat, and a long overcoat covered his clothes but revealed a pair of shiny black boots to which his skates were fastened.

The lady—Christy caught her breath. It might almost be her, with its tightly curling dark hair worn loose about the shoulders, the round face and well-developed figure. Vivid blue eyes gazed back at her, mirroring her own.

She stared very hard at the ball, afraid, though she didn't know why. Slowly, almost against her will, she inverted it. The ivory flakes swirled, enveloping the skaters. . . .

The world about her spun dizzily. Everywhere, white flakes filled her vision. She couldn't feel the cement beneath her feet, she couldn't feel anything, not even the icy cold. Only the ball between her hands seemed solid, real. . . .

In slow motion, she toppled over, falling, tumbling through

23

space. The ball slipped from her nerveless fingers, shattering about her on the snow-covered paving. For one disoriented second, it seemed to explode, to envelop her, as if it drew her *into* it and she became part of the scene. . . .

Her world settled. She extended a hand, found she sat on the snow-covered ground, and tried to right herself.

A man cannoned into her, tripped, and sprawled across her, knocking her flat. He rolled off, and something whizzed past Christy's nose to bury itself in the snow. She gasped, staring at the bone handle of a knife, still quivering from the impact, only inches from where the man's back had been a moment before.

Chapter Three

The man rolled to a crouch, ready to spring to safety, his gaze darting back and forth. Christy huddled where she lay, staring about in horror. No punks or gang members bore down on them, no men cloaked in an aura of danger. No one, in fact, appeared particularly interested in them at all. The people continued to skate on the pond or—

Christy blinked. Or ride in horse-drawn carriages? And their clothes! Everyone dressed so strangely. Had she stumbled into a Dickens Christmas festival?

Only their costumes dated to an earlier period—like the snow scene in the ball. . . .

The snowdome! She looked about, frantic. She'd dropped it. . . . The fragments of glass, the wooden base, the enameled figures. . . . Where were they? She *had* to find them.

She brushed snow aside, searching through the mounds of dirt-encrusted white. The pieces should be there somewhere. They couldn't have simply vanished. . . .

And her purse. It *wasn't there*. Could it have been snatched, so fast? But the snowdome. . . .

"Are you hurt, miss?" A deep, well-modulated voice sounded behind her.

Unsteadily, Christy turned to look up into a commanding face dominated by a pair of wide-set eyes so dark as to appear black. Thick auburn lashes ringed them. Her gaze rose to his matching, waving hair.

He extended a hand down to her. "I'm sorry I ran into you. As you may have noticed—"

Another knife, thrown from the opposite direction, landed in the snow barely inches from where Christy sat. With a gasp, she grabbed the offered hand and the man dragged her to her feet. Trembling, she clung close to his side as she stared about, wide-eyed with shock.

"Hell and the devil confound it!" Still holding Christy's hand, he pulled her to the partial shelter of a shrubbery.

She followed, too stunned to protest. "What's going on?" she managed.

He positioned himself in front of her, so his body completed the shelter offered by the hedge at her back. "Please accept my apologies for entangling you in this absurd situation." He didn't glance at her as he spoke. His frowning gaze scanned the sparse crowd. Apparently nothing threatening presented itself, for the tenseness eased out of his shoulders. "It should be safe for you to go, now. You should be in no danger. I'm very sorry to have involved you."

"Was someone really throwing knives at you?" she demanded, still not quite believing it.

The lines about his generous mouth tightened, lending his countenance a grim cast. "Jokesters. But it is me they are intent upon annoying, no one else. Had I not been so clumsy as to have run into you, you would not have been subjected to this odious prank."

"But throwing knives! That goes beyond joking. Someone could get killed. Do you want me to find a policeman?"

"The watch—" he began, then broke off. For the first time, he actually looked at her. A long moment passed as his arrested gaze remained on her face, then slowly traveled over the rest of her.

"A bobby?" she tried. "I'm sorry, I'm an American. I don't have all the terms down right. Don't ever let anyone tell you we speak the same language."

"An American," he repeated, as if that explained everything. He appeared to be transfixed by her high-heeled boots, the

26

sheepskin that rimmed their top, and the hem of her calf-length black wool skirt.

"*Would* you like me to get help?" she repeated.

He dragged his bemused gaze back to her face. "Is that the fashion in America?"

"Yes. Look, you're really not worried about this? I mean, someone hurls a couple of knives at you, but you're just going to pretend it never happened?"

"No one is trying to kill me—at least, not seriously."

"Not seriously," she repeated, incredulous. "My brothers and I used to get up to some pretty weird practical jokes, but we never did anything really *dangerous*. Not like this."

A grim smile just touched his firm lips. He had a very attractive face, it occurred to her. Strong, with a straight nose, high cheekbones, and a jutting chin. Lines of worry etched the brow beneath that thick auburn hair.

She lowered her gaze to the heavy overcoat he wore. It hung open, displaying an elaborately tied cloth about his neck and an old-fashioned green coat. A waistcoat peaked out from beneath. His pants—She'd never seen anything like them, outside of pictures, and as for those gleaming black boots that reached almost to his knee! She caught her breath, intrigued. He must be one of the performers for whatever pageant took place about them.

And that explained the knives. One of his fellow players must have thrown them closer than the script required.

Relief flooded through her. "Is this a mystery or thriller or something?" She grinned, determined to enter into the spirit of the seasonal gaiety. "I'm sorry I got in the way. I hope I didn't ruin the performance."

The creases in his brow deepened. "What performance?"

"Isn't this some Christmas production? All of you wearing those costumes? Aren't you part of some acting troop?"

"What are you talking about?"

She shoved her hands in her pockets, reeling. The fingers of her right hand encountered the sack of chocolate chips, and she grabbed a couple. "What *is* going on?" she demanded.

He ran a well-formed hand through his hair, looked about on the ground, then picked up a delightfully furry hat with a low crown and curly brim. He placed it on his head and turned back to her. "Perhaps I do owe you an explanation. This harassment began back around October, with a seeming accident. The shaft on my carriage had been tampered with. Since then, I have suffered three more similar accidents. All potentially lethal, yet not one has worked properly."

"So you're not worried."

His mouth compressed. "Last week, the harassment came in the form of someone shooting at me, but missing. And now, the knives. This is the first time, though, anything has been tried when other people are about."

"Have you any idea why? Or who's behind it?"

"No. But at a guess, I would say someone wants me scared, but not necessarily dead. I'm afraid I have offended a number of people of late."

"Have you?" She found his calm acceptance of the absurd situation fascinating.

"I am a writer, you see—at least, I am an advocate of social reform, and I use the written word to further my cause. If you will permit me to introduce myself? Major Holborn, entirely at your service."

"Holborn—" She broke off, staring at him. In her mind, she again heard Amanda's cheerful rendition of the "Twilight Zone" theme. Talk about weird coincidences. . . .

He awarded her an elegant bow right out of another era. "Again, forgive me for intruding upon you with my troubles." He tipped his hat, then paused, his expression altering as he regarded her.

Her confusion must show on her face, she reflected. With tremendous effort, she pulled herself together and managed a shaky smile.

"Is there no one with you?" he asked suddenly. "This is no neighborhood for a lady to be alone."

"Isn't it? I—I didn't realize. I was thinking about something, and just walking, and when I looked around, I had no idea where I was." She glanced back at the snow where she had fallen, but neither the fragments of the snowdome nor her purse were anywhere to be seen.

"Allow me to escort you to your destination. If you are

28

not afraid of my company." He offered her his arm.

Feeling silly, she took it. It was a sweet gesture, so very — well, old-fashioned. She honestly couldn't think of another word for it. But it described him perfectly, from his clothes, to the formal way he talked and his charming manners. He seemed perfectly at home that way, too. It was only she who seemed out of kilter.

She shook off the eerie, dizzy sensation. Maybe she'd hit her head when she fell. Or maybe she was coming down with the flu. That would explain why she kept reading strange things in that book. And the fact this man's name was Holborn — that was one of those freaky little quirks of coincidence. Stranger things happened every day. Just generally not to her.

People milled about them, pausing to watch the skaters, then moving on. The men all wore those same period clothes, she saw, and a number of them swung canes as they walked. The women wore long, high-waisted coats and hats of various shapes and sizes. Some had their hands stuffed into fur muffs.

Christy might have minimal knowledge of historic costumes, but these sure looked authentic to her. There were so many variations on the basic lines, they must have been made from copies of original patterns rather than a store-bought all-purpose one. Whatever was going on, the local people certainly participated to the hilt. She didn't see a single person in modern dress.

A shiver ran through her and her fingers tightened on the man's arm. Had the police cordoned off this area, closing it to those who didn't take part, and she had blundered through without noticing?

"May I know your name?" Major Holborn led her around several people who stood in a small knot, talking.

"Christy. Christina Campbell."

"You are an American, I believe you said, Miss Campbell? Have you been in England long?"

"No. I only arrived the day before yesterday."

"Was it a difficult crossing?" He glanced down at her from his imposing height, and his gaze lingered on her face.

"I'm beginning to think it must have been. Look, I'm sorry. I'm feeling a bit disoriented."

They reached the street, and she stopped dead. "Where are

29

the cars? Where did all those *horses* come from? How could they clear such a large area? What's—what's going *on?*"

Gently he pried her fingers loose from his coat sleeve. He retained her hand, holding it in a comforting clasp. "You need have no fear. If you will tell me at which hotel you are putting up, I will convey you there and give you into the care of your woman."

She nodded. "The Edgemont. It's on Piccadilly." But how did he know about Amanda?

His brow furrowed. "I don't believe I am acquainted with that hostelry. But never mind. I'm sure a jarvey will be able to find it." He tucked her hand once more through his arm and started forward.

Maybe it wasn't the flu. Maybe she was just dreaming, *had* dreamed the whole ridiculous situation. She gave her head a brisk shake, setting the thick mass of her tight curls bouncing about her shoulders.

It didn't help. The impossible scene about her remained the same. So did the man walking at her side. At least she showed excellent taste in men, even if he was an hallucination.

"I'll probably wake up in a few minutes," she informed him, her tone purely conversational. "I do have peculiar dreams, but not usually in this much detail. They make about this much sense, though."

He looked down at her, frowning, but did not respond.

Christy's gaze traveled from his face to her surroundings. Fascinated, she regarded the variety of horse-drawn carriages that passed. Everything looked too authentic. She had a vivid imagination, she *could* have created all this, but it looked so *real.* Maybe the flu theory was the best, after all. She didn't feel asleep.

A small, closed carriage approached, pulled by a single horse, and Major Holborn stepped forward. Christy joined him, then stopped in her tracks. Across the street stood *Williams and Sons,* the antique shop where she'd purchased the snowdome.

She had to go back into that shop. It was something familiar, something she recognized. Maybe that man could tell her what happened. She pulled away from Major Holborn, ducked around a husky man in a threadbare coat, and darted into the street.

Miss Campbell lunged away from him, and Major James Holborn, acting out of instinct, darted after her. Catching her arm, he dragged her out of the path of an approaching horse. She struggled, but he retained his grip.

Where the devil did she think she was going? Escaping from him? If so, why?

There was something more than a little peculiar about her, about the way he tripped over her right at the moment someone hurled a knife at him. He didn't like mysteries, and he intended to solve the riddles this young woman presented before letting her out of his sight.

His frowning gaze rested on the desperation of her expression, and his suspicions wavered. Either she was honestly alarmed and disoriented, or she was the best actress he had ever encountered.

And she herself had mentioned actors. His gaze narrowed. Again, she tried to free herself. "I've got to go in there!"

"Why?"

"It might explain everything. Please, let me go."

"Permit me to escort you. I would be very glad to hear a few answers, myself. Wait –" He pulled her back once more as she started impetuously forward. "It isn't safe to run into a street like that."

"True. You drive on the wrong side of the road." A laugh broke from her, rising toward the hysterical. "Come *on!*"

"Very well." Retaining his hold on her arm, he led her across, wending his way between the carriages and carts.

As they reached the flagway, she drew ahead, hurrying toward the store. She glanced at the window, and stopped short.

"Is something wrong?" James came level with her.

"The display has changed."

"Has it? You probably have the wrong shop."

"I don't!" She jerked free and glared at him. "This is the spot. Even the name is the same." She drew an unsteady breath, and the defiance in her expression faded to confusion. "Only there were framed Victorian prints in the window, with holly draped over them. Now there are all those Chinese vases and statues."

"How long ago were you here?"

"Only—" She broke off. "I *thought* no more than an hour ago. Maybe it's been longer."

"Would you care to go in?" He opened the door, and a tiny bell tinkled as he led her, unprotesting, inside.

She stopped again just over the threshold, her startled gaze flying about the large room. "It's different! Everything's different."

"Shall I ask the shopkeeper if he's recently changed his stock?" he asked.

She nodded, mumchance.

For the moment, at least, she showed no tendency to run away. Leaving her staring about with that blank, lost look on her face—her very pretty face—he approached the middle-aged man who stood behind the counter, polishing silver. With the man's assurances his displays had not been touched in months, he returned to Miss Campbell.

She listened to him, then shook her head. "This is impossible," she breathed. "*All* of it. It *has* to be a dream. Oh, God, I wish I could *believe* it's a dream."

"Do you recognize the shopkeeper?" he asked.

"No. This one's much younger, and he's got sandy hair." Impulsively, she pushed past the major. "Excuse me?"

The man looked up. "Yes, miss?"

"Is there another man who works here? Older? He was wearing an overcoat and a cap, and he had a fringe of wispy white hair."

The shopkeeper laid down the spoon he held. "No, miss. There's only me, the other lad, and the gentleman what owns the shop."

"Is he older?"

"No, miss."

"But there was one, he was in here earlier."

The clerk cast an uneasy glance at the major. "I've been in here since opening, miss."

"What about yesterday?"

James took her arm once more. "It seems you've made a

mistake, Miss Campbell. There must be several shops that appear similar from the outside."

"But it's in the same *place!* On the same corner. And the name's on the sign. How could I mistake that?"

"It seems you have." He drew her firmly but gently toward the door. Her confusion appeared genuine. Perhaps he had been too quick with his suspicions. He could see no purpose to such an elaborate charade.

She shook her head, her large blue eyes clouding, and turned back to the shopkeeper. "Have you ever had a snowdome in here?"

The man chewed his lower lip. "Well, miss, it would melt pretty fast, it would. We keep the coal burning. Not stingy, the master. Not stingy at all."

"I mean a glass ball, filled with liquid. There are figures inside, and flakes of plastic. When you turn the ball over, it looks like it's snowing inside."

"Does it, miss?" He regarded her, fascinated. "What's plastic?"

She opened her mouth, then shut it again. After a moment, she said: "Little flakes of something white."

The shopkeeper shook his head. "That sounds like a rare treat to see, it does. Never heard of an oddity like that, before."

Miss Campbell rubbed her eyes with the heels of her hands. "I bought one here," she insisted.

"No, miss. Must have been another shop, it must. I'm sorry."

"And you've never seen a snowdome before." Her voice sounded hollow. Slowly, she pivoted around on her heel, her uncertain gaze seeking out the major. "Where *did* I get it, then?"

Her bewildered, frightened, tone landed him a leveler right to his chivalric instincts. No threatening mystery, but a maiden in distress. He would not let her down. After tilting at so many windmills, it would be a pleasure to embark on so simple a quest.

Dazed, Christy allowed Major Holborn to lead her from the shop. She stood on the sidewalk while he flagged down one of those small horse-drawn carriages. Hansom cabs? No, those were Victorian, and everything around here looked earlier. Regency-era-ish. These would be called hackneys.

He helped her inside, and for a moment she clung to his hand, the one stable element in this freakish world.

"What was the name of your hotel, Miss Campbell?" He waited, one foot still on the cobblestones.

"The Edgemont." She could hardly wait to get to her familiar room in the familiar hotel. She brought her voice under control. "It's on Piccadilly, near the Green Park Underground station."

"The what?"

"The cabby should know." She leaned over, forcing Major Holborn to step back. "The Edgemont, please," she called.

"The what, miss?"

"This isn't funny. Will you just take me to Piccadilly? You can't miss it, once you're there."

Major Holborn swung up into the carriage and closed the door. With a slight jolt, the vehicle moved forward. Christy huddled back on the seat, wishing something—just *one* thing—would make sense.

After a few minutes, they turned a corner and she peered out the window. Once they got away from that little park, maybe everything would return to normal. Seeing a familiar sight—like a car—would do her a world of good.

But though they turned several more corners, not a single automobile met her uncertain gaze. A chill crept through her that had nothing to do with the iciness of the weather. Something was wrong. Something was eerily, crazily, wrong.

Dear God, it was wronger than she thought. There was Hyde Park, and Hyde Park Corner. . . . *Where was the traffic?* There was no possible way all of London could be cleared of cars! The place was a madhouse, at any hour of the day or night. There should be flashy shop fronts and neon lights and people dressed like *her*, not like this man who sat so calmly next to her.

How could he not be panicky, too? The whole world had gone crazy—or had it only done so for her? After all, he seemed to fit in perfectly, he acted entirely at home.

The carriage drew to a halt, and Christy looked out, anxious. Nowhere did she see the glass facade of the multi-storied hotel. The buildings were old-fashioned, yet not old—like everything else.

"Where to from here, miss?" the driver called.

"Keep going. It's tall—at least twenty-two stories, I think. And it's all glass."

An astonished whistle escaped the man. "Well, now, miss, I can't say as I've ever seen a building like that in London, afore."

"But it's *got* to be here!" She pushed past the major and thrust the door wide. Everything seemed familiar, yet not quite the way she remembered it. She jumped to the pavement—the *cobblestones?* She ran forward, only to stop and turn slowly about, searching for any fragment of the modern London she thought she knew.

"Everything's *wrong!*" she cried.

Major Holborn climbed down from the carriage. Christy stared at him, then turned and ran, blindly, wanting only to escape. People stepped aside, getting out of her way. Strangely dressed men and women stared at her, their expressions shocked. And London remained different, as if it were younger, untouched by the passage of a couple hundred years. Almost, she might have stepped back through time. . . .

An hysterical giggle rose in her throat, and her shoulders trembled with the effort to contain it. Laughter broke from her, and she couldn't stop. She just stood there, shaking with the humorless spasms.

"Miss Campbell!" The major's strong hand closed on her shoulder.

She turned toward him and buried her face against his shoulder. He stiffened, then slowly his arms closed about her. "Where *is* it?" she managed to gasp.

"It will be all right, Miss Campbell." His tone tried to soothe her. "Come, let me take you to a place where you can rest."

She nodded, too confused to do anything other than accompany him. He led her back to the hackney, which awaited them, and helped her inside once more. He called something to the driver, but Christy didn't hear. Her ears rang, and a wave of dizziness washed over her. She sank back against the cushions and closed her eyes.

"Are you feeling ill? Do you have a vinaigrette with you?"

"A what?" She looked up. They were moving, they had turned onto a side street, and still everything seemed like she'd walked into a living museum. Everyone wore those antique clothes . . . only they looked new. "I—I haven't got anything. I've lost my purse."

"Sit still, then. I'll be able to give you into the care of a very kind woman shortly."

"Thank you." She managed a shaky smile. "You are the one being kind. You must think I'm crazy. I'm beginning to think so, myself."

"Just a little disoriented, I expect. You might be taking ill."

"I hope so," she murmured. She looked up at his strong, aristocratic profile, the dark eyes, the auburn hair. She was lucky she had run into such a considerate man. He might have turned out to be a real creep. Instead, she'd roused the protective instincts of an extremely good-looking *gentleman* whose manners and bearing made every other man she had ever met seem rough and uncouth. Yes, she liked Major Holborn. . . .

"What is your first name?" she asked suddenly.

His thick auburn eyebrows rose a fraction. "James."

"James," she repeated. "Major James . . . Edward . . . Holborn . . . ." Her voice trailed off.

"That is correct. How did you know about the Edward?"

The hysteria rose within her again. "I—I think I might have read a book you wrote, once."

"Did you? *Social Injustice?*" He sounded surprised, and pleased.

She shook her head. *"Life in London."*

He blinked. "You must have it confused with another. I've been thinking of using that as the title for the volume I am currently writing, but it is still a long way from being published."

"Is it?" She slipped her hand into her coat pocket, and closed her fingers about the thin volume that rested there. *His* book . . . ?

Nausea alternated with the dizziness, and she stared out the hackney window, watching the unfamiliar traffic pass by. They turned once again, and even Christy's untutored eye detected the difference in the neighborhoods. Gone were the stately mansions and elite shop fronts. Now they traveled through narrow, dirty alleys lined with buildings that could do with massive repairs. People no longer dressed with flair or elegance. Ragged children, cripples, men who looked like they knew their way around the inside of a jail, women who plied their age-old trade on the street corners. . . .

Christy shivered. No one would go to this much trouble to create an aura of poverty from an earlier era.

Somehow, incredibly, she really had stepped back in time.

Chapter Four

Stepping back through time.

No, that was impossible. It simply couldn't be done. Yet how else could Christy explain the evidence of her eyes and ears? Her logical mind insisted all of this had to be an illusion or hallucination, some cruel hoax her imagination had cooked up for her. But *was* it?

Impulsively, she turned to Major Holborn. "What year is it?"

"It is still almost three weeks before the new year."

"What *year?*"

His frowning gaze rested on her. "Eighteen-Ten."

Eighteen-Ten. The date on that snowdome. She opened her mouth, then closed it again. She had wanted her fears denied, not confirmed. After a moment, she hazarded: "You aren't just making this up, are you? For a joke?" She tried to keep the pleading out of her voice.

"I would do nothing to cause you distress.

"No." Her lingering hopes faded. "I don't think you would." Generally, her snap judgments about people proved accurate. Either he was the greatest actor she had ever encountered, or he was exactly what he appeared to be.

She drew an unsteady breath. "Look, I think I'm in a bit of trouble, here." Now *there* was an understatement. "I seem to be in

London a—a little earlier than I expected." About two hundred years earlier, but at the moment she wasn't up to explaining that.

"And you have forgotten where you are staying?" Only kind encouragement sounded in his voice.

"It may be worse than that." Her inventive brain whirled, then hit on an explanation. "I was to join some people, some chance acquaintances I met on the"—not plane—"on the boat. They took my luggage with them."

"We will insert an advertisement in all the papers. They will be quite alarmed when you do not arrive as expected."

"I don't think so. They—they were so very specific about the hotel, its name and description. I think they must have been con artists."

"Con—?"

How did one describe a con artist? "It was deliberate, to steal my bags."

His brow snapped down. "Far too much of that sort of thing has been going on. Usually it occurs after the ship has docked, though. A man offers to carry your luggage to your hotel, then simply disappears with it."

Did that mean he believed her story? For that matter, did she believe the whole situation?

She still sat in a horse-drawn hackney, not a heavy black London cab. The people outside the window still wore those Regency-era clothes, though they looked seedier by the minute. Apparently, it was all real.

But how was she to get home?

"This is not perhaps the district to which I should bring you." Major Holborn broke the silence that had stretched between them. "It is not the most savory area of London."

"No, it doesn't look like it." She hesitated. "Where *are* you taking me?"

"To some friends. The Reverend Mr. Runcorn and his wife. They operate a small orphanage in Saint Luke's, off Golden Lane."

Christy considered this. "I haven't any money. My purse has disappeared."

"Do not concern yourself. It will be all right."

They fell silent again until the carriage pulled up before a dilapidated old building. Not even in its better days could it have boasted any semblance of elegance or grandeur; now it seemed earmarked for a wrecking ball. At least it would, Christy corrected herself, if one had been invented yet.

The major jumped down and paid the driver. Christy descended to the filthy street after him, and looked about with uncertainty. If she'd still had her purse, she would have hidden it under her coat. This was no neighborhood in which to go out either at night or unarmed.

A slovenly woman, with unkempt hair and a tattered shawl which failed to conceal her too-skimpy bodice, swaggered up to the major and smiled at him, inviting. He tipped his hat to her, then offered his arm to Christy and led her up the stairs. From what Christy could see, these must be the only ones on the entire street that weren't rickety. Someone kept them tended—and swept.

He knocked, and less than a minute later the door opened to reveal a young maid in a high-waisted gray uniform with a white apron, and blond curls of an unbelievable hue protruding from beneath her mobcap. Delight transformed her face as she saw him.

"Well, guv'nor, you're a sight for sore eyes, and no mistakin' that. Been days, it's been. Now, you come in, you don't want to go temptin' them as oughts to know better with your flash tattler."

"My watch stays in my pocket, Nancy."

"That's as I was sayin', guv'nor. I could 'ave it out of there in a twinklin', meself, I could."

"But you wouldn't."

"No." She sounded almost regretful. "A right beauty it is, too. Well, you come into the sittin' room, and I'll go fetch the missus. Upstairs keepin' the boys at their lessons, she is." Her curious gaze fell on Christy.

Major Holborn ushered Christy inside, and she glanced about. Several bright hunting prints covered the newly painted white walls, and a small table, over which hung a rectangular mirror, stood opposite her. Several closed doors led to other rooms, and at the back of the hall a stairway rose to the next floor. The smell of leather mingled with that of lemon oil and wax.

The major led the way into a small room at the front of the

house, overlooking the street. Nancy, with a marked sigh, set off on her errand.

Christy stared after her, fascinated. "Who is she?"

"A former pickpocket, but reformed now, I assure you. She serves the Runcorns as a maid."

"And she's familiar with your watch?"

A soft, unexpected chuckle escaped the man. "That was how we met, you might say."

Christy couldn't help but smile. "Apparently you make a habit of picking up strays."

He sobered. "Let us say I don't like to see anyone in trouble. Particularly a young lady of gentle birth, who is alone and far from her own home. London would not have proved kind to you, Miss Campbell."

"But you have, and I want to thank you. I'm sorry about how I acted earlier. I must have seemed pretty crazy. I'm still confused, but I think I can cope, now."

His gaze rested on her face. "You Americans have an unusual way of expressing yourselves. Delightfully so," he amended.

"As incomprehensible to you, as you are to me, I suppose." Christy advanced another step into the room, and looked around.

The same cheery brightness that characterized the hall greeted her here. Four comfortable chairs stood around a table, and an antique piano rested against the back wall. A faded couch, only slightly patched, faced a hearth in which a merry fire burned. Christy crossed to it and held out her chilled hands.

Her gaze fell on the mantel, and she frowned. "They haven't decorated for Christmas, yet," she said. "I expected boughs of holly or something."

"It's too early." The major joined her. "The holly and mistletoe are never brought in before Christmas Eve. Is it different in America?"

"The retailers begin the day after Halloween." She caught herself. "We start early, to make the most out of it, I guess."

The warmth of the room enveloped her, making her sleepy. She yawned, surprising herself. After what she'd been through, she should have been keyed up, frantic — if not an out-and-out jibbering idiot. Instead, the tension eased from her muscles, leaving her oddly relaxed.

And hungry. She couldn't remember when she'd eaten last. She'd only had a cup of coffee in her room that morning before starting out. Nor had she ever gotten around to that lunch she'd promised herself. At the moment, she didn't even have any idea what time it was—at least in relation to *her* day.

The door opened behind her, and she spun about to see a frail little lady enter the room. Silvery white hair wound in a braided crown about her sweet face, which was dominated by a pair of laughing brown eyes.

"James, how delightful of you to call upon us." She swept forward, her hand extended.

He bowed over it in that stately manner Christy liked. The elegance that characterized this time charmed her.

"I have come for your kind assistance, Elinor." He retained his hold on that gentlewoman's hand, and led her to where Christy remained before the fire. "I have encountered a young lady in considerable distress. May I introduce Miss Campbell? Miss Campbell, this is Mrs. Runcorn."

An expression of gentle inquiry touched the woman's lovely eyes. "How do you do, my dear?"

Christy bit her lip. "I'm afraid I'm about to impose on you."

"Indeed? What may we do to be of assistance?"

Christy cast the major an uncertain glance.

A slight smile touched his firm mouth. "It appears she has been the victim of a cruel hoax, and has been robbed of all her possessions."

"How dreadful. Are you far from home, Miss Campbell?"

"Very far. I'm an American. I've only just arrived in England, and I don't know anyone."

Mrs. Runcorn nodded, and wisps of soft, silvery hair fluffed about her face. "You did very right to bring her to us, James. Now, you must not fret, my dear. Take a seat while we decide how best to begin. Would you—Ah, here is Nancy with some refreshments."

The door opened inch by inch as the maid eased her way in with a tea tray. A large white china pot decorated with little rosebuds, four cups and saucers, a creamer, and a sugar bowl crowded together on one side of it. Christy barely scanned these before her gaze lit upon a plate piled high with cookies. Another held slices

42

of a rich-looking cake. Her mouth watered, and a growling in her stomach reaffirmed how long it had been since she'd last eaten.

Mrs. Runcorn settled on one of the chairs, and Nancy set the tray before her. Christy hesitated by the blazing fire, but the lure of food won out. She joined the other two.

"Will you find Mr. Runcorn and see what is keeping him, Nancy?" Mrs. Runcorn checked the pot, then left it to steep.

"Be along afore the cat can lick 'er ear, 'e will, missus. Little Alfie done gone and stubbed 'is toe. Cryin' fit to break your 'eart, 'e was," she added cheerfully.

As Nancy retired from the room, a slender gentleman in his early sixties, garbed in the black coat and dog collar of a clergyman, caught the door for her. His silvery white fringe of hair bordered a lined face dominated by a patrician nose. Nancy grinned at him, and her off-key whistle floated back to the salon as she went on her way.

Mr. Runcorn closed the door, then straightened his spectacles and peered at the assembled company. The warm gaze of his blue eyes rested fondly on his wife, then moved to the major.

"James. How good to see you. Just the man I wanted, at that. You must come with me to view the latest improvements. The attic chambers no longer leak, thanks to you. They have even been refurbished."

"Then perhaps you will allow me to present a candidate for occupying one of them."

The Reverend Mr. Runcorn turned his kindly, inquiring gaze on Christy, and warm color rose to her cheeks in response to his scrutiny. The major once more launched into her story.

Christy lowered her gaze, unable to meet the sympathy in all three faces. Guilt surged through her, as if she lied to them for some evil purpose! She'd tell the truth, if she could—or if she could be certain what it really was. Traveling through time. . . . Her logical mind still fought against the evidence of her senses. Sight, hearing, smell. . . .

Smell. Vividly, she became aware of the plate of cookies on the table before her. How she wanted to try out taste! Unable to help herself, she reached for a golden circle filled with walnuts and raisins.

"A biscuit, my dear?" Mrs. Runcorn instantly picked up the plate and held it out to her.

"Thank you." Her hand hovered over the selection for a moment, then she gave up and grabbed several. At this moment, she didn't care what was polite for a lady of this time. She was hungry.

Mrs. Runcorn smiled, apparently unoffended, and poured tea. Christy accepted both cream and sugar, which her hostess added with a liberal hand. For several minutes, Christy concentrated on her mini-feast, assuaging the worst of her hunger. With some carbohydrates inside her, the whole world seemed to settle. Unfortunately, it remained a very alien and old-fashioned world. She swallowed the last cookie, and Mrs. Runcorn immediately offered her the other plate filled with cakes. Christy took two.

At least she felt better. With food no longer her major concern, she allowed her attention to focus on other things.

Major Holborn — it still seemed impossible he could really be *her* James Holborn — sat near the paned window, discussing the problems of the orphanage with Mr. Runcorn. His auburn hair caught the light of the westering sun, and came alive with flame. Every feature of his striking face seemed animated as he leaned forward, gesturing, describing a plan for further renovations. She found herself fascinated against her will.

Damn it, she didn't need to think about *him*. She needed to concentrate on getting home, where she belonged.

She turned back to her hostess to find that elegant little lady watching her with a puzzled frown. "I look strange, don't I?" Christy asked, blunt as always.

Mrs. Runcorn shook her head with more politeness than truth. "I daresay those are your traveling clothes, my dear. Have you indeed lost everything?"

"I have." She bit her lip. "I don't like imposing on you, but at the moment, I'm afraid I don't have any choice."

"We are delighted, my dear. We are always glad to do a favor for Major Holborn."

Christy glanced at that gentleman. "You know him well?"

Mrs. Runcorn laughed softly. "Indeed, yes. It is he who is the kind patron of our orphanage."

"He is?" He must have some money, then, she reflected. "But I can't let him pay for me," she added, finishing her thought aloud.

44

"Now, you mustn't worry about that, Miss Campbell."

"But I don't have any money! I don't have anything."

"You will stay here until some other solution has been found for your difficulties."

Christy drew a deep breath. Going home didn't seem to be an option at the moment. That being the case, she might as well concentrate on discovering what she was doing here in the first place. And since Major James Holborn lay at the center of that mystery, she'd do best to remain in his vicinity.

She didn't want to be dependent on him, though. That didn't seem right. "I'm going to need a few things," she said slowly.

"I'm sure I can provide—"

"Could you hire me?" Christy broke across her words.

"Hire you? My dear, there is no need, not if the major wishes us to take you in."

"I want to earn my keep. I'm going to need clothes, and—and a toothbrush. I don't even have a *hair* brush." Or her makeup, or cleanser or anything else she considered essential. The horror of her situation began to hit home: they didn't have chocolate chips in this era. She was dead!

Mrs. Runcorn patted her hand. "I am sure we can come to some arrangement, my dear."

Christy turned to the men. "Major Holborn? If I promise to stay here and work as a maid for at least the next week or two, do you think you could advance me a little money for wages?"

"A maid!" For a moment, astonishment flickered in his eyes, then disapproval settled over his strong features. "You are not to be thinking of going into service. That is not in the least suitable for a lady."

"I'm not a—" She broke off. She wouldn't try to argue with his notions of class system. At least not while she seemed to be on the winning end of it. "There is so much I need, and I won't impose on everyone. Please, let me earn it."

His chin jutted out in a stubborn manner.

She sighed, recognizing a brick wall when she ran into one. "All right, not a maid. But there are any number of things I can do to help around here. If you won't let me clean, what about cooking?" She read the unyielding set of his jaw, and tried again. "How

45

about if I help with the children? Perhaps I can teach them something?"

The Runcorns exchanged an arrested glance.

It did not escape the major's notice. "Are you in need of instructors for the boys? Why didn't you tell me?" he demanded.

"We didn't want to bother you with unnecessary expense," Mr. Runcorn admitted after a moment. "Elinor and I have been able to teach them well enough, though it has sometimes occurred to us they might respond to a—a younger person."

Relief rushed through Christy. "It's settled, then," she announced before any of them could change their minds. Then the rashness of her offer dawned on her. "How old are they? And how many?"

"There are only eight," Mrs. Runcorn assured her. "They range in age from nine to thirteen."

"Nine to thirteen," Christy repeated, trying to keep the dismay from her voice. Just what she needed, a pack of preteens. Well, it might be worse, though she was more experienced with younger children. Being an aunt came in useful.

"May I ask your salary requirements?" Amusement returned to the major's dark eyes.

Christy blinked. "I have no idea. What's the going rate?"

He burst out laughing. "I believe two hundred pounds is a reasonable figure."

"A week?" she hazarded. That didn't sound like much, but then she had no idea how much a pound was currently worth.

A puzzled frown creased his brow. "A year," he corrected, gently.

"A—" She broke off, shocked. "Well, now I've got an idea about the exchange rate, at least." She saw his frowning face, and grinned. "Sorry, I didn't mean to embarrass you with an outrageous demand. From what I've seen of you, I'll bet that's a very generous salary."

"I am sure you will do an admirable job." The major turned back to the Reverend Mr. Runcorn, in the manner of one dismissing a matter now settled.

"Have things been quiet for you since we had the pleasure of seeing you last?" The clergyman helped himself to a thick slice of cake and fixed his concerned gaze on his visitor.

The major hesitated. "There has been another occurrence," he admitted.

Mrs. Runcorn's delicate hand fluttered at her breast. "How dreadful. What happened this time?"

The major glanced at Christy. "Someone threw a couple of knives at me while I was walking across a small park."

"Oh, if only they would play off their foolish tricks in the daylight, so you might see who is responsible!" Mrs. Runcorn clasped her hands.

"This time, they did," Major Holborn said. "It happened just over an hour ago."

"Did you see anyone?" Mr. Runcorn demanded at once.

The major shook his head. "I'm afraid they got away—again."

"If only you could have caught one of them," Mrs. Runcorn cried, distressed. "Then at last you might have demanded an explanation."

"There is no point in repining. Perhaps next time—"

"Perhaps next time," Mr. Runcorn interrupted, "they will hit their mark, and you won't be able to ask them."

"It was because of me, wasn't it," Christy said suddenly. "If I hadn't—stepped—in front of you and tripped you, you could have seen who threw those knives. Couldn't you?"

"There is no way of knowing that," came his calm response.

"You should be mad at me instead of being so nice. I'm sorry."

"Do not distress yourself. It is in no way your fault. Had I been paying more attention to where I was going, I would not have knocked you down. It is I who should apologize."

Guilt flooded through her. It had been her unorthodox arrival into the past, literally tripping him up, which prevented him from catching, or at least seeing, the knife thrower. If she hadn't appeared, he might be well on his way to solving his riddles. Or the knife might have hit its mark. . . .

A chill crept along her spine, and she swallowed a mouthful of tepid tea. What had she gotten into? *Time travel*, of all things. And attempted murder.

And possibly a revolution?

Chapter Five

The cup rattled in her saucer, and Christy stilled her trembling with an effort. Why *her?* The book with the print that changed only for her, the skaters in that ball who moved only for her. And James Edward Holborn himself, providing the link between them. What had *he* to do with her? And what was she doing in *his* time?

Mrs. Runcorn rose. "We are being thoughtless, my dear. You have undergone a great ordeal. Allow me to show you to your room, where I make no doubt you will want to rest before we dine."

"Thank you. I — I think that might be a good idea." Christy searched for her purse, remembered she no longer had it, and stood. To her relief, her legs held her.

Mrs. Runcorn looked her over, her expression thoughtful. "We are much of a size, I believe. I shall find you a gown and night rail. Tomorrow we shall set about replenishing your wardrobe."

Amid Christy's renewed thanks, her hostess led her from the chamber and up the staircase at the end of the narrow hall. As they reached the first landing, children's voices shouted, laughed, and argued.

"Don't worry, I won't show you around our orphanage until tomorrow. And the boys are very good, I assure you."

48

A high-pitched wail rose at that moment, followed by Nancy's sharp reproof to someone named Sammy. Another voice piped up with the information that Alfie always whined, and it didn't mean nothin'.

"Now, no more mischief from you, Jem," Nancy declared. "Davey, get your 'ead out of them clouds and 'elp Tom clear the table. And mind, Bert," she added, her voice fading with her retreating footsteps, "the missus don't want to see that sullen face at the dinner table."

"Eight of them?" Christy asked again.

"Poor things. The weather has been so dreadfully cold, they haven't been able to go outside as much as they would like. There, I'm sure the novelty of having you for a teacher will have them on their best behavior. The schoolroom and the boys' rooms are on that floor," she added as they passed it. "And we are all up here."

Christy emerged into the upper hall and looked about, favorably impressed. The wainscoting boasted a fresh coat of white paint, and flowered paper covered the walls above. The rug might be threadbare, but not a single speck of dust or lint lingered. Polished tables displayed an assortment of china and glass knickknacks, and a bowl of flowers lent a bright touch.

"In here, my dear." Mrs. Runcorn opened a door at the end of the corridor. "I'll have Nancy tidy it a bit for you, and remove the Holland covers."

Christy stepped inside, and shivered at the chill air that greeted her. Slowly, her gaze traveled over the small chamber. It, too, had been recently painted, only this time in a light yellow. Christy's taste ran to bright, primary shades, but she found nothing at which to complain. A narrow bed stood against the center of the far wall, with a small but adequate fireplace opposite. A window let in faint sunlight, which fell across the white sheets that covered the other pieces of furniture.

"Don't bother Nancy. It sounded like she had her hands full with the kids. I can fix this up myself."

"You don't mind, my dear?" Mrs. Runcorn sounded surprised.

Christy smiled. "You'd be amazed how capable I am. Now, is there a bathroom nearby?"

"A—" Mrs. Runcorn broke off. "Would you wish a tub carried up here?"

Christy blinked. "Oh, no, that's not what I meant. Where do you wash your hands?"

"There is a basin, over here." Mrs. Runcorn swept a cover off a small chest, revealing a china basin painted with a delicate rose pattern. On the shelves inside the cupboard stood a matching pitcher and a chamber pot.

Christy swallowed as the real deprivations of her new situation came home to her. "Is the outhouse *very* far from the back door?" she asked.

"Do you mean the necessary?" Delicate color touched the lady's cheeks. "Not *very* far."

"Well, I always did enjoy an adventure. Now, where can I find towels, soap, and water?"

Mrs. Runcorn assured her these would be brought shortly by Nancy, then after only a few more protests, allowed her unusual guest to pull off the Holland covers, and returned to her own work.

As the door closed behind her hostess, Christy exposed an oak bureau. Next she found a matching dressing table and chair, then an armoire. The bed, when she bounced on it, proved to be comfortable enough. Two pieced quilts lay folded over the foot of the bare mattress. She'd have to add sheets to her list of requirements.

She turned to the last cover, and unearthed an ancient upholstered chair. She sat on it, then leaned back against the padded cushions. Not bad. She stifled a yawn. Maybe she'd just sit here for a few minutes. It had been rather an eventful day. She huddled into her down coat and closed her eyes.

When next she opened them, darkness engulfed the room, broken only by the dancing light from the fire in the hearth. It burned low, and the chill had vanished from the chamber. Christy yawned, stretched her arms over her head to ease her cramped muscles, then froze, suddenly wide awake.

The tiny room, the narrow bed, the chair in which she sat—this wasn't the Edgemont in Piccadilly. She was at the Runcorns' orphanage, somewhere in one of the poorer districts of London, almost two hundred years before she'd been born.

There went her last hope this entire impossible situation had been nothing but a bad dream. She'd been asleep now for several hours, at a rough guess, and she was still here. Unsteadily, she rose to her feet.

A small clock stood on the mantel over the hearth, and she peered at it. Nine-thirty? She'd been asleep longer than she realized. If only she'd been able to pull a Rip Van Winkle, and return to her own time.

An extra pillow and two more blankets now graced the bed, which had been made up with mended white sheets. A plate with rolls, cheese, an apple, and a knife stood on the dressing table, and someone—probably Mrs. Runcorn—had laid over the wooden chair a high-waisted gray dress with long sleeves topped by puffs at the shoulders, one of those long wool coats that buttoned to the high-waisted bodice, and a white nightgown. A comb now rested on the bureau, the soap dish held a scented cake, and a linen towel hung over the washstand door.

Christy looked for the pitcher, then finally spotted it on the hearth where the fire had kept the water warm. Touched by this thoughtfulness, she carried it to the washstand and poured some into the basin. She dragged off her coat and high-heeled boots, then pulled the blue turtleneck over her head and slid the wool skirt over her hips. She hung her clothes in the wardrobe as neatly as possible. An iron of some sort she could probably obtain, but dry cleaners were another matter.

She stood at the dressing table in only her royal blue camisole and slip with their black lace trim, and combed out the tangled mass of her dark brown hair. All she had with which to tie it back was the huge blue clip bow she had been wearing that morning. Next time she went time traveling, she'd have to pack a few things. Like hair pins. And makeup. And more chocolate.

She lit a candle with a spill from the hearth, washed her face, then as an afterthought rinsed out her underthings and hung them by the fire to dry. What she wouldn't give for a change! She pulled on the cavernous nightdress, climbed into bed, and quickly drifted off once more.

"Coo," a female voice exclaimed in tones of reverential awe.

51

Christy dragged open her eyes. Daylight streamed in through the window. By the washstand stood Nancy, holding up the camisole.

The maid eyed Christy with respect. "I ain't never seen the likes of this, afore. Major 'Olborn's below, askin' after you."

Christy climbed out of bed, feeling ridiculous—and somewhat floundering—in the tent she wore. Normally, she slept in an oversized T-shirt. "I'll be down in a few minutes. What time is it?"

"Gone on nine, it 'as. You missed breakfast, but I've brung you a tray. Are you puttin' this on?"

Christy took the camisole and slip from her. "I'll be down as fast as I can," she repeated.

As soon as the maid took her leave, Christy dragged off the tent, pulled on her underthings, then turned to the wardrobe. She'd better not wear her own clothes today. Major Holborn and the Runcorns had accepted her appearance without comment—so far, at least. If they had a chance to study the garments in more detail, though, it might lead to some ticklish questions. Zippers hadn't been invented yet. She'd better start conforming to the local—and temporal—standards.

By means of minor contortions, she managed to fasten the buttons at the back of the gray gown. The fact it fit a bit too tight didn't help any. Christy might be small, but she was generously endowed.

She ran her hands over the seams of the gown, and a new problem struck her. No pockets. And what was worse, no tissues. She'd have to get a handkerchief from somewhere. She dragged on her pantyhose and boots and, still chewing a slice of cold toast, hurried down the several flights of stairs.

Sounds of the boys reciting a dull lesson reached her as she passed the first-floor landing. She continued to the ground level and entered the sitting room she'd been in the night before.

The major stood near the hearth, leaning over to examine a paper Mrs. Runcorn held out to him. Christy stopped in her tracks, and drew a slow, appreciative breath. That was one man who would never disappear in a crowd. The power of his presence wrapped about her, making her vividly aware of him. A tingling sensation danced along her flesh. Sheer animal magnetism, wasn't that the trite phrase? At the moment, she couldn't think of a better.

The door closed behind her; he looked up, directly at her, and the penetrating assessment of his gaze sent her back a pace. Suspicion tempered yesterday's concern, and an element of challenge lay in the depths of those marvelous eyes. A thrill of nerves raced through her, leaving a hollow sensation in its wake.

His searching scrutiny rested on her a moment longer, then he awarded her a sketchy bow. "Good morning, Miss Campbell. I trust you are now rested?"

"Yes, thank you." Damn, the man unsettled her. She looked away, unable to meet the intensity of his regard. "Mrs. Runcorn, I'm really sorry about last night. I'd only meant to sit down for a minute, not fall asleep like that. Please forgive me."

"Of course, my dear. There is nothing to forgive. Now, the major has had the most delightful notion. He wishes to take you to the shops himself."

Christy cast an uneasy glance at him. "Do you? Are you quite certain? I don't want to put you to any trouble."

"It will be my pleasure. I am sure we have much still to discuss, Miss Campbell."

Even through that calm exterior, she caught the note of determination in his voice. Well, she couldn't blame him. He'd acted on generosity of spirit yesterday afternoon. By now he'd had time to reflect — and ask himself a few questions about her. Like how she happened to turn up so opportunely in his path, and in such desperate straits as to instantly appeal to his chivalry. In his position, she'd be suspicious of herself, too. And be out to learn a thing or two about this protegée.

That meant trouble time, for her.

She ran back up the stairs and grabbed the borrowed coat, then slowed as she started back down. He'd had his friends take her in before he'd had time to reflect. Did that mean he might change his mind and have them throw her out? Or would he keep her here, where they could watch her for him? He'd probably feel safer knowing where she was — and whether or not she tried to hurl a few knives at him, herself.

What *was* she going to say in response to the probing questions he must have planned for her?

Stick to the truth, she reminded herself—at least, as far as possible. That way she wouldn't trip herself up in a web of lies.

He waited in the lower hall. His gaze ran over her, and he nodded as if in silent approval—or as if one of his nagging uncertainties had been quieted. Apparently, she'd passed muster—this time, at least. She'd have to study everybody she saw, and copy the appropriate mannerisms and figures of speech, if she hoped to keep him from guessing how *very* much out of place she really was.

He escorted her outside to where a low-slung carriage stood before the door, with a little man holding the head of one of the matched gray horses harnessed to the rig. The major handed Christy into the seat, climbed up beside her, and started the pair. The man—a groom, she supposed—stepped back, then swung up behind as the carriage passed him.

Fascinated, Christy looked about, noting details she had been too upset to notice yesterday afternoon. A living museum surrounded her, with costumes, professions, and customs that would vanish with the coming of industrialization. And here it was, for her to see—and experience.

Again, they made the abrupt transition into a better neighborhood, and she leaned forward, trying to take in so many strange sights and sounds. A man in ragged clothes swept snow from a crossing with a stick broom. Vendors wandered the streets, shouting their wares. And so many people rode horses!

"Do you find London so very different from New York?" He cast a sideways glance at her. "That was where you said you were from, was it not?"

The first of his tests. She swallowed, and settled more decorously on the seat. "No, I'm from a tiny town in Connecticut. And yes, it's very different." That much, at least, was the truth.

Their carriage slowed behind a wagon filled with crates, and Christy swiveled about to watch the passing people. One of the horsemen behind them pulled up abruptly and turned away.

"How many days did the crossing take?" Major Holborn whipped up the team, and they swept past the obstructing vehicle.

"It seemed like forever." How many days *did* it take, at this time? She couldn't ever remember hearing. The Clipper Ships hadn't been developed yet, of that she felt certain. But did that mean months — or just weeks?

"You don't remember the date on which you set sail?"

Christy managed what she hoped was a convincing laugh. "It was postponed so many times. Our departure, I mean. The weather was bad."

He stiffened. "Indeed?"

Bad answer. She bit her lip. "There was something about the cargo not arriving on time, and the captain refusing to sail without it." That had a better sound to it. Most occurrences in life seemed to be motivated by finances.

She returned her attention to the passersby, hoping he'd accept her hazy responses for abstraction rather than evasiveness. Everything *did* enthrall her, after all; it was so very different from the world she knew. She leaned out to watch a huddled figure with a scarf wrapped about her head, who sat before a cart on which a small fire burned beneath a huge urn. The woman poured a cup of steaming liquid and handed it to a boy in exchange for a coin.

Christy craned her neck to look back, and out of the corner of her eye caught sight of a horseman pulling up short and turning away.

"That's the third time that same man has done that!" she exclaimed.

"What?" Major Holborn glanced at her, a frown creasing his brow.

She told him. "He's about half a block back, now, but he's been with us for some time. I don't think I'd have paid any attention to him if he didn't keep turning away like that."

"Indeed." He sounded grim. "Kepp, did you hear the lady?"

"Yes, sir," came the response from the groom.

"Will you keep an eye out for him? And can you contrive it so he doesn't know you're watching him?"

"That I will, sir."

They started forward once more. The major swung left at the first corner, then again at the next. After a fourth jaunt down a side street, he pulled out of the flow of traffic and brought his pair to a halt.

"Well, Kepp?"

The groom swung down. "He's still with us, sir. Begging your pardon, but it might prove mighty interesting if'n I was to have a word or two with him. Mighty interesting, indeed."

"No." A gleam lit the major's marvelously dark eyes. "That is a pleasure I intend to reserve for myself. I'm tired of being followed about." He inclined his head toward Christy. "If you will excuse me, Miss Campbell?" He tossed the reins to his groom, swung down from the carriage, and set off with a rapid, determined stride.

Chapter Six

"What's he doing?" Christy demanded of the frowning groom. "He's not going to tackle that man alone, is he? What if he's dangerous?"

"The major can take care of hisself, miss." Still, the groom directed an uneasy glance over his shoulder.

Christy sprang to her feet, setting the carriage rocking. "He may need help."

"If you please, miss?" Kepp steadied the horses. "He'd rather you didn't go getting yourself involved, like."

"Tough." Christy cast him a scathing look and jumped to the ground, only to trip in the unfamiliar long, narrow skirt. With a muttered oath, she hiked it up and set off at a run after Major Holborn. Already, he was far ahead with his long, swinging stride. His height, though, made it easy for her to spot him. He was a very striking figure, she realized.

And far too easy to follow. That thought left an uncomfortable sensation in the pit of her stomach.

She hurried on, jostling through the crowd. People stared at her, she suddenly realized. Apparently, ladies weren't supposed to run through the streets.

Standing on tiptoe, she tried to catch another glimpse of the major, but he'd vanished. Probably he'd rounded the corner.

57

She increased her speed, reached the end of the block, and collided with him.

He grabbed her and steadied her against his chest. For one breathless moment, she stared into his dark eyes, and the sheer power of the man slammed into her. Everything but the strength of his hands on her arms faded from her consciousness. Abruptly, he released her, and for a moment she floundered.

"Did he get away?" she managed.

He nodded, and the lines etched themselves more deeply about his mouth and eyes. "You should have stayed at the carriage."

"What, and let them pitch knives at you with no one to help you?"

"No one threw anything." His gaze rested on her, and after a moment, he added. "I am accustomed to being obeyed."

"That I can believe." She pulled herself back together. "I'm not one of your employees or servants or whatever you call them, though."

A slow smile lit his dark eyes. "Aren't you? I thought that was what you wanted, last night."

She swallowed. She could think of something else she was beginning to want, and it only confused the matter. She couldn't ever remember being so forcibly aware of a man before. She took refuge in offense, and faced him squarely. "You don't trust me, do you?"

He didn't answer at once. He offered her his arm, and led her back toward his carriage. At last, he said: "I don't know quite what to make of you. You warned me I was being followed."

"Just when you'd about decided I was one of your enemies? I'm not, though."

"What are you, then?"

"A very lost person, who's as confused by what's going on as you are. Come on, let's get on with this shopping trip. I'm in crying need of a toothbrush."

"And a number of other things, I should imagine."

She cast a sideways glance at him. "Why did you offer to bring me? I've never yet known a man who liked to shop."

"You have vast experience with the matter?" Again, that suspicious note crept into his voice.

58

"Well, my father always refused to go, and so do my brothers. My sister's husband only goes along to control how much she spends."

"You have a large family?" He fastened on this new topic.

"There are five of us kids. We—" She broke off. She missed them, more than she had thought possible. If she were never able to see them again . . . The thought sent an aching pang through her. She couldn't bear it if she missed Jon's and Melany's wedding, or never got to see Matt and Shelley's new baby. . . .

"Is your father a landowner?" His question dragged her back from her wallow in self-pity.

"No, a minister in a small town. He died three years ago."

"And what brought you to England?" They reached the carriage and he handed her in.

"I have a business—I deal in rare books and prints. I—"

"Indeed?" He broke across her words, surprised. His assessing gaze rested on her once more as he climbed in beside her.

"I came over on a buying trip," she continued, trying to ignore the unsettled sensation that rippled through her. "But things got a little crazy."

The major took the reins, the groom once more swung up behind, and they set forth. He headed the horses down another narrow lane, and slowed.

"The houses in this block are in a shocking state of repair," he informed her.

The most casual glance would be sufficient to tell anyone that. Paint peeled back to reveal layers of earlier colors, holes gaped in steps, ready to trap unwary feet, smashed panes of glass in the windows alternated with ones which were merely cracked. The icy wind must blow right through the rooms. Everywhere, piles of filth sullied the snow, and the stench couldn't be ignored. The children playing in the street wore such pitiful rags, they must be cold, always cold. And hungry. . . . Christy looked away, feeling ill.

"It distresses you?" His voice held a curious, intense note.

Her grasp tightened on the side of the carriage. "How can people be so darned heartless? Look at them, what chance have they got? From the time they're born, all they see is failure and poverty. They don't even know what it's *like* to succeed."

"You don't think this is normal? That if they worked harder, they could get out of this situation?"

So that was what he was getting at. "Quit preaching to the converted," she advised. "I've spent enough time working in homeless shelters to know every single person has a different story. Look, I'm all for doing something about living conditions, here and everywhere. You don't have to convince me to see your side of it. I already do."

"I am pleased to hear it." Still, skepticism sounded in his voice.

He didn't believe her. That meant, she supposed, she would be in for more of these tours while he tried to win her over. What would it take to convince him she was not in cahoots with his enemies, trying to silence his crusading voice?

And she wanted to convince him. She wanted his trust. She respected the strength of his convictions, admired him for them, and wanted his good opinion in return. That was all. There wasn't — there couldn't be! — anything more personal about it.

Major James Holborn cast a sideways glance at his companion, and fought against a tug of attraction. She was confoundedly pretty — though her appeal lay more in her lively manner and unusual charm than in any perfection of feature. Her gleaming hair massed in a riot of dusky ringlets about her rounded face. Today she didn't wear that bright blue bow that had fastened her curls at the top of her head. Too bad. It had suited her.

And what was he to make of her — enemy or damsel in distress? The neighborhood through which they passed honestly seemed to distress her. Was she, as she claimed, the daughter of a clergyman? That she was an American, he accepted without question. Being brought up in a savage land so far from the civilizing influences of London would explain the many oddities about her.

It would also explain her lack of missishness, and her casual avowal of dealing in books and art. What a very strange place American society must be, to have produced a young lady of such decided opinions. He found her refreshing.

Yet he fought his impulse to trust her. The possibility remained his nameless enemies had planted her on him. She might well be nothing more than an accomplished actress, hired to insinuate herself into his good graces. It behooved him to keep her near, watch her closely, and woo her support.

Unfortunately, the prospect appealed to him a little too strongly.

He wended his way through another poor district, and at last emerged into territory belonging exclusively to the elite of London society. She still evinced the same fascination, as if all this were new to her. She leaned from the curricle, staring about, eager to see every sight, distressed by the poverty, enthralled by the elegance. If he weren't suspicious, he would be convinced she had never before been in London — or even any large city.

He drew to a halt in Jermyn Street before the shop of a modiste with whom he had dealings before. The unconventional Miss Campbell would not alarm Madam Hendricks.

Miss Campbell eyed the front critically. "It looks expensive."

"I am quite able to afford it." He found her caveat irritating. Had part of him wanted to discover her as willing to dip into his pockets as the dubious ladies of his acquaintance? In a way, it would be easier to find this to be the case, to learn his first impression of her had been wrong, that the air of quality which distinguished her had been feigned. Then at least he would know what to make of her.

She regarded him with a troubled expression haunting her huge eyes. "I'm *not* able to afford it," she said bluntly. "This is coming out of my salary, remember, and I don't want to spend more than I'll be able to earn." She offered a smile, as if to soften her stubbornness: "Look, I'm only going to be teaching, and I don't even know how long I'm going to be here. Isn't there somewhere cheaper that would do just as well?"

"Cheaper, if you mean less dear, certainly. But not just as well. Under the circumstances, I require you to dress as a lady, to avoid any unfortunate incidents."

"What do you mean?"

He clenched his jaw. Was she truly so innocent he had to spell it out for her? That possibility both intrigued and disturbed him. "You will be residing in a less than elegant district, Miss

61

Campbell. You will encounter men who might not behave toward you in a gentlemanly manner unless they are imbued with respect for you."

"You don't think I can take care of myself?" Her vivid blue eyes danced with a challenge.

He found it hard to resist. The devil! She stirred some very ungentlemanly impulses in him. "We will go in," he said shortly.

She clambered down without waiting for his assistance, which further irritated him. "Walk the horses, Kepp," he snapped. The groom accepted the ribbons from him, though fixed such a reproving regard on him as to bring him up short. James raised a coolly inquiring eyebrow. "Is something the matter, Kepp?"

"You shouldn't ought to be taking a lady like her down some of them streets, sir. As well you know."

"She isn't your usual sort of lady, Kepp."

The groom snorted. "You ain't never said a truer word, sir. That's one as is real quality. Not one of them simpering misses, but one with a bit of spirit."

"You like her?" He regarded his henchman in surprise.

"She's a right 'un, sir, no mistaking that."

"Isn't there?" The major turned away, frowning. Kepp was not one to lightly bestow his approval.

He followed Miss Campbell into the intimate front room of the shop. Long, gilt-trimmed mirrors hung on every wall, interspersed with several fetching creations of lace and gauze. He found her critically examining these with a look of disapproval on her expressive features.

Despite his uncertainties about her, he smiled. "You don't like them?"

"They're so—so frilly." She wrinkled her upturned nose. "Isn't there anything practical here?"

"I didn't think ladies were overly concerned with that."

"You certainly go in for chauvinistic stereotyping, don't you? If I'm going to be teaching a pack of preteen boys, I'm going to need something sturdy. And warm."

"So you will." He turned to the gaunt-faced woman who stood in the doorway at the back of the shop.

Madam Hendricks held herself stiffly, eyeing Miss Campbell with the unloving smile of one about to forcibly have an intruder

62

evicted. One glance at James, though, apparently changed her mind. "Major Holborn." She advanced toward him. "What would the young person wish to see?" she added in cool but civil tones.

"The young *lady*," he corrected, "has need of two morning gowns, a pelisse, and an evening gown or two. Something that can be delivered on the morrow, if you please."

"On the—" The woman broke off. "We have a few samples, of course. I am sure they will suffice."

James inclined his head. "Please see to it. Miss Campbell, I will return for you in about two hours. If by any chance you finish before that time, you will find a haberdashery two doors down on the left. I should have returned before you have completed your purchases. If not—" He broke off and drew a small purse from his pocket.

She took it, then looked at it as if she didn't know what to do with it.

"I would suggest you purchase a reticule." He bowed over her hand, then directed a curt nod toward the modiste.

From what little he had seen of Miss Campbell, he had few doubts she would manage very well. With only a minor qualm about letting her out of his untrusting sight, he set forth for the St. James's parish workhouse in Soho. No matter his personal problems, the overcrowded conditions at this establishment demanded immediate attention.

He returned two hours later, scowling. He had hit upon no remedy for the workhouse's pitiful conditions, but he had mentally composed the next segment of his social commentary. The wealthy elite must be brought to notice the plight of those less fortunate. Haranguing, as he had tried earlier, only had won him enemies. To make his cause popular, he would have to entertain his audience, make them laugh, provide a way in which they could draw enjoyment from helping others. He had to make it fashionable, and that was not going to be easy.

He entered the modiste's, but saw no sign of Miss Campbell. As he turned to go out, though, fabric rustled and the curtain separating the front of the shop from the back parted.

The proprietress emerged. "Major Holborn. Do come back. Miss has been enjoying a cup of coffee while she waits."

His eyebrows rose a fraction, and he preceded the woman into her workroom. Never before had he entered this portion of the establishment, and he glanced about at the tables laden with fabrics and the group of women industriously stitching by the light of candles.

A young lady, not in her first blush of youth but with a quiet elegance, sat before a large desk on which a coffee-pot, a plate of biscuits, and two cups sat on a tray. Her white muslin gown, sprigged with tiny roses, boasted a low-scooped bodice filled with netting to her throat, where it fastened with a delicate bow. A delightful high poke bonnet framed a round face with startlingly vivid blue eyes and a full, laughing mouth. Clusters of tight dark ringlets hung about her neck. With a sense of shock, he recognized Miss Campbell.

"Is this all right?" she asked.

The devil! He hadn't noted before how husky and sweet her voice could be. For the first time in a very long while, he floundered for a permissible answer.

"I prefer bright colors," she went on, "but Madam Hendricks says it 'wouldn't be at all the thing.'" She glanced at the older woman. "Did I get that right?"

"You did." The modiste eyed James. "Miss has been telling me what a dreadful time she has had."

"Dreadful, indeed," he agreed. "Miss Campbell, you look quite delightful."

"Madam Hendricks has been terrific, Major," Miss Campbell declared with a rush of warmth. "She told me what I needed to buy at the other store—what you call things over here. And when I got back, they'd already altered this to fit me." She rose and moved to where he could see her. "Do I look like a teacher, now?"

"No," he said before he could stop himself, then could have bitten his tongue as her face fell.

"I *knew* it should have been simpler. I'll have to return this," she told Madam Hendricks. "And he'll never approve of that evening dress."

"Indeed, I most likely shall. You will not be an instructress forever, remember. Your difficult situation will be rectified as soon as you have sent a letter to your people in America."

She opened her mouth, then closed it again, and his suspicions surged once more to the forefront. Damn this vacillating. Why couldn't he make up his mind about her? *Could* her situation be rectified? Was she impoverished, sent by her American family to try her fortunes in England? Or was she an adventuress—or even in the pay of his enemy?

Part of him objected to that last possibility. Yet with knives landing within inches of his back, he was in no position to take anything—or anyone—on trust. Despite her provocative voice and very kissable mouth. His gaze rested on her full lips, his pulse quickened, and a most unwelcome longing stirred in him.

"Have you finished here?" he asked abruptly. "Then I had best take you back to the Runcorns."

They accomplished most of the return journey in silence. He ought to be pointing out more instances of poverty and despair among the denizens of the back slums, but he found her mere presence disturbing. It would be best if he avoided her company in future. He drew up before the orphanage in record time, and Kepp carried her packages inside.

She descended to the paving, then looked up at him with a hesitancy that sat oddly on her vivacious features. "Thank you," she said simply.

"My pleasure." He touched the brim of his curly beaver, and set his pair in motion without allowing himself to look back at her. He needed to concentrate on his work, on recording the expedition to the workhouse before the right tone slipped irrevocably from his mind. The last thing he needed was a very lovely—and possibly treacherous—distraction.

Not until late the following afternoon did he finish his new chapter, and only then did he permit his thoughts to return to Miss Campbell. He should visit the Runcorns, he supposed. Not that he had any desire to see Miss Campbell, of course. He merely needed to assure himself all progressed as it should, and she filled her position to their satisfaction.

He drove himself to the disreputable alleys off Golden Lane, left Kepp with instructions to walk his pair until he returned, and ran lightly up the steps and rapped on the door. A little over a minute passed before Nancy appeared.

Her easy smile brightened. "Lord love you, guv'nor, we

thoughts as you'd be 'ere right early this mornin'.'"

"Is something amiss?" He handed over his hat, pulled off his gloves, and shrugged himself out of his greatcoat.

"No, ain't nothin' amiss." She laid his beaver aside and accepted his other things. "Everythin's gone right, it 'as. That lady you brung is a wonder. The boys'll do anythin' she says, just to 'ear 'er talk."

Above them, footsteps pounded the length of the hall, and the ceiling shook. Startled, James looked up. After a brief pause, the thundering resumed, headed in the other direction.

"What the devil — ?" He looked toward Nancy.

She giggled, and jerked her head toward the steps. "You go on up, guv'nor." She started down the hall in the direction of the kitchens.

Several childish voices rose in laughter, then faded beneath the mad dash for the other end of the room. Intrigued, he made his way to the floor above, then down the hall to the large chamber allocated for the boys' lessons. He entered as the rush started once more.

"Remember, it has to be spelled *right!*" Miss Campbell's husky voice shouted over the hubbub.

He stopped in the doorway, scanning the room. Mrs. Runcorn sat in a chair near him, chuckling softly as she watched the scene. Six of the boys stood at one end arranging blocks, each with a letter painted on it. The last two boys reached them, only to be left behind as the others took off for the other side, where they scrambled among a large pile of wooden cubes, seeking the letters they needed.

"What, in the name of all that is holy, is going on?" he demanded.

Miss Campbell, attired in a becoming gown in a deep shade of rose muslin, jumped up from her chair in the middle. "Wilfred, you give that back to Alfie. He had it first. You'll have to find another one."

The wiry little nine-year-old turned his tousled dark head to glare at her. "Ah, Miss Campbell — "

"You heard me, Wilfred. You try that again, and it's back to the slate board for you."

"Yes'm," the boy muttered, chastened, and dove once more

66

into the pile of blocks. The others began their run to the opposite side of the room, and grumbling, Wilfred followed several seconds later.

"Done!" A slender, fair twelve-year-old raised his hands over his head.

The next moment two more finished as well, and the stragglers ran up with their last letters and shoved them into place.

"Very good!" Miss Campbell surveyed the blocks. "Round three goes to—no, it doesn't. Tom, you've got the wrong letters. 'School' is spelled with a 'ch,' not a 'k.' Remember?"

"*I* remembered," shouted the boy who had finished second. "*I* win."

Miss Campbell scrutinized his efforts. "So you do, Jem. Very good, all of you. Why don't we—"

"Miss Campbell!" One of the younger ones interrupted her, jerking his head toward the door.

She looked up, eyes bright and laughing, and a soft flush lent becoming color to her cheeks. "I didn't hear you come in, Major."

"No, I'm surprised you could hear anything, with all that running and shouting."

To his consternation, her lips tightened and her shoulders trembled. Instantly, he regretted his words. "I didn't mean—"

Her laughter cut off his apology. "I'm sorry," she managed when she could speak again. "You looked so shocked. I *know* this isn't the way you teach at—over here, but it's easier to learn when you're having fun. Isn't it?" she asked of the children, and got a chorus of agreements.

"Where did you acquire your teaching methods?" he demanded, torn between amusement and uncertainty at her unorthodox approach.

"Sesame Street," came her prompt response.

"Where?"

She laughed again, an easy, mischievous sound that enveloped him, warming in its richness, unsettling in its effect on him.

"It's a place that makes learning fun," she explained. "My nieces and nephews watch—go there. And Gina—my sister who

67

teaches second grade—swears by it for helping kids with the basics."

"What else do you have planned?"

She raised her chin, as if challenging him to object. "Tomorrow we're going to start on accents and manners."

"On what?" That took him by surprise.

"Accents and manners. They're all young enough to change the way they talk. You don't want to grow up to be street sweepers, do you?" she asked the boys.

Several shook their heads "no," but not with certainty. "What *will* we do?" the fair, slender boy asked.

"Anything you want, Tom," Miss Campbell said. "Would you like to work in an office? Be a clerk, maybe?"

"Don't be daft, miss." One of the older boys waved his hand in denial. "We ain't goin' to get no jobs like that."

"Why not? If you talk and act like office clerks, that's exactly what you'll become. Then no more of this hand-to-mouth existence in these slums. You'll earn money—*real* money—and be able to live in comfortable houses and buy whatever you need."

"Cor," another breathed, apparently awed by this picture of security.

James's lips twitched, and he fought them into a stern line. "You are undermining the social class system, Miss Campbell."

She inclined her head in acknowledgment. "Thank you. I try."

"If all Americans are like you, it must be a very strange place," he said, with feeling.

Her grin broadened, staggering him. He had thought her large, startlingly blue eyes dominated her charming face. But when her incredible smile flashed, it took his breath away.

"Miss," Tom piped up. "We wants another word."

"Spell 'school,' " she shot at him. He did, stumbling only a little over the 'ch,' and she nodded. "All right, pick the next one."

A minute later, all eight boys dove into the pile of blocks for the first letter of "carriage."

"Remember the spelling rules we covered earlier!" she shouted over the commotion.

"Will they?" He raised a dubious eyebrow.

"I should think so. We made up rhymes until they got the idea."

"Do you make everything a game?"

"If possible. It's a lot more effective."

"A lot noisier, too."

She smiled and shook her head. "That's a small sacrifice. Besides, it's too cold to take them outside to run off their energy. This way we're having a lesson and recess combined. Maybe you'd rather come back tomorrow morning when we're doing math. I have a quiet game planned for that."

They watched in silence, until a shout from one of the boys and a chorus of groans from the others announced that someone had succeeded in spelling the word. Miss Campbell congratulated Davey, then encouraged the others to finish, as well.

Mrs. Runcorn rose. "It is time for their chores, Miss Campbell."

The young lady nodded. "You heard Mrs. Runcorn. I want all the blocks put away and the tables straightened. Or there won't be any games tomorrow," she added as a dark threat.

James leaned against the jamb, watching with approving eyes as the boys scurried to straighten the mess caused by their games. Miss Campbell had a knack with children, he had to admit that. No, he corrected himself the next moment, she had a knack with everyone. Energy and enthusiasm bubbled from her. She made him want to run laughing through the meadows in a game of tag, which he hadn't done in nearly thirty years. She made him want to—

The blood pounded through his veins, and he cut off that thought. Despite his suspicions—and her free and easy mannerisms—she did not have the appearance of a straw damsel. He would not—*could* not—insult her. He would learn more about her, though.

He moved aside to allow the boys to file past and up the stairs to begin whatever chores awaited them. "Miss Campbell," he said softly as she followed.

She stopped and turned her steady gaze on him. The uneasy sensation shot through him that she wished to know as much about him as he did about her. "Will you drive with me?" he asked.

She started to agree, then glanced at Mrs. Runcorn.

"Of course, my dear," that lady said at once. "You have already done far more than I expected."

"Put on your pelisse." He watched as she hurried past and ran lightly up the stairs. She almost bounced, so light and energetic was her step.

"She is the most charming creature." Mrs. Runcorn's gaze followed her. "I vow, James, I could not be more pleased with her. You see how the children adore her, and they memorized so many rules today, which I have never been able to make them do before. She makes everything a treat."

"Has she said anything about herself?"

"She comes from a large family, that is certain. Her father was a vicar, I believe, and so is her eldest brother."

He nodded slowly. No contradictions in her stories yet. But was it all real — or a carefully rehearsed pretense?

She returned more quickly than he expected. A becoming bonnet now covered the top of her hair, which escaped in a riot of curls about her neck. The new pelisse of brown wool must have been delivered that morning. On the whole, he found himself favorably impressed with the picture she made.

"Did everything you require arrive?" He escorted her down the stairs.

"Yes, Madam Hendricks was so kind. And you have been, too. Thank you so much."

Her rush of warmth unsettled him. The devil take it, he found her far too attractive for his own good. If his enemies had planted a spy on him, they could not have made a better choice.

Disturbed by how much he enjoyed her company, he led the way outside, where they waited in the icy wind for Kepp to return with the curricle. Two minutes later, the grays swept into sight, moving with an ease that still commanded his admiration.

Kepp drew them to a halt, jumped to the ground and handed over the reins. "Bit of a breeze blowing up, sir," he said. "Looks like it's coming on to snow."

His comment was an understatement. Dark clouds gathered overhead, and the wind whipped Miss Campbell's skirt about her shapely ankles. James dragged his gaze from the sight. Today he would show her how the poor suffered in such weather. Christmas could be a very bleak time of year.

Miss Campbell scrambled into the curricle in a manner that would have drawn shocked exclamations from the fusty matrons of society. He found it quite taking—as he did most of her unconventional ways. Annoyed with himself, he took his place at her side and set his pair in motion.

As they turned the corner at the end of the short street, something shot past his head and hit the back of the seat with a thud. He caught his horses' mouths, then released them the next moment as he saw the firm ball of white snow rolling down to the cushions.

Miss Campbell picked it up, started to toss it over the side, then brought it back. Her gloved fingers dug through the tightly compacted flakes, and a soft exclamation escaped her. "There's a rock in here! A large, sharp one. Now where—"

The next landed on the rump of the near horse. The animal lashed out, kicking the traces with a blow that sent the curricle skittering sideways over the icy paving. The other horse reared, and the carriage snapped back into position, setting the first horse bucking as the pole rammed into it. The vehicle teetered on the off wheel, Kepp cried out in alarm, and too late, James tried to catch Miss Campbell as they overturned into the gutter.

Chapter Seven

Christy floundered to her hands and knees in a snow drift made deep by the clearing of the street. At least something broke that fall, it would have been awful —

Her unsteady gaze fell on Major Holborn, where he lay slumped in the shallow layer of new-fallen flakes over the cobbles. She stumbled clear of the bank and ran to him, as he dragged himself to his feet.

"Are you hurt?" she cried.

"No." He pushed past her, his movements stiff, and made his way to where the horses struggled on the ground, kicking and striking out in their attempts to regain their feet. He grasped the headstall of the nearest. "Kepp!" he shouted.

The groom limped over from the other side, soothing the off horse with gentle words. The major ran his hand down the near animal's neck, reached the harness, and tugged it free from the shaft. Kepp supported the carriage bar while the major unbuckled another strap. The gray lunged upward, caught its balance, and stood quivering, covered in nervous sweat, barely touching the off hind leg to the paving.

Christy grabbed the torn remnants of a rein and led the frightened beast a few yards away. It trembled, blowing hard, neck and chest drenched. Its ears twitched, and blood from a jagged cut seeped down its flank. She stroked the horse's shoulder, murmuring softly.

A minute later the two men freed the other gray. While Kepp held the animal's head, the major knelt and examined its legs, then stepped back and nodded to Kepp. The groom led the horse forward.

"Naught but a strain, I shouldn't think," Kepp called back, a heartened note in his voice.

The major nodded, then turned to Christy. "Thank you, Miss Campbell."

"He's got a nasty cut." She continued her soothing stroking of the animal's withers and neck.

"Let's have a look at it."

Allowing Christy to retain her hold on the horse, he cast a cursory glance at the bloodied flank. His mouth tightened in an angry line, but he turned his attention to the more pressing matter of the beast's legs. He ran his hand along each, feeling the muscles and joints. On the off hind, as he reached the cannon bone, the animal jerked away.

"Poultices tonight, I think." He patted the gray's rump. "Let's see what you've done, here." He bent once more, this time examining the flank, and his brow creased. "Now, how did you do this, old boy?" Without looking up, he called: "Are the shafts broken, Kepp?"

The groom led the horse he held back to the wreckage, and studied the tangled mass of wooden poles and leather straps. "Looks sound, sir," he called back after a couple of minutes.

"Could the other one have kicked him?" Christy suggested.

"This wasn't caused by a shoe." Frowning, the major flicked remnants of snow from about the wound. "I believe that second snowball also had a rock in it."

"Why—" She broke off and stared at him, horrified. "Look, you've got to go to the police or whatever you have over here. This is awful! Playing practical jokes on you is one thing, but hurting the horses goes beyond all limits! Are you going to report this?"

His steady gaze rested on her face.

Warmth flooded her already heightened color. "All right, so I'm an animal lover," she snapped. "Is there anything wrong with that?"

73

"Nothing in the least," he said. "I applaud it. But what, precisely, am I supposed to tell the watch? That someone threw a couple of snowballs with rocks inside? Thank you, but I have no desire to become the laughingstock of the local magistrate. I would probably be told not to drive a sporting vehicle through a district where its cost could support all the residents in comfort for the better part of a year."

"Could it?" Christy glanced at the vehicle, still lying on its side, then her slow gaze traveled across the people who had gathered to watch, some jeering, some silent, their faces masks of antagonism. Not one of them had moved to help, she realized.

A wrenching fear stirred in the bottom of her stomach. Riots in the streets, one version of his book had read. A revolution against the upper classes — which he so completely epitomized in his manners and appearance.

She swallowed. "Let's get out of here."

The major turned toward the watchers, singled out a boy, and gestured him to come forward. When the lad did, the major drew several coins from his pocket. "Are you familiar with the Golden Lane Orphanage?" he asked.

The boy eyed the coins. "Aye, guv'nor.

"Have a couple of your friends help you take my curricle there, will you? A guinea each?"

Two more boys rushed forward and eagerly set about hoisting the vehicle back onto its wheels. The horses started and stamped uneasily, but settled again. The carriage must have been light, for the boys righted it with ease. One of them held Kepp's gray while he examined the undercarriage.

After an intent survey, the groom nodded in approval. "No obvious damage, sir. Still, I'd like to see it gone over afore you're fixing to drive out again."

The major nodded his agreement, then watched the boys back the curricle in a circle, one holding each of the shafts, and a third supporting the middle pole. They set off at a trot toward the orphanage.

The major dusted his hands on the sides of his buckskins, then took the long reins from Christy. "Again, thank you, Miss Campbell. You have shown excellent presence of mind."

74

She grinned. "No problem. Are you all right? We landed pretty hard."

A slow smile twitched the corners of his lips. "You are a remarkable young woman, Miss Campbell. Under the circumstances I would expect you to indulge in a fit of the vapors."

"The what?" She laughed. "What on earth is that?"

He shook his head. "Something I would be willing to wager is very far from your nature." He started after the boys, slowing his steps to accommodate the lame horse. "I regret our expedition has come to naught."

She shrugged. "It doesn't matter. Maybe we can go out again another time. Was there something particular you wanted to show me?"

"I want you to know London as I do." The steadiness of his voice barely covered the force behind his words. "I want you to see how these people must live, especially at this time of year."

She looked at a group of women who stood by the side of the narrow street watching them, at their ragged garments which were insufficient to keep out the cold. "You don't have to show me. In San Fr — in the place where I live, I work at a homeless shelter. I've seen people who've lost everything, who don't have a roof over their heads or enough food to eat, and God, how I hate it." She shivered. "England hasn't cornered the market on poverty, you know."

She huddled into her pelisse and wished she'd worn her down jacket instead. The days were far too short — and cold. At least she had *something* warm to wear, unlike so many of these people. She tried to put her hand in her pocket for her plastic bag of chips, but her fingers met only solid fabric. No pockets. She'd left the bag in the other coat.

She sighed. "I need chocolate."

His mobile eyebrows rose. "Would you care to stop at an inn for a pot? You look chilled, and you've been through a very traumatic experience."

"Pot, nothing. I want the chewable kind."

At that, he frowned. "I greatly fear there isn't a confectioners in this quarter of town."

"Terrific." If even one of those would do her much good. If memory served — and when it came to chocolate, it usually

75

did—there wasn't supposed to be any of the solid eating stuff until 1847. That meant for the next thirty-seven years, she'd only find something vastly inferior. Of course, cocoa butter came along about 1828. She considered the eighteen-year wait and shuddered. She'd never survive.

It made one more reason why she had to return to her own time, and as quickly as possible. Her meager supply of chips couldn't last much longer.

They turned off Golden Lane, onto the narrow alley leading to the orphanage. Mr. Runcorn, huddled in his greatcoat, stood outside with the boys and the curricle, staring up the street to where Kepp approached with the sound gray. His hands shielded his eyes. As Christy and the major came into view, Mr. Runcorn hurried forward to meet them.

"James!" Concern showed on his every feature. "What happened?"

Briefly, Major Holborn explained about the snowball.

The elderly man shook his head. "This is getting serious, James. Miss Campbell might have been seriously hurt."

"But I wasn't," she said quickly.

"My horse may have been." The major bent to run a hand over the animal's leg again.

As Mr. Runcorn joined him in a gentle probing of the tendon along the cannon bone, an unwieldy carriage rounded the corner. Its body perched precariously above wheels which were over five feet in diameter. Christy watched in fascination as the driver bounced along, and wondered when he would be thrown out.

One of the blacks harnessed to the shafts shook its beautiful head, setting the harness bells jingling, and its companion danced daintily sideways. Christy whistled softly. "There's someone asking for trouble. That turnout must have cost a small fortune. What is it?"

Major Holborn looked up to follow the direction of her gaze, and a slight smile relieved the severity of his expression. "That, Miss Campbell, is my cousin, Saint Ives."

"I meant, what is he driving?"

"Ah, a swan-necked phaeton. Have they not become popular in America, yet? You shall have to have the dubious honor of riding in one."

"No, thanks."

The major cast her an amused glance, and stepped forward to greet the new arrival.

Christy regarded the major's cousin with interest, from the graying sandy brown hair that protruded from beneath his high-crowned curly hat, to the sharp face which appeared to consist primarily of a thin beakish nose, narrow mouth, and pointy chin. The heaviness of his coat did nothing to hide the slenderness of his build.

St. Ives's gaze fell on her, and she stepped back, suddenly uncomfortable. An overly polished, cold-fish type. His upper lip appeared to be curled perpetually into a sneer.

He returned his regard to the major. "Dear Coz, a carriage accident? You?" A flash of humor lit his steely eyes.

Major Holborn merely smiled. "A badly misplaced snowball. What brings you here?"

"You, dear boy, what else would induce me into this benighted neighborhood?" An exquisite shudder ran through St. Ives. "I've had the merry devil of a time tracking you down, too. Wickes finally told me you were here." He glanced at the building again and the curl of his lip deepened. "You have an unaccountable fondness for this district."

"For the people," the major agreed. "And what is of such urgency you permit it to drag you into so unsavory a neighborhood?"

"The pleasure of your company, what else? I'm having a gathering at my house for dinner tomorrow night, and thought you might care to join us."

Major Holborn raised an eyebrow, and Christy gained the impression this was an unusual invitation, and not one motivated by any desire for the pleasure of his company, either. Uneasy, she pressed the major's arm in silent warning.

He ignored her. Smiling, he said: "Who else will be there?"

St. Ives rattled off several names with titles, all unknown to Christy. They obviously made an impression on the major, though.

He frowned. "You have a number of important members of the government. Why do you want me?"

St. Ives's smile thinned. "With your appalling hobby,

77

Coz, I thought you might like the opportunity."

Major Holborn nodded slowly. "Does this mean I have free rein in what I say?"

A slow grin spread over St. Ives's narrow face. "Anything you can make them listen to, dear boy, anything at all."

The man was up to something. It struck Christy that the major might well be walking into a lion's den. If that were the case, now was not the time for good manners. She couldn't let him go alone to face . . . who knew what?

She managed a soulful expression. "What fun! Oh, what a wonderful evening you will have, Major. I wish—" She broke off in pretended confusion.

Major Holborn cast a shrewd glance at her, and clamped his mouth closed.

St. Ives raised his eyebrows and glanced at the major. "You have not, dear cousin, introduced me as yet to this charming creature."

Christy gritted her teeth at the phrase and smiled. She didn't want to tell him off—yet.

The major hesitated, then said: "Miss Campbell, an American visitor. This is my cousin, the earl of St. Ives."

St. Ives swept off his hat in as elegant a version of a bow as could be managed from his precarious perch. Christy batted her long lashes in feigned delight at making his acquaintance. The earl extended his invitation to her, as well, and Christy thanked him. His mission apparently accomplished, St. Ives touched his hat once more and drove off.

Major Holborn turned on her as soon as the carriage pulled out of hearing range. "What the devil are you about?"

Christy folded her arms and stuck out her stubborn chin. "I don't trust him."

"Why on earth not?"

"Someone's out to hurt you, in case you've forgotten."

His brow snapped down. "And you think it's St. Ives?" He shook his head. "You are fair and far out, my girl. Why should he want to? We are cousins. I was raised by his father. I have known him since my cradle."

"Are you sure he isn't harboring some old grudge?"

"The idea is ridiculous."

78

She glared back at him. "He's up to no good. He wants something from you."

"More likely it is his wife who wants me present, to drive a couple of old bores away from her dinner table at an early hour."

Christy considered. "Are they? Old bores, I mean?"

"Devil a doubt. Have you ever known a person in government who wasn't?"

At that, she smiled, albeit with reluctance. "Some things never change, I guess. I haven't embarrassed you too much, have I?"

He inclined his head. "I can see that having the charge of you, Miss Campbell, is going to tax even my inventiveness."

He took his leave of her to care for his horses and carriage, and she went inside to be greeted by Mrs. Runcorn with a cup of hot tea.

St. Ives's motive behind that invitation continued to trouble Christy as she stiffly made her way to her room. The earl did not appear to be a man bent on the selfless purpose of helping his cousin's work. She would have to wait until tomorrow night, she supposed, to find out what he was up to. At least she had assured the major would not attend the gathering without a friend.

A friend? She lay on her bed and frowned at the blazing fire. That brought up the whole issue of why she was here in the past. The major must be a key actor in some event shortly to take place, that much *seemed* clear. Otherwise, his would not have been the only book to shift between versions of what occurred. *But what was going to happen?*

Her gaze strayed to the clothes cupboard, where she had secreted his *Life in London,* wrapped in her sweater to keep it hidden. What was her role? To help the major—or hinder him? *And why her?* She slammed her fist into the mattress in frustration. If only she could talk to him about it, *warn* him, maybe together they could find some answers.

She envisioned the result and cringed. He'd talk to her, all right—the whole time he drove her to the local mental hospital. Bedlam, wasn't it? If she kept at this much longer, she'd belong there.

Her restless fingers plucked at the coverlet. Okay, she'd ignore the *whys* for now. She'd work on the *hows.* Such as how, when she knew so little about history, was she to prevent some action of the major's from starting a revolution?

She shied from contemplating that horrendous responsibility. Instead, she spent the evening creating mathematical crossword puzzles for the boys, aimed at determining their various skill levels. This accomplished, she turned her attention to devising a fun way to memorize the multiplication table. That occupied her thoughts for the better part of an hour, and saw the demise of two more of her precious chocolate chips. At last, she admitted herself temporarily stumped.

The following morning, interspersed with spelling, math, and reading lessons, Christy began the boys' instruction in the subtle art of rising above their class. At every opportunity she corrected speech and manners, then challenged the boys to do the same for each other. Mrs. Runcorn observed this process with considerable approval, while Nancy watched with absolute awe.

At first, Christy noticed the maid finding chores to do right outside the schoolroom door. As the lessons progressed, Nancy did less actual work and more just standing and listening. Finally, Christy invited her to join them, saying the boys needed interaction with a lady.

"Me, miss?" Nancy laughed, though with little humor. "I ain't no lady."

Christy fixed her with a firm stare. "You are if you act like one."

Intrigued, Nancy joined them, and worked with a determined intensity that piqued Christy's curiosity. After she at last dismissed the boys to their chores, she helped the maid straighten the room. The girl continued to practice, holding her shoulders straighter, even bobbing a clumsy curtsy to a desk as she passed.

Christy watched her, wondering what lay behind this dedication. She replaced the last of the books on the shelf, then regarded the maid. "What would you like to do with your life, Nancy?"

The girl leaned back against a chair, a dreamy halfsmile just touching her lips. "Mr. Wickes — what is valet to Major 'Olborn — says as it's a good life bein' a lady's maid. I won't never talk flash enough for that, though. Not to 'is likin', least ways."

"And why not?" Christy demanded.

The girl shrugged. "Mr. Wickes, 'e don't 'old with a mort what forked a tattler or two in 'er time. You'd think as it was 'im as was earl, and not the major's cousin."

She took herself off, leaving Christy to fathom the meaning of her cryptic utterances. She finally decided the valet must disapprove of Nancy's former profession as a pickpocket. On the whole, she couldn't blame him. There were worse ways, though, Nancy might have made her living.

Evening—and the dinner party—at last approached, and with trepidation Christy faced the task of transforming herself into a respectable lady of this era. She donned her new high-waisted gown of amber crepe, then regarded her reflection with misgivings. A suitable dress wasn't enough. Her hair was all wrong, her face didn't look right without makeup, and who was *she* to be teaching the boys manners? She had no idea how to behave, herself!

A gentle rap sounded on the door, and Nancy stuck her head inside. "If'n you don't mind, miss, I'd be right glad to lend a 'and. If you'll 'elp me talk more genteel?"

"Of course." Christy regarded the maid in relief. "Do you have any idea what to do with my hair?"

"I've 'elped the missus a time or two," Nancy offered, though her tone implied the results had been less than desired. "It can't be that 'ard, it can't."

After several initial mishaps, and considerable pauses to explain points of grammar, they at last achieved a creditable arrangement of the thick masses of Christy's curls. Christy stood before the mirror, regarding herself with a critical eye. She felt like she was going to a costume party.

It would be much easier if she were. Then she wouldn't have to worry about what she said or how she behaved. She hadn't been brought up to the world she would enter tonight. She was a twentieth-century American, and not of the upper classes, either. Her manners were far too free and casual for this time period.

She tried, unsuccessfully, to calm the fluttering of nerves in her stomach. What if she embarrassed both herself and the major? She dreaded proving a source of ridicule for that St. Ives.

There was only one thing to be done. She went in search of Mrs. Runcorn, to ask about any blatant taboos.

She hurried straight to the sitting room, but that cozy apartment stood empty. Christy's heart sank, and she bit her lip. So little time, so much to learn. Mrs. Runcorn probably busied herself in the kitchens, where Christy's frantic questions would be an unwelcome interruption. She hoped the woman would understand, and forgive. Once more, she set off in search of her.

She had taken no more than ten steps down the hall, though, when a sharp rap sounded on the front door. She hesitated a moment, then shrugged and went to answer it. Probably she breached all sorts of social rules, but it seemed ridiculous to just stand there and wait for Nancy to drop whatever she did.

She swung the door wide, then stared in awe at the impressive figure on the porch. The light from the hall fell on Major Holborn's black wool cloak, which parted in front to reveal a black velvet coat, a white waistcoat, and black satin knee breeches. He removed his hat, and the flickering candles glinted off his auburn hair and highlighted the planes and contours of his face.

She faltered back a pace, unable to drag her gaze from him. She'd been aware of his rugged good looks before, but considered him the outdoors type—someone who'd fit into flannel shirts, jeans, and fisherman knit sweaters to perfection. She hadn't expected him to blend into such elegance. At least not so perfectly. . . .

A wave of attraction swept through her, compelling and undeniable, leaving her breathless in its wake. Oh, no, the thought drifted through her mind, she couldn't be that much of a fool! They were two hundred years apart, and not only in time, but in their outlook on life, how they had been brought up, undoubtedly in their goals and expectations. She would not let herself fall for a man from another time.

Abruptly, she turned away. "Do I look all right?"

For a long moment, he said nothing. She glanced over her shoulder and met his critical regard—and an unfamiliar spark in the depths of his dark eyes. Slowly, his gaze moved over her in a manner that caused a warm flush all over her and quickened her pulse.

"You will do very well." His voice held a note of reluctant admiration.

Damn, why did his approval have to matter to her so much? His distrust had been safer. Holding herself under strict control, she walked into the sitting room.

He remained where he stood, his brow furrowing. "What is the matter?"

I like you too much for my own good. With difficulty, she kept from blurting that out. Instead, she concentrated on the question that had worried her since yesterday. "Why did your cousin invite us?"

A slow smile lit his eyes. "After what you said, it would have been impossible for him *not* to invite you."

She waved that aside. "I know I was rude, or ill bred, or whatever. You don't have to rub it in. Why did he invite *you*? I'll swear you're not friends."

He came up to her, stopping a bare pace away. "I can think of no reason why he should wish me harm. It's true, we have not always been close. Ten years separate us, and we have never had much in common."

She looked up into his face. Big mistake, she realized. His closeness sent a yearning seeping through her veins, alluring— and impossible.

At least the major didn't seem to be affected. She should be glad for that—but she wasn't. She crossed to the hearth, putting a safe distance between them. "Isn't it odd he should suddenly go to so much trouble to find you just to invite you to dinner?"

"I believe the answer lies in his newfound responsibilities. Our relationship underwent a rather subtle change after the death of his father, you see.

She looked up quickly. "In what way?"

"I believe he is taking his role of head of the family quite seriously. He inherited the title and all the estates, along with the responsibilities that entails. Looking out for the other members of the family is one of those."

She digested this. "It is not one he appears to care for, in your case, at least."

He shook his head. "You wrong him. He has made a point of checking up on me with astonishing regularity since shouldering

83

his duties. And now, shall we go? Where is your wrap?"

She ran back upstairs, then hesitated over her choice of coats. It was too darned cold outside for the thin wool of the pelisse. She'd take a chance on the down. It was three-quarter length, and had passed before without comment.

By the time she returned to the hall, the Runcorns had joined the major. He now held a towel-wrapped oblong under his arm. The Runcorns wished them a pleasant evening, then returned to their own occupations.

Major Holborn escorted Christy out the door, gently touching her back as he ushered her through. Abruptly he stopped in his tracks and stared at the slick material. "What is it?" he demanded.

"A down coat."

"Down," he muttered. "In a coat." He ran his fingers along the fabric. "I've never felt anything like this."

She tensed. "You've seen it before," she reminded him. "And touched it."

"I had gloves on."

Gloves. . . . She tried a smile, but knew it to be shaky. Now, his gloves protruded from the pocket of his coat. Oh, damn, why had she taken the chance?

She wasn't about to try to explain nylon to him. She wasn't even sure how it was made, but she knew it wasn't a natural fiber. "It's a material they're using quite a bit in America," she tried, hoping he'd accept her evasion.

He touched it again, his expression curious, but he said nothing more. Speculation, though, remained in his eyes as he studied her, and a sinking sensation once more assailed her stomach. He wasn't going to let the matter drop. He'd allow it to ride for the moment, but something in the set of his jaw warned her he grew more and more determined to get to the bottom of the mysteries she presented. And when Major James Edward Holborn set out to do something, she had an uneasy feeling he accomplished it.

Chapter Eight

Christy stepped out the door, and the icy wind whipped the flimsy amber crepe of her evening gown about her legs. Even with Major Holborn staring at the nylon of her down coat as if it had been imported from another planet, she was better off in it than in the pelisse, she decided. The chill would cut right through the fine wool. She could do with her boots, too. These slippers were hopeless.

She glanced up at the threatening clouds, which hung low in the sky, obliterating any light from the stars. Darkness closed about them, and she shivered. "It looks like it's going to snow before much longer."

"You are probably correct." He ushered her down the steps, and opened the door to a carriage.

A covered one, she realized with relief. One of those hackneys. Thank heavens he hadn't brought his curricle. She climbed inside and hugged herself as she settled on the seat.

He called the direction to the driver, then jumped in beside her. "Here." He placed the bundle he held at her feet.

Warmth radiated about her legs, and she pulled her skirt aside for a better look. "What is it?"

"Only a hot brick."

"You're kidding. What a terrific idea."

He frowned. "Do you not use them in America?"

85

Another blunder. She struggled for an adequate response, then gave up and said the first thing that came to her mind. "Of course. Only I hadn't expected you to put one in a hackney." She gave an elaborate shiver and changed the subject. "It's freezing. Everything about the weather screams Christmas, but there aren't any decorations up. It doesn't seem right."

He chuckled. "What do you want? Banners hanging from every sign on the streets?"

"Yes." She tried hard not to find his deep voice enticing, but failed. "That's exactly what I'm used to, from October on."

"October?" This time he laughed outright. "No, Miss Campbell, I will not be taken in by one of your hums. October, indeed. Do you not find it sufficient to celebrate for the twelve days?"

"We don't. Celebrate them, I mean. We have our decorations up, and the parties start right after Thanksgiving—the end of November, I mean. But after Christmas Day, things are sort of quiet until New Year's Eve. Then it's all over. There aren't many of us who still remember Epiphany."

"I had not thought your country had strayed so far from the old customs."

"You'd be surprised," she muttered.

She directed her attention out the window, and stared at the feathery flakes that drifted down, softening the fastness of the night to a swirling gray. Here and there, the fitful glow of a dim oil light announced their passage to the more fashionable quarter of town. At last, they turned onto Portman Square, and the driver pulled up before one of the many towering mansions which lined the street.

The major jumped down, paid their jarvey, then helped Christy to the snow-covered pavement. She followed him up the shallow steps, keeping her head lowered against the icy wind.

He sounded the knocker, then glanced down at her. Once more, a deep chuckle escaped him. "You have snow in your hair." Gently, he dusted the flakes from her curls, then hesitated, an arrested expression in the depths of his dark eyes.

Her gaze met his, and awareness swept through her, strong and tantalizing. Her breathing quickened. She tried to look away, to break that mesmerizing contact, but she remained a prisoner of his compelling regard.

She couldn't be this crazy. She couldn't fall for him, she couldn't be drawn into the powerful emotional vortex that reached toward her. What life could she share with this man, even if she remained trapped in his time? They shared no common ground. . . .

Or did they? They both worked for the betterment of living conditions for the poor. They both cared for animals. Maybe, just maybe . . .

The door opened, breaking the spell, and in relief she turned—only to come up against the most pompous-looking man she had ever encountered in her life. He peered down his nose at her, taking in every detail of her appearance, then turned and inclined his head in a supercilious manner to the major. He stepped back to permit them to enter.

"Good evening, Doring." The major took off his hat and cloak and handed them over, then assisted Christy with her coat.

The butler accepted it, then held it gingerly, regarding it as if it were some foreign object. Well, it was, Christy realized. She only hoped he wouldn't comment on it. That might start the major questioning her again.

Luckily, Doring had been trained too well—or considered it beneath him to take notice of a visitor's garments. His features rigid, he merely laid her coat aside.

Christy cast an uncomfortable glance around the hall, and remained where she stood. The major appeared very much at ease—yet made no move to locate his cousin. Instead, he waited for the butler to complete his tasks, then with Christy on his arm, he headed up the steps in the man's wake.

That struck her as odd. Major Holborn must know his way around—he must have lived here, in fact, while he was growing up, since his cousin inherited the mansion. Under the circumstances, she would have expected him to barge ahead. It's what she would have done. Instead, he allowed Doring to lead the way along the upper hall to a room from which voices could be heard.

Propriety, she realized. The major adhered to a strict code of behavior, the basics of which escaped her completely. Apparently, one had to follow the rules, no matter how ridiculous.

She hung back, nerves tangling in her stomach. She would

make a fool of herself, and have no idea what it was she had done. She would embarrass the major by doing something so silly, not even the explanation of her being an American could excuse it. Hers was not the world of these stuffed shirts. She didn't fit into it — probably not even into his class.

Doring threw open the door, and the major drew Christy into a spacious apartment decorated in the rich tones of deep crimson and gold. Gilt-trimmed mirrors and ancient, elaborate portraits lined the walls, and three incredibly beautiful and intricately patterned rugs covered the floor. Delicate china ornaments, painted with an expert hand, lined the mantel. Everywhere, candles flickered in silver holders.

The flagrant display of wealth overwhelmed her. She tried not to think of the number of homeless shelters that could be funded with the money represented here, but failed. Almost, she blurted out that thought, and was relieved when she caught herself.

Relieved? Good heavens, what was happening to her? She wasn't one to let *any* society's mold dictate her priorities. She'd never before guarded her tongue, why did she do so now? She should speak up, and possibly pave the major's path to make his comments on social conditions.

But she wouldn't. Her outspokenness — or any such serious breach in her manners — would embarrass him.

Damn, she was behaving like a wimp, not standing up for what she believed in, and all because she felt like a freshwater fish suddenly adrift in a very salty ocean.

She emerged from her frustrated reverie to discover all the men had stood at their entrance. One came toward her, a slender gentleman with a developing paunch, whose calves and shoulders had been padded out in a very unnatural manner. Jewels glittered in his neckcloth and on his fingers, and an eyeglass hung about his neck on a black ribbon. His features appeared set in a perpetual sneer, which Christy could not forget. St. Ives.

"Coz." He rolled the word out in a slow drawl. "And Miss" — he hesitated a fraction longer than necessary before finishing her name — "Campbell, was it not?"

The realization she had just been put properly in her place unsettled her. Well, she wasn't about to let him guess he had succeeded in discomfiting her. She straightened her shoulders, and managed a bright facsimile of a smile. "What an excellent memory you have, my lord."

He directed a sharp look at her, as if he suspected—but couldn't quite believe—her insolence. She fluttered her lashes innocently, and a self-satisfied smirk settled over his features. He inclined his head with infinite condescension, and returned to his other guests.

"Do you think it possible for you to remain within the bounds of propriety?" the major demanded, his tone hushed. He regarded her in a mixture of amusement and exasperation.

"I couldn't help it. Darn it, I can only take just so much of his sneering." She met his stern gaze, and shrugged. "All right, I'll behave."

"Thank you." He took her arm and led her toward the fireplace.

A young woman in an elaborate robe of silver silk over a white satin underdress stood before the hearth, her restless fingers playing with one of the delicate figurines on the mantel. A cloud of soft brown curls framed a pale, narrow face with no pretences toward beauty. Her large gray eyes rested on St. Ives, then transferred to the new arrivals. With a sense of surprise, Christy recognized a lurking sadness in her expression.

The major took the woman's hand and raised it briefly to his lips. "May I present Miss Campbell to you, Margaret?" He drew Christy forward. "Your hostess, Miss Campbell, my cousin's wife, the countess St. Ives."

Christy froze, and directed a frantic look at the major. Should she curtsy? Not with much grace, that was certain. Why hadn't she thought to ask before they got here?

The countess extended a delicate hand. "How do you do, Miss Campbell? I am so pleased you could come. As you can see, we are the sole females present. Lady Paignton has been summoned to her daughter in Yorkshire. Only imagine, all three of their little boys have the whooping cough. Is it not dreadful?"

"It certainly is." Christy smiled back, relieved. She had expected St. Ives's wife to be as formidable and disagreeable as he. What had this gentle, sad-eyed woman to do with that supercilious snob?

"I feared I should be quite alone, with both Lady Paignton

89

and Lady Sophia withdrawing like that at the last moment." A tremulous smile just touched the countess's lips.

"Were Lady Sophia and Sir Dominic expected?" the major asked. "I do not remember St. Ives mentioning him."

"Of course. He was the reason—" She broke off.

St. Ives strolled over to them and cast his wife a quelling glance. "Sir Dominic has taken ill, I'm afraid," he told his cousin. "He sends his regards to you."

"Does he?" The major frowned. "I do not believe we have met these six months or more."

"Nevertheless, he has always shown a vast interest in your welfare."

Major Holborn inclined his head. "How very flattering. I must remember to thank him."

St. Ives moved off, and his wife rushed into speech. "I understand you have only just arrived from America, Miss Campbell. What adventures you must have had. I should so love to hear about them. But now you must meet our other guests. James?" She directed a pleading look at the major. "If you would be so kind?"

"My pleasure." He led Christy away.

She slowed her steps. "Who is Sir Dominic?" Something nagged at her about the name, as if it were familiar but she couldn't quite place it.

"Sir Dominic Kaye. He is one of the Opposition leaders."

"Sir Dominic . . ." Her voice trailed off. Sir Dominic Kaye, recipient of the letter from the regent—the future regent—which had brought her to England. Good heavens, was she actually to meet the man? What an exalted crowd she'd fallen in with.

She glanced back with renewed interest at Lady St. Ives, who went to her husband's side and touched his arm. He spoke too softly for Christy to catch his words, but his wife shrank away. Her thin arm encircled her protruding stomach in a protective gesture.

Christy blinked. "She's pregnant!"

Major Holborn directed a pained look at her. "In the family way, I believe you mean."

Christy made a face at him. "You and your euphemisms. No wonder she looks so pale. She should get off her feet and rest. It must be an awful strain organizing a political bash like this. Have they had a fight?"

"I do not know what you mean."

"He just snapped at her."

The major drew a deep breath. "Even marriages of convenience require a period of adjustment, Miss Campbell. It is best not to interfere."

"Convenience." She glanced again at Lady St. Ives, who had returned to her position before the mantel. "The poor woman."

"On the contrary. She is considered very lucky. She has traded her breeding for a title, a considerable fortune, and an enviable position in society."

"What a cold-blooded way to put it." She glared at him. "I suppose you plan to arrange a suitable marriage for yourself."

"You mistake. I have nothing to offer a lady of birth and breeding. And how did we come to be discussing me?"

"Most men find themselves to be a topic of considerable interest." She awarded him her sweetest smile.

For a moment, he struggled, then his deep chuckle escaped him. "Miss Campbell, you are incorrigible. Come and meet your fellow guests—provided you promise to be on your best behavior."

"If I don't, can I get out of this?" She hung back, eyeing the gentlemen with misgivings. She could do with a shot of Dutch chocolate courage.

"You invited yourself," he reminded her.

He led her in the direction of a middle-aged gentleman, only to be brought up short by the most impossibly handsome young man Christy had ever beheld. Rich brown hair swept back from his forehead, and his bright hazel eyes held a knowing gleam as they rested on her. Lines of dissipation belied his angelic expression.

"Holborn." He nodded to the major. "One hears your efforts on behalf of the poor continue. Really, your energy is quite amazing." He covered a yawn with one delicate white hand.

"Brockenhurst!" The older man joined them and shot the other a quelling look, his countenance somber beneath his unruly graying hair. "Good evening, Holborn. Pleasure to see you."

James greeted him, then presented Christy. "Viscount Brockenhurst," he gestured to the younger man, "and Sir Oliver Paignton."

Brockenhurst inclined his classically handsome head and moved away. Sir Oliver, as if to make up for his friend's rudeness, bowed over her hand in a courtly manner and murmured a polite acknowledgment. His gaze rested on her a moment, and a slight frown creased his brow.

He turned to the major. "Dreadful business, this proposed regency," he said. "They'll bring it to a vote soon, you mark my words, Major. Then we'll be in a dreadful fix."

Christy looked up quickly, fascinated. "Do you think so?" She'd read in the library about there being some controversy. "The king's son seems the only possible choice. He's his heir, after all. Who else should have the nominal rule when his father is incapacitated?"

With one forefinger, Sir Oliver Paignton tapped the small enameled box he held, and his serious gaze fell on her once more. "You mark my words, my dear," he repeated. "The people will never accept Prinny as regent. His extravagances, his morals!" He shook his head. "I greatly fear what the outcome will be."

Another man joined them. "A revolution in the streets, after the manner of the French, I shouldn't wonder."

Christy spun about to see an impeccably attired gentleman of about the major's age, with a tall, muscular build and thick black hair barely touched by gray. An air of energy hung about him.

The steady gaze of his frowning brown eyes rested on Sir Oliver. "The bill must be defeated when it is brought to a vote."

"Why?" Christy looked at each of the men in turn, and encountered their surprised regard. Warm color crept into her cheeks. "He isn't *that* unpopular, is he? I mean, he doesn't really have anything to say in government policy, does he? I thought your kings weren't much more than figureheads . . ." Her voice trailed off.

"Lord Farnham." A slight tremor of amusement sounded in Major Holborn's voice. "Permit me to introduce Miss Campbell. An American, as I believe you may have guessed."

"Indeed?" Lord Farnham fumbled at his breast, grasped a black ribbon and raised the eyeglass that hung from it. Through this, he regarded Christy. After a moment, he allowed it to drop, and his features relaxed. "You must forgive us, Miss Campbell. It is far too easy to discuss matters important to us, even in the presence of ladies. We forget our conversations can be of little interest to your fair sex."

"Actually, I find it *very* interesting. But what makes you think there'll be a revolution? After all, your prince will inherit soon enough, anyway, and no one will be able to prevent it, then. What does it matter if he takes over a few years earlier?" She glanced at the major.

He set his jaw, but still it quivered. A gleam of suppressed laughter lit his eyes. "Indeed, she has a point."

St. Ives turned from his conversation with Brockenhurst and strolled over, his lip curled. "Now is the time for a Stuart to once more claim the throne."

"Very true." Sir Oliver Paignton exchanged a glance with Lord Farnham. "A new Pretender, as Sir Dominic is always saying, would meet with far more success than did Bonnie Prince Charlie."

Christy blinked, and ran her limited knowledge of British history through rapid review. Charles Edward Stuart, whose claims to the throne had been denied at Culloden Moor in the 1740s. Over sixty years ago.

"What, Jacobite sympathies?" Major Holborn shook his head, mocking. "It is a shame Prince Charlie's only son was stillborn."

"So there isn't a Stuart heir?" Christy looked from one serious face to another.

"On the contrary, Miss Campbell." St. Ives drew a small chased silver box from his pocket, flicked it open, and helped himself to a tiny pinch of the powder within. "Prince Charlie had a brother—Henry—but he is a bishop."

"Catholic," the major explained. "His religion makes him unacceptable for the British throne."

The other men exchanged glances again, and Christy's foreboding grew. She didn't trust them, any of them. Did they hope to turn Prinny's unpopularity into a coup, not for the Scots but for the Catholics? Something, perhaps, similar to the modern struggle between England and Ireland?

Dear God, was this what changed James Holborn's book? Cold, sick, she turned away. Did these men incite the lower classes of England against the profligate Prinny? Did they then bring Henry, the last Stuart, from wherever he lived in exile?

She closed her eyes, and visions of an unquenchable revolution rose to haunt her, even bloodier than the one prophesied by Sir Oliver. And everyone would join in, with the poor rising against their oppressors, and fighting in the streets. . . .

"Miss Campbell?" The major's quiet voice sounded in her ear. "Are you all right?"

"Yes, of course." She managed a shaky smile. "I'm sorry."

Doring entered, announcing dinner. The major firmly took her arm and led her after the others down the hall and into a magnificent apartment. Christy stopped just over the threshold, taking in the elegance, the rich furnishings, the abundance of gold and silver plate.

The blurring lines from the major's book forced themselves once more into her mind. Would this be one of the houses stormed by the angry mobs? Would St. Ives and his unhappy lady be dragged into the street to be beaten and stabbed?

Major Holborn led her to a chair and pressed her into it. She sat without protest, then looked about the table at her fellow guests. Had they any idea of the horrors their plans might produce?

It didn't appear likely. Throughout the protracted meal, talk around the table continued to center on the debates raging through the houses of Parliament. Christy listened to the fears of these men, and found her own growing. They all looked sensible, not at all like alarmists.

What if they were right? Was that the action Major Holborn must perform, to somehow make Prince George more acceptable to his people?

She glanced up the table to where the major engaged in earnest conversation with Brockenhurst. Apparently, the major took this talk seriously, for he joined in the discussions, his manner concerned.

Did all this lay the basis for the ending of his next book? To hear these government officials talk, all it would take for utter catastrophe would be one unpopular decision by the houses of Parliament. She barely tasted the various dishes, so intent was she on the reactions of the men.

At last, Lady St. Ives cast an uncertain glance at her husband. He paid her no heed. After a moment's hesitation, she rose and looked toward Christy.

Christy cast a frantic glance at Major Holborn. With the slightest jerk of his head, he indicated she should go with her hostess. She did, following that lady from the room and down the hall.

Accompanied by the soft rustling of her silk gown, Lady St. Ives led the way to a spacious, richly appointed apartment, not the one where they had gathered before dinner. A piano and harp stood at one end of the room, and a grouping of sofas and chairs stood before the hearth. The countess seated herself in one of these and gestured for Christy to join her. Christy did, feeling distinctly uncomfortable.

"I am so glad James brought you." The countess managed a shy smile. "I always feel so very much alone, especially when I am the only lady present at one of these functions. But I must not expect him to arrange parties for my pleasure." Color flooded her too-pale cheeks, and she looked away. "Have—have you known James long?"

"We only encountered each other a couple of days ago. I am—rather new to this country."

"Of course." Lady St. Ives regarded her clasped hands, as if she found making even the most trifling of polite small talk to be a chore. "Are you involved in his work?"

"I am assisting some of his friends—the Runcorns. Are you acquainted with them?"

"I—no. St. Ives says they are not at all the thing, and I am not to call upon them."

"I see." Christy clamped her teeth together to keep her unruly tongue in check. The Countess needed a lesson in liberation, not to mention a short course in self-assertiveness. And St. Ives needed a good swift kick in the seat of his chauvinistic pants. The "convenience" of this marriage obviously had been designed for the earl, to assure him a timid wife who

95

didn't dare possess an opinion not of his choosing.

"Do you play the pianoforte?" Lady St. Ives asked after a moment's silence. She regarded her guest with a shy hopefulness.

"No, I don't," Christy admitted. "I would love it if you would, though."

The Countess flushed with real pleasure. "Would you? It has always been a favorite pastime of mine."

With all the air of one making good her escape, the countess retired to the instrument. She didn't bother selecting any music, she simply started to play with a facility that indicated long hours of dedicated practice.

Christy sank back against the cushions of her chair in relief, and closed her eyes. Slowly, the knots of tension untied themselves.

She had almost drifted off to sleep when the gentlemen joined them at last. She roused herself, opening her eyes to find the major standing before her, frowning. The strains of Mozart still filled the room. Apparently, her hostess had not noticed her inattentiveness.

"We had best be leaving." Major Holborn turned to his cousin. "Both of us must be up betimes on the morrow. Thank you for a most interesting evening, St. Ives."

"Delighted, little cousin, quite delighted."

Lady St. Ives turned from the instrument. "You cannot stay?" Honest regret sounded in her voice.

Christy shook her head. "I'm afraid not. I had a wonderful time, though."

Becoming color flooded the countess's cheeks. "You must come again, Miss Campbell. James, I cannot thank you enough for bringing her."

The major's mobile eyebrows rose. "My pleasure," was all he said.

Amid repeated thanks, they escaped the room and headed down the stairs to the front hall, where the efficient Doring waited to assist them with their things. He offered to send a footman running for a hackney, but the major waved this aside. They would find one at the corner, he assured the butler, and escorted Christy outside.

"Thank heavens that's over with," she breathed as the door closed behind them.

"Bored?" he asked.

"No. How could I be? Look, is everyone really worried about a revolution, or are they just working themselves up over nothing?"

The gentle amusement faded from his face. "It is a distinct possibility. Prinny has not endeared himself to the common people. He—" He broke off and glanced behind them.

"What is it?" Her tiredness evaporating, Christy spun about.

The major turned more slowly, and his grip tightened on her arm.

Three men approached, all garbed in dark clothing. Even their faces appeared unnaturally shadowed. The next moment, Christy realized they wore masks covering their eyes and noses.

Her rapid heartbeat pounded in her ears, and her hand closed over the major's in sudden fear. "What—"

One of the men raised his arm, and the deafening explosion of a pistol filled the air. The major's hat flew from his head, and he staggered backward.

Chapter Nine

Christy froze, too shocked to react. Major Holborn's hat . . .

Another man raised a pistol and her paralysis vanished. She grabbed the major's arm, and together they ran, bending low, maneuvering in a zigzag pattern. Either that first man was one colossally good aim to be able to miss at so short a distance, or this was a serious attempt at murder that very nearly succeeded.

The other gun fired behind them, its explosion deafening in the snowy stillness. Christy ducked around a corner a bare pace ahead of the major, ran a few yards, then darted through a narrower opening.

The major passed her, grasping her hand as he pulled into the lead. His long-legged stride would have outdistanced her, but her panic pumped adrenaline through her system, sending her racing along at his side.

"Here!" The major's voice reached her through the pounding in her ears.

He veered sideways through an opening in the darker shadows she hadn't noticed. Where they were now, she had no idea at all. She ran on, stumbling over piles of rubble.

She stepped on a jagged brick, and bit back an exclamation of pain. Her slippers must be in shreds. Her toes were so numb from the cold she could barely feel them — which was a blessing, under the circumstances.

"Steady." Major Holborn caught her as she tripped again. His tension sounded in the grim note in his voice.

Her heart pounded in her chest and she gasped for breath, but still she ran after him, twisting and turning through a maze of back alleys. Behind them, the sounds of pursuit dropped away, fading, as their trail eluded the men. Abruptly, the major lunged to the left again. Christy staggered after him, and they stopped at last.

She leaned against an icy cold wall, panting, her fingers clutching the uneven surface in an attempt to keep her strained leg muscles from collapsing under her. Numb as they were, her feet ached. She stood on something uneven. And sharp. She kicked aside a large chunk of broken brick — one of the many strewn in untidy heaps — and rubbed her injured feet.

She leaned back again and realized she trembled, with both the exertion and the fear of what would happen if they were caught. She glanced at the major. "This —"

He clamped his hand over her mouth and drew her closer to him. "Quiet." The word sounded on the merest breath of air.

With difficulty, Christy forced herself to breathe slower, so her ragged gasps wouldn't be audible. Then she, too, heard the crunching of the snow, the footsteps the major's quicker ears must have caught. Somewhere close — too close — a cat hissed and howled, and a small dog let loose a volley of high-pitched yapping. A deep voice muttered words Christy couldn't quite catch, and another answered.

She tensed, pressed against her wall. As her eyes grew accustomed to the darkness, a dim, rectangular shape took form beside her — a door into the building. Blackness engulfed their surroundings, making it impossible to see farther away. For all she knew, they had chosen a dead-end alley in which to hide.

The footsteps paused, and Christy cringed back, willing herself to disappear. She held her breath, desperate to make no noise, then the soft crunch of snow receded as the man continued on his way. Her heart resumed beating with a painful jerk.

Limp with reaction, she sagged against Major Holborn. His arm circled about her, supporting her, comforting in his mere presence. Far too comforting. She'd be happy to stay there for a very long while. Corny clichés about safe harbors drifted through her mind, and she allowed her cheek to rest against the smooth wool of his cloak.

Her breathing had almost slowed to normal when his arm slipped from around her and he caught her hand once more. Again, his voice barely reached her. "I think it's safe to go now."

She stood on tiptoe, one hand on his shoulder to reach his ear to whisper back: "Will you finally admit someone is trying to kill you? Those men weren't muggers, and they certainly weren't playing games."

He hesitated a moment, then returned a very unsatisfying: "Possibly."

Couldn't that exasperating man get it through his thick skull he was in serious danger? He persisted in considering these assaults on him mere harassment! Whether he believed it or not, someone wanted Major James Edward Holborn dead. And Christy desperately didn't want that to happen.

She cast a sideways glance up at his tall, broad-shouldered figure in the heavy cloak covering his elegant evening dress. No, she didn't want anything to happen to him; she would do everything in her power to prevent it. She looked around, then hugged herself in frustration. "I feel so darned vulnerable."

An unexpected touch of amusement crept into his voice, and his warm breath misted as it hit the icy air. "Arm yourself. There should be plenty of weapons at hand." He peered through the darkness. "Hard to see, though. Which under the circumstances is lucky. Our footprints would be all too visible in the snow."

Christy stooped, but no projectile of a comfortable size met her searching fingers. She wouldn't mind a *little* bit of light. The major inched forward, still holding her hand, and perforce she followed.

Two steps later, a bruised toe led her to a brick fragment of the right size. She tucked it into the pocket of her down coat, encountered the plastic bag, and fished out one more of the precious chocolate chips. She needed the energy. She shied from considering what she'd do when she ran out of them. She couldn't survive thirty-eight years without her favorite fix.

She found several more chunks of stone and brick, and

crammed them into her pockets. The major paused at the corner to check both ways, then drew Christy after him.

"Which way?" she whispered.

He shook his head, a gesture barely visible in the darkness of the narrow alley. Again, they wended their way through a maze of short turnings, and emerged at last onto a wider street. Before them . . .

Christy came to an abrupt halt. Directly in front of them stood two men in heavy dark coats, their faces in deep shadow, their eyes completely obscured by masks.

Christy gasped. For one moment the men stared at them, as startled as they, then one raised his pistol. The major caught Christy's hand, and as they turned, the pistol fired with a resounding explosion.

A sharp exclamation escaped the major, and he clasped his upper arm. Frantic, Christy caught his good elbow and thrust him ahead, then swung back as she pulled a brick piece from her pocket. With all her energy, she heaved it, only to miss the man by a bare inch. His companion raised his pistol.

Steadying her rising panic, she hurled another chunk, this time hitting their assailant in the shoulder as he released the hammer. A spark flickered from the pan, pale smoke puffed from the barrel, and the ball whined past her ear. It hit the side of a brick building, and buried itself harmlessly in the snow.

She heaved the last of her limited arsenal, then grabbed the major's arm and pulled him once more through a crazy maze of rapid turnings, down more dark alleys and mews, until the sounds of pursuit once more faded away. She collapsed against a wooden fence, it gave way behind her, and she fell backward.

A gate. The major followed her through, shoved it shut, and crouched against it.

Christy picked herself up and brushed off the snow. For a long minute she huddled there, until her breathing steadied enough for her to speak. "How bad were you hit?"

He remained silent. She could feel his tension, the tautness of his muscles as he leaned against her. She covered his hand which gripped his arm, and warm blood oozed over her fingers. She swore softly.

Startled, he stared at her, and a soft chuckle escaped him.

101

"You have taken the words out of my mouth, Miss Campbell, but I assure you, they would have been better left there."

She searched for an appropriate response. "Hell and the devil confound it," she said evenly, borrowing his own phrase.

His broad shoulders shook, and a spasm of pain flickered across his face. He sobered at once.

She stood. "Let's get you home."

"I believe we will do best to go to the Runcorns'."

His voice sounded tight, forced, so unlike himself it scared her. She located a handkerchief she had stuffed in her pocket, now crumpled from being buried under the broken bricks. It missed by two inches being long enough to tie around his arm. Frustrated, she folded it into a pad. He took it from her and pressed it to his arm.

"Will you be all right?" Even in the darkness, she could see the strained set of his jaw.

"Confound it, Miss Campbell, this is not the first time I've been grazed by a ball."

"Is that all? A graze?" She wished she could believe him. She eased open the gate, gestured for him to pass through, then closed it behind them.

Cautiously they advanced, and turned the next corner. To Christy's surprise, they emerged onto a major thoroughfare. Oil lamps burned fitfully at distant intervals, and a number of carriages swept past.

"Oxford Street." Satisfaction sounded in the major's voice. "Very good, Miss Campbell."

"Of course," she said, somewhat hollowly. "I brought us here on purpose, you know."

She stepped forward, and spotted one of those covered carriages that looked like the ones they'd ridden in before. "A hackney?" she asked, then hailed it. To her relief, it stopped. She urged the major inside, gave the direction of the orphanage, and followed him within. With a sigh, she sank onto the seat, and the pain in her feet began at once.

"You seem to be a very capable young lady." A waver of determined amusement colored his words.

"You don't have very great expectations for women," she countered.

He leaned back against the cushions and closed his eyes. As they passed near one of the few street lights, she caught a glimpse of his tense face, his thinned lips — proof of the pain he tried to ignore. Christy watched him closely, wondering how much blood he had lost. He was quite right about being glad for the darkness. Once he had been hit, their assailants would have been able to follow the trail of dripping crimson.

At last, the hackney drew up before the orphanage off Golden Lane. With a sharp order for the major to stay put, and not leave the carriage under any circumstances, Christy jumped out and ran up the steps. The door was locked, so she applied the knocker with vigor.

A long minute passed, and Christy cast an uneasy glance about. Then the door opened and Nancy stood there, yawning, a warm shawl wrapped about the shoulders of her dressing gown.

"They've shot Major Holborn in the arm," Christy said. "Help me get him inside, we've got to take care of it."

Mr. Runcorn appeared in the lighted hall behind the maid. "What's this? Miss Campbell? Did you say James —"

"He's been shot." Tears of reaction started to her eyes, and in annoyance she dashed them away.

"Fetch hot water, Nancy, and alert Mrs. Runcorn." The clergyman pushed past Christy and started down the steps.

"Make sure the water boils!" Christy shouted after her, then hurried after Mr. Runcorn.

The major stood in the street, paying the driver. The hackney pulled away, and he turned to regard them with disapproval. "I am quite capable of walking on my own, Miss Campbell."

"You are also capable of being a target." She positioned herself at his side. "If you think your association with this place is unknown, you're being naive. Don't you think your enemies will have someone watching this house as well as your own?"

He glared at her, but held his tongue as they escorted him indoors, one on either side, using their bodies as shields.

Mrs. Runcorn met them in the hall, a pile of torn linen strips and a couple of small bottles in her arms. She followed them into the parlor. "Nancy will be back in a few minutes with the water," she said.

"Make sure it's boiling." Christy cast a pleading glance at the woman.

"Whatever for, my dear? We don't want to scald him when we wash the wound, do we?" Mrs. Runcorn set down her supplies. "Now, don't be in such a pucker. I've tended innumerable injuries before. He will be quite all right, you'll see."

Mr. Runcorn helped the major out of his evening cloak, then turned his attention to his ruined coat. "Can you slide your arm free?"

Christy watched, biting her lip at the strain on the major's face. Still, he made no concession to his wound, refusing to acknowledge the obvious pain. "Aren't we supposed to cut the fabric away?" she asked, calling on her knowledge of various low-budget costume films she'd seen.

"I fail to see the need to further damage my apparel," Major Holborn informed her coldly.

Mr. Runcorn eased the heavy cloth off the major's shoulders, and helped him slide his good arm from the sleeve. Blood soaked the other a deep shade of purple. Crimson drops fell from his fingers.

Trying hard not to disturb the wound any further, Christy helped inch the velvet fabric down his arm. It had been so elegant, and now it had been reduced to a rag.

One short intake of breath was all that betrayed the effort this maneuver cost the major. At last, his hand emerged and Christy let out a sigh of relief. She tossed the ruined garment aside.

"Be seated, James." Mr. Runcorn pressed him into a chair. "Let's have a look at this."

A hole tore through the once white fabric of his shirt. Now, blood soaked the entire area, even staining the side and front. Mr. Runcorn drew a knife from his pocket, opened it, and sliced through the fabric.

For some reason, Christy felt no sensation of pleasure at having anticipated this step. Instead, she cringed for the major, who remained frozen, immobile, obviously trying very hard not to react at all. Finally, Mr. Runcorn pulled back the fabric six inches on either side, exposing a nasty tear in the skin from which blood oozed sluggishly.

"It's clotting nicely," Christy managed, hoping her voice

didn't shake too much. A distinct sensation of nausea washed through her. "Can we get him to a doctor?"

"There is no need." He kept his voice even. "He would only want to bleed me."

"What? You've lost enough blood!"

"My sentiments exactly, Miss Campbell." He leaned back in the chair, staring fixedly ahead, his jaw set against the pain he refused to acknowledge.

"Won't it need stitches?" She looked from one to the other of her companions.

"I assure you, Miss Campbell, it is not in the least necessary," the major said through gritted teeth. "I am far more familiar with wounds of this nature than are you. Unless I am much mistaken, the graze is neither wide nor deep. You may examine it for yourself if you do not believe me."

"All right, I will. Is there more light?"

Mr. Runcorn slid a table into position on the major's left side, and Mrs. Runcorn placed a three-branched candelabrum on its surface. By the flickering illumination provided by the tapers, Christy forced herself to look at the wound.

When was penicillin developed? She knew the history of chocolate backward and forward, and could provide dates on every major breakthrough, up to and including the production of the first chips. But she hadn't the foggiest idea when the concept of hygiene was developed. Later than this, though, of that she was certain. Hadn't she read more people died of infection than of their wounds at this time?

Nancy pushed the door open and carried in a large kettle between two towels. This she set on the table, then stood back. "Well, guv'nor, you've gone and got yourself into a real fix this time, ain't you?"

"Haven't you," Christy corrected, never taking her gaze from the major's arm.

Gently, Mrs. Runcorn set Christy aside, dipped a towel in the warm water, and applied it to the wound. The major winced, and every tendon stood out on his neck. With deft strokes, the woman washed the area.

The blood started once more, but now Christy saw he had been right, the wound was not as bad as it first appeared. Still, she wished she had some aspirin or ibuprofen or anything to offer him.

Mr. Runcorn placed a glass in the major's free hand. His fingers tightened about it, and he swallowed the contents in one gulp. Mr. Runcorn took it back and refilled it.

The major waved it aside. "I need to keep my wits about me."

"You need do nothing of the kind, James. You will stay here tonight."

The major made no answer. He gritted his teeth again as Mrs. Runcorn patted the wound, this time with a dry cloth, then sprinkled the contents of a bottle over the area.

"What is that?" Christy peered over her shoulder.

"Basilicum powder. It will help it heal."

"But will it stave off infection? Don't you have *any* antibacterial agents?"

"Any what?" Mrs. Runcorn didn't look up from her work.

"Nothing." Christy closed her eyes. If she'd only known she was going to wind up two hundred years before her own time, she would have read up on all sorts of things. Time travel, though, was one thing for which she'd never thought to prepare herself. If only she could take him back to her own era, to competent doctors who would give him a good shot of penicillin, who would keep it from getting infected, who might even stitch it closed to minimize the scar. He would bear one, of that she was certain.

She looked up again to see Mrs. Runcorn had placed a pad over his arm and now wrapped another strip of cloth about it to hold it in place. This she fastened, then stood again, smiling.

"There, Major. That will hold for now. You are not to move that arm any more than is strictly necessary. Is that understood?" She took another long strip of fabric and slipped it around his lower arm, then about the back of his neck where she knotted it into a sling. "You are to let it rest," she informed him. "Nancy, have we a bed prepared for the major?"

"Don't bother," he said quickly. "Miss Campbell, I would like a word with you though, before I go. Alone."

"Would you?" She glanced uneasily at the others.

Nancy collected the water and the soiled cloths, and Mrs. Runcorn picked up the clean ones and her basilicum powder.

Mr. Runcorn handed the major the glass, then held the door for the others to exit. They deserted her, Christy reflected. She crossed to the hearth and stared into the fire.

"Miss Campbell."

The sheer force of his voice and willpower caused her to turn toward him.

"It is time you answer a few questions." He held her gaze. "You are obviously not trying to kill me, but I must have some answers before I can trust you."

She nodded, but said nothing.

"I have never met anyone like you, before." He rose and took several unsteady steps toward her, only to stop a foot away. "I don't know what to think of you. What the devil is an 'antibacterial agent?' "

"Something that hasn't been developed here in England, yet." Even to herself, her voice sounded feeble.

"Are you an expert in medicine?"

She shook her head. "Where I come from, we are a little more advanced in many ways – both socially and scientifically."

"I see. Is this knowledge you can share?"

She shook her head. "It has to be learned the hard way."

"The way I must learn about you?"

She stared at her hands. She didn't want to create a web of lies between them. She wanted – Longing swept through her, intense and terrible. She wanted to know the real James Edward Holborn, to share her fears and hopes with him, to turn over to his capable hands the dreadful burden of the truth. She wanted the impossible.

"Please," she said at last. "There's nothing more I can tell you. What little I know for certain sounds too preposterous to be believed. You'd only think I was lying, and be furious with me for thinking you'd accept anything so bizarre."

"And what do you expect me to draw from that?"

"Only that I would tell you if I could make sense out of it, myself."

He extended his good hand, and the liquid sloshed in his glass as he touched the nylon sleeve of her down coat. Bewilderment flickered across his face, only to fade beneath determination. "I am going to find out who you are, where you are from, and what you are doing in my life," he said. "I give you fair warning. I intend to have answers from you, and I will not be put off."

If only she had her purse, some dated identification, some *proof* . . . but she didn't. She stared at him, helpless. His dark eyes closed in his thoughts, impenetrable, yet coldness emanated from him, chilling her.

She shook her head. "I would do anything to be able to tell you more. I don't know how I got here, or even why."

"I see." The two syllables fell like ice. "Good evening, Miss Campbell." He turned on his heel, picked up his cloak, and attempted to slip it over his shoulders.

"Here." She helped him wrap it about himself.

The defiance of his departure somewhat diminished, he gave her a curt nod and stalked into the hall.

The Reverend Mr. Runcorn awaited him. "You won't go, will you, James?"

"I will."

"But there is no carriage," Mr. Runcorn protested. "I can fetch the cart—"

"There is no need."

"At least let me accompany you to the corner, until you can find a hackney."

"And don't take the first one that stops for you," Christy said.

The major turned and stared at her for a long moment. "I am not a fool, Miss Campbell, despite what you appear to think."

Over the major's renewed objections, Mr. Runcorn accompanied him out the front door. Christy leaned against the jamb, eyes closed. She needed to come up with a believable story, anything to drive away that distrust. She still stood there, replaying that uncomfortable scene in her mind, wondering how to make things right between them, when Mr. Runcorn returned.

He stopped in the hall and fixed her with his compelling regard. "They were waiting for you when you came out of his cousin's house?"

Christy nodded. "It wasn't chance. The first shot almost hit him in the head—it took his hat off. They mean to kill him." To her dismay, her voice broke and tears started to her eyes.

"He is a sensible man, Miss Campbell." He patted her shoulder gently. "He will take care of himself. Come, the hour is late."

Together, they picked up the candles at the foot of the stair and climbed the several flights to the floor with their rooms.

The evening had started out such fun, Christy reflected as she twisted and contorted her upper body, trying to reach the buttons on her gown. At last, she freed herself and pulled it off. She shivered in the chilly night air; the fire had burned down, so she threw a fagot onto the smoldering coals. What she wouldn't give for a bit of forced air heating right about now.

She washed her face, then pulled the pins from her hair and let it tumble down below her shoulders. Sitting at the dressing table, she tried to drag a comb through the thick curls. How could the night have ended so badly?

The familiar occupation of untangling her mass of hair soothed her, and the tension ebbed from muscles that began to ache. She could use a hot shower — or half an hour in a Jacuzzi. She wasn't used to running a marathon practically barefoot over broken bricks through twisting alleyways. She stifled a yawn, then gave up and crawled into bed. Not even her troubled thoughts could compete with the exhaustion that crept through her.

She awoke in the morning to the sound of a herd of elephants descending the steps at breakneck speed. Shouts and laughter emanated from the stairwell, and in a moment her sleep-fog mind cleared. The boys, on their way to breakfast.

She stretched, discovered a few more stiff muscles that had jumped on the bandwagon, and groaned. Given her choice, she would stay right here, snuggled beneath the down comforter. She had to earn her keep, though. And she wanted to find out if the major had arrived at his rooms safely.

She swung her bruised feet out of bed, washed with the water Nancy must have brought in while she slept, then dragged on her muslin gown. A few minutes later, she hobbled down to seek her own meal.

By the time she reached the dining room, the boys were just finishing, and Nancy had begun gathering the empty plates. Mrs. Runcorn sat at the foot of the table, papers spread about her, jotting down notes to herself.

Mr. Runcorn, at the head, stood. "Our chores first this morning, boys."

All eight of the orphans rose and filed out without a murmur of protest, winning Christy's surprised approval.

Mr. Runcorn smiled at her. "Lessons this afternoon, Miss Campbell. You have the morning free."

Christy thanked him. "And Major Holborn?"

"Everything is fine. He sent a message when he arrived home last night." With a reassuring nod to her, he followed the boys.

Relieved, Christy filled a plate and carried it to where Mrs. Runcorn worked. "How may I help you?" she asked.

The woman sighed. "There is always so much to be done. We need a side of mutton, and I do not know when I am to find the time to go shopping."

"I could do it for you."

Mrs. Runcorn tilted her spectacles and regarded Christy over their tops. "Could you, my dear? I vow, it would be the greatest help if you could do so, from time to time."

"I'd be delighted." Christy settled at the table. "Where do I go?"

"For this once, I had better spare Nancy to you. She can show you which stalls have the best meats, and what we need, and how not to be taken in."

"It'll be a pleasure, it will." Nancy paused in her gathering of dirtied cups and flatware. "I'd like another of them lessons, if you don't mind, miss."

Christy agreed, keeping her reservations about her own suitability to herself, and finished her breakfast. She then joined Nancy in the kitchen and helped with the washing up, over the girl's protests. Twenty minutes later, they set forth in a rough cart owned by the orphanage for transporting supplies — and occasionally taking the boys on outings. Jem, the eldest, rode in the back to take charge of the horse while they shopped.

Nancy drove the Runcorns' aging chestnut mare through the streets with less than expertise, but at last they arrived at a courtyard teeming with people, which she identified as Leadenhall Market. For once, the sky held no threat of snow. Nancy turned the cart over to Jem, who scrambled onto the seat.

Christy jumped down, fascinated by the activity. Nancy steered her through the first court, filled with leather hides and the people bargaining for them.

110

"This is the Green-yard," Nancy announced as they entered the next. She led the way to a cart, greeted a rough man with a teasing word, and he responded with her name. She entered into lively negotiations for a side of mutton, obviously a familiar routine to both of them.

This settled to their mutual satisfaction and the money exchanged, the man dispatched two of his assistants to carry her purchase to the waiting wagon, which they seemed to know well. With a cheery wave, Nancy then led the way to the shops set into a huge building. "Fish," she explained.

Christy nodded, staring avidly about, taking it all in. So much business, so many people. . . .

She shivered with that eerie sensation of being watched. She looked quickly around, searching for some familiar figure, and to her dismay she focused on a man of medium build in a heavy garment Major Holborn had called a "frieze coat." The man turned away, but didn't move off. Something about him seemed all too familiar.

Forcing herself to remain calm, Christy strolled forward and pretended to examine the contents of the stalls and shops. At least the icy weather kept the meats cold. It would probably make her sick to come here in the summer. She paused, glanced casually to both sides, and found that same man had followed, keeping his distance yet keeping her in sight.

"Is there another way out of here?" Christy asked Nancy in an undervoice.

"What's the matter?" The girl looked up quickly.

"There's a man following us."

Nancy rolled her eyes. "Is 'e 'andsome?"

"I think he's the same one who followed the major before, on horseback."

The roguish twinkle faded. "Is 'e, now?" Nancy looked about, and her tiny chin jutted out. "You just show 'im to me, miss, and we'll see 'ow much followin' 'e does, we will."

"That might not be safe. Can we just slip out of here?"

Nancy bit her lip, her eyes narrowing. "There're a number of passages, miss, leadin' to the streets. Lined they are, with various shops. We needs a cheese, anyways. Through 'ere," she announced, and led the way into a third court and approached a

111

man selling herbs. A few minutes later, armed with a basket filled with lavender, basil, and rosemary, they strolled aimlessly through the other herb stalls.

"Cast your daylights about, miss. Does you see 'im?" Nancy asked *sotto voce*.

"Yes." Christy stared at the man. He glanced up, met her gaze for a split second, then abruptly turned and wandered off a few paces. With exaggerated fascination, he studied an array of hanging garlic.

"Let's go," she breathed. She caught Nancy's arm and together they darted behind a stall, then worked their way through an assortment of crates until they reached a passageway lined with stalls. Behind them, they heard the crash of someone falling over obstacles.

Nancy slowed, but Christy clutched her elbow and quickened their pace until they ran. More crashes followed, then silence. Christy risked a glance back and saw her pursuer emerge from the maze of stalls and set off after them.

Chapter Ten

Christy grasped the basket and ran, heedless. Behind her, Nancy struggled to keep up. And farther back — she didn't dare think what that man did. She only wanted to reach their cart, return to the orphanage, and send a message to the major telling him what occurred.

They emerged onto the street, then hurried along this until they neared the entry to Leadenhall Market where they had left Jem. The lad lounged on the seat, hat pulled low over his eyes, arms wrapped about himself to keep warm in the chill wind. Christy tossed the basket into the back and scrambled up.

Nancy grabbed the reins from the boy. "Come on, you young sluggard." She shoved him over, sandwiching him between herself and Christy. She released the brake and urged the horse into an ambling trot. "Is this the best you can do, you bone-rattler?" she demanded.

"What's ado, miss?" Jem yawned and stared at Christy, wide-eyed.

Christy looked back the way they had come, but no frieze-coated figure lumbered after them. "I think we lost him," she said at last.

"Not for good, you 'asn't," Nancy said. "Lord love you, miss, that gave me ever such a fright."

"You and me, both." Christy shivered. "Why would someone follow *us?*" She met Nancy's gaze, and knew there was no need for an answer. Someone wanted the major, and she had been marked as one of his companions. Apparently, she, too, would now be watched. That prospect left her ill. "Keep an eye out behind us, will you, Jem?" she asked.

The boy nodded and scrambled into the back of the wagon, along with the side of mutton, the wrapped fish, and the basket of herbs.

"If you see a man on a horse who seems to be keeping us in sight, let me know."

"I sees several," the lad offered.

"Can you take us around a few corners, Nancy?" Christy kept her gaze focused behind them. "Just to see if anyone follows?"

The girl nodded, her expression grim. At the next corner they turned left, then left again, and at the third they headed right.

Christy glanced ahead, then back again. "Well, Jem?"

"That cove there, what's on the bay prad. Wearin' the frieze coat?"

"Thanks, that's him." Christy huddled onto the seat, chilled by more than the wind. Why didn't he approach them? Why only keep them in sight? After the violent attack of last night . . . She shuddered.

She leaned forward, wishing the poor animal between the shafts might be a high-spirited racehorse that could whisk them away from their shadow. They'd probably wind up overturned in the ditch, though, the way Nancy drove. They lumbered along, caught in the slow-moving traffic. Definitely, if she had to stay for any length of time in the past, she was going to learn to drive and ride sidesaddle. She didn't like being at the mercy of somebody else's abilities.

They finally turned onto Golden Lane, then into the narrow alley leading to the orphanage. Christy looked back once more. The man rounded the corner behind them, then reined in, as if keeping a vigil. Her heart beat faster and her nerves screamed.

Two of the boys came down the steps and hailed Jem. Together, they hoisted the side of mutton from the cart and carried it up the steps. Nancy armed herself with the basket and fish while Jem once more took charge of the cart. Christy cast one last look at the solitary horseman, then ran up the stairs and into the house.

She slammed the door behind her and leaned against it, breathing hard. *Why?* What did that man want from her—from Major Holborn?

She had to warn him—and as soon as possible. She started up the stairs in search of someone, only to encounter Mrs. Runcorn coming down. "Where is Mr. Runcorn?" she demanded.

The woman regarded her with concern. "In his study, my dear. The major has called. Is something wrong?"

"Not now." Relief surged through Christy, only to vanish the next moment. Unwittingly, she had led the major's enemies right to him. . . . No, that was ridiculous, they already knew about the orphanage.

"Well, you are not to worry about the boys this afternoon, my dear." Mrs. Runcorn's warm smile flashed. "Since this is already a special day, and it is growing so very close to Christmas, we have decided to combine two traditions into one. But you will learn more about that presently."

Christy's lips twitched into an ironic smile. Finally she was about to experience a truly old-fashioned yuletide tradition, and she was too upset to enjoy it. She thanked Mrs. Runcorn and hurried along the hall to her husband's study. She burst through the door without knocking, and both men looked up in surprise.

The major, his complexion too pale and the sleeve of his coat bulging from the bandage beneath, rose. "What has occurred?"

She resisted the temptation to throw herself in his arms. Damn the man for being so attractive—so calm and reassuring. She drew a ragged breath to bring herself under control. "We were watched in the market," she managed, "and the same man followed us home. He's in the street, back at the corner, and—"

The major set her away from the door and stormed out. Christy dove after him. He took the front steps two at a time, reached the paving, and strode toward the corner. By the time she caught up with him, though, no sign of the man could be found.

He turned back, his brow heavy. "Was it the same one who followed us before?"

"I couldn't be sure. I *think* it was, but I never got a good look

115

at his face. There was something familiar about him, which was how I spotted him in the market."

He swore softly. Together, they retraced their steps to the orphanage.

Mr. Runcorn stood just inside the doorway, waiting, his expression anxious. "Nothing, again?" he asked as they entered.

The major shook his head. "It's confoundedly cold out there. I can't blame anyone for not staying around. It seems," he added, looking down at Christy, "his purpose must have been to discover where you went this morning, and once having followed you back here, perhaps his duty was over."

"But *why?* Why *me?*"

"Because as little as you may like it, Miss Campbell, you are now associated with me."

Actually, Christy liked that idea quite a bit. Her gaze rested on him, moving across his striking countenance, to his broad shoulders. A slight tremor shook them. "You're freezing," she said suddenly. "Or is your arm hurting? You shouldn't have taken it out of the sling."

"I assure you, Miss Campbell, I have sustained far worse injuries and dealt with them with considerably less fuss."

"Come." Mr. Runcorn led the way down the passage. "Let us return to the fire."

Christy trailed after them. They entered the study, a cozy apartment lined with books, with a large desk standing in the center of the room. A grouping of chairs had been arranged before the fireplace, with a low table in their midst. Handfuls of papers lay scattered on its surface.

The men returned to these chairs, and Christy joined them. Her gaze moved over the papers, and with a shock she deciphered some of the words. "Your book—" She broke off, and an eerie sensation rippled through her.

"Yes." The major gathered some of his notes. "My last was a scathing attack on society's heartlessness. As you possibly have guessed, I earned no friends from that, certainly none to my cause. And possibly a few deadly enemies. This time I intend to give the *ton* what it desires."

"Which is?"

"Something to amuse them."

She picked up one of the sheets. "It isn't easy to amuse someone when you're pointing out poverty and injustice, is it?"

A half smile just touched his lips. "If you can make someone laugh, you will gain their attention, and they will remember what you say. If I present members of the *ton* as social heroes, perhaps I can make helping others into a popular pastime."

The Reverend Mr. Runcorn shook his head. "If you do, James, it will be the first time anyone has ever succeeded in softening the hearts of the wealthy."

"But it is worth a try." The major leaned back against the cushions.

Christy raised her gaze to his face. "Do you hope the publication of this book will stop the attacks on you?"

His eyes darkened even more, becoming solid pools of black. "I am more concerned with the other effect of this book. Besides hoping to influence society, I anticipate it will earn a fair amount of money."

"To fund our orphanage and other such projects," Mr. Runcorn said. "He has done so much, already."

The major waved that aside. "There are benefits from this I enjoy very much. Remember, today is Saint Thomas's Eve."

"What is that?" Christy looked from one to the other.

Mr. Runcorn latched onto the new topic in relief. "Do you not celebrate it in America? Tonight is a night of harmless divinations. I cannot approve of taking such things seriously, of course, but the boys enjoy it. We have also made this the day for cutting our holly and ivy."

In spite of her fears, Christy's spirits lifted. "How much do we get? And do you decorate the whole house, or just one room?"

Mr. Runcorn shook his head, and a smile eased the solemnity in his features. "We cannot bring it in until Christmas Eve, my dear. We must store it outside until then."

Anticipation for the expedition warmed Christy, until it dawned on her a great deal of her pleasure lay in the prospect of spending the better part of the afternoon with Major Holborn. Trying to cover her consternation, she examined the sheet she held; she remembered this page.

And well she should. A frisson of fear tingled up her spine. It was the section directly before the one that rewrote itself. He would shortly begin on Chapter Ten, and that meant their decisions and actions over the next few days might well decide the version of history which would become reality — an innocuous house party, or a riot of bloodshed and death.

And what role did *she* play? Did events alter because she came back through time — or was it her presence here in the past that kept history the way it should be? Dear God, why couldn't it have been someone more adequate to sorting out history and politics than she?

Her legs buckled, and she sank onto a chair. What had she gotten herself into, this time? She always knew she was impulsive, but how did she get into this mess?

"You are going to have to be more cautious." Mr. Runcorn's words broke through the fog of horror surrounding her. She looked up, but he addressed the major.

James Holborn shook his head. "Cautious, certainly, but I have another plan."

She stared at him, aghast, and caught the intent gleam in those dark eyes. "You *want* them to make another attempt on you!"

"I do, but in a way I can control. I am going to get to the bottom of this." His tone left no doubts about his determination. "I will not tolerate this any longer, not when someone else is placed in danger."

His gaze flickered across her, startling her as she realized his concern was not just for others in general, but for her in specific. He cared what became of her.

"Miss Campbell," he continued, "I do not want you going out alone under any circumstances, is that understood?"

She nodded. "Don't worry, I won't let them use me as a pawn against you. But I'm not going to just sit around if something is happening to you, either. Will you go to the authorities now?"

He drew a deep breath. "I did. Last night, after I left here."

"Then —"

He shook his head. "They didn't take it seriously — any more than I did myself, at first. Their only aid was to advise me to leave town for some secret destination. They also suggested I publish a conciliatory book in the near future, before making my whereabouts known again."

"That's *all* they did?" she demanded.

He nodded, humor glinting once more in his eyes. "You are even more indignant than I, Miss Campbell."

She swallowed. "Are you going to do it?"

"I am not." The gleam faded, leaving in its place a trace of steel. "I will not be intimidated."

"And hopefully not killed," she added—but too softly for him to hear.

She left them and started up the steps, only to encounter the boys on their way down for the midday meal. She hurried to the kitchens, and over Nancy's halfhearted protests assisted her in carrying the food to the dining room.

The major joined them at the table, and entertained the boys with a highly colored account of his exploits in the war. Ned broke in on his narrative, demanding even more details than the major provided—or made up, Christy guessed as the tale became more absurd. The boys guffawed, and he switched to a story of a Christmas season spent huddled around an inadequate fire with the sounds of cannon punctuating their caroling.

The meal completed, Jem and Tom, the two eldest, ran to the stable to harness the aging mare once more to the cart. It would be a slow drive, Christy reflected, as twenty minutes later she watched the animal plod up the street to the orphanage. The boys piled into the back of the wagon with alacrity. Kepp pulled up with the curricle only minutes later, and the major handed first Christy, then Mrs. Runcorn onto the seat.

The carriage had been designed to hold only two people, Christy realized, as the woman slid in beside her. Luckily, Mrs. Runcorn was a slender woman. Christy herself might be well rounded, but only in proportion to her minuscule build. She scooted over as close as she could to the other woman to provide room for the major. There was nothing small about him.

Quarters were close, and she found herself pressed against him, intriguingly so. Far too intriguingly. She studied the road before them with fixed concentration, willing herself not to be aware of every jostling bump that bounced them together.

The major cast a frowning glance at her. "About what are you thinking, Miss Campbell? You are far too silent and solemn for such a festive expedition."

"I was only thinking how cold it is," she said, improvising.

Thick clouds hung overhead, menacing, as they had been almost constantly since her arrival. There would probably be snow again before they returned. Fortunately, the curricle had a hood that could be drawn up, rather like riding in a convertible.

As they passed out of the disreputable district, she cast an uneasy glance behind them. No men on horseback tried to hide from her searching gaze. Their only shadow was Mr. Runcorn and the cart. Still, she kept watch, afraid to relax her guard.

The buildings became spaced farther and farther apart, until long stretches of heath spread out on either side of them. Christy shivered, and wondered if there might be any hope of a hot drink where they headed. Probably not. She huddled instead in her pelisse.

At last, they left the buildings completely behind and found themselves on an unbroken expanse of rolling ground with shrubs and woods. Other carriages sped past, filled with laughing passengers, probably bound on the same errand. The ancient cart plodded behind them.

The major turned onto a narrow lane and guided them deep into a wooded section. He drew up, tossed his reins to his groom, and helped the ladies down. A few minutes later, Mr. Runcorn's unwieldy contraption pulled up behind them and the boys jumped forth, each armed with a knife. They took off with whoops of delight, and in moments disappeared into the underbrush.

Mr. Runcorn beamed after them. "A delightful expedition, James. I only wish there was more we could do with them in the countryside."

The shrieks of laughter continued, punctuated by loud arguments over who discovered certain choice branches of holly and who was to carry the mistletoe back to the cart. Smiling, the major went after the boys to settle their disputes.

Christy followed, enjoying the crisp, cold air and the feeling of freedom, of being away from London. All too soon, heaping armloads of greenery filled the wagon, and the boys reluctantly climbed in on top.

"It's a shame to go back." Mr. Runcorn pulled himself onto the box and collected his reins.

"Why don't we stop at Hyde Park?" The major kept his voice low. "I saw children ice skating on the Serpentine earlier, perhaps the boys would enjoy it."

"How very kind." Mrs. Runcorn cast a hopeful glance at her husband, who agreed at once.

The major called to the boys, asking if they would care for this treat, and instantly a fight broke out between two as to which was the better skater. The major commanded quiet, and announced it would be determined in a contest, with the other six boys being the judges.

It took some maneuvering to turn the cart, but at last Mr. Runcorn accomplished the feat and started back toward the city. Within a very few yards Major Holborn passed him, then led the way, wending through the maze of streets. At last, they pulled up before the orphanage.

Nancy opened the door for them, as the boys piled out waving branches of the holly and mistletoe at her. "A right regular time you've been 'avin' of it," she said, pleased.

"To the shed, boys," Mr. Runcorn called.

Armed with their greenery, they headed toward the back of the house.

Mr. Runcorn watched them with a benevolent smile, then turned to the maid. "We are to go skating, Nancy. Do you care to come?"

The girl shook her head, setting her brassy ringlets dancing. "Not me, sir. Never could get used to them things. Miss can use my skates, if'n she'd like."

"I'd love to," Christy declared. "Thank you." That left her with the task of finding shoes suitable for strapping on the blades. Her high-heeled boots wouldn't work, of that she felt certain. Nor did her foot size, large by current standards, make borrowing easy.

Mrs. Runcorn came to her rescue, finding her a pair of boots outgrown by an older boy before he left the orphanage. She apologized for their bulky weight and shabby condition, but Christy waved that aside.

"They fit, that's all that matters," she assured the woman.

Twenty minutes later, loaded with a selection of skates, scarves, and gloves, they piled back into the vehicles and set

121

forth to Hyde Park. Christy resumed her vigilance, but still she could detect no threats to Major Holborn's safety. Almost, she began to relax as they pulled through the Grosvenor Gate and onto the carriage drive.

They completed almost a full half circuit before they came in sight of the frozen lake, on which children and adults alike skated. A collection of booths and stalls clustered together, with a large number of people milling among them, creating a fairlike atmosphere. Was this a regular occurrence, Christy wondered, or did some wily vendors merely take advantage of a golden opportunity? Wonderful smells drifted forth. Gingerbread and cinnamon rolls—or the current equivalent.

The major took the boys for hot chocolate, and brought steaming mugs back for Christy and Mrs. Runcorn, as well. They settled on a bench, and Christy took a tentative sip, then wrinkled her nose at the bitterness. She could use a few marsh-mallows on top. She might be able to get cream and cinnamon if she really tried, but it just wouldn't be the same.

Their drinks finished, all busied themselves strapping the blades to their shoes. Major Holborn finished his own, then knelt before Christy. He took her left foot in his hands, and shook his head over her clumsy boot. She could only be glad she didn't wear her own high-heeled ones, with their zipper closing only partly hidden beneath the tabs. *That* would have taken some explaining.

With the skates fastened at last, and adjusted to the major's satisfaction, he assisted her to stand. Already, the boys made tentative forays on the frozen lake, the elder skating with vigor, the younger with more awkwardness. They didn't seem to mind.

"Miss Campbell?" Major Holborn offered her his arm.

She took it, and allowed him to help her across the uneven ground separating them from the Serpentine. As soon as they reached the ice, he struck forward with an even glide, and she clung to him, following perforce. The blades felt different from the shoe-skates to which she was accustomed.

They progressed in silence, his good arm supporting her, until she found her balance. She liked the feel of his hand pressing against her back, gently assisting her. Flakes of snow started to fall as he took her gloved hands and glided into the first movement of a dance.

"No." She pulled back, effectively stopping him. "You'll have to teach it to me, first. I don't know the steps."

"We have to adapt it to skating, as well."

He demonstrated the first pass, then helped her through it. After one round of the cordoned off "rink," repeating the steps, she announced herself ready to give it a try. He whistled an opening bar, then glided forward into the first step.

A dance. Skating. Snow. The enameled scene in the snowdome. . . . The shock of her realization numbed her. She stumbled, and landed on her tailbone.

"Are you all right?" Major Holborn grasped her elbow and drew her to her feet.

"Yes. I —" She steadied herself against him, shaken. "Yes." She regained her balance and looked around. If he wanted to know what happened . . . "Where are the boys?" she asked, hoping to divert him.

"Forming a whip."

"Won't the younger ones get hurt?" She moved forward, and discovered her muscles weren't as young as they used to be. That fall hurt.

The major caught her arm and swung her back. "You need have no fear, they will be all right. They are far more resilient than you or I."

"They'd have to be," she admitted. "They could hardly be less. I'm going to be sore tomorrow." She brushed herself off. "I suppose I shall have to teach standing up for the next couple of days."

A soft chuckle broke from him. "My dear Miss Campbell —" He broke off, as if recollecting the impropriety of her comment. His gaze traveled back to the boys. "If it would make you less uneasy about them, I will join them and assure that their games do not get out of hand."

"You do that." She shook her head as he set off across the ice. If the man wanted to join a whip, why didn't he just do it? Afraid of damaging his macho image by enjoying a child's game? *Did* they have macho images at this time? She considered, and decided they undoubtedly did. That had to be a sex-linked male characteristic, as old as the race.

As he reached the boys, an argument broke out among them, which the major settled summarily by himself anchoring the whip. Keeping his injured arm close to his body, he held out his good one to the first of the boys. Others joined, not of their group, and soon Christy and Mr. Runcorn were among the very few skaters not part of that human chain.

Christy eased herself around the outer perimeter, wincing at the pain in her hip, stretching her injured muscles. The boys showed no such hesitation. The major skated a zigzag pattern in the lead, picking up speed, and the end of the whip swung wildly from side to side. He laughed and made a sharp turn, obviously enjoying himself every bit as much as the littlest of the children.

It was one of his most endearing traits, this ability to shrug off his fears and play the role of surrogate father. Emotion rushed through her, warm and enticing. He possessed a number of appealing qualities. . . . Watching him, she, too, could almost forget the danger that perpetually lurked just a step behind them.

The end of the chain broke lose, and three boys shot out toward a roped-off area. They recovered their balance, then headed off to explore, ducking beneath the boundary. Christy caught her breath as they skated toward an unfrozen portion of the lake.

With a word to the boy behind him, Major Holborn untangled himself from the whip and bent low, striking off in pursuit. Christy started after them, fear welling in her. The boys were light, they probably wouldn't disturb the thin ice, but the major was another matter.

He was so far ahead, beyond the reach of any help. If he fell through, no one could reach him in time. . . .

No, she wasn't the only one chasing after the major. Relief left her weak. Mr. Runcorn sped across the slick surface with sure, easy strides, closing the space between them. At that speed, he would overtake him just beyond the ropes.

Christy's heart lurched, as a vision of the Reverend Mr. Runcorn's tentative, tottering forays on the ice rose in her mind. Frantic, she scanned the rink, and saw the clergyman sitting on a bench beside his wife. Then who—?

She peered at the man, barely able to make him out in the

124

fading light that filtered through the heavy clouds. A voluminous greatcoat enveloped him, and a hat rested low on his head. They might keep him warm, but they also provided an ample disguise, one to which no one would pay any heed until later, when they tried to remember what he looked like. . . .

Abandoning all caution, Christy struck out as fast as she could. He was a far better skater than she, much stronger, and outdistanced her with ease. Abruptly, he glided to a stop in a shower of ice shaved by his blade.

Major Holborn stood less than ten yards from him, bending over, talking to the three boys. The man raised his arm, and a stray beam from the vanishing sun glinted off the polished barrel of his pistol.

Chapter Eleven

"Major!" The scream tore from Christy's throat.

As if by instinct, James Holborn ducked, grabbing the boys and dragging them down with him, shielding them with his body.

A flame spurted from the pistol, and the explosion of sound ricocheted over the ice. For a split second, the man stood as one transfixed, then he struck out with swinging strides. The major launched himself in pursuit, his skate caught on the broken ice, and he went down on one knee. The shattering fractures spread beneath him, and he retreated with care. His assailant reached the far side of the lake, clambered over the bank, and ran through the snow to a waiting closed carriage. As the major regained his feet, the vehicle pulled away.

Christy, trembling and wobbling on her skates, reached the major's side and threw her arms about him, holding him as tightly as she could, desperate to reassure herself he was all right. A broken sob escaped her and she buried her face in his greatcoat.

His good arm closed about her, and for a long minute he held her in his embrace, cradling her against his chest. He murmured something too soft for her to catch the words, but just the sound of his voice filled her with an emotion so intense it brought tears to her eyes. She raised her face to his, and forgot to breathe as she read there a reflection of her own growing need.

Abruptly he stepped back, releasing her. The excited voices of the boys finally penetrated to her as they babbled, demanding to know what happened.

"Did someone really let off a barker at us?" Sammy asked, obviously thinking this raised their status in importance.

The major forced a note of cheerfulness into his voice. "Not at you, at me."

"Aw." Sammy, at least, seemed disappointed.

Oh, for the resiliency of youth. Christy could use some of that right now. Her gaze strayed back to the major's grim face; their gazes met, and she couldn't look away. Tension, as intriguing as it was powerful, raced between them—a bond she couldn't—and didn't want to—deny. Vaguely she remembered they came from different worlds, from different times, but at this moment, what did that matter?

Major Holborn broke the trance, turning his attention to the boys with a determination that effectively blocked her out. He sensed it, too, this unbearable awareness. Of that she felt certain. Yet he intended to ignore it, refuse to give in to it. With his back to her, he collected the boys, delivered a stern lecture on skating near thin ice, then herded them toward where the others still skated.

The Runcorns stood on the snow at the edge of the rink, watching as they approached. Mrs. Runcorn stepped forward, her expression anxious, and beckoned her charges to her.

"No one looks worried about anything except the thin ice. Have they simply ignored the gunshot?" Christy demanded of the major. In her own time, it might have been mistaken for a car backfiring, but not here.

"They must have thought something happened in one of the stalls." He helped her onto the bank. "It is amazing what people can overlook."

He could have been murdered, and no one would have realized what went on right in front of them. . . . Cold seeped through Christy's veins, as if her blood passed through a freezer unit. This attempt had been bolder, better planned. . . . "It was different," she blurted out.

The major touched her lips with one finger and gave a slight shake of his head. He signaled the boys and announced: "Hot chocolate and gingerbread time."

The boys cheered and scrambled off the ice, and for some time they all busied themselves removing their skates. The major pressed Christy onto a bench and knelt before her, grasping her foot.

"This man was different," she repeated. "He was so confident. He never looked back, he never looked around, he concentrated on *you*. He never seemed to doubt he could kill you." She forced herself to say the words.

"Then he should have taken better care of his weapon. Did you notice the flame from the barrel? He used too much oil."

"Will you not take this seriously?" She clasped his hand between both of hers. "Next time, he won't make that mistake. Or any other, for that matter."

He released her foot, rotated his hand so his gloved palm clasped hers, and at last met her gaze. "Then I had better know who it is by then, and why he is after me."

She shivered. It didn't seem possible to be any more frightened or cold, yet she managed it. His enemy came too close, but at least now he openly acknowledged the reality of the danger. If only that could prove enough.

He rose, and she joined him in collecting the boys' skates, which they sent back to the cart with Jem and Tom. When the lads returned, they all set forth for the hot chocolate stand.

Christy glanced about, and spotted a booth of far more interest to her. "There's one with mulled wine," she said. "I could use some of that, if you don't mind."

He nodded. "I think we both could." After paying for the mugs of chocolate, he distributed coins among the boys and told them to buy gingerbread or brandy snaps or fairings, whatever took their fancy. They evaporated like a cloud of mist in the hot sun.

"James." Mr. Runcorn caught his arm. "That man on the ice—Sammy said he shot at you."

The major nodded. "They have made their attempt for today, we should be quite safe, now."

He offered Christy his sound arm, and she took it, her hand closing tightly over it. "Major—" she began.

"Not now."

She bit her tongue to keep back her words of warning, and clung to him for comfort.

The snow drifted down again as they purchased their hot spicy wine. They wandered through the booths, sipping the warming beverage, and she tried hard to savor the experience. Her thoughts, though, could not stray far from the major's danger. Her fingers clenched on his sleeve as she glanced about, unable to shed her nervousness. "Don't you think—"

"No, I do not," he interrupted. "If that man was as confident as you think, he will not have provided for a second attempt today."

"I'll feel a lot better when you're safely indoors."

"If you think I intend to spend the rest of my life cowering in fear, Miss Campbell, you are much mistaken."

She shook her head, and her lips twitched into a rueful smile. "No, that isn't like you."

They returned their mugs to the booth and found the boys had finished their purchases. One—Ned—showed off his proficiency with a ball and cup toy. The major sent Jem to obtain a container of roasted chestnuts, and went himself to where a bonfire burned. There he purchased several bricks which had been heating in the flames.

Christy continued to cling to him, knowing she provided inadequate protection, yet unwilling to let go. At last, to her relief, they returned to the carriages and the waiting Kepp. She and Mrs. Runcorn climbed once more into the curricle, the major placed one of the wrapped bricks at their feet, and Mrs. Runcorn fussed with her skirts, settling herself in comfort.

"So kind, such attentions," she murmured.

The major waved that aside. "Nonsense, it is too cold to be without them."

The boys, meanwhile, scrambled into the back of the wagon and argued over the remaining bricks. Christy huddled over theirs, glad for its warmth.

Darkness closed about them, and now she only could make out dim shapes of people and objects. Kepp had brought up the hood against the falling snow, and she hoped it afforded the major some protection—though she greatly feared it didn't. As they started once more through the streets, she peered from one side to the other.

"Be still, Miss Campbell," the major murmured. "Do not alarm Mrs. Runcorn."

That lady apparently didn't hear. She snuggled into her woolen pelisse, her hands clasped in her muff where they held a small heated rock wrapped in cloth.

"You've got to be more careful," Christy whispered back, and knew she sounded like a broken record.

They reached the orphanage, and the major assisted Christy and Mrs. Runcorn down. Mrs. Runcorn hesitated, looking up at him with a thoughtful expression in her brown eyes. "I believe you should come in."

He nodded. "I left my papers in the study." He told Kepp to return in fifteen minutes, and accompanied them up the stairs.

The cart pulled up before the house, and the boys piled out. The two eldest again took charge of the wagon, and drove off to settle the horse for the night.

Mr. Runcorn mounted to the porch and ushered them into the house. "James," he said without preamble, "I think you should remain the night."

"Just what I was thinking." Mrs. Runcorn turned in relief to her husband. "It would be the very thing."

"There is not the least need." The major looked from one to the other of them, exasperated. "Do you think I am not capable of taking care of myself?"

"I think you're capable of being shot at, James." Mr. Runcorn led the way into the sitting room. "You escaped this afternoon, but it wasn't by much. By now, that man will have had time to recover and be ready to make another attempt."

Christy clasped her hands before her. "It would be far too easy, while you're driving. Your carriage is unmistakable. Your beautiful horses—they're so distinctive."

"What do we have to do to convince you?" Mr. Runcorn regarded him, his expression somber. "If you won't do it for yourself, then do it for us, for we will not be able to sleep a wink all night for worrying whether or not you are safe."

The major shook his head. "It would only be to delay the next attack. If indeed someone lies in wait for me tonight, then what is to stop him in the morning when I leave here?"

"Daylight may prove your friend," Mr. Runcorn said. "It will be best if you refrain from now on from going out toward evening. A man can hide in shadows even in the dimming light."

130

"He can do that in broad daylight." The major's expression remained grim. "Do you think I fear the ghosts? They are said to walk from tonight until Christmas Eve, remember. I can hardly skulk indoors for the next four days."

"Please, James." Mrs. Runcorn laid her hand on his arm. "We have the extra room. I assure you, you will be quite comfortable. You may even send Kepp for Wickes. You need want for nothing while you remain with us. And you will be far safer than at your lodgings."

"Your man can bring your night rail and shaving kit," Mr. Runcorn added.

The major's gaze rested on him a moment, traveled to his wife, then settled on Christy. "And you, Miss Campbell? Have you no entreaties to add?"

She shook her head. "I've never yet known a man to take sound advice, so why should I expect you to listen, now?"

A short laugh escaped him. "It seems I must stay, if only to prove you wrong."

Mrs. Runcorn smiled in relief. "How *un*handsomely said, James."

"Indeed," he admitted. He turned his softened gaze on Christy. "Do you, also, think it unsafe for me to go out this night?"

"This night, especially. Our friend from the rink will be furious with himself for failing. And that means he's all the more likely to strike again, fast, without due reflection, if the opportunity is presented to him. And that might make him all the more deadly."

The major crossed to the fire and stared into it for several silent minutes. "Very well, then," he said at last. "I accept your hospitality, with thanks."

Relief left Christy weak. For this one night, at least, he would be safe.

Noises in the hall announced the return of the boys. Mr. Runcorn opened the door and called to Jem.

"Aye, sir?"

"When Kepp returns with the major's curricle, will you hold the horses for him while he steps in, please?"

Jem took off with alacrity, not, Christy noted, delegating the task to one of the younger boys. All of them seemed pleased to do

131

the major the most trifling service. She could understand that. He inspired loyalty.

Kepp arrived a few minutes later, then took himself off to fetch Wickes. That matter settled, Mrs. Runcorn headed down to the kitchen to see how Nancy progressed with the dinner. Christy followed, wanting to be of assistance. With the major joining them, she felt certain something special would be prepared.

She was right. Major Holborn, she learned, had a fondness for vacherin, a mixture of strawberry preserves and whipped cream, spooned into meringue baskets. Christy set to work steaming vegetables, and as soon as Nancy finished basting the main course of roasted mutton, she set about fixing the special dessert with Mrs. Runcorn's aid. Her own task completed, Christy, over their protests, took herself off to oversee the setting of the table by the boys.

She started back up the stairs from the kitchen, only to stop short at the sight of a strange and very elegant man in his early forties descending toward her. Thinning blond hair receded from his high forehead, and a broad, blunt nose dominated his square face. His black coat fitted smoothly across his shoulders, and the faint spicy scent of a cologne hovered about him. He bowed to her and stepped aside to permit her to pass.

She hesitated. He seemed too much at home to be an intruder. But who — ?

"Miss Campbell, don't you go — " Nancy stuck her head out of the kitchen and broke off. "If'n it ain't Mr. Wickes. 'Ere, now, don't you go a-scarin' miss by creepin' around. You ups and tells 'er who you is."

"It was my intention." His pained gaze rested on Nancy's vivid brassy hair, and he permitted himself a slight shudder. Pointedly, he returned his attention to Christy and bowed to her once more. "Mr. Wickes, miss. I have the honor to serve Major Holborn as his valet."

"Of course." Christy held out her hand. "I'm pleased to meet you. And I'm glad you're here. He didn't hurt his arm any more today, did he?"

A muscle twitched in the valet's cheek, and he stared at her hand. After a moment, he took it. "Thank you, miss. And no, miss. He did not reopen the wound."

132

"Good. Excuse me, I've got to go check on the table." She passed him, aware she had probably just broken every social rule on the book. She only hoped she hadn't offended him too much.

The meal proved to be a lively affair, the boys full of their day's treat. No fear of their hot chocolate and gingerbread affecting their appetites, Christy noted; they ate everything in sight. She leaned back in her chair, listening to their excited chatter, watching their animated faces. This was no normal orphanage. This was more a home. She was very fortunate to have fallen into such hands.

When they finished eating, Nancy and Mrs. Runcorn directed the boys in their cleanup. Christy tagged along, and stacked dishes on the shelves after Alfie dried them. Mr. Wickes, she noted, tended to the pots and pans, which in no way diminished his supercilious expression.

"Above 'isself, 'e is," Nancy informed Christy in an undervoice. Her gaze rested on the valet, and she sniffed. "Keeps to 'isself over there, wont 'ave nothin' to do with the likes of me."

Nancy returned to scrubbing the large wooden table, and Christy glanced over her shoulder to where Wickes hung a frying pan on its metal rack. The valet glanced at the girl, then immediately looked away.

Christy bit her lip and accepted another damp plate from Alfie. Poor Wickes. He might have convinced Nancy he despised her, but he didn't seem to have convinced himself. An ever so proper gentleman's gentleman and an ex-pickpocket? Her smile faded. In this era, that was probably as impossible as a duke and a chambermaid.

The last cup returned to its place, they put away their scrubbing brushes and hung the towels to dry. Wickes declined Mrs. Runcorn's invitation to join them in the sitting room, and took himself off to the major's chamber to arrange his things. The others trooped up the stairs to play a divination game before bed.

Already, Major Holborn and Mr. Runcorn arranged apples and knives for the boys on the table. The children swooped down on these, jockeying for positions, arguing over who got the largest apple or the sharpest knife. The major silenced this squabbling with a word, and the boys went to work.

Christy stood in the doorway, her gaze resting on his dark

auburn head as he bent toward the youngest of the boys, helping him pare his apple in one long piece. Considering someone tried to kill him just a couple of hours ago, he appeared amazingly relaxed. In fact, she would swear he enjoyed himself. In his position, she'd be terrified.

She went to his side, unable to stay away, and took the chair next to him, near the hearth. "They are certainly involved in this, aren't they?"

He shot her a humorous smile. "We have changed the rules a trifle. The original game supposedly showed the initial of one's true love. They do it for the first letter of their future jobs or apprenticeships."

Alfie finished his spiral, held it aloft for the others to see, then tossed it over his shoulder. "What is it?" He spun around for a better look.

"A 'C,' " Jem declared. "You're goin' to be a chimney sweep, you are."

"I don't want to be," Alfie cried.

"Why not a clerk?" Christy suggested. "Or a constable."

"Or a corporal," the major added, joining in the game. "What else can you think of that begins with a 'C?' A cook?"

This diverted the boys, and they became more outlandish in their suggestions for each of the letters. At last, Mrs. Runcorn announced it was past their bedtime, and sent them upstairs. Sammy opened his mouth to protest, but the major cut him short by threatening to pull an inspection on them in fifteen minutes, with dire consequences if they weren't asleep. Laughing, the boys ran to their preparations.

"Which is a wonderful change, we usually have at least one straggler," Mrs. Runcorn said with a sigh.

"I'll withdraw also, if you don't mind." The major rose. "I cannot neglect my work." He retreated down the hall to the study.

Christy watched him go, then mounted the steps to her room and closed the door firmly behind her. Major Holborn planned to work, presumably on his book.

Curious, she drew the copy of *Life in London* out of its hiding place in the bottom of her clothes cupboard and unwrapped it from her royal blue sweater. For a long moment she stared at the title page, studying his name in print, then she turned the pages over one at a time, scanning the typeset words. The lines remained clear, the words solid and unchanging—except for a rare, occasional one that blurred.

She passed sixty-odd pages that way, then turned the next into Chapter Eight. Part of this first sheet remained legible, the rest shifted before her eyes. A light-headed, dizzy sensation swept over her as her fingers traced the letters, trying to force them to hold a single shape.

This must be the section he currently wrote. He had yet to complete it in final form, so the words continued to shift between the possible alternatives. The same held true for those few words in the earlier chapters, which either he or a publisher would change before printing.

She leafed through the next fifteen pages, and at least half of the words altered. He still had a lot of rewriting to do, she surmised. She turned another, and froze; the type ran out after only three lines. The rest was blank.

Startled, she flipped through the remaining forty-odd pages of the book, but they remained empty, all the way to the end. She closed the volume and stared at it. The section he had yet to begin. Her history, his future. As yet uncast.

She hugged herself, cold with more than the icy chill of the December night. St. Thomas's Eve, December Twentieth, the night of divination. How appropriate. Which course would events take? She had always assumed history was a given, once lived it couldn't be changed. Yet here she was, knowing events to have occurred one way, and seeing before her the evidence that they could alter.

If this revolution came about, would that be the reality she knew, the one she tried to preserve, the one *all* history books would record? And what else would change? The ripple effect through time boggled her mind. How many subtle differences would there be?

Would she even exist, or would history create different patterns that would prevent her parents—or grandparents, or even great grandparents—from ever meeting? Would she simply vanish? Then would the effect be retroactive, so she never came to this time at all, since she never existed? One little change now, and how very different life could become two hundred years in the future.

Her gaze returned to the volume she clenched in her hand. During the next week or two, James Holborn would either record a house party he had yet to attend, or riots would break out in the streets. And somehow, his actions, and probably her own, would determine the course of history.

She opened the book once more, to the last pages with writing. As she watched, several lines ceased their shifting and became solid. She swallowed. He worked on it now, put something in its final form. A shimmering line formed on the almost blank page.

What did he write? The word "pistol" stood out for one moment, then vanished into a hazy blur. She didn't remember anything about guns in the printed book, at least not until she reached Chapter Ten and the tale of the rioting. A chill crept through her that refused to be banished. Had they begun on the sequence of events which would lead, ultimately, to bloodshed and death?

She had to stop him from recording more of his danger, from recording anything having to do with violence, lest that version become the permanent one! She shoved the book into the reticule which hung at her wrist, grabbed up her candle, and shielded it as she ran from her room, down the stairs to the study where the crackling of a fire and the warm glow of light indicated someone worked within. She pushed wide the partially open door, then stopped on the threshold.

James Holborn sat at the writing desk, quill in hand, his brow creased in a frown as he studied the page before him. Her gaze fell on his scrawling copperplate.

"What are you writing?" she demanded.

He looked up, and his eyebrows rose in polite inquiry. "I am finishing a chapter of my book."

"I know that, but—"

"You do?"

She bit her lip. "I mean, I saw you weren't quite done with it. Naturally you're polishing it a bit."

His gaze rested on her face. "What has distressed you?"

"Why are you writing about pistols?" she blurted out.

All expression faded from his face. "How did you know I was?"

She closed her eyes, aghast. How could she have been so *dumb* as to say that? But it was all she could think about.

He rose and came around the side of the desk and positioned

himself directly in front of her. "I asked you a question, Miss Campbell."

"It —" She broke off, not able to come up with a single explanation, believable or otherwise. She clutched the ribbons of her reticule, then glanced down at it. She shouldn't have brought the book with her. . . .

"What have you in there?" He caught the cloth bag.

She tried to pull it back. "Nothing. It — it's just a book. Your earlier one." He met her frantic gaze with a penetrating one of his own, and she looked away, desperate. She couldn't let him see it.

"May I?" He dragged it from her wrist and pulled it open.

"No!" She caught at it. Or did part of her *want* him to see the book, to end the pretences between them, to warn him of the dangers that threatened ahead?

He pulled the bag free of her grasp and drew out the thin leather volume. "It is certainly a beaten-up copy, isn't it?" He turned it over, and his expression froze. *"Life in London,"* he said at last. "That was not the title of my first book. Rather, it is the one I have considered for the manuscript on which I currently work."

For one long, heart-stopping minute, his gaze rested on her stricken face. At last he lowered it to the book, and leafed through the pages. Silence filled the study, broken only by the crackling of the fire. Then he looked up once more at her, and she fell back a pace under the force of the anger in his flashing eyes.

"I think, Miss Campbell," he said, his tone rigid, "it is time for those explanations you avoid so well."

Chapter Twelve

This time, James determined, he would not be put off, not be distracted by Miss Campbell's taking ways or her lovely eyes and enchanting smile. This time, he would force the truth from her.

Slowly, as if compelled against her will, she looked up to meet the challenge of his gaze. She looked away at once, her shoulders slumping. For a long minute she stared into the fire, and seemed to draw courage from the glowing coals. "You're not going to believe what I have to say," she said, her voice so soft he could barely hear.

"Very probably not," he agreed. "I have never met anyone like you, before. And this" — he tapped the book — "this, my dear Miss Campbell, defies logical and reasonable explanation."

A slight smile twisted her lips. "You're not kidding."

"Do you have any idea how it feels to leaf through the pages of a published book that *isn't* published — let alone finished — yet? This is impossible."

"I'd noticed. The whole situation is impossible."

He sat back on the edge of the desk. "I'm very much looking forward to what you will have to say about it."

"Right." She drew a deep breath. "Just for a moment, consider the possibility I come from a time two hundred years in the future. How does that hit you?"

138

"Do you want the truth, Miss Campbell?"

She grimaced. "No. I just need you to believe me."

"I'm listening, let's leave it at that."

She crossed to the fireplace and stared into the flames. "I really do come from the future. I'm a rare book and antiquities dealer, which is how I got into this mess." She spun about to face him. "I *flew* to England, Major Holborn. On a ship that travels through the air. It's powered by engines that—oh, damn, you don't even have *steam* engines yet. How am I going to explain gasoline? Never mind, but it only takes hours, rather than weeks, to cross the Atlantic."

"Indeed." He folded his arms and allowed his lip to curl. "Are you certain you are not a writer of lurid novels, Miss Campbell?"

"Only if you're the writer of ones that shift their lines," she shot back. "I came to England for a purpose—for an auction at Sotheby's. I bought that book—" she gestured toward it—"as part of a lot. The first nine chapters stayed solid. The rest shifted back and forth between two very different versions. From Chapter Ten on—the part you're about to start writing. The part that's blank now."

His fingers whitened on the volume. Pointedly, he glanced at the mantel clock. "It grows very late for fairy stories, Miss Campbell."

"Fairy tales? Look at your book again, Major. Is that a fairy tale? The type is shifting, isn't it? *Isn't it?*"

He gritted his teeth, then unclenched his fingers and leafed once more through the pages. It wasn't possible, it simply wasn't *logical,* yet the letters altered themselves, forming different words and sentences. The basic content remained the same, except one version read in a more polished form, as if he had cleaned up his notes. . . .

Hell and the devil confound it! If he weren't careful, he'd find himself believing this nonsense. "What do you claim the rest of the book is about?" With an effort, he kept his voice even.

"Neither version ever got clear enough for me to really read it. I only caught glimpses of them." She hesitated, then plunged on. "One described a Christmas house party, at which a number of government officials were present."

"And the other?"

She paced to the chairs, and clutched the back of one. "The other spoke of riots and bloodshed in the streets, and a revolution like the one the French had."

"This is nonsense." He surged to his feet and started to slam the book onto the table, only to stop himself with it halfway down.

"I knew you wouldn't believe any of this. That's why I've avoided your questions." She brushed the dark curls from her eyes in a frustrated gesture. "Remember how crazy I acted on that first day when you met me? How would you feel if you suddenly looked around and found yourself transported back to *Sixteen* Hundred, and the buildings and landmarks you knew had vanished, and everyone dressed and talked *differently?*"

He crossed to the fire and stared at it for a long moment, then turned back to her. "Have you any explanations about why this should have happened?"

"Only a pretty scary one. I checked other books written at this time, and none of them shifted like this. And I showed your book to other people, and they only saw the tale of the house party. The words only changed for me, and only in your book."

"And your conclusions?"

"As far as my time is concerned — and for that matter, as far as all other books from *this* time are concerned — no revolution takes place. I can only assume some action on your part — and possibly on mine — either causes or prevents the rioting. History seems to be in our hands."

"That is quite a responsibility you choose to place upon my shoulders, Miss Campbell."

"I didn't make the choice. I wish I'd never gone to that damned auction — *or* seen your stupid book. Then history could have just gone on without me."

"History." His lips twisted into an ironic half smile. Was that the way she thought of him? Some ancient relic from the distant past? The devil, she had him doing it, almost believing this ridiculous story of hers.

His gaze strayed back to the book, and his frown deepened. There might almost be some justification for that belief. He raised his gaze to her once more. "If you're really from the future, how did you get here?"

"That snowdome you made."

"That—" He broke off. "Do you mean snowball? What you would make if you pack a handful of snow for throwing?"

"I wish. Don't you remember, I described it to that man in the curio shop? The place where I bought it—except that was two hundred years in the future? It's a glass ball, filled with a liquid, usually with a scene inside and little flecks of something white. When you shake it, the flecks drift down on the scene like snow."

"And?" he prodded.

"This one showed a man and woman ice skating, with a carriage and gray horse in the background. As I looked at it, the couple danced—the same dance you showed me today."

"And what did you mean about my making it?"

She drew a shaky breath. "It had your signature on the bottom. The figures were cast from silver and enameled, to keep them from tarnishing in the liquid."

He set his jaw. "I do cast in silver, and I sometimes enamel the pieces. Jewelry making is a hobby of mine. Anyone could have told you that. I have never, though, made such an object— indeed, I have never heard of such a thing before."

"Well, you'd better get to work on it. You dated it Eighteen-Ten, which gives you only a couple of weeks to complete it."

"And what makes you think I intend to do anything of the kind?"

"If you don't, it won't exist in the future to bring me back through time."

"Which is the best argument I ever heard for *not* carving any wax for the next month," he shot at her.

She shook her head. "I'm here, aren't I?"

He strode to the window and gazed out at the snow falling in the narrow alley behind the house. "If I don't make it, what happens to your history, then? What happens to you?" He glanced over his shoulder at her.

She sank onto the chair. "I don't know. Maybe you have a revolution instead of a house party. It's the book, though, not the snowdome, that shows the potential disaster. What if you don't finish it, so it's never published?"

His gaze fell on the manuscript pages scattered on the table, then transferred to the volume he still clutched. No, it was his

141

work, what he believed in. Only his death would prevent him from finishing it. Only his death. . . .

Icy tentacles crept through him. Only his death, which someone seemed very determined to bring about.

He dragged open the book, watched the shifting type, studied the blank pages at the end. Nothing was settled. It was true, he didn't yet know what he would write in this section. He had no plans, though, to attend a house party—and certainly no intention to witness a revolution in the streets.

A revolution in the streets. Some part of him feared that possibility already. A chance existed, a very real chance. Sir Oliver Paignton, Lord Farnham, Viscount Brockenhurst—their comments at St. Ives's dinner party returned to haunt him. If Prinny, with his spendthrift ways, became regent, would the poor of the city rise up in protest, demand a portion of that vast fortune he wasted on frivolities to obtain the basic necessities for themselves?

A revolution, like the one in France.

And somehow, he was involved, or it would not be his book alone which altered its words.

"Rioting," he repeated aloud, and turned to face her.

"Something is going to happen within the next couple of weeks, and I don't know what it is," she declared. "That regency bill?"

He shook his head. "I have nothing to do with that. I have no influence in government circles—much to my regret. My sole influence rests with the people who have read my writings on civil reform. If, as you suggest, this matter hinges on me, then it must be these writings that are responsible." His fingers clenched on the book. "I will do everything in my power to prevent such a bloodbath in England."

"Got any bright ideas?"

He drew a deep breath, considering his options. "I think," he said at last, "we will do best to speak to Saint Ives."

"Your cousin? Why?"

"He takes a considerable interest in government policies, gathers about him men of influence. All of the people at the dinner party—except us—were important in the government."

"Then you think these are the men who might cause—or prevent . . ." Her voice trailed off as she sat up, her eyes sparkling, animated. "Could they be induced to prevent problems? To possibly pass a bill—"

"Or *not* pass one," he interrupted her. "Confound it, I have been blind! My writings on social reform combined with Prinny's taking the regency will be the destruction of England! Come on." He grabbed her hand and started for the door. "Get your bonnet and pelisse."

"Where are we going?" She hurried after him, barely keeping up with his long strides.

"To Saint Ives. I want a word with him, and I want you to listen."

He threw open the door, propelled her down the hall, and took the stairs two at a time. By the time he'd fetched his greatcoat and beaver, she had only just reached her chamber. He waited while she collected her things, then helped her into the pelisse.

"Will he still be up?" she asked.

He gave a short laugh. "Knowing Saint Ives, he will be entertaining again this night. He rarely seeks his couch before three in the morning." He started down the stairs, then realized she wasn't following.

"Is this safe?" Lines of worry creased her lovely brow, her features so expressive of concern—for him.

"It's a chance I'm prepared to take," he said. "Are you coming?"

For answer, she followed him.

The icy night air chilled him to the bone as he stepped onto the front porch. What it did to Miss Campbell in that flimsy gown he didn't want to think. At least her pelisse was of sturdy wool.

It wasn't going to be easy finding a hackney, despite the fact it lacked only twenty minutes before eleven. No jarvey with any respect for his life lingered on Golden Lane—or anywhere in St. Luke's, for that matter.

He quickened his stride, then slowed as her ragged breathing reached him through the muted stillness of the snow-filled darkness. He strained his ears for the sound of pursuit, but none came. He cut down Barbican Street, and at last they emerged onto Aldersgate. Here, a number of carriages—some of them hackneys—passed.

The fourth he signaled stopped for them. He bundled Miss Campbell inside, then gave the direction of his cousin's house. The driver raised an eyebrow at this exalted address, cast a speculative eye over the major, then jerked his head for his passenger to enter.

"Not on his usual route, I should imagine," Miss Campbell said.

James acknowledged this, then fell silent, staring out the window. What a devilish situation. He couldn't abandon his life's work, yet to pursue it might result in a far worse situation than existed now. Should he act—or do nothing? Which course led to the preservation of England—and the betterment of the lower classes? This remarkable—and possibly mad—young woman couldn't tell him.

At last the driver pulled up in Portman Square and let them down. James paid him, then strode up the stairs, drawing Miss Campbell with him. He knocked, then waited, one hand shoved in his pocket, the other about her elbow, and wished it weren't so damnably cold.

At last the door opened. Doring stared at him, surprise flickering across his normally impassive countenance. "Major Holborn!" He stepped back and gestured for them to enter. "His lordship is entertaining this evening."

James nodded. "I expected as much. Might I have a word with him alone, please?"

"Certainly, sir." Doring escorted them up the stairs and into a small salon at the front of the house.

A sudden burst of laughter sounded from down the hall, and several deep voices rose in a jovial exchange, then faded to silence. Miss Campbell crossed to the fireplace and held out her hands to warm them. After a moment, James joined her.

The welcome heat reached his fingers, relieving their numbness. "We could have picked a better time of year for this adventure," he said.

She smiled, but shook her head. "Oh, no, you wouldn't want to take all the challenge out of it, would you?"

"Of course not." Somehow, she made it all seem not quite as

bad. His gaze rested on her face, on the lock of curls which hung over her forehead in delightful disarray. Normally, he liked extreme neatness in a lady. But Miss Campbell defied all the rules.

She wasn't exactly a beauty, he decided. Just breathtaking. No cool ice maiden this, not at all the sort of female toasted by the *ton*. She vibrated with passion, vivacity, and a depth of emotion he could barely comprehend. Not to mention a reprehensible sense of humor.

Desire for her surged through him with an intensity that drove all from his mind except its unexpectedness, its unfamiliarity in his dealings with ladies of virtue, and its incredible strength. Stunned, he gazed into her huge, luminous eyes.

They met his in a look half startled, half rueful, which faded into a yearning that mirrored his own. Against his will, against his better judgment, he stepped toward her, his hand reaching out to brush that stray curl from her forehead. His finger trailed to her cheek, then traced her lips. They parted, and her soft breath fanned his flesh. Such very kissable lips. Why had he not yet availed himself of their promise?

Because he was a gentleman. Abruptly, he turned away, folding his hands into fists to prevent them from returning to her. Confound the woman! Couldn't she see the effect she had on him? A man of honor did not — *could* not — so far forget himself with a defenseless female under his protection.

The door opened, and with a concerted effort he pulled himself together and greeted St. Ives.

The earl, resplendent in a coat of deep blue velvet and a white satin waistcoat, paused just over the threshold and raised his quizzing glass. After a moment, he allowed it to drop. "Dear Coz, what brings you out on such a night? And Miss — Campbell, is it not? How delightful."

He crossed to the chairs and gestured for Miss Campbell to be seated. She perched on the edge of one and leaned forward, elbows on her knees, in a most unladylike manner James found endearing. She raised her gaze to his face with an expression of such uncertainty mingled with trust in his judgment, that James was hard put to it not to kiss her on the spot. Confound her enchanting ways!

"Well?" The earl lounged back on a sofa, his elegantly pantalooned legs extended before him toward the fire.

James strode to the window and stared out over the street. A barouche drove by, a crest emblazoned on its panel. Lights flickered from the carriage lamps on the box, glinting off the metal accoutrements of the harness, and the soft jingling of the bells reached him. So very different from Golden Lane.

He turned back into the room. "As you know, I move among a different order of society than do you."

St. Ives raised sardonic eyebrows. "Indeed, Coz? Do you know, it had occurred to me."

"What might not have occurred to you," James said, "is that I hear a very different view of political events from those to which you are exposed."

"Is this view supposed to be of interest to me?" The earl covered his mouth with the tapering fingers of one hand and yawned. "Do get on with it, dear Coz. I have guests waiting."

James clenched his jaw. "I am hearing a great deal of discontent among the poor and the elderly."

A sharp laugh escaped St. Ives. "Dear Coz, not even *you* can think this is a matter of any remarkableness. It is not in the least unusual."

"No, it is not, and that is the problem." He positioned himself directly before his exasperating cousin. "It is far too usual, and it is also rapidly becoming dangerous."

"Do you mean those attacks on you? I have told you repeatedly not to stir up the rabble of this poor city. If you insist on behaving in so unseemly a manner, then you will have to take the consequences."

"I doubt it will be me, alone. The discontent may soon go beyond the grumbling stage. You cannot tell me you have never seriously considered the possibility of a revolution?"

St. Ives's eyes narrowed. "Do you hear rumors of violence?"

James glanced at Miss Campbell. "I do," he said, his voice level.

"Confound it!" St. Ives surged to his feet, his affected manner dropping away. He strode to the hearth, then abruptly about-faced. "That damnable regency bill!" he exploded. "The masses will never tolerate Prinny's wastrel ways." He shook his head, and all expression faded from his face. "Perhaps they are right,

146

after all."

"Who? About what?" James demanded.

St. Ives slammed his fist on the mantel. "Prinny. He'll be the death of us all."

"No!" Miss Campbell's gaze flew from St. Ives to James. "It's something else that has to change. I know for a fact your Prinny won't cause any trouble by being appointed regent."

"Do you?" St. Ives raised his quizzing glass once more and regarded her through it. His sneer returned. "By Jove, what a remarkably well-informed young lady."

James rounded on her, ignoring his cousin. "What changes? What do we do that makes him acceptable?"

"*We?*" St. Ives shook his head. "I, for one, have not the influence."

Again, James paid him no heed. "How many possibilities are there?"

"Only the two, I should think." She shook her head. "Either you attend a house party or—or you know the other choice."

"*I* don't," St. Ives pointed out.

"Riots in the streets," James agreed.

"Then by all means, dear Coz, attend this house party." The earl's lip curled. "It seems the most sensible course."

James fixed his cousin with his steady regard. "Do you know, Saint Ives, I believe you are right. Somehow, I must attend this house party. There seems little we can do until then."

"Excellent. Allow me to offer mine, then, if it will prevent these riots you fear. I have two other guests remaining with me this night. Will you not join us?"

James cast a questioning glance at Miss Campbell.

"I don't know," she said slowly. "This isn't exactly a Christmas house party, is it?"

"How grieved I am to inform you it is not. Merely an expedience for two members of the Home Office who do not wish to travel in this inclement weather. Sir Oliver and Lord Farnham. Brockenhurst is with us, as well, but he does not, I believe, intend to remain the night."

Miss Campbell glanced at James. "It *might* be the one. There are certainly members of the government here."

"Very well, then." He nodded. "Thank you, Saint Ives. We

147

will be delighted to accept your hospitality. Only let me send a message to the Runcorns to assure them we are unharmed."

St. Ives's eyes narrowed. "*Have* you been having more of that problem?"

James's lips twitched into a rueful smile. "In fact, I had promised the Runcorns to remain for the night with them, rather than risk going out after dark."

St. Ives tugged gently at his quizzing glass, a frown darkening his blue eyes. "There is no question but that you stay, then. I will send someone for your man and your things. Miss Campbell's things as well, of course."

"Thank you." Her voice, though, held a note of skepticism.

The earl dispatched a footman on the errand, then led the way down the hall to the drawing room. The faint odor of heady wine mingled with the beeswax from the multitude of candles and the smoke from the fireplace. The chimney needed sweeping.

Lady St. Ives sat with Farnham at a small card table near the hearth, and the other two gentlemen rattled a dice box on another topped with a green baize cloth. Sir Oliver Paignton laid down the ivories, and Brockenhurst's hazel eyes widened at sight of the newcomers. He cast a questioning glance at St. Ives.

Sir Oliver reached across the table, touched Brockenhurst's arm, and shook his head.

"Fresh blood?" Lord Farnham folded his cards, his gaze speculative. He leaned back in his chair and ran his fingers through his windswept black hair.

Lady St. Ives rose gracefully in a cloud of pomona green silk, which did not quite conceal her advancing pregnancy. A dyed ostrich plume curled from her fashionable crop of blond ringlets and just brushed her cheek. "James? How delightful. But what brings you here so late?"

"I fear we are joining your party, Margaret." He took her hand and awarded her an elegant bow. "I believe you remember Miss Campbell? I have placed her in an awkward position, and must beg your chaperonage of her for this night."

"Of course I remember, and shall only be too delighted." A shy smile lit her pale blue eyes. "Would you care for a game of cards? I fear I bore Lord Farnham."

"Impossible," that gentleman declared at once.

"He does not mind in the least playing for penny points." Margaret cast him a grateful glance.

"Like you, dear Coz." St. Ives's cool gaze rested on Farnham, and his sneer settled over his narrow features. "Ever the defender of damsels in distress."

Farnham awarded him a mock bow.

"It was very kind of him," Margaret said, quick in his defense. She turned her resentful regard on her husband. "He—he realized I have no taste for high stakes."

"Do you not, my dear?" St. Ives tugged at his quizzing glass. "Now, why had I not realized this before?"

"I don't, either," Miss Campbell said quickly. "In fact, I don't think I know any of the games you play here. Is there a simple one you could teach me?"

Lady St. Ives at once offered her assistance, and Lord Farnham rose and strolled over to the other gentlemen at the dicing table. James, also, joined them.

Sir Oliver smoothed down his unruly graying hair, then extended his hand. "What a delightful surprise, Major. How are you?" A smile sat uneasily on his lips.

"Major." An unidentifiable emotion flickered through Brockenhurst's bright hazel eyes, and he stood. "Good evening."

James raised his eyebrows in mild surprise. "What, not a single comment about my slumming in Mayfair? You must be castaway."

Brockenhurst's slender frame stiffened. "I have never meant to give offense."

James shook his head. "You never could hold your wine. For heaven's sake, be seated. What the devil are you about? You never stand upon ceremony with anyone except Prinny."

"Sit down, sit down." Sir Oliver tugged at the tails of the viscount's exquisitely cut coat. "Don't be a demmed fool, boy. Well, Major, what's your pleasure? Faro? Hazard? Or the bones? I'll warn you, they're throwing devilishly contrary tonight."

James shook his head. "Don't let me interrupt. I'll join whatever it is you play."

After some polite deferring to one another, Sir Oliver persuaded Brockenhurst to start a faro bank. Farnham and St. Ives withdrew to another small table, and joined in hand after hand of piquet. They appeared oblivious to the others.

The remainder of the evening and the early hours of the morning passed in the dedicated pursuit of gambling. Sir Oliver, once in possession of his cards, had eyes for nothing else. Brockenhurst lounged back in his chair, playing as if he had little interest in the proceedings, yet winning a considerable amount.

They at last rose from the table with Sir Oliver jovial, despite his heavy losses. James found himself some fifty pounds to the better, and was glad for Sir Oliver's sake St. Ives insisted upon keeping the stakes low.

Margaret at last gave vent to the yawn she had been trying to smother. Miss Campbell stood at once.

"You shouldn't have stayed up so late," she said. "I'm sorry, you must be exhausted."

That lady shook her head, setting the plume jiggling once more against her cheek. "It would be unthinkable to retire before my guests. Come, Mrs. Munchken will have prepared your room long ago." She crossed to the hearth and pulled the bell rope.

A sour-faced woman in apron and mobcap entered a minute later, as if she had been waiting just outside for the summons.

Margaret handed Miss Campbell into her care, then turned to James. "You know your way to the green room? Then I will bid you good night." With a halfsmile of apology, she went to her husband's side.

James followed as the housekeeper escorted Miss Campbell to a small chamber at the back of the next floor. Through the door, he glimpsed Nancy dozing by the fire, and relief surged through him at the Runcorns' thoughtfulness. Miss Campbell would be far more comfortable with someone she knew to look after her.

He himself occupied a spacious apartment one flight up. Wickes greeted him at the door, and over his man's shoulder he could see his things arranged with comfortable familiarity.

Only the mildest reproach showed in Wickes's face as he stepped aside to permit his master to enter. "Are we settled this time, sir?"

"We have only moved twice, this night," James pointed out, amused.

"Indeed, sir."

Wickes set about removing his boots, and in a very short time James dismissed him. After finishing his preparations for bed, he extinguished the candles and settled in a chair with a glass of brandy. Lord, what a night this had been. He wasn't at all sure what he was doing here, either. Miss Campbell and her preposterous stories. Yet the print in that book . . . *his* book. . . . None of this made sense.

And there went his primary argument against Miss Campbell's claims she came from the future. Logic and sense played no part when it came to her. *Damn* the chit! She had him behaving as if he *believed* her. And what was worse, he realized the next moment, he actually did.

He glared into the hearth, annoyed with himself. How could he be so gullible, so —

The soft creak of the handle turning cut across his thoughts. He rose, reaching for the fireplace poker, as the door inched open. A pale round face, surrounded by a cloud of dusky ringlets, peeped inside.

With a sigh, Miss Campbell slipped through the opening and closed the door behind her. "Thank heavens! I *thought* this was your room, but if I'd been wrong —" She giggled, and clutched a muslin wrapper about her. "Wouldn't you have liked to see Sir Oliver's face if I'd waltzed in on *him?*"

James returned the poker to its stand and glared at her. "Please leave, Miss Campbell. You have no business being here."

"Well, that's a fine welcome. I just came to make sure you were all right."

"And why shouldn't I be? This is my cousin's house."

"That's exactly why. I don't trust him. There's something peculiar going on. All those men, particularly Lord Brockenhurst, kept staring at you. It was enough to give me the willies. I couldn't sleep." Her bare feet made no sound as she crossed the carpet to stand before the blazing hearth. She shivered, and inched closer.

The thick mass of her hair fell well below her shoulders, the tight curls haloing about her head in a riot that made him long to run his hands through them. What else it made

151

him want to do registered itself in a very marked manner.

A rush of heat surged through him. Lord, she was lovely, so full of life and vitality. And so very desirable. Unable to resist, he brushed her hair back from her eyes. Such beautiful eyes. A flame danced in their depths. Reason told him it was the reflection from the firelight, yet his heart cried out it was her passionate nature. His hand buried itself in her curls, clasping the back of her neck. Those lips. . . .

His mouth brushed hers, testing with a feathery soft touch. She swayed toward him, her arms encircling his waist, her fingers tracing a tantalizing pattern up his back. Her lips caressed his chin, and a low groan rose from the depth of his being as his control wavered on the brink.

With an enormous effort, he set her aside. "You have assured yourself as to my well-being, Miss Campbell. You may now leave."

He turned away, cursing himself for a fool. Never had he wanted a woman so much, never had he faced so wrenching a choice between honor and passion. The females who usually stirred his desire belonged to a very different order, were his—or any man's—for the taking. But not Miss Campbell. Not . . . Christina.

From behind him, her arms crept about his waist once more, and he stiffened. "Miss Campbell." He grasped her hands and loosened her hold, knowing his action was the opposite of what he wanted, and knowing his willpower—and his self-respect—hung by a very thin thread. It would be so easy to give in to the need that raged through him—and so unforgivable for taking advantage of a lady under his protection.

"This isn't why I came here." Her cheek pressed against his shoulder blade, and her body molded itself to him. "I honestly only meant to check on you. But—James?"

The huskiness of her tone battered the walls of his defenses. "No." His voice rasped in his throat. "You can have no idea where this will lead, my dear." He faced her, clasping her hands between his own. "No lady should ever come to a gentleman's room. The situation can get out of control far too rapidly."

"Good." She barely breathed the word. "James, I—"

Once more, the eerie creek of the handle reached him. He

grasped Miss Campbell's wrist and shoved her behind the curtains which surrounded his bed. "Keep down and keep quiet!" he hissed. He grabbed up the discarded poker and swung around to face the door as it inched silently open.

Chapter Thirteen

Christy opened her mouth, then shut it as the soft rustle of satin reached her. Someone entered the room. She tensed, then drew her legs under her so she crouched. The bed curtain might provide a hiding place for her, but if this intruder dared harm James . . .

"Ah, you are still awake?" St. Ives's silken drawl reached her. "Dear Coz, I thought you would have been asleep by now."

"Did you? What a peculiar time to call upon me, then."

St. Ives laughed, though it sounded somewhat tense. "I fear it was not the pleasure of your company I sought. Rather, to assure myself of your safety."

"Indeed?"

The earl sighed. "Yes, as odd as it may seem, I do find I have a certain fondness for you. And a certain interest in keeping you alive. I came because I thought I heard someone moving about the house. The stairs are in the most dreadful habit of creaking, you must know. Has anyone come near your door?"

"My man came a few minutes ago," the major lied easily. "Might it have been him?"

"I suppose it is possible, but the person I heard used the main stairs, and I did not hear him leave."

"Ah. A mystery then. A ghost, perhaps? After all, it is Saint Thomas's Eve."

154

"More likely the house settling. Very well, if you are quite safe, I shall bid you good night." His muffled footsteps crossed the rug. "Lock your door after me," the earl advised. A soft click indicated his departure.

Christy rose from behind the bed to see the major turn the key in the lock, then toss it on the table. He placed his ear against the door and waited. She inched forward, wondering if the earl peered in through the keyhole. Just in case, she stayed out of the direct line.

The major waved her back, and she stopped, then sank down on his bed. Two minutes passed, ticking by their slow seconds, and at last James nodded to himself. He gestured Christy to silence, crossed to the fire and poked at the embers. He threw on another log.

At last, he came to her side and bent close. "I didn't hear any retreating footsteps." His voice made the merest thread of sound. "It will be best if you wait for a few minutes before leaving."

"Fine. I don't trust him" His nearness set her pulse beating erratically. She forced her concentration back to his danger. "What if he hoped to find you asleep? What's to have stopped him from killing you?"

"A sense of family?"

His breath fanned her cheek, and an aching longing seeped through her. "He doesn't like you," she managed. She caught his hand, and temptation proved too great. She drew him down beside her. "That scared me when he came in. I really thought he'd come to attack you."

"No." He stroked her hair, soothing. "It's all right."

Closing her eyes, she reveled in the sensations caused by his simplest touch. She rested her cheek against his shoulder. "Now it is," she agreed.

"Miss Campbell—" He set her aside.

No, she couldn't bear it if he withdrew from her. Not now, not tonight, not when he filled her world, when the sound of his deep voice sent a thrill through her very being. She'd never felt like this before. She'd never felt such depth of emotion, such certainty she had found the one man . . .

She gazed into his eyes. The smoldering glow she encountered

155

there robbed her of breath. He felt it, too, this desperate need, this sense of oneness between them. They belonged together, but he'd fight against it. . . .

This was too important to let his ridiculous noble instincts rule his heart. She slid her arm across his broad chest, then pushed hard, so he fell back on the comforter. She stopped his struggles by pinning him by both shoulders.

"Miss Campbell—"

"Christy," she whispered, and trembled with nerves at her audacity. "I'm doing this for your own protection, you know. *Someone* needs to stay with you tonight. Just to make sure you're safe, of course."

In spite of himself, his lips twitched. "And who's to make sure I'm safe from you?"

"Do you really want to be?"

For a long moment he remained silent, gazing at her. At last, he said: "What I want and what is right are vastly different things."

"No, they're not! James, it's not like this at *all* where I come from. I haven't been brought up with these ridiculous constraints. The rules of your time just don't apply to me, so don't judge me—or us—by them."

His fingers brushed across her curls. "It couldn't have changed that much."

"Oh, yes it could. You need a lesson in our modern ways. Now—in your time—no one thinks the worse of a man for sleeping with a woman, do they? In *my* time, men and women have become equal that way. If what we share is as *special* as this. . . ." She broke off, unable to put the feelings and sensations into words.

"You are under my protection. I cannot take advantage of you."

"I'm over the age of consent and capable of making my own decisions."

"And apparently mine, as well." A gleam lit the depths of his dark eyes, and he pulled her to him. His mouth brushed across her cheek, then found her lips.

She closed her eyes, savoring the fierceness of the pressure. His hands moved over her shoulders and back, tantalizing and teasing, as he deepened the kiss, demanding an even greater response from her. She gave it. His arms tightened, crushing her against him, and the passion flaming between them sent wonder surging through every part of her.

He released her slowly, lingeringly. His hand slid to her cheek, then cupped the nape of her neck. "Does that measure up to the standards of your time?"

A shaky laugh escaped her. "Beats them all hollow," she assured him. "Maybe I'm the one who needs a lesson."

His finger trailed down her throat to the scooped neckline off her muslin wrapper. "This is your last chance to withdraw."

"Are you kidding? And miss my chance to learn from a master?"

A slow smile of purely male triumph spread across his features. "You desire me to instruct the instructress, then?"

"Very much," she breathed. "I think you'll find me a very attentive student."

"Then let us begin the lesson." With a gentle tug, he freed her sash, then eased her shoulders and arms free of the flimsy fabric. For a long moment he gazed at her, then with a groan, he dragged her once more to him in a crushing embrace.

"I'm going to like your homework," she murmured as he lowered her against the pillows.

Christy awakened slowly to the feel of James's arms still wrapped about her. She sighed, and stretched in luxurious contentment. Predawn light seeped into the room, bathing the bed in a soft glow. It was tempting—so *very* tempting—to remain right here, touching him, reliving the joy of the love they had shared. If they were discovered, though, he would never forgive her.

With a regretful sigh, she eased herself away from him, drew on her robe, then gazed down at his recumbent figure. He lay sprawled in the massive tester bed, the bedclothes all askew. His deep, even breathing assured her he remained fast in much needed sleep. She kissed the top of his auburn hair and slipped quietly from his chamber.

Noises from below stairs announced the fact the servants were up and about. If she ran into one, James would be furious with her. She grinned at the thought of the so-proper major explaining what had occurred between them to his cousin. Almost, it was tempting. James needed some loosening up. Dear James. Dear, wonderful, sexy—beloved—James.

She reached the next floor down and made her way to her chamber, where she built up her fire before climbing into her cold, empty bed. She'd much rather be sharing his, still. Damn his sense of propriety. But his lesson last night had been heaven itself.

She drifted into a hazy doze, from which she was disturbed over two hours later by an indignant Nancy. The girl swept into the room, a tray in her hands, talking as she came.

"The hours the gentry keeps, Miss Christy. We'd of been up and doin' long ago, what with our tasks. Such idleness!" She set down her tray, and her impish smile flashed. "And don't I just wish I could be one of 'em!"

Christy laughed and picked up the cup of hot chocolate. "Boy, I'm hungry. Any hope of breakfast anywhere?"

Nancy sniffed. "Not for another hour, at least. Mr. Wickes says as the gentry don't leave their rooms until noon."

Christy rolled her eyes, then settled cross-legged on the bed with her cup in hand. "What do you think of this place?" she asked.

Nancy turned from the cupboard with Christy's sprigged muslin. "I knows a few cracksmen what would give their right arms to mill this 'ere ken."

Christy blinked. "Mill a—You mean rob it?"

"*I* wouldn't," came the affronted reply. "I told you, I don't 'old with that no more."

"What do you think of the people?" Christy tried again.

To her surprise, a dull flush crept up the maid's cheeks. "Oh, they's all right, as flash culls go. Can't say as I'd like to work for that 'atchet-faced twiddlepoop what walks about on cat stalks, cousin of the major's or no. But some of them others, they ain't so bad."

"Oh?" Christy's gaze rested on her. "Any one in particular?"

Nancy sniffed. "No matter what Mr. 'Igh-and-Mighty Wickes says, *some* gentlemen don't sneer just because

158

a girl don't talk flash."

That one of the guests had set himself out to charm Nancy, Christy felt certain. She could guess with what purpose in mind, and it angered her. Nothing further, though, would Nancy divulge, leaving Christy to worry whether the girl would abandon her plans to join the respectable ranks of the upper servants in favor of a temporary and far less respectable liaison with an upperclass roué who knew how to turn a girl's head.

When Christy at last made her way to the breakfast parlor, the morning was considerably advanced. To her pleasure, only one other member of the house party as yet had emerged. James stood before the sideboard, a plate in one hand, the cover of a chafing dish in the other, as he examined the contents. He replaced it and tried the next.

Christy closed the door behind her and leaned against it. "Alone, at last," she breathed, at her most dramatic.

He stiffened. "Good morning, Miss Campbell."

" 'Miss Campbell?' " She crossed the room and slid her arms about him. "Are you mad at me for slipping away without saying goodbye? I was afraid if I woke you, I wouldn't get away at all, and then your valet would catch us."

"Christy, please." With his free hand, he attempted to extricate himself.

She wouldn't let go. Instead, she used his maneuverings to place herself in front of him.

"Can you never behave?" The reluctant smile in his eyes denied the exasperation of his tone.

She took the plate from him and placed it on the sideboard. "Why should I? There's no one here."

"What if someone walked through that door?"

"I have it on good authority *no* one gets up this early. Now, what's *really* the matter?" She clasped her hands behind his neck and forced him to look at her. After a moment, she said: "You're feeling guilty, aren't you?"

He moved away, and ran unsteady fingers through his already disordered auburn hair. "You confuse my sense of right and wrong, and that is not a sensation I enjoy."

"I can think of a few you did."

His lips twitched. "Baggage. But I am still a man—a

gentleman—of this era. Give me time, Christy."

"I'll try." She managed a smile and turned to the row of chafing dishes and found a plate. Time. Nearly two hundred years of manners, social development, women's lib, the sexual revolution. It all lay between them. She couldn't expect him to loosen up overnight any more easily than he could expect *her* to conform to the circumscribed behavior of his society. But then she didn't want him to change *that* much. She liked him old-fashioned, with his sense of honor and noble standards.

James filled a tankard with ale, then carried his breakfast to the table. When he glanced up at her, his expression reflected his usual imperturbable calm. Yet in the depths of his dark eyes, a spark remained.

He wrapped the proprieties of his era about him like a suit of armor, she reflected. Only she detected the chink. She eyed his broad-shouldered figure, the fascinating lines of his face, and determined to undermine his good intentions once more at the earliest opportunity.

As she settled in a chair across from him, the door to the parlor opened and Sir Oliver and Lord Brockenhurst entered together.

James looked up in surprise. "You here, Brockenhurst?"

The viscount, elegant in a neat blue coat that emphasized the classical perfection of his features, hesitated in the doorway. "I am not quite sure how it came about, though I believe it had something to do with a fourth bottle of claret."

Sir Oliver shook his shaggy head, "This younger generation, Major. Can't hold their wine. Though I distinctly saw him walk up the stairs." He turned to Christy and bowed low over her hand, raising it fleetingly to his lips. "Ah, to be fifteen years younger." He sighed.

"I wouldn't mind losing a few years, either," Christy assured him. Like about two hundred, but she kept that thought to herself.

Brockenhurst made his selections at the sideboard, then took a place near James. "You are up betimes, Major," he said.

"I have work to do this morning."

"Ah, yes, the poor." St. Ives, already dressed for the day's session in Parliament, crossed the threshold. "Good morning."

160

He nodded to the others, then addressed himself once more to James. "The poor are always with us, are they not?"

"You might, of course, suggest another bill," James offered. "Trim a little of Prinny's spending and provide more training and assistance for those condemned to the workhouses."

"You would make an excellent head of government, would you not, Major?" Sir Oliver looked over his shoulder from where he stood before the chafing dishes, and a slight frown creased his already lined brow. "Such concern for the masses."

"Have you considered what your life might have been like had you been born of their number, and not to your family and estate?"

St. Ives shuddered. "Please, dear Coz, *not* while I'm contemplating my breakfast."

Brockenhurst looked up from his plate. "As it happens, that is very much the subject under discussion right now."

"The regency bill," James agreed. "Prinny cannot be allowed to enrage the people with his wastrel ways. Have you considered the potential consequences?"

"Indeed we have, Major," Farnham said from the doorway. "Indeed we have." His serious brown eyes clouded, he paused on the threshold to survey the assembled company, then made his way to the pitcher of ale. "What, are we all gathered?"

"Do you intend to speak in today's debate?" James asked him.

Farnham rubbed his waistcoat with a meditative hand. "I believe I will, Major." He swallowed a mouthful of ale, then nodded his head. "Yes, I believe I will. Someone must make certain all options are considered before a dreadful mistake is made."

"My cousin is of the opinion there will be rioting if Prinny is appointed," St. Ives informed him.

"That is not what I said," James corrected. "Only if the interests of the poor are ignored."

"They are one and the same." Sir Oliver drained his mug and slammed it on the table. "None of these German Hanovers have the interest of the people at heart. We need a Stuart, Major. A king born and bred of the British."

"Scots, actually," Christy murmured, but no one paid her any heed.

161

"A pity Henry is a bishop," James agreed. "Still, there must be other candidates. One of the royal dukes, perhaps?"

Sir Oliver snorted. "Damned fool idea. There isn't one of them worth his salt."

Christy looked from one to the other of the serious faces. "You've misjudged the people's reactions to your Prinny. Have you considered the possibility his appointment *won't* start a revolution? That everybody *expects* him to become regent?"

Brockenhurst turned an indulgent smile on her. "You Americans," he said. "I find it hard to believe it has been so very few years since we were all one country."

Farnham shook his head. "Come, come, Brockenhurst. A lady is entitled to her opinion."

"Provided she keeps it to herself?" Christy demanded. "Would it be so terrible if your Prinny *did* become regent?"

Viscount Brockenhurst possessed himself of her hand and patted it. "Very dreadful, my dear. Politics is a man's world, don't trouble your lovely head over such matters. Gentlemen, we forget our manners. We have a delightful visitor among us, yet all we can speak of is our upcoming debate."

"Oh, don't give it a thought," she said.

James rose, and fixed her with a compelling eye. "If you are done, Miss Campbell? We had best be off. You have much to do this day, I am certain."

"Yes, knitting and cooking, I expect." She flashed him a false smile.

"Excellent, excellent." Sir Oliver rose. "Miss Campbell, a pleasure as always. I hope we may meet again soon."

Christy turned that falsely sweet smile on him, then joined James in thanking St. Ives for his hospitality. After saying their goodbyes to the assembled company, they went into the hall. Below, in the entry, Nancy and Wickes stood side by side, pointedly not looking at one another. Several bags stood by the door, awaiting their departure.

Lady St. Ives descended the stairs, only to stop at sight of them. "Are you going so soon, James? I had hoped—" She broke off.

"I fear we must." James took her hand. "We were just coming to find you."

She waved aside their thanks, and accompanied them down the last flight of stairs. "Let me send a footman for a hackney."

"Never mind. Wickes?"

"Certainly, sir. Two vehicles, I believe?" The valet bowed, and set off on his errand.

Wickes returned less than ten minutes later, and, with the help of the jarvey, loaded the baggage into the first carriage. Nancy, with a lingering glance over her shoulder, climbed in next. Wickes followed.

Christy started down the stairs to enter the second vehicle, only to come to an abrupt halt. Two houses down, about twenty feet from the corner, two frieze-coated figures stood close together, deep in conversation. Quickly, she hurried ahead and jumped into the vehicle.

"James!" she hissed as he set foot on the step. "Those are the men who've been following us. There, near the corner. I've never seen them together before."

"Wait a minute," he called to the jarvey.

James pretended to examine his boot while the two men spoke for a moment longer. One strode off, and the other glanced toward their hackney, then quickly crossed the street to the garden at the center of the square.

James straightened at once. "I want you to follow that man," he told the jarvey, gesturing in the direction of the first. "Without him being aware of it, if possible." He swung into the vehicle and it started forward. "The changing of our watchdogs, I should imagine." He sounded pleased.

"Do you think we can keep him in sight?" Christy leaned forward, craning her neck to catch a glimpse of the frieze-coated man.

"I very much hope so. If he is indeed going off duty from keeping an eye on us, it seems very likely he will make his report to his employer."

Christy caught her breath. "You mean—?"

He nodded. "I may at last find out who is behind this non-sense."

Chapter Fourteen

Apparently oblivious to his pursuers, the man strolled to the corner. A number of carts and fashionable carriages jostled past, but no hackneys. James caught the edge of the window, ready to call to his jarvey to slow, when the man strode up to a covered chaise and entered it without a word to the driver. That individual gave his pair the office, and they pulled into the flow of traffic.

"Well, well, well," James murmured.

Christy caught his hand in a warm clasp. "We *must* be right," she breathed. "It was there, waiting for him. Maybe it brought his replacement."

He covered her fingers fleetingly, recognized the danger of such an action, and released her. "We very well might find out." He leaned out the window and called to the Jarvey: "Follow him!"

He sat back, but kept the window down despite the cold, watching the town chaise as it wended its way through the traffic. One would think that with all this snow, people would find excuses to remain indoors. Yet the entire population of London appeared to be abroad this morning.

Beside him, Christy shivered as the wind whipped through the carriage. The devil! If only he had thought to obtain a hot brick for her feet, she must be chilled to the bone. His gaze lingered on her riotous hair, then traveled to those marvelous eyes, brilliant blue and filled with laughter, even now, when they headed into possible danger. He never should have included her on this chase, he should have sent her back inside — or sent her on to the safety of the Runcorns in another hackney.

Her infectious smile flashed and she squeezed his fingers. "Don't look so worried. We're getting somewhere at last." She let down the window on her side and peered out. "I can't tell, but I *think* that other man is following *us*. What a parade we're making."

James spun about, staring hard out the window. Confound it! Of course that other man would pursue them, since that appeared to be his job. "When we arrive at our destination, we may well be at a considerable disadvantage," he said.

She nodded. "Sandwiched between them. I wonder if they brought any mustard?" she mused, then shuddered. "Let's just hope it isn't catsup."

He let that pass. Questioning her cryptic utterances invariably led to even more confusion. At least she didn't go off into strong hysterics like any other woman of his acquaintance would. Made of stern stuff, his Christy.

His? He cast a considering glance at her. Yes, his, for however long he could keep this vibrant, loving woman at his side.

Yet how long would that be? For the next week or two, at least, of that he felt certain. She had been thrust into his world for a reason, to help prevent a revolution. Surely she wouldn't be torn away from him until they completed that task.

But what about after that? Would she remain stranded in his time, separated from her family, from everything she knew — with him? Or would she return where she belonged?

His gaze rested on the enchanting curve of her lips, the long sweep of her dark lashes, the impish gleam in her brilliant eyes, and he knew he didn't want her to leave. She'd crept into his life, into his being, until he couldn't imagine existing without her.

"I wonder how much farther?" She peered once more out the window. "Do you suppose he knows we're following him, and he's leading us on a wild-goose chase?"

He drew a steadying breath and forced his attention back to the problem at hand. "I don't believe so. We are not directly

165

behind him, he should have no reason to be aware of us, as yet."

They proceeded for some time through the drifting snow, turning first onto Oxford Street, then onto Tottenham Court Road. As they continued, without changing direction, James drummed his fingers along the edge of the door panel. The buildings grew farther and farther apart, until at last they passed out of London and onto Hampstead Heath.

"Perhaps we should have brought our suitcases," Christy said. James shook his head. "It can't be much farther."

"He'll notice us, if it is." She looked back the way they had come. "There are other carriages, at least."

"Let us hope he is not aware of us." He glanced at Christy and frowned. What the deuce was he to do with her if trouble began? He doubted the jarvey would be willing to enter any fray; he wished Wickes had selected a more robust driver, one who might welcome a bit of home-brewed.

He touched Christy's hand. "If our friends ambush us, I want you to stay in the hackney. Crouch low on the floor. They might not see you."

"Of course they will." She bristled. "Do you think I'd let you face an attack alone?"

"Christy!" He possessed himself of her cold fingers. "I won't place you at risk."

"Is that what you think of me? That I'm helpless? I'll have you know I've taken two self-defense classes, and I've got a couple of pretty good karate kicks."

"A couple of what?" As usual, she had lost him.

She thrust out her delightful chin. "I mean, I'm perfectly capable of taking care of myself in a fight."

"You—No, that's impossible." The thought was ludicrous. "You don't know what you're saying."

"Oh, don't I? You don't work in San Francisco's Tenderloin without being prepared."

"You—are you saying you have learned to *box?*"

At that, she laughed. "Of course not. I'm not nearly big enough for that. I fight dirty." She eyed him, a martial light kindling in her eyes. "I could probably teach you a few tricks."

"I'll bear that in mind," he managed.

The hackney slowed, and instantly his attention switched

from his unconventional lady to the countryside. Deep drifts of snow covered the fields, with bushes poking through at intervals. White-laden branches hung low beneath their icy burdens.

They turned onto a narrow lane, and after a few moments their pace increased once more. A mile later, the hackney slowed and pulled onto the snowy verge.

Christy peered out through the flurry of flakes that whirled about their carriage. "Has he stopped?" she called to the driver.

The man swiveled around on his box, and his narrow face peered down at her. "They've gone into a drive, miss."

"Do you know where we are?"

"About five miles outside of London, miss."

James swung down. "Stay here, Christy."

She scrambled after him. "Forget it! I'm not letting you go anywhere alone."

"Christy!" He caught her shoulders. "This could be dangerous."

"And I suppose being shot at and chased through the alleys of London isn't? Come on, are you staying or coming?"

James glared at her, then turned to the jarvey. "Wait for us. It will be well worth your while when we return."

The little man eyed him with interest. "It's too cold to keep old Frederick 'ere standing, sir. Doesn't take the snow the way he used to."

"Walk him, then, but keep within sight of this place. We may be leaving in a hurry."

The man's eyes narrowed. "Not milling any kens, are you, guv'nor?"

James smiled, in spite of his tension. "No. But if we do not return within an hour, you might do well to lay information in Bow Street."

The man nodded. "That I will, guv'nor."

Hugging her arms about her against the cold, Christy started across the narrow lane, only to pull up short as a heavy closed carriage lumbered toward them. Bells jingled on the harnesses of the four flashy chestnuts pulling it. A coat of arms was emblazoned on the panels. It passed without slowing, and the occupants—a stout, older couple—paid them no heed. Probably

167

some wealthy aristocrats on their way to a Christmas house party.

A shiver raced up her spine. A house party. That's where James needed to be. She started once more across the way, only to have him catch her arm.

"Not up the main drive. Do you really want them to know I'm walking right into their lair?"

"Well, it might bring faster results," Christy pointed out, though that was the last thing she wanted. Apparently, he'd accepted the fact she was going with him, and that relieved her. She didn't want to spend every step of what ought to be a surreptitious trek through the snow on arguing with him.

They crept down the lane, away from the gate, searching the hedges for an opening. After about fifty yards, he located a likely spot amid the leafless branches, and slipped through. Christy, on hands and knees, followed.

They emerged into an open expanse of what was probably lawn beneath the white blanket. James took her frozen hand and, bending low and running, led her along the line of hedge until they reached a wooded stand about a hundred yards away. The jingling of bells and the muffled hoofbeats of a single horse made Christy jump, but they proved to be coming from the other side of the hedge, approaching along the lane from the same direction as they had come.

Christy shivered. "Do you have any idea whose house this is?"

He frowned. "I'll know better when I see it from the front, though I'll swear I've been here before."

She rolled her eyes. "I *knew* we should have gone up the main drive." They crept through the woods, circling around until they faced the back of the house. "Look familiar?"

A dog barked, a deep, reverberating woof that set her heart pounding in her chest. There weren't any trees nearby to climb, and by the sound of it, that hound probably had teeth to match the woof.

"Very familiar," James muttered. "The devil! I know I've been here."

"How delightful. Do all your friends want to murder you?"

He shook his head. "It only takes one, my dear, it only takes one."

168

They ran for a shrubbery, leaving footprints behind them, she reflected ruefully. Some surreptitious expedition this was, with them alerting the animals and leaving tracks all over the place. Again, the crunch of hooves on gravel reached them, and Christy ducked low.

"I believe *our* tail has finally shown up," she said.

"No, that can't be. If he'd followed us—" He broke off as the sound grew more distant. "He must be leaving. That must have been him we heard earlier."

Christy sighed. "Shall we just walk up to the front door and announce ourselves?"

"I doubt there's any need at this point. I think we will do best to leave as quickly as possible. As soon as I discover whose house this is."

They followed another hedge to the edge of the stable, crossed behind it, then dashed the few exposed yards to the low shrubs lining the drive. Christy crouched and followed this toward the gate, then at last stopped to look behind her.

"We're clearly visible from the house," she said in disgust. "Someone is probably having a pretty good laugh at us."

James nodded, his expression grim. "Then why haven't they come after us?"

"Maybe they're arranging a reception at the front gate for when we try to leave."

By mutual consent, they abandoned their pretenses of hiding and walked erect, following the curve of the drive until at last they obtained a clear view of the facade of an elegant Georgian manor. For a long minute, James stared in silence.

"Well, well, well," he said at last.

"Is it? Well, I mean?"

"You've even heard of him."

"I have? Who?"

"This is Briarly. The home of Sir Dominic Kaye."

"Sir—" The blood drained from her face, leaving her clammy. "Oh, James, what a tangle!"

"My sentiments exactly."

"No, there's more you don't know. Look, I told you I came to England to buy a letter. It was written by your Prinny, and it was addressed to Sir Dominic Kaye, requesting his support in passing the regency bill. This Sir Dominic must be aware of some threat you pose—your books, perhaps—and is trying to get rid of you."

James frowned. "Just because he *received* a letter does not mean he supports Prinny's regency."

"But that *must* be it. Unless you can think of another reason why he'd want you assassinated?"

A grim smile just touched his lips. "Not at the moment."

"Could he have been the one on the ice who shot at you?"

"He is not a robust man."

"All he needed to be was a good skater." She shivered. "What have you ever done to him to make him take such drastic measures? Couldn't he just *talk* to you? Ask you not to cause trouble?"

He drew a deep breath. "I have met him upon many occasions, but I cannot really say I know him." He shook his head. "Our mystery, it seems, deepens. For now, let us get out of here."

They continued along the line of shrubs toward the lane. No one appeared, no one challenged them, no dogs raced in frenzied pursuit.

Christy shuddered. "How could somebody you know, a gentleman, a friend of your cousin's, *do* this to you?"

"I don't know. But I intend to find out." His tone left no room for doubt.

They reached the gate, and Christy moved ahead to look up and down the lane. The soft jingle of bells preceded their hackney, which rounded a curve toward them. Christy ran forward, waving to him.

"Has anyone come out of this drive?" she asked.

The driver nodded, glowering at them. "Quite a nip in the air, miss," he said, pointedly.

James's lip twitched. "Would there be anything in your regulations against taking us to the nearest inn for a warming drink? I don't believe I'd notice, of course, if you had one as well."

The man smiled broadly. "Mighty kind of you, sir, mighty kind indeed."

"Did anyone come out?" Christy repeated.

"Yes, miss. Another 'ackney."

"Another—it was our tail!"

"What happened?" James asked.

"Oh, 'e arrived 'ere just after you two disappeared through that there 'edge. Pulled abreast of me, 'e did, then the passenger told the jarvey to turn into that there gate. Come out again after no more than fifteen minutes I'd say."

Christy cast James a rueful glance. "Now what?"

"Let's go back, I think."

"Any particular inn you was thinking of, guv'nor?" the jarvey asked, his tone hopeful. Obviously he didn't intend to let them forget the promised treat.

"One of your liking," James said, and helped Christy into the carriage.

"What is this, a standoff?" She slid over to make room for him. "They now know that we know who they are."

"Do we?" He leaned back and closed his eyes. "I know whose house they went to. What I cannot understand is Sir Dominic's involvement in anything so mystifying. The more I think about it, the less likely it seems."

"Unless he really supports Prinny."

James shook his head. "He's a member of the Opposition—as are most of my cousin's friends. And very outspoken about Prinny's extravagances. You may remember that from Sir Oliver's comments."

"*Everyone* your cousin knows is outspoken about that." She sighed. "That also provides an innocent explanation for the letter, doesn't it? Or *could* his opposition all be a cover on his part, to make you think he supports what you do when in fact he's trying to kill you?"

"I can't think of a single reason why he should want to. It seems I shall have to ask him."

"*We* will. You are not meeting him anywhere alone."

James regarded her through lowered lids. "He would be hard pressed to murder me in our club," he pointed out.

"And do you think he'll go there now he knows you know?" She shivered. "He'll probably have to strike fast, now. Why didn't they just trap us there?"

"One can only assume he has his reasons."

She glared at him. "Possibly one being the presence of our

171

driver in the road. They must have guessed you'd tell him to go to the authorities."

"Possibly." James fell silent for a very long while, staring out the window of the carriage.

The heath behind them, they drove through the outskirts of the city, then pulled into the yard of a respectable inn. James handed the driver some coins, then took Christy inside where he ordered a couple of coffees. He steered her to the inglenook, where they sat on a wooden bench and stared into the fire.

"It's creepy," Christy said at last. "Somebody you *know.*"

"Very few people are murdered by strangers," he pointed out.

"Except for psychopaths." But the truth of what he said sank in. She came from an era jam-packed with random drive-by shootings and serial killers. But this was different. This was the systematic stalking of one man, for a specific reason. In some way, James must jeopardize someone's existence.

"Is it only when you do something in particular?" she asked suddenly. "They seem to follow you all the time, but they don't always try to kill you. They didn't this morning, they didn't now, and there have been other occasions, too. Why is it that sometimes they attack, and others they don't?"

He shook his head. "Opportunity, perhaps?"

"Or if they think you are about to do something to harm them?"

"How could I have possibly harmed anyone while skating on the Serpentine?"

She drew an unsteady breath. "No, I suppose you're right."

"There's only one thing to be done. I will confront Sir Dominic and demand an explanation."

"Do you think he will talk to you?" She looked up at him, worried.

"If he doesn't, I will call upon him — and in a manner he is not likely to find pleasant."

They finished their coffees and returned to the hackney. The jarvey once more sat on his box, looking considerably more pleased with his lot in life. James gave the direction of the orphanage, and once more they set off, wending their way through the snow-filled streets.

Christy stared out at the blank coldness of the view that met her gaze. "It doesn't feel like only a couple days before Christmas. There should be lights everywhere, and garlands and banners."

"I almost wish I could see this world of yours. It sounds so very different from my own."

"It is," she agreed. "I miss it, terribly. I thought I hated it, with all its pollution and crime and commercialism, but it's *mine*."

He covered her chilled hand. "There's a very good chance you'll go back to it. It's where you belong."

But not completely what she wanted, not after what they shared last night. . . . A longing filled her, to stay in this alien time with James—yet she missed her brothers and sisters. The ache in her heart deepened, tearing at her. Whether she remained or returned, she was going to lose someone she loved.

She blinked back the moisture that stung her eyes. "Do you know what it is to be close to a family?"

A long moment passed. "No," he said at last. "I had only my uncle and cousin, and not by any stretch of the imagination could we have been considered close."

"I'm sorry. You missed out on a lot." She strove for a lighter note. "Do you know, my oldest brother's getting married next week, and I'm supposed to be one of the bridesmaids."

"Maybe you will be. That's still at least seven days away—" He broke off.

"Exactly. Seven days and almost two hundred years." She managed a facsimile of her usually bright smile. "That ought to give me enough time."

They reached the house off Golden Lane, and James handed over a considerable number of bills. The jarvey promptly offered his services at any time in the future if they should need to follow anyone again.

James's lips twitched into a smile. "Thank you, but—" He broke off. "Will you wait for a few minutes?"

"What are we doing next?" she asked as he came up the steps.

"Flinging down my gauntlet."

Her gaze narrowed. "You're going to send a message back with the driver?"

James nodded. "It seems the easiest. I wouldn't wish to risk sending a friend or someone in my employ, who might be taken

173

hostage and held. A jarvey they would have no reason to treat as anything other than a messenger."

"Any idea how to word this?"

"I'll think of something, I feel quite certain."

Nancy opened the door, and her face broke into a wreath of smiles. "There you are, guv'nor. About to send the watch out after you, we was. Where ever've you been?"

"On a slight side excursion." He strode through the door.

"The missus is that worried about you, Miss Christy." Nancy shook her head.

"I'll go to her at once and apologize." Christy ran lightly up the stairs. From the schoolroom, she could hear the boys' voices raised in repetitions of the multiplication table. She winced, remembering her own struggles with that—and her failure to think of anything better.

She opened the door and stuck in her head, and instantly the lesson came to a standstill. The boys gathered about her, demanding to know where she had been, and if she would take over in their studies. She shook her head, silenced them at last, then apologized to Mrs. Runcorn for her absence.

"It's quite all right, my dear. As long as you both are safe."

"For a bit longer. I must go back down and keep James from doing anything too rash."

Elinor Runcorn's eyebrows rose, and a slight smile touched her lips. "Of course, my dear. No," she silenced the boys as they protested. "Miss Campbell will return when she is able. I suggest you continue with your lessons, so you may all surprise her with how much you have learned. Remember, later this afternoon you are to go out Thomassing."

"What?" That stopped Christy.

"Thomassing. It is a very old custom, but one we still observe. Perhaps you have abandoned it in America. The children go from door to door, begging the ingredients for Christmas frumenty."

Christmas frumenty. Another tradition she would love to learn more about. But not now, not while James remained in such danger.

She headed down the steps to the resumption of the chanting of the times tables. At least they were memorizing it, if not

174

actually learning it.

As she reached the hall, James entered the house once more. "Have you sent the message already?" she demanded. "Where are you to meet?"

"A very public place, I assure you. I have no taste for assignations at midnight in the ruins of an old abbey."

"Well, you *do* like to take all the fun out of things, don't you?" In a way, that was almost what she feared from him. "Where?"

"The British Museum, in the Egyptian Room."

"You're kidding. That sounds the perfect place for some intrigue."

"I thought you'd be pleased."

"When?"

"I suggested four o'clock. Two hours from now. We shall wait and see."

Christy did wait, though with rapidly dwindling patience. She slipped up to her room and sought comfort from a chocolate chip, then returned to pace the study with James. Most of the allotted time passed before the jarvey returned, bearing Sir Dominic's agreement. A thrill of nerves danced along Christy's spine as she read the scribbled note. Whether or not they did the right thing, they were now committed.

Again, James retained the services of the jarvey, whose open grin indicated he regarded James as a Father Christmas personified. Christy climbed into the vehicle and sat back against the now familiar cushions, and stared out the window as the snow increased. At last, they pulled up in Great Russell Street before the British Museum.

She stared at it, startled. It bore little resemblance to the structure she had visited so very long ago, in the future.

"Want me to wait, guv'nor?" the jarvey called as James climbed out. A note of complacency sounded in his voice.

James actually smiled. "Please do."

He escorted Christy down the path and through the front doors. As they wended their way to the Egyptian Room, Christy clutched his arm, nerves dancing through her stomach. Desperately, she tried to keep at bay the "what ifs" that crowded her mind.

"It will be all right, nothing can happen here," James said

175

softly.

"Where have I heard that before? You'd just about fit into one of the mummy cases, if someone shoved you in. Look, shouldn't we have gotten some help?"

"We're just here to talk. Maybe we can clear everything up."

"Oh, right. His trying to kill you is all a misunderstanding. Of course."

He shook his head. "We'll find out in a moment."

They entered the rooms devoted to the Egyptian antiquities captured from the French. Christy sauntered at his side in what she hoped was a fair imitation of a tourist.

"There," James breathed.

She looked up quickly. At the far end of the first room, a dapper little man sat on a bench, his hands folded over the rounded head of his walking stick.

"That's Sir Dominic?" she demanded. "He could *never* have been the man on the ice. He's much to frail."

"We shall see." James led her forward.

Sir Dominic Kaye rose as they approached, and awarded James a deferential bow. James introduced Christy, and the elderly gentleman raised her fingers briefly to his lips.

"A pleasure, Miss Campbell."

"I believe we have much to talk about," James said, his voice steady.

"More than you realize, Major. Very much more than you realize. I have a great deal to tell you of considerable importance." A slight frown creased his brow. "I had hoped not to have to reveal this to you as yet, but we are agreed the time is now upon us when you must know all—"

"About that, at least, I agree," James said.

Sir Dominic held up a fragile hand. "I fear you are under a misapprehension, and for that I am greatly to blame. What I must tell you involves the reason someone wishes to kill you—and why I have placed a guard on you for your protection."

"Protection? Is that what you call having someone fire at me?"

Sir Dominic shook his grayed head. "Never would I order such a thing."

"Forgive me if I find that hard to believe."

Sir Dominic's grip tightened on his cane. "I can understand your distrust. It saddens me, yet it doesn't surprise me."

"I am willing to listen to explanations."

The man nodded. "Not here. I would be grateful if you would agree to join a house party at Briarly over Christmas."

"The house party!" Christy's grip tightened on his arm.

James silenced her. "Why should I?"

"There will be a number of people there, all well known to you, who share in this secret we have kept for so long. Your cousin Saint Ives will be of our number. And there, I promise, the whole will be disclosed to you."

"You're not going without me!" Christy declared.

Sir Dominic smiled. "To be sure, you will be most welcome, Miss Campbell." He turned back to James. "Will you come, Major?"

James glanced at Christy.

"The house party," she repeated. "I think we should."

He raised his eyebrows. "Do you? Very well, then. We accept."

Sir Dominic let out the breath he had held in a long, relieved sigh. "On the Twenty-third, then? We will expect you in the early afternoon. Miss Campbell? Major?" He directed a bow to them both and, leaning heavily on his cane, exited the room.

Christy turned to stare after his departing figure.

"We've agreed to walk into the lion's den," James pointed out.

Christy nodded. "It's a Christmas house party. You've got to attend one—and record it, remember? But—"

"But?" he prompted as she hesitated.

"I don't trust him. I don't trust any of them. I don't know what we're getting into."

"No," he agreed after a moment. "Neither do I. But it is certainly going to be interesting finding out."

Chapter Fifteen

James stood in the marble-tiled Great Hall of Briarly as his gaze traveled over the elegant house, with its oak-paneled walls hung with ancient tapestries. Behind him, Nancy and Wickes ordered the distribution of the luggage, and two footmen set forth to carry the various valises and portmanteaux to their destinations.

He turned to watch Christy, who stared about, an expression of awe on her lovely face. "What do you think?" he asked.

"That I'll feel a lot better when you've written your forty pages and we can go," she said bluntly. "Honestly, James, it gives me the creeps. What can he possibly say to you? What secret can they *all* be keeping?"

A slight noise caught his attention, and he looked up to see Sir Dominic Kaye descending the grand staircase with the help of his cane. Behind him came a slight woman, whose short-cropped curls formed a silver halo about her lined face. She supported herself on the banister, then caught her husband's arm as they reached the Great Hall.

"Perhaps we shall now learn our answers," James said.

"*If* he tells the truth. We probably shouldn't have come."

"The house party, remember?" He stepped forward to greet his host and hostess, then introduced Christy to Lady Sophia Kaye.

That lady took her hand, and a sad smile just touched her lips. "We are delighted you could join us," she said, her voice soft and low. "This is a time we have long anticipated."

"But not with pleasure?" The note of regret in her voice had not escaped James.

She shook her head. "Whether it is for good or ill we have yet to learn . . . Major."

"It is for the good," Sir Dominic asserted. "Come, would you care to be shown to your rooms, or will you join the others? They await your pleasure in the Green Salon."

"They have *all* arrived?" James's eyes narrowed.

Sir Dominic inclined his head. "I felt, under the circumstances, it would be best for you to be the last."

James's fingers twitched. He had only his knife slipped inside his boot. His carriage pistol remained in his valise, and was even now en route to the chamber he would occupy. He straightened his shoulders. "Very well, then. Let us get this over with."

Sir Dominic nodded, as if pleased with James's response, and led the way through one of the several doorways opening off the Great Hall.

Christy stepped close to James; the warmth of her presence reached out to him, steadfast and loyal, no matter what dangers might lurk. The thought of having her once more under the same roof for the night sent a distracting surge of desire through him. Her hand crept into his, and he squeezed it with reassuring pressure.

"Miss Campbell, you are an American, I understand?" Lady Sophia's sweet voice broke the silence. "You must tell me all about life in our former colonies. How very long it has been since I have had news from there. My cousin went to live in Boston, you must know. Before that dreadful war." The elegant little lady shook her head. "So very long as it takes to receive word."

James caught Christy's mischievous glance and frowned at her. She was far too capable of telling her hostess that for her it had taken less than a day to cross the Atlantic — and that communications could be established in the winking of an eye through a collection of cables and wires. He still found that one hard to believe. Once started, he could well imagine the other tales of wonder Christy might divulge.

To his infinite relief, she merely returned a noncommittal answer. One could never be quite certain with Christy what whimsy might seize her. It was part of her undeniable charm.

Sir Dominic opened the door, and it swung wide. James stepped inside and came to a halt. Four gentlemen—the members of his cousin's house party, in fact—sat within, gathered about the fireplace.

Viscount Brockenhurst, an ingratiating smile on his handsome face, rose at once to his feet. Sir Oliver Paignton, whose unruly mane of graying hair appeared rumpled more than usual, followed suit. After a moment, Lord Farnham stood also. St. Ives joined them, and raised his quizzing glass in a pointed manner.

Sir Dominic limped forward, leaning heavily on his cane. "As you see, Major, these men are all your friends."

"Acquaintances, at least," James agreed smoothly.

Sir Dominic inclined his head in acknowledgment of this correction. "Over the past months—or years—as our secret has been revealed to each of them, they have made it their concern to pursue this acquaintance with you."

"I am flattered," James made no attempt to disguise the dryness in his tone.

St. Ives crossed to the fireplace and leaned an elbow on the mantel. Idly, he swung his glass by its riband. "It has not, I assure you, been solely for the undeniable pleasure of your company."

James regarded him for a long, thoughtful minute. No love lay between them, but he would have sworn no open enmity existed, either. Yet since coming into the title—and possibly into this mysterious secret?—an added edge existed in everything his cousin said.

Sir Dominic gestured toward one of the two chairs which had been unoccupied. "Will you not be seated?"

"No, I thank you. I am quite comfortable where I stand." He was also nearer the door, in case it became necessary to leave quickly. And, he judged, he had enough room to retrieve and throw his knife. He met and held Sir Dominic's gaze. "I am, however, running very thin on patience. I should be glad to know what importance I hold for these gentlemen, what you know of these attempts that have been made on my life, and why you have felt it necessary, as you claim, to set a watch on me."

The men exchanged resigned glances—as if they did not relish the prospect of providing the answers.

Sir Dominic folded both hands over the ball of his walking stick and leaned forward. "What do you know of Charles Edward Stuart?"

James's eyes narrowed. "The Young Pretender? I'm no Jacobite."

"Really, my dear—Major." St. Ives shook his head. "A son should support his father, however little he agrees with his politics."

"His father?" James spun to face his cousin. "What the devil are you talking about, Saint Ives?"

Sir Oliver nodded, setting his graying hair bouncing about his robust countenance. "It's long since time he knew the truth, Dominic. I always said it should not be kept from him."

Sir Dominic shook his head, a sad, gentle smile on his aging features. "What we did, we did for the best. For his own protection."

With difficulty, James kept a hold on his temper. "Will someone please explain what is going on?"

"It is really quite simple," St. Ives drawled. "You are not my cousin."

"The devil I'm not. Who am I, then?"

Sir Dominic answered. "You are the legitimate son of Louise von Stolberg and Charles Edward Stuart."

James looked from one to the other of them. Had they gone mad? Did they think *he* had, that he would believe such nonsense? "Their only child was stillborn."

"So the world was led to believe. I, however, hold the documented proof that this was not the case."

James drew a slow, deep breath, stilling his rising anger. "I don't know what nonsense this is, but if you expect me to believe anything so absurd—"

His gaze fell on Christy and he broke off. Absurd. Like a beautiful young lady falling through time and landing at his feet? What had happened to his life of late, that reason and logic no longer applied?

Slowly, he advanced into the room. When Lord Farnham offered him a chair, he sank onto the edge. "There must be a fascinating reason why this child was declared to be stillborn. I am waiting to hear it."

Sir Dominic took the seat opposite him, and the others resumed

181

theirs. "Your father was fifty-eight at the time of his marriage. Your mother was eighteen. Both were Catholic, and any child born to them would have been raised in the Catholic faith."

James returned the level regard and nodded. "And as such," he said, "their child would not be acceptable for the British throne. I am well aware of that."

"You are not aware, perhaps, that a great number of people would be glad to see the Stuarts once more upon that throne. They went so far as to devise a plan to make it possible."

James drew a slow, deep breath. "I believe I begin to see."

Sir Dominic nodded. "The child was spirited away at its birth and replaced with a dead infant. Those involved in this conspiracy, including the midwife and attendants at the lying-in, all signed documents attesting to the identity of both children. You are the image of your father, in coloring," he added.

James stared at his clasped hands. "This child—me, you would claim—was then placed with a noble family to be raised in the Anglican Church?"

Sir Dominic smiled. "You have a quick mind, Major. By this simple change in your religious upbringing, you are now an acceptable candidate for the British throne."

James surged to his feet. "This is absurd."

"Is it?" Sir Dominic glanced at the other men. "Lord Brockenhurst?"

The viscount, who had sat in silence, lifted a leather satchel from where it lay on the floor beside him. From it, he drew forth a miniature portrait. "Prince Charles Edward Stuart," he said, and handed it to James.

James sank once more onto his chair, and stared into a rendition of what might have been his own face. The visage might have been longer, but a painted version of his own black eyes stared back at him from beneath a wave of identical dark red hair. The features bore a striking resemblance to his own.

He raised his head and looked from one to the other of the intent faces watching him. Whether any truth lay in their claim or not would be determined later. Right now, he wanted to know what, precisely, their intentions were. Though with a sinking sensation, he realized he knew.

Lord Farnham and Viscount Brockenhurst exchanged a significant glance. Farnham ran his hand through his thick black hair, rumpling the faint streaks of gray. He cleared his throat. "You are well aware of the unrest throughout our country."

"Of the unpopularity of Prinny." Brockenhurst leaned his slender frame forward, regarding James with intensity in his hazel eyes.

James nodded. "And of the fact Parliament is even now debating a regency bill. I doubt there is anyone in England not aware of this."

"It cannot be much longer." Sir Oliver sprang to his feet with the energy of his athletic stature. "I fear our days grow short, for there can be no denying this time our good king is unlikely to recover. At the moment, Prinny, as unpopular as he is, must be acknowledged the most likely choice."

"The effect on the country," Brockenhurst said quietly, "will be devastating, with a bloody revolution the most likely outcome."

"But there is another possibility," Sir Dominic said. "You, a Stuart, a known supporter of the poor and underprivileged, can prevent this. Come forward at once and declare yourself the best choice for regent, then king upon the eventual death of King George."

For a long minute, silence filled the salon, broken only by the crackling of the fire. James looked from one to the other of the intent faces—all focused on him. He leaned back in his chair and turned to Sir Dominic, the apparent spokesman for this bizarre group.

"You don't really expect me to believe any of this nonsense, do you?" he asked at last.

"We have considerable documentary evidence. Brockenhurst?" Sir Dominic held out his hand to the youngest member of their conspiracy.

Lord Brockenhurst drew a handful of sheets from the satchel and gave them to Sir Dominic, who held them out to James.

James hesitated, then accepted them. Vaguely, he was aware that Christy stood behind him, looking over his shoulder. Why hadn't she warned him of this? Surely she must have known—unless not a single word of truth lay in it. Then why go to this elaborate charade? If they wanted him silenced . . .

His thoughts roiling, he picked up the first of the papers and read the statement affirming that the baby boy born to Louise von Stolberg had been healthy, but switched with a stillborn infant. The real Prince James Edward Stuart had been placed into the keeping of Martin Holborn, fifth earl St. Ives, to be raised as his nephew until such time as it was deemed prudent to enlighten the boy as to his true identity. It bore the signature of Juliana, Countess St. Ives, who had been in attendance at the birth.

The next related a similar account, with the title Farnham scrawled at the bottom.

James leafed through the remaining sheets. All contained much the same information, in various hands from illiterate scrawls to elegant copperplate. Nine documents in all, each providing a variety of corroborating details, up to and including the deep red of his hair and the existence of an oval birthmark on the inside of his right thigh. As he stared at the sketch of this mark, made by the midwife, the identical one on his leg seemed to burn.

This wasn't possible. None of this could be true. Yet that mark . . . Memories came to him of his youth, of instructions given to him by his uncle—his *supposed* uncle—about duty and self-sacrifice for the good of those under the sphere of his influence. At the time it had seemed odd, for he possessed no estates, no armies of tenants or employees for whose interests he had to concern himself. With an elder cousin, he had no expectation of stepping into his uncle's shoes. Yet the words had been repeated often, until James had taken them to heart.

"Do you not recall my father's violent objections to your choice of a military career?" St. Ives's voice broke across his thoughts. "Then how he suddenly relented and purchased your pair of colors?"

James looked up into the face which for once did not bear a sneer.

"I believed my father afraid of losing you, at first. But when I succeeded to his room, I learned the truth."

Sir Dominic nodded. "We feared for your life—for the continuation of the Stuart line. But at the time there seemed little danger, and a Stuart who had served his country with a distinguished military career might be all the more acceptable to the populace."

"I see." James's fingers tightened on the papers he still held. "You can have no idea how honored I am by your concern, gentlemen."

Lord Farnham gave a short laugh. "You must admit to your significance."

"*If* any of this is indeed true." James studied the serious face, with the brown eyes that never seemed to smile. "This Farnham," he said, holding up the paper. "Was he your father?"

The man nodded. "He died only three years after that, preventing someone from assassinating the prince."

"Then your family has served the Stuarts well," James said softly. The burden of guilt, of responsibility, of the entire Stuart legacy, descended on his shoulders like a mantle of granite. He straightened in a conscious effort to bear the suffocating weight.

"His grandfather," Sir Oliver said, adding another layer, "died at Culloden Moor."

The Stuart legacy. James rose and turned away, needing time to assimilate this, time to think—time to recognize the enormity of what they expected of him in return for all their conspiracy had done.

Warm hands caught his, and he opened eyes he hadn't realized he'd closed and gazed down into Christy's drawn face. "Well, my dear?" he said softly.

"I need to talk to you," she said.

He nodded. Lord, it would be good to slip away with her, to lose his concerns in her full lips, her generous love, her throaty, infectious laugh. Only she wasn't laughing, now.

She gripped his hands. "Please, James?"

He touched her cheek with one finger, and an infinite sadness flowed through him, leaving a vast yearning in its wake. If, indeed, all this were true. . . . And with a painful certainty, he knew it was. It explained so many puzzles—and the reason someone wanted him dead.

He turned to the circle of men behind him. All of importance, all prominent in the government, and all waiting on his next words. Sir Oliver Paignton and Sir Dominic Kaye, both men whose names frequently appeared in the pages of the *Morning Post* in connection with their debates in Parliament. Lord Farnham, Viscount Brockenhurst, and Earl St. Ives, each an expert in a different office, each a commanding figure among his colleagues.

185

The significance of this new reality dawned on him. As a Stuart, as regent, as king, his concerns would not be mocked. He would speak with power and authority, and men such as these, men who dictated the country's policy, would listen — and act. How much good he could do . . .

"James!" Christy tugged at his arm. "Now."

His gaze lowered to her frantic face, and a slight smile twitched on his lips. "If you will excuse us, gentlemen?"

"Of course." Sir Dominic rose, leaning heavily on his cane. "We will leave you."

"No." James stopped him with a wave of his hand. "Don't let us disturb you. Is there another room, perhaps, where we could talk?"

"You may use the salon next to this, if you wish."

James caught Christy's arm and led her out, forestalling Sir Dominic's obvious intention to escort them there himself. "Does he think I can't find my way for a journey of twenty feet?" he muttered to Christy.

She shook her head. "Bear in mind your rise in status around here. If you play with them, you're going to have to get used to a lot of kowtowing."

"If I play with them." He closed the door of the next apartment behind them. "Do you think I have a choice?"

"I don't know." She crossed to the window which looked out over the drive. "Do you remember creeping along that just a couple days ago? It feels like it's been forever."

He came up behind her and rested his hands on her shoulders, drawing her back so her head leaned against his chest. "What did you want to say?"

She tensed beneath his fingers. After a long moment, she said: "I'm afraid."

"Why?" He turned her to face him. "Christy, do you see what they offer me?"

She nodded, her expression strained. "Bloodbaths and revolution."

"No!" He released her and paced to the hearth, then spun about. "No, no rioting in the streets. There wouldn't be any *need!* Can't you see? I could prevent all that. I could give the people what they want, the chance to lead decent lives."

186

She shook her head. "Can't you understand? You *don't* become regent. Prinny does, that's the way history occurs. And it doesn't cause any revolution or bloodshed!"

He froze, studying her face, seeing her fear. "You mean *I* am what causes all that disaster? A Stuart coming forward to claim the throne?"

She nodded. "It must be that. Oh, James!" She buried her face in her hands, then looked up at him once more. "I saw two possible courses for history in your book. Prinny could be named regent and all would continue smoothly, and you record the events of this house party. Or there is a bloodbath, and the aristocrats are slaughtered in the streets—because a Stuart tries to claim the throne."

In four long strides he reached her and grasped her hands. "Think, Christy. Did you see anything about a Stuart in my book?"

She stared at him, her expression confused, then she shook her head. "No."

"Then that must be it. There are three—or even more!—possible courses of action. No," he silenced her as she opened her mouth to protest. "Just think, Christy. This is Eighteen-Ten, not whenever you lived. The history you know *hasn't happened yet.* And as we've seen from the unwritten portions of my book, it *can be changed!*"

"That's what scares me!"

"No, listen. What if the riots occur because I do nothing? There is so much I could do. We could rewrite the history you know, make it better, relieve so much suffering."

"James—"

He gazed beyond her shoulder, unseeing, ignoring her interruption. "Prinny *is* a wastrel, and very unpopular with the commoners. They would welcome a ruler who had their interests at heart, whose concern lay with the people."

She stared at him, her expression aghast. "You're having delusions of grandeur."

Slowly, he leveled his regard on her. "They don't appear to be delusions."

Chapter Sixteen

Christy clenched her fists. "James, listen to me! Stay out of this. Prinny may not be popular, but people love to grumble. They may complain a lot about him, but they won't *do* anything. They don't care enough. But you — your situation — would be different."

"Why?" James shot at her.

"Because you're a Stuart. I don't know that much about English history, but the Stuarts caused a lot of suffering. They had the right to the throne, but not the support. Do you want to start it all over again? Lead an army against your countrymen and see your followers slaughtered on the fields? Or in the streets? Maybe *that's* what your book referred to."

He shook his head. "I wouldn't come to power by war, but by an act of Parliament."

"And what if you're *not* accepted by the government? What do you think would happen then? The fact a Stuart exists — and one who's a supporter of the poor, at that — isn't going to remain a secret for long. The common people will see you as a champion for their cause. What's to stop them rising up in protest, demanding you be made regent?"

He ran his hands through the thick auburn waves of his hair. "Confound it, Christy, if I *am* a Stuart —" He broke off.

"So what if you *are?* Do you think this is your divine destiny, or some corny tripe like that? Damn it, James, don't hide behind stupid clichés. Think this through!"

She studied his face, and saw pigheaded stubbornness in the set of his jaw. Now was not the time for bludgeon tactics.

She went to the window and gripped the blue velvet drape. Deep breaths, she told herself. Calm down. It would be too easy to push too hard, force his pride into making the wrong decision. There had to be alternatives, ones that didn't demand he deny his newfound heritage.

If only he had been left with his true parents, raised a Catholic and a pretender prince, he might have been content to live in exile in Italy. And she never would have met him, never would have found the book he never would have written. . . .

Never. The mere thought of that, of never having known him, of never holding him in her arms, tore at her, leaving an aching void in her heart. Tears burned in her eyes, but she blinked them back. Dear God, she loved him.

She went to him and held him tightly, pressing her face against his chest. One of his strong arms wrapped about her, the other hand stroked her unruly hair.

"Of all the things I thought Sir Dominic might have to say, I never expected this." His lips brushed the top of her tight curls. "But now that I know, you cannot ask me to deny it."

"No," she agreed in a very small voice, "but — " Slowly, she raised her head and looked up into his frowning face. "You can proclaim yourself a Stuart, but there is nothing that says you have to try for the regency, is there? Wouldn't your very existence prove a sufficient threat to your Prinny? He might be willing to make concessions in his own habits and for the poor, just to *prevent* you from causing an uprising."

"We shall see." His expression remained unreadable. "You are quite right, today is not the time for decisions."

She nodded, but in her heart, doubts remained. His very existence threatened the stability of the government. As long as he lived, there would be someone, somewhere, anxious to see him dead.

A knock sounded on the door, and it opened. Sir Dominic hesitated on the threshold. "Major?"

James released Christy. "I have accepted what you have told

me," he said, his voice steady. "I have *not,* however, made any decisions on how that will affect my future actions."

To Christy's consternation, Sir Dominic bowed. "As you wish, Major. Now, if you will permit me, I will show you to your rooms. We keep country hours at Briarly."

To her relief, Christy found she and James had been placed in the same wing and on the same floor. It made it easier to keep an eye on him, to make sure no one—other than herself, of course—crept stealthily into his chamber at night. Satisfied, she entered her own apartment and greeted Nancy, who sat moodily stirring the embers in the grate.

"What's wrong?" Christy drew up a chair at her side.

Nancy shook her head. "I was just wonderin' 'ow the missus and the boys was gettin' on with that maid the major 'ired."

"They'll be fine. And she's only there temporarily, so don't you worry about not getting your job back. I'm very grateful to Mrs. Runcorn for sparing you to me." Her gaze narrowed on the girl. "What's *really* the matter?"

"Ain't nothin' you can do a lick o' good about, Miss Christy. I just wish—" She broke off and stabbed the poker into the side of a log.

"I can listen, at least."

Nancy sighed. "Did you ever makes plans for your life, miss, then 'ave 'em go all astray?"

A short laugh escaped Christy. "Yes. Badly. Have yours? What did you hope for?"

"I never knew nothin' but thievin', Miss Christy, not 'til I prigged that tattler of the major's. Then suddenly—There was a whole new world, miss, with people the likes of which I never seen afore. And gentlemen—" She broke off.

"Men who treated you with a bit of respect?" Christy suggested.

Nancy nodded. "I swore I'd do whatever it took to make—a man—not ashamed of me. But it didn't work. And then when I finds one what doesn't mind 'ow I talks, all 'e offers is to set me up with my own carriage and say as I can dress up as fine as five pence."

"What is it you *do* want?"

Nancy sniffed. "Well, I don't mind the carriage part, nor the

190

fine fallolls. But I don't want no slip on the shoulder." She drew a shaky breath. "I want someone to love, Miss Christy, but I ain't no fit wife for a decent man."

"You're getting there. Just give it time. You're using far fewer can't words all the time. Hadn't you noticed?"

Nancy nodded, and wiped her eyes on the back of her sleeve. "I tries to talk right, miss. Not as I see where it's doin' me no good, though. No man what knows my past would 'ave me. Leastways, none as I could care about."

"Maybe you just haven't met the right one, yet," Christy offered.

Nancy's expression closed over. "And maybe I 'as." She straightened, and shook her brassy curls. "Now, Miss Christy, you shouldn't of gone and let me run on like this. Addlepated, that's what I am, to go a-worriting myself over some mackerel-backed old looby. Settin' up as a doxy wouldn't be 'alf bad, it wouldn't. Could make my fortune, I could."

Christy opened her mouth to protest, then shut it again. Love and a comfortable life. Who didn't want that? Still—"Don't do anything rash."

"No, miss," Nancy said, though she didn't sound at all convinced. A deep, resonant gong reverberated through the house, and Nancy rose, as if relieved at the interruption. "Time you was gettin' dressed for dinner, miss."

No more confidences was the maid willing to share, so Christy allowed herself to be assisted into the gown of amber crepe. Her hair took some time to arrange to Nancy's satisfaction, but at last Christy hurried down the stairs to the salon where the house-guests would gather before dinner.

Margaret, Lady St. Ives, sat before the hearth, her pale face bent over the tiny robe she embroidered. She looked up, and a tentative smile touched her lips, which did nothing to alleviate the sadness in her eyes. "Good evening, Miss Campbell. I am so glad you are here. I dread these political affairs, do not you?"

"I'm new to them. Sore back?" Christy brought her a pillow and slipped it into place. "My sister always had an awful time sitting when she was pregnant."

A soft flush crept into Lady St. Ives's cheeks. "It is very kind of you," she murmured, and returned to her embroidery.

191

Another unhappy woman, Christy reflected. The men of this time had it too much their own way. What with the countess being ignored by her husband, and Nancy being snubbed by Wickes and propositioned by—by whom? She really had to figure that one out.

Lord Brockenhurst entered, poured himself a glass of wine, and glanced about the room. His gaze fell on Lady St. Ives, and with a sly smile he went to her side and said something Christy couldn't catch. The lady looked up at him, an expression of consternation—or was it fear?—on her face. He laughed softly and moved away, and Lady St. Ives lowered her gaze to her embroidery. It was a very long while before her needle moved again.

One by one, the others put in an appearance, and Christy positioned herself where she could watch as many of them as possible. James started toward her, only to be waylaid by the jovial Sir Oliver. Farnham and Sir Dominic caught him next, and kept him talking until after the butler entered to announce dinner.

The meal passed with ceremonial pomp, and with all due deference paid to James. Whether the servants knew the real identity of their guest of honor, or if they merely had been ordered to accord him every mark of subservience, Christy couldn't tell. She didn't like any of this, though. Even the lofty dining room, with its heavy carved furniture, ornate tapestries, and gleaming silver, oppressed her. She'd gladly exchange it all for a pizza in front of the TV set in her own airy apartment.

James, to her dismay, appeared all too much at his ease in his present elaborate surroundings—as if he took the advancement of his status and the respect of the others as his due. Maybe it was, but that didn't mean he had to seem so at home with it. With a sinking heart, she acknowledged he belonged here—and she very much did not. No matter how much she tried to deny it, the fact remained James was a Stuart, born from long lines of princes and kings, and he now displayed his ability to take his proper place among them.

She wished she didn't feel so out of place. She glanced around the table, uncomfortably aware of her lack of social training. Lady St. Ives sat opposite her, with Lord Farnham on her left, and Brockenhurst on her right. The countess concentrated on her plate, onto which a footman scooped a serving of fish in a lemon-colored sauce. At the foot of the table, Lady Sophia brought to a close her conversation with St. Ives and turned her attention to Brockenhurst.

If she watched enough, Christy reflected, she might get the hang of this. She turned to Sir Oliver, on her own right, a smile pinned firmly on her lips, only to have it slip awry.

He watched her through half-lidded eyes, a frown creasing his forehead. "You are well acquainted with Major Stuart?" he asked. He didn't even hesitate over the change in name.

"Not very," she admitted, and saw the relief register in his face. "I'm sort of a bodyguard," she ad-libbed. "My job is to protect him."

Sir Oliver's eyebrows shot up. "Is it, Miss Campbell? I am amazed."

"That's American women for you. We'll surprise you every time."

He nodded. "I am very glad, for your sake, then."

She stiffened. "And why is that?"

He cast a sideways glance across the table, to where James sat at the right of Sir Dominic, speaking to Farnham. "Because he *is* a Stuart, my dear. Forgive me if I speak out of turn, but it is his duty to marry a princess. It had occurred to some of us—" He broke off with an apologetic smile. "I am glad to hear it is not so."

"I see. You were afraid I'd upset your little applecart."

"No, no. You're a sensible young lady, and he is a man of honor. I just wanted to make certain— Well, that is neither here nor there, is it, for you tell me there is no such question between you?"

"No," she agreed, her voice hollow. "How could there be?" How, indeed? Emptiness seeped through her, robbing her of her appetite, leaving her cold and lonely. She ached for James, for the reassurance of his arms about her.

She turned away, to St. Ives on her other side, but he paid her no heed. His gaze rested on James, his expression intense. Almost, Christy thought, as if he waited for his erstwhile cousin to make some gauche mistake, thereby proving himself unworthy of the high estate to which he had been born, if not raised.

The meal at last drew to a close, and Lady Sophia rose, giving the signal for the ladies to withdraw. Christy trailed after the other two, glad to escape, yet wishing she could remain near James.

She needed him — and she needed to know what they would say to him, what arguments they would present that she wouldn't hear. And how willing was he to listen to them? She desperately wanted to know the answer to that question.

The ladies entered a drawing room where several card tables had been laid out, and a pianoforte and harp stood at the far end, away from the hearth. Lady St. Ives seated herself at the pianoforte, leafed through the music, then began to play. Lady Sophia settled on the sofa, picked up her embroidery, and invited Christy to take the seat at her side.

"Have you found everything to your comfort?" The elegant little woman set a neat stitch.

"Yes. What lovely work," she tried, desperate to keep the conversation away from herself.

The needle flashed as her hostess set another. "I do hope my husband's guards have not discomfitted you unduly."

"Oh, no. I much preferred them to the ones with the guns and knives."

Lady Sophia clicked her tongue. "There, I do not know how those dreadful men were able to get so close to you. Dominic's guards *should* have spotted them and gotten to you first."

"Fortunately, the assassins were equally as inefficient." Apparently, good help was hard to find in any day. Christy drew a deep breath. "I hope Sir Dominic has something more effective in mind for the future."

To that, Lady Sophia murmured an assent, and they fell silent, listening to the countess playing a ballad on the pianoforte and singing quietly to herself.

After about a quarter of an hour, the gentlemen joined them. Sir Dominic, with the able assistance of Sir Oliver, arranged his guests at the various card tables, and within minutes the sound of the pasteboards being shuffled filled the room.

Christy rose and went to stand behind James's chair to watch him play with Sir Dominic. Piquet, she remembered from a previous evening. She looked at the others and frowned. Lord Brockenhurst beckoned to Lady St. Ives, but she refused to meet his gaze. Instead, she accepted Lord Farnham's invitation with patent relief.

Sir Oliver drew out a considerable pile of coins and placed them at his side, then glanced about, his expression hopeful. After a moment, Lord Brockenhurst took the chair opposite and followed suit. St. Ives joined them.

Christy watched the intensity with which they played for a few minutes, then returned her attention to James. He lounged back in his chair, a glass of wine at his side, and studied the cards in his hands. It appeared little would be accomplished this night aside from gambling. She stifled a yawn.

James glanced up at her. "Why do you not retire for the night, Miss Campbell?"

"Are you sure —" She broke off. She could hardly ask him if he thought he was safe.

Amusement lit his eyes. "Quite sure. You may relax your vigilance for once."

She wouldn't mind escaping this party. Even aside from her worries about James's safety, and her distrust of these conspirators, she wasn't enjoying it. She could spend her time far more delightfully in planning her next assault on James's defenses.

She excused herself to Lady Sophia, smiled a good night at Lady St. Ives, and made her way up to her room. She prepared for bed without summoning Nancy, then settled before her mirror, experimenting with her unruly hair. She would have to ask James if he preferred it worn up, in the local prevailing fashion, or loose about her shoulders.

She regarded the current result, but a vision of James's strong features hovered in her mind. Dear James, what a day this had been for him. To learn he was a Stuart, of royal blood. *Not* plain Mr. Holborn, but Prince James Edward Stuart.

Prince James. . . . A chill crept through Christy, and she stared at her reflection with unseeing eyes. A prince, who by birth was so far above a lowly Miss Christina Campbell that it created an insurmountable barrier between them. It was hopeless. . . .

Sir Oliver's gentle warning had been no mere expression of

what he thought best, but a statement of inescapable fact. James had no choice in the matter. He owed a duty to his name, to his heritage, to marry a princess. . . .

She turned away, hugging herself, sick at the thought. James, tied in a bloodless marriage to some German frump of high birth, producing children with her to carry on the line. That was no life for him, not for a man of his passion and spirit, of his generous character. He deserved so much more. Surely somewhere there must be a princess of passable looks and temperament, who could make him happy.

The possibility he actually might come to *love* his princess tore her apart.

Yet even if he hadn't been a prince, what could there ever have been between them? Had she honestly been so foolish as to expect them to share something permanent? No matter how much she loved him, they were the products of different times, raised in different worlds.

And at any moment, she might be dragged back to her own, separated from him by nearly two hundred years.

Blindly, she pulled the pins from her hair and sought her empty bed. For a very long while, she huddled beneath the covers, hugging a pillow, and finding no comfort.

The clicking of her door handle disturbed her some time later. Her eyes flew open, but the fire had burned low, and it was too dark to see. Slowly, she dragged herself up onto one elbow.

A dim shape slipped into her room, enveloped in a flowing garment. She'd recognize the broad shoulders anywhere. A pang of yearning shot through her.

"Christy?" James's soft voice reached her. He felt his way to her bed and sat down on the edge. "It's ten minutes until three. Officially Christmas Eve morning. I thought we should celebrate."

He'd come to her. . . .

"It's cold in here." He crossed to the fire and tossed on another log. A taper stood on the mantel, and he lit it, then brought it to the table beside her. "I want you to see something." From his pocket he drew forth a dark lump, and held it out to her.

The light flickered across the carved figure. A woman skating.

"Me. You've started the snowdome to bring me back." That

knowledge warmed her.

He set it aside, and his serious gaze rested on her face as he once more sat on the bed. "Have you considered the possibility it might also take you from me?"

A way home. It was what she wanted, what she *had* to want. She shivered, and didn't meet his steady regard. "I wish I knew if I had a one-way or a round-trip ticket."

"So do I." Apparently, he had no trouble deciphering her meaning. "I have done a great deal of thinking during the past several hours."

"Have you?" she asked, cautious.

He brushed her curls from her shoulder, and his hand cupped the nape of her neck. "This—my being a Stuart—changes a great deal."

"I'd noticed. Your name alone could start that revolution we have to prevent."

"Which makes it all the more important for me to have you with me—to discuss my best course of action." His mouth brushed the sensitive skin behind her ear. "How is that for a first step?"

Her lips twitched into a sad smile. Obviously, he hadn't thought things through. Longing overcame sense, and she ran her fingers through his hair, loving the tousled result. "I thought you didn't approve of this sort of thing," she murmured.

He slid the thin muslin of her nightgown aside and kissed her collarbone. "The situation is different, now."

She tried to ignore the sensations that rippled through her. "Yes, it's worse, not better."

"Why? I resisted before because a liaison with a gentleman could only have brought you the contempt of society. But a liaison with the Stuart pretender will bear no such stigma. You will hold a position of importance and influence."

"I see. The Stuart heir's mistress."

"I promise you, even though I must make a marriage of convenience, I will assure it makes as little difference to us as possible. I will set you up in a house in a fashionable quarter of town. You may have a *carte blanche,* anything you wish, and I will visit you as often as I can."

She stared at him for a long moment, as the full, insulting

197

reality of his words sank in. "Your mistress," she said at last, and fury ignited within her. "You mean your expensive prostitute. Is that what you think of me?"

"Christy." He caught her agitated hands. "How else to you expect to live if I don't provide for you? You have no family, no money, no one else to turn to."

"So I should join the oldest profession to support myself?" His brow snapped down. "I didn't say that."

"It's what you mean, though, no matter how you try to disguise it."

"It's a perfectly acceptable arrangement. In this time—"

"This time isn't *my* time." She inched back, farther away from him. "And you don't have to worry about me. Do you think I'd stay in *this* time, where you lousy chauvinists have it all your own way? Marriages of convenience and mistresses! Honestly, don't you ever think of a woman as a *person?* Someone to share your life with?"

He stiffened. "As a Stuart—"

"Damn your royal blood! As a *Holborn,* you at least showed a sense of decency."

"I cannot expect you to understand the obligations that have descended upon me, or the—"

"Oh, no, how could I? I'm just a mere woman, a plaything for you *important* men."

"Christy—"

"Oh, get out! Or are you planning to give me a hundred bucks or pounds or whatever to pay for tonight?"

His mouth thinned, and he surged to his feet. "I would not so demean either of us. I will be far better employed finishing these figures." He snatched up the one that rested on the table. "Perhaps that snowdome really will take you home—away from me." He spun about on his heel and stalked out the door.

Damn him, damn him, *damn* him! Christy fell back against the pillows, choking back furious tears. How could he so cheapen everything they'd shared? She offered love, and he talked in terms of a business arrangement.

The sound of a door opening down the hall reached her, and she realized James hadn't fully closed hers. Who else would be up and about at this hour? She certainly didn't want them looking in on her. She climbed out of bed, and peeked into the hall in time to see Lord Brockenhurst creeping toward the stairs, his greatcoat gathered about him, his hat on his head, and his boots in his hand.

The peculiarity of his actions penetrated her unhappiness. He was going out, obviously. At three-thirty on a very cold and snowy morning. Not on any legitimate business, of that she felt certain.

Images of knife throwers and gun shooters sprang to mind.

Fears for James's safety drove her hurt from her mind. For his sake, she had better learn more.

Chapter Seventeen

Christy crept down the stairs, leaning on the banister to keep her weight off the aging boards. If one squeaked, and Lord Brockenhurst turned—or worse, waited for her on the next landing . . . She shivered, and was glad the oil lamps burned so low, barely providing sufficient illumination for her not to stumble. They also kept her in deep shadow.

An eerie creak from below broke the stillness of the night, and she gasped and drew back. For several heart-stopping seconds she clung to the rail, her mind screaming retreat, her legs too wobbly to move. Silence surrounded her, like a comforting blanket, and she drew a shaky—but noiseless—breath. She descended another cautious step.

At the next landing she crouched low and peered over the railing. Brockenhurst's coated figure cast a dim shadow which wavered, then vanished as he reached the Great Hall. Not so much as the whisper of his stockinged feet on the bare tiles reached Christy, not a clue as to which direction he might have gone. Yet the boots and coat indicated he must be going out. And apparently not by the front door.

Christy continued down, until her bare toes encountered the icy chill of the marble floor. Why couldn't she have worn slippers? Or something warmer than her muslin dressing gown?

How did people *survive* this insufferable, everlasting cold? She missed forced air heating. And hot showers. And an electric blanket.

She wanted to go home, back to her familiar comforts, away from James!

She blinked away the moisture that filled her eyes. If only Sir Dominic had kept his rotten revelations to himself for just a little while longer, she might even now be in James's arms, celebrating the joyous season, instead of freezing in this dark hall.

Which brought her back to the question of *why* Lord Brockenhurst crept about in the middle of the night. Not for any good purpose, of that she felt certain. He must be going out to meet someone — and what, tell whoever it was that James now knew his real identity?

Christy clutched the newel, her thoughts racing. Before, there had been no hurry to murder James. Now, though, he might step forward at any time to claim the throne. And someone, possibly some loyal supporter of Prince George, might well go to any length to prevent that.

She started forward, running silently over the tiles, searching through the blackness for any sign of movement, any indication where another door might be located. Nothing.

She stopped and peered about, struggling against her rising anxiety. How many corridors opened off this main room? She couldn't remember. Three? Or four? Each one led to a different area or wing of the house. And each one might have any number of exits to the outside.

Why hadn't she explored the house more thoroughly when they arrived? She *knew* James would be in danger, she'd even suspected a trap! But all that talk of his being a prince, of his possibly becoming king of England, no wonder she'd slipped up.

At least James couldn't be killed yet. Not until he'd written the account of the house party.

Unless someone else finished the book for him.

A chill settled in her already aching heart. Was that why the words shifted? Because one of several different people might write one of several different endings? She had to find Viscount Brockenhurst. Maybe he'd left a candle burning somewhere. . . .

On the third corridor she checked, a dim glow greeted her eyes. Heartened, she hurried down this hall, glad of the soft carpet that enveloped her frozen feet. At the end, a door stood slightly ajar, and within the room she glimpsed the flickering light of a fire burning low in a huge hearth.

She inched the door wider and slipped inside. A library. And in the wall next to the fireplace stood a long French window, with its curtain pulled askew. Christy touched the handle and found it unlatched. Bingo.

She opened the door, and snow pelted her, whipped inside by a moaning wind. Prudently, she shut the paned glass panel again. Barefoot and wrapped in thin muslin was no way to go outside in weather like this. Yet by the time she put on something more suitable, Brockenhurst would be long gone and his trail buried beneath the new flakes.

With a sigh, she sank into a chair conveniently pulled up before the fire, its back to the French window, and extended her freezing feet to the lingering warmth. Fat lot of good she'd done. At least she knew Brockenhurst was up to something, if not what. She could make a few guesses, though, and they all boded ill for James. She'd better tell him.

Going back up proved easier than going down, for she worried less about noise. At last she reached her own floor and went to James's room. She turned the handle, but it wouldn't open. Surprised, she tried it again, then realized he had locked it.

She hadn't expected him to take such an elementary precaution for his safety, not when he thought he was among friends. Relieved to discover he retained that much sense, at least, she returned to her own chamber and threw another log on the fire, then curled into her lonely, cold bed.

A persistent banging in the room awakened her some time later. She opened one heavy eye to see Nancy rummaging through a clothes cupboard. She dragged out Christy's rose-colored muslin and hung it over a chair.

"What's going on?" Christy asked.

Nancy sniffed. "Didn't think nothin' would wake you, miss. Dead to the world, you was."

"Well, I'm not anymore. What time is it, anyway?"

"Half past nine, Miss Christy. And what Mrs. Runcorn would say, you sleepin' the morning away like that."

Christy yawned. "Maybe that's why she's been so generous about letting you come with me. To keep me in line."

Nancy snorted. "There ain't nothin' she wouldn't do for the major. Nor nothin' the reverend wouldn't, neither."

Nor Christy, for that matter, she reflected ruefully. She sighed and shook off her grumpiness. Nancy didn't deserve to be snapped at. *"I'm* certainly grateful," she said. "I don't know what I'd have done without you."

The maid nodded, though without enthusiasm.

Christy packed three pillows behind her back, located her hot chocolate and took a sip. It was still warm. "What's wrong?"

The girl sniffed again. "Don't see as where anythin' should be wrong, miss."

"No, but it is, isn't it?"

"Men!" She shook out Christy's shawl with an angry snap and hung it over a chair. "Don't you never go trustin' one, miss. They ain't worth it. After everythin' 'e promised —" She slammed a drawer shut with enough force to relieve considerable tension.

Christy's eyes narrowed. "Your gentleman is someone in this house?" she asked.

Nancy opened another cupboard door, apparently for the sole purpose of slamming it. "A title don't make no man a gentleman."

A title. "Lord Brockenhurst?" she hazarded.

Nancy nodded. "And don't you never believe anythin' as that flash cull tells you."

"No, I don't think I will," Christy said slowly.

"Didn't bother to come see me last night, like 'e said 'e would, and after that pretty speech 'e made me."

"When was that? That night we stayed in Portman Square?"

Nancy sank down onto a chair. "What with Mr. Wickes lookin' down 'is long nose at me, I was blue deviled, I was. Then along comes 'is lordship and calls me a saucy piece and makes me an offer fit to stare." She sighed. "I should've knowed it was a take-in."

"Did he ask you questions about the major?"

Nancy shrugged. "Nothing much."

So, that fine, mocking dandy had been cultivating Nancy in order to spy on James. And last night he stood her up — because he had a more pressing engagement, perhaps with an accomplice who wanted James dead? Anger welled in her anew. Brockenhurst. At least now she knew in which direction the danger to James lay. She set down her cup and climbed out of bed. "Do you know if the others are up yet?"

"That lot?" Nancy sniffed. "Shouldn't wonder if we don't see 'ide nor 'air of 'em till dinner."

Christy nodded, and went to wash her face with water from the pitcher that stood before the fire. Twenty minutes later, dressed and with her riotous hair arranged with some semblance of propriety, she hurried down to the breakfast parlor. As prophesied by Nancy, that apartment stood empty. Christy helped herself from one of the dishes, ate enough without really tasting it to stave off hunger, and went in search of any life.

She found James in the Great Hall along with Lady Sophia, two footmen, and armloads of holly, ivy, and mistletoe. Christmas Eve, she realized. Her spirits lifted, only to plummet the next moment. Christmas Eve, and her family was thousands of miles and almost two hundred years away. She missed them all terribly. And she'd alienated the only person she had in this time — which would be making her miserable if she weren't so mad at him.

No, she would *not* indulge in self-pity. She would concentrate on settling matters here as soon as possible, make James finish that snowdome for her, then use it, somehow, to take herself home.

Away from James.

He looked up, saw her watching him, and his brow snapped down. He handed the holly garland he held to a footman, and strode up to her. "I want to talk to you."

She nodded, mustering her defenses against the awareness that surged through her at his nearness. She needed to talk to him, too, to tell him what occurred during the night, warn him one of Sir Dominic's select little conspiracy might well be a traitor. She glanced at the closed mask of his face and shuddered. He looked set to deliver a tirade.

She managed a false smile. "It's Christmas Eve. Shouldn't we enter into the spirit?" She scooped up a handful of mistletoe.

"An excellent suggestion. There's a front room over there we can decorate." He retrieved his holly and led the way to the nearest door.

She hesitated a moment, then followed. After shutting the door behind her, she crossed to the window to stare out over the snow-covered landscape. The soft jingle of carriage bells reached her, carried on the icy wind. She braced herself.

He tossed his greenery on a table. "I meant no insult to you last night, Christy," he said without preamble. "I fear the problem lies in the conventions of our different times. Forgive me for expressing myself in a manner that was not acceptable to you." He held out his hands to her. "How, in your era, does a gentleman deal with his love when he cannot offer her the protection of his name?"

She swallowed. "I would support myself. But we would share a home, and every aspect of our lives. . . ." Her voice trailed off.

"Do you think I do not desire that?" he demanded, his voice harsh. "Christy —" He closed the space between them and gathered her into his arms.

She pulled back, found herself captive, and abandoned the struggle. She leaned her cheek against his shoulder.

He drew a deep breath. "My world seems to have turned upside down in the past twenty-four hours. Don't send me away from you again, my love. I need you with me."

She clung to him, knowing this was what she wanted. If her only option in this time was to be called his mistress, then so be it. His royal mistress. . . .

All the horrors that such a position would entail descended on her, and her tantalizing glimpse of happiness evaporated.

"James —" She shook her head. "It wouldn't work for me, you know it wouldn't. I don't fit into your society. These stuffed shirts make me uncomfortable. And I don't want to be the subject of constant gossip, of caricatured cartoons. I'd make gauche mistakes, and everyone would think me inferior and unworthy of you." Pain seeped through her. "I — I'm not cut out to be a Stuart prince's mistress."

"But you are cut out to be my love." He kissed her forehead. "I'll purchase a small country estate, and you can earn your own keep by managing it for me. It will be our private retreat, and I won't let any of these bores come near us."

"Would they let you?" She covered his shoulders with her hands, and pushed herself away so she could look up into his face. "It sounds like they're mapping out your life for you. If they make you regent, could you escape to be with me? And even if they don't . . ." Another reality returned to plague her, which she'd tried to thrust from her mind. "It's not that simple, James. I'm only going to be a complication in your new life."

"A very delightful one." His mouth sought hers.

She avoided his kiss. "No, don't you see? You said it yourself. As a Stuart, it's your duty to marry."

"Into a royal line," he agreed, his tone one of distaste.

"But she'd be your *wife*. How could I be so cruel as to play the role of the 'other woman' to make her life miserable? And you wouldn't want me to, either." Tears burned her eyes, and she blinked them back. "When you make your dynastic marriage, you know perfectly well you'll want to make the best of it. Whether or not you come to love her, you'll be faithful to her. You're too damned noble for anything else. And you'd better believe they're out there, right now, making up a list of candidates."

"My duty," he repeated. "How am I ever to give you up?"

She pulled free from his slackened hold. "You already have," she said with more firmness than she felt.

"Now look who is being noble," he said softly.

She tried to ignore his words. "From now on, I'm just your bodyguard and advisor. We have a revolution to prevent, remember? I'm here in your time for a reason." She had to concentrate on that, keep her thoughts from her hopeless love, from all she was losing. Last night— "James! I—I actually forgot! I think I know who's trying to kill you."

He froze. "Who?"

"Brockenhurst."

For a long moment, he said nothing. Then he startled her as a reluctant chuckle broke from him. "That *dandy?* My love, you've had some wild notions, but this one knocks the others all to flinders. What possible reason would Brockenhurst have for wanting me dead?"

"He mocks your helping the poor, doesn't he? He's probably afraid any country under your regency would play Robin Hood."

His brow snapped down. "You are being absurd."

"Am I? James, if you become regent—"

"Oh, no, Christy, not today. I have enough to assimilate as it is, without considering my next actions."

"No, just listen to me. Brockenhurst went *out* last night. And he was *sneaking*. And he's been cultivating Nancy. Why else would he do it if he wasn't trying to spy on you?"

"Possibly because Nancy is a very pretty girl."

"James—"

"Not today!" He ran a hand through his already disheveled hair. "Not today. This is Christmas Eve, Christy. Let's try to enjoy the season, while we can."

She drew a steadying breath. "I wish we were back at the Runcorns with the boys. Christmas should be spent with children."

He looked away, but not before she glimpsed the bleakness of his expression. Her heart went out to him. Poor, dear James. He suffered, sacrificing his personal happiness to his sense of duty. He was so vulnerable—and right now, so was she.

She picked up her mistletoe. " 'Tis the season to be jolly," she said, and tried to smile.

"Then let us try." He also gathered his greenery, and determinedly they set about decorating the room.

She lacked any joyous spirit, though. At least she could be near James, know he was safe and unharmed. That would have to be her comfort.

By the time she trailed him back to the Great Hall, Lady St. Ives had joined the group there. While two maids sorted the piles of greenery, the countess assisted her hostess in weaving garlands. Already, several long strands waited.

As Christy crossed the marble tiles, Lord Farnham bore down on James. That gentleman stopped short and awarded the major a deferential bow. "Sir," he said. "We have much to discuss this day."

"We have nothing to discuss today. This is Christmas Eve. I intend to spend it in an appropriate manner." He selected one of the finished garlands and began to wind it about the mahogany banister.

Farnham shook his head, his gaze resting thoughtfully on James. Slowly he turned and saw Christy, and his brow furrowed. He strode up to her, and when he spoke, he kept his voice low. "Miss Campbell, it seems the major is reluctant. He must be convinced, for the sake of our great England."

"You're telling me." She didn't bother pointing out, though, that they hoped to influence him in opposite directions. She said nothing more, and after a moment, he wandered away.

Next down the stairs came Brockenhurst. Christy stiffened as he approached James, but he merely greeted the major with a marked degree of respect and moved on. Christy watched him, her gaze narrowed, but he made no other move toward James.

At last she relaxed her vigil and joined in the decorating. Within the hour, the other members of the house party joined in the morning's labors. Sir Dominic called for his valet, who was an accomplished fiddler, and soon the Great Hall filled with the strains of Christmas carols. Christy listened, trying to identify the unfamiliar tunes.

Where were her favorites? She needed them to cheer her, to remind her of home—and happier times. "The Twelve Days of Christmas," though, began life as a Victorian memorization game, and Franz Gruber didn't get around to composing "Silent Night" until 1818. At last the man played one she recognized, and she blended her voice with the violin strains on "God Rest Ye Merry, Gentlemen." After a few seconds, the others joined in, as well.

This was more like it. Almost, if she closed her eyes, she could envision her sister Gina playing her guitar, her family about her instead of these strangers. It was Christmas, a season of hope. She looked toward James and saw his brow less furrowed, his expression less troubled. He, too, it seemed, found a measure of comfort in the message of the season. She hoped it would sustain them both through the difficult days ahead.

Sir Oliver handed her a sprig of mistletoe. "Can you find a suitable place for this, Miss Campbell?"

"Indeed, I can." She tucked it into a bare spot in a holly garland. "There, that looks better."

"A very capable young lady, I see." He eyed her in a contemplative manner.

Another one. Her heart sank. "Not very."

He shook his head. "Now, I feel quite certain, if you put your mind to it, you would be able to use your influence with the major to encourage him to declare his right to the throne."

"Do you? That's funny. I get the distinct feeling he isn't easily influenced by anyone." At least, she hoped so. She gave Sir Oliver a false smile and moved away, joining the violin with "Adeste Fideles."

She had barely reached what she mistakenly thought of as safety when someone touched her arm. She broke off her stumbling rendition of the Latin words and turned to see Viscount Brockenhurst.

A serious expression marked his undeniably handsome countenance. "Miss Campbell, you count yourself a friend of Major Stuart's."

She managed a smile. "Too much so to bring any pressure on him at the moment. Give him time."

Or should she suggest they pursue him with relentless vigor? Her lips twitched. That might turn him against the whole scheme. And somehow, he had to be turned against it. With a sigh, she wondered if all of them would try to get to him through her.

She learned the answer to that question all too soon. Before the party retired to the breakfast parlor for a cold collation at two o'clock, every person present had approached her, including Lady Sophia. Lady St. Ives, admittedly, did so with reluctance, but her pleas held a discouraging ring of sincerity. To each of them, Christy returned a polite refusal, and no longer blamed James in the least for demanding a day or two of peace.

She could, of course, tell them the truth, that they were on the wrong track. Yet without proof of the success of Prinny's regency—of the potential danger of James's very existence—no one had any reason to believe her. And on one point she had to agree with these men. James would make a far more worthy ruler than Prinny in every respect.

But would he ever get to prove it? What if, after all, only the two possible versions of history existed? Then either James

209

would quietly disappear, unheard of by anyone outside these walls, or his appointment as regent would trigger a revolution that would destroy the England they all loved.

James drummed his fingers on the table. If he remained indoors one more minute, he might start throwing things. Admittedly, he had enjoyed the decorating—or at least he would have, had he not contended with five gentlemen's gazes boring into his back. Their determination was almost a tangible force, and an infectious one at that.

Almost, he conceded the good he could do as regent. Almost Christy's warnings troubled him, and he found he could not dismiss them. Were there only the two choices for history, though? If there were others, if he could make a better life for the poor, if his struggles for social equality could actually take on reality. . . .

Yet at what cost? The Stuart name always stirred controversy. And here he was, a Stuart yet a Protestant, with a chance to retake the throne for his family honor. A Stuart. . . .

Hell and the devil confound it, it was enough to make his head ache, trying to determine the possible consequences. He slammed down his mug of ale and came to his feet in one fluid movement.

"Sir?" Sir Dominic rose, leaning heavily on his cane. "What is it you wish?"

To be left alone! But he didn't voice that thought. He wanted to escape. . . . "Are there horses? I would like to ride."

"Of course. I will have mounts brought around for us all as soon as you are finished with your meal."

James smiled with what grace he could muster. A crowd wasn't what he had in mind, yet how could he avoid it without being rude?

Christy looked up, frowning. "I'm not very good—"

He threw her a rueful smile. "Stay here, then, where it's warm. It seems I will not lack for chaperonage." But he'd far rather have her at his side. He could teach her to ride—only she'd refuse, and try to keep a distance between them.

His lips twitched with the irony. Somehow, they had changed

210

places. Now it would be he, trying to undermine *her* good intentions. She was stubborn, his Christy. Yet so was he. He would win her back to his arms where he needed her, warm and caring.

He turned and strode from the room, and the others scurried in his wake. Lord help him, was that another thing to which he would have to grow accustomed? This damnable deference? Was Christy the only one still prepared to argue with him and risk his displeasure? If they but knew it, they did their cause no good by this treatment of him.

He took the stairs two at a time, headed for his chamber to change into riding dress. He took no pleasure in the fact that those of the gentlemen able to bound after him, did so.

Thirty minutes later, all six men set forth, five on horseback and Sir Dominic in his curricle. The bright, clear day, the crisp wind blowing in his face, everything about the glorious afternoon beckoned James to take the nearest fence flying and gallop across the heath. He set his teeth and resigned himself to a dull trot along the road. This was almost as bad as driving with the Four-in-Hand Club to Salt Hill.

Before twenty minutes dragged by, he found himself wishing heartily for a blizzard, anything that would drive the others back indoors. His companions rode in a respectful silence that further distanced him from them. Even St. Ives's acidic tongue remained still.

If he raised a finger, would they fall over themselves, fawning, to ask his bidding? He didn't want to find out. He had more important problems to puzzle through, such as the relative good he could do for England weighed against the probable alterations to the history Christy knew.

Right at this moment, though, *her* history lay far in *his* future. It could all happen differently, not at all as she knew it, and for the better. Would that not be worth any risk?

Yet Christy didn't think so. He dug his heel into his mount's side, and it swished an annoyed tail and lunged forward into a canter. He guided it over a ditch solid with frozen mud, then onto the verge beyond. Ice crackled beneath its hooves.

He drew a deep breath of pure freedom, leaned low, and urged the animal into a gallop. Behind him, hoofbeats pounded in pursuit. He started to push his mount faster, realized he tried to escape his escort, and drew in, annoyed with himself. After a few more paces, he reigned to a halt, and regarded his self-appointed court.

"There is no need for us to stay together, if any of you would rather turn back. Forgive me, Sir Dominic, I find myself in the mood for a long gallop."

"Of course." Sir Dominic glanced at Sir Oliver.

His friend nodded. "With your permission, sir, may I accompany you?"

"I do not require attendants," James said, as gently as he could through his rising irritation.

"Not as an attendant. I, too, enjoy a good gallop."

Probably, he did. Advancing middle age had done nothing to slow this robust man. He could not refuse the company.

St. Ives also elected to join the cross-country run, leaving Brockenhurst and Lord Farnham to turn back with Sir Dominic. Three down, two to go, James reflected, and urged his horse forward.

St. Ives pulled abreast of him. "Have you been thinking about what they said, yesterday?"

"I have. You must have been delighted to discover I am not really your cousin."

St. Ives laughed, but it contained little amusement. " 'Dear Coz,' " he said. "It has a far more familiar ring than 'Sire.' "

"Good God," James said, and shuddered.

A slow smile almost disguised St. Ives's sneer. "Just so. I believe I shall return, as well. It's devilish cold, and I find what little mud has melted is spattering my top boots. With your permission, Sire?"

"Go to the devil," James told him, only joking in part. He turned his horse toward the fence that bordered the road and cleared it, without looking back.

Sir Oliver followed, but his shout brought James to a halt. He turned back to find the older man swinging to the ground.

"I think he may have strained a tendon." Sir Oliver frowned. "I'm afraid I'll have to lead him back. I am sorry to curtail your exercise, sir."

"There isn't any need. I'll go on by myself."

The other shook his head. "I should not leave you."

"Do you think I cannot sit a horse? I wish some exercise. I shall not run away or come to grief, and if I did either, I assure you there would be nothing you could do. I promise to return within the hour. It is my wish," he added, exasperated.

Sir Oliver regarded him, his expression troubled. "If you would indeed rather be alone—?"

"I would."

Before any more arguments could be put forward, he spurred his horse onward. For a full quarter of an hour, he allowed his mount its head as the mad dash eased his tension. At last the animal slowed, and James patted its streaming neck as he brought it to a walk.

Only then did the folly of his actions dawn on him. He'd permitted his temper to get the better of him, to drive away his protectors. Well, he could take care of himself, and so they would learn.

He'd come a good distance, but he would still have time to walk back, cooling his mount, before his watchdogs became anxious. He followed a stream, now frozen over and partly covered in snow, until he encountered a stone wall. For once he experienced no desire to jump it. Nor did his mount, which plodded along, head lowered, still blowing from their freezing dash through the countryside.

James patted the animal's neck again. "Well, old man, shall we—"

A gunshot exploded, all too near. The horse reared, slid on the icy mud, and fell over backward, throwing James against the stones.

Chapter Eighteen

Aching pain roused James back to consciousness. For a long moment he lay still, trying to discover a portion of his anatomy that didn't hurt, then abandoned the unequal attempt. At least nothing seemed to be broken. Everything responded when he tried to move it.

With a concerted effort, he dragged himself to his feet and dusted off the clinging snow. Cold seeped through to his bones from lying in that muddy drift. His horse was nowhere in sight. Well, that didn't surprise him. If it had any sense, it probably had gone home. Which was what he should do.

With only a few uncomplimentary thoughts about mounts which deserted their riders, he set off on foot for the journey back to the house. His head throbbed dully, as if the animal had delivered a swift kick to the back of his skull before departing. More likely he had struck the wall. He probed the area with a gentle hand and found an impressive goose egg already well developed. His fingers came away streaked in blood. Now how—

He came to an abrupt halt as memory flooded back. He hadn't been clumsy, someone had fired a shot. Why hadn't that person finished him off, while he was unconscious? It would have been all too easy.

He swore under his breath. He'd walked—or ridden—right into that one by shaking off his protectors. Still, the question remained of why he wasn't dead.

Three possible answers occurred to him as he resumed walking. His assailant might have been pressed for time, or might have thought he'd succeeded. Or it might all have been an accident, caused by a careless hunter. The last seemed the likeliest. At any rate, he seemed safe enough at the moment.

Trudging through the mounds of snow proved close to impossible. Either he sank in past the tops of his riding boots, further drenching his leather breeches, or his heel skidded on the ice slick. Twice, he sprawled unceremoniously on a particularly slippery patch.

At last he reached another stone wall, and beyond it lay the road. By dint of gritting his teeth, he clambered over the obstacle, finding a few more protesting muscles in the process, and stepped gingerly across the ditch. With more confidence, he struck out along the muddy surface of the lane.

Some twenty minutes later, as he neared the shrubbery boundary of Briarly, three men on horseback cantered into the lane from the drive. Behind them came Sir Dominic in his curricle. Brockenhurst reigned in, effectively blocking the others, and allowed James to approach.

"Your horse came home without you . . . sir." Only the slightest hesitation sounded before that final word.

Deference might color his tone, but James also detected the amusement in the man's eye. Could this have been a practical joke?

"What happened?" Sir Oliver demanded, his expression grim.

"Some poacher in the woods, I believe. My horse spooked at the firing, then had the misfortune to slip on the ice. Has he strained anything?"

Brockenhurst snorted. "Saint Ives is in the stable with him now."

"Of course," James murmured.

"Confounded poachers." Sir Dominic, who had reached them in time to hear the account, glared down the road. "Damned rascally fellows."

"Probably just trying to obtain something for their Christmas

215

Eve dinner." James winced as he climbed into the seat of the carriage.

Sir Dominic turned the equipage and started for home. "Miss Campbell is quite concerned."

"What kept her from coming after me?" James asked, interested. It would take a great deal to keep his Christy away.

Sir Dominic chuckled. "My wife. She insisted Miss Campbell would only be in the way, and set her to tearing bandages to wrap your supposed wounds. Your Miss Campbell has an amazingly strong will for a female."

"I'd noticed."

They rounded the curve of the drive and came into sight of the house. By the time they pulled up before the front door, Christy had reached the porch. She ran down the front steps, then came to a halt barely inches from James.

"Are you all right?" Her anxious gaze searched his face.

"As you see. Somewhat bruised," he added, as she showed signs of checking on the spot.

"That's all? What happened?"

He eased himself down to the gravel drive, and instantly she caught him, as if she could bear his weight into the house. He waved her aside, but as usual she ignored him. As they went up the stairs, he told her.

In the hall he found himself confronted with Wickes, Lady Sophia, Margaret, and both the butler and housekeeper. He waved away all suggestions of potions, vinaigrettes, liniments, and pastilles, but accepted the offer of a stiff brandy and a bathtub to be carried to his room. What he wanted more than anything, he confessed, was a long soak in a hot tub to ease his muscles.

Christy trailed him to his chamber, but caught his arm before he entered. He studied her anxious face for a moment, then gestured for Wickes to precede him.

"Yes?" he asked softly.

Christy glanced through the doorway, to where the efficient valet laid a new fire in the hearth — out of hearing distance. "Damn it, James, I've been worried sick about you! Can't you take even the simplest precautions? You *know* someone is trying to kill you. How could you

216

be such an *idiot* as to send everyone home?"

His eyes narrowed. "I wanted to be alone. Obviously that was the wrong choice. Never mind, you may bear me company now."

She regarded him, suspicion rife on her lovely face.

"Come scrub my back for me," he suggested. She bit her lip, and the longing in her eyes set his pulse rate racing.

Determinedly, she shook her head. "All you need is a soak. If you have to dance tonight, you don't want to be stiff." Abruptly she turned and hurried away.

Before she could give in to temptation, perhaps? That thought made him feel considerably better.

Christmas Eve, Christy reflected, and she had spent most of the day among virtual strangers. And James. . . . No, she couldn't give in to the love that filled her. Every minute she remained in his world proved to her she didn't belong in it. Once the novelty of his new status wore off, and he no longer needed the security she offered, he, too, would begin to see how poorly she fit in among the elite. She couldn't bear to see his love fade, or watch him turn to another, more suitable, woman.

Hands off, no matter how painful, was the safest policy.

She grimaced at her reflection in the mirror. She couldn't delay this any longer, she supposed. She was as ready as she could be without any makeup to give her confidence. She arranged the shawl she'd borrowed from Lady St. Ives about her shoulders, and headed for the door.

She reached the Great Hall as Lady Sophia, a vision in dull gold lace and silk, swept out of the salon. Three ostrich plumes decorated her soft, silvered curls, which clustered about her powdered face. Her husband, resplendent in a mulberry velvet coat and black satin knee breeches, followed, leaning on his cane.

"Ah, my dear," Lady Sophia cried, seeing Christy. "You look lovely."

Christy blinked. What she looked was inappropriate to the occasion, if these two were anything to judge by. She'd known there would be dancing, but the fact of it being a formal *ball* hadn't sunk in until now. She should have stayed in her room.

She hadn't realized how *elegant* these people could look in their old-fashioned clothes. She felt like a frump.

"Will there be many people here tonight?" She cast an uneasy glance at her amber crepe gown, and knew it to be lacking.

"Oh, no, my dear. It will be quite a small ball, under the circumstances. No more than twenty couples."

She did some rapid arithmetic. Forty people. And she'd be standing out like a weed at an orchid show.

Sir Dominic clasped her hand. "Have no fear, Miss Campbell. The guests have been selected with care. Only those friendly to our cause — or in ignorance of it — will attend."

"Oh." She closed her eyes and turned away. Surely no one would dare try to assassinate James with so many people about. He must be safe, at least for this one night.

They sat down twenty to dinner. The others, Christy gathered, would arrive later. The meal, perhaps due to the addition of so many guests, all in a festive spirit, proved a far livelier affair than that of the previous night. The wine passed freely, and Christy found her glass refilled with alarming regularity. The dining room itself had been transformed, with boughs of holly, ivy, and bay draped across the sideboard, surrounding two thick candles wrapped with holly. Bright red berries glistened everywhere.

James, much to her dismay, sat near the head of the table with a beautiful young lady on either side. Sir Dominic must be regretting he hadn't had the foresight to snare a European princess or two to dangle like bait in front of him. Though she feared James was already far too willing to listen to Sir Dominic's schemes.

And why shouldn't he? After all, he would be following in his family's tradition. If it weren't for the potential consequences, she would be behind this herself.

Christy buried her sorrows by sampling such delicacies as pheasant pie and preserved ginger, and a traditional dish of wheat boiled in milk and seasoned with sugar and spices, which Sir Oliver called frumenty. So that's what the boys had gone "Thomassing" to get the ingredients for.

She had barely finished her minced pie when the footmen cleared the table and refilled her glass with a spiced wine. One of

218

the older gentlemen near the head began a lively story, but the arrival of the first of the ball guests brought this to a rapid conclusion. Lady Sophia and Sir Dominic led the way to the ballroom, where they were kept busy for some time receiving the flow of visitors.

When the majority of the guests had arrived, the butler threw wide the huge double doors leading into the Great Hall, and two grooms, assisted by the footmen, wheeled in a barrow in which rested a gigantic tree root. This they conveyed to the cavernous hearth. With great ceremony, the butler unwrapped a charred brand, lit it from a taper, and held it to the Yule log until at last it caught. The guests gathered about, and Sir Dominic led them in the singing of a carol while the wood smoldered. For a minute smoke gushed, then the flames grew brighter and the draft drew through the chimney.

The musicians took their place in their balcony, and the cacophony of strings tuning and warming up filled the vast chamber. The guests mingled, arranging partners, and Christy found herself standing alone. She made her way to a refreshment table on which stood a bowl of spiced, but nonalcoholic, cider. She procured a cup of this and located a comfortable seat to watch.

"You are not preparing to dance?" Lord Farnham bowed before her. "May I have the honor of adding my name to your card?"

Christy shook her head. "I don't think I know any of your dances. I'd hate to embarrass some poor—" She broke off. Not far from her, James bowed before a curvaceous blonde and took her hand. Christy gritted her teeth and turned back to Lord Farnham.

He shook his head. "There will be any number of gentlemen desolated."

Christy managed a false smile as he moved on to Lady St. Ives. Just how hard *were* these dances, anyway?

The musicians struck up the first piece, and the couples arranged themselves in four long lines. Christy leaned forward, studying the movements as the participants bowed or curtsied, then changed positions back to back with their partners. They chasséd, cast off, then changed face to face with their opposite corner. So this was where square dancing originated. But she

219

liked this stately form far better than the livelier version. And as long as she kept an eye on the others, it couldn't be too hard, could it?

James certainly knew how to dance. He moved through the steps with studied grace—as did his partner. They obviously enjoyed themselves, and the movements showed the girl off to her best advantage. Christy bit her lip, and watched as the blonde raised her laughing face to look at James.

The first dance ended, the gentlemen escorted their partners from the floor, then went in search of their next ladies. James led out a flame-haired beauty in a fluttering lace gown which left little to the imagination. Christy watched, temper smoldering, willing that brazen flirt to make a blunder.

"Miss Campbell?" Sir Oliver bowed low before her. "We cannot have you sitting alone like this."

"You're welcome to join me." She managed a bright smile, and hoped he'd think she enjoyed herself.

He directed a speculative glance at her, then to where James took his partner's hand and circled with her. "Do you find our dances so very different?"

"I wish I'd taken a few lessons," she admitted.

"There are only just so many basic steps, which are combined in different ways. That is a half poussette," he said as the couples took hands and exchanged places once more. "And this is four hands around," he added as groups of four joined hands and walked in a circle.

By the time the dance ended, Christy recognized a number of moves. She thanked Sir Oliver as he took his leave of her, then studied the next dance as it began.

Periodically over the next two hours, Sir Oliver or Lady St. Ives, whom the older man appeared to have recruited, sat at her side to continue her instruction. Christy's confidence rose as she recognized the repeated movements, until she almost felt ready to try herself.

Abruptly a gong sounded. Christy started, and glanced at Sir Oliver, who currently kept her company.

"It is time for supper." He rose and bowed before her. "Lovely lady, will you be my partner?"

She smiled. "This is one event I know I won't flub, at least.

220

Thank you, I'd be delighted."

Out of the corner of her eye, she caught a glimpse of James standing in a small knot of people. He'd been very busy this evening, never lacking a partner. And never even offering to sit out a dance with her. Had he already begun to realize he was better off without her? Suddenly, irrationally, she longed to prove him wrong. She took Sir Oliver's arm and allowed him to lead her out.

The dining room once more had been transformed, this time into an elaborate buffet. Strains of music drifted through the door, along with muffled laughter. From the servants' hall, she realized. They held their own celebration this night. She accepted the plate Sir Oliver handed her and made selections from the delicacies laid out.

James entered, and on his arm hung one of his pseudoprincesses, a tall, willowy blonde who seemed to float rather than walk. Christy suppressed an urge to trip her as they passed. Titled ladies, all of birth, beauty, and undoubtedly fortune as well. Why should he spare even a passing glance for a mongrel like herself?

Suddenly, she wanted very much to go *home,* to her mother's tiny house. The whole family would be gathered about the fire, singing carols while Jon and Gina played their guitars, drinking hot spiced cider and eating the cookies they would have all spent the day baking. Would they miss her if she weren't able to get back to them? She would rather be there than here, any day.

Why had fate — and that damned book — upset her life? She'd be much happier if she'd never heard of Major James Edward Holborn Stuart.

She looked up, across the room, directly into his eyes, and her heart constricted. She had already lost her family for this season, she couldn't bear to lose him as well. Somehow, in the short time they had been together, he had become her world.

She escaped from Sir Oliver with a murmured excuse, only to collide with Brockenhurst before she could attain the door. He swept her an elegant bow and directed a smile at her that probably dazzled ninety-nine ladies out of a hundred. It left her cold.

Apparently oblivious of this, the viscount, still beaming at her, returned her to the ballroom where the musicians had once

221

more taken up their positions. "Are you spoken for?" he asked.

Through the door she saw James approach, his lovely partner still clinging to his arm. Rashly, she turned back to Brockenhurst. "No, I'd be delighted."

He led her onto the floor and into one of the lines.

"You may have to prompt me," she said nervously.

"Indeed?" His lip curled into a sneer that would have done St. Ives credit. "Surely you jest."

She'd made a big mistake. Her courage failed, and she took a step backward, only to collide with someone. She spun about and looked up into James's calm, smiling face.

"Excuse me. Permit us to join you." He positioned his partner—Lady St. Ives—next to Christy and himself stood beside Brockenhurst.

"Don't worry," the countess whispered to Christy. "We'll prompt you. James was quite high-handed, you must know. As soon as he saw you with Brockenhurst, he dragged me away from my partner and begged my assistance."

Her surprised—and grateful—gaze flew to James, and the warm gleam in his eyes left her breathless. He did this to save her.

The music started, and she had time to think of nothing but the steps, called softly to her by Lady St. Ives. She made several stumbling mistakes, but somehow it wasn't as bad as she'd feared. Brockenhurst might look down his aristocratic nose at her, but the encouragement of the other two carried her through. James and his thoughtfulness filled her heart.

When the music ended, it was James and not Brockenhurst who claimed her. He raised her fingers and brushed them with his lips, and she caught her breath.

"You will now partner me," he said.

The possessiveness of his tone set her pulse racing. She looked up into his dark eyes, and longing swept through her. She shouldn't, her rational mind warned—but what chance did logic have when he was here, at her side, gazing at her like this?

With an effort, she looked away. "You've just seen a sample of my lack of ability," she warned. "I'll be quite a letdown after your other partners. Are you sure you want to do this?"

"Very sure. You'll begin with a curtsy, then take my hands for a full poussette." Quickly, he ran through the steps in order while

222

the other dancers took their positions. "And remember," he finished softly. "You are supposed to look into my eyes."

The music began, she looked up at him, and found she couldn't drag her gaze away. He took her hands, and she remained mesmerized, moving at his guidance, aware of little beyond him. Why hadn't she realized how sensuous and just plain *romantic* this kind of dancing could be? No wonder society's rules wouldn't let a man stand up with a woman more than twice in one evening.

At last he stopped and stepped back, a smile touching his lips that left her breathless. Several seconds passed while she gazed at him, caught up in a spell solely of his weaving, before she realized the other couples were leaving the floor. Warm color crept into her cheeks.

"Welcome to my world." He carried her hand once more to his lips, then tucked it within his arm. "You see, it is not as difficult to fit in as you feared."

To fit in—with his society, with his life. Perhaps it could work—perhaps she could *make* it work. It would be worth anything to remain with him, to share their love again—and again. She could adapt, learn the rules and play the game. At least she'd be with James. . . .

With James, as regent? With a rush of horror, she realized she had come to accept that possibility. And where did that leave *her* world?

Blindly, she broke from him. She heard his surprised exclamation as he called her name, but she ignored it. She needed time to think. . . .

She made it to the door, and slipped out into the Great Hall. At the far end, the Green Salon stood closed. That should provide temporary asylum. As she darted inside, darkness greeted her, broken only by the glowing embers of the fire which had burned so merrily before.

She couldn't be so crazy as to forget what lay at stake. She didn't belong in this time, she was a product of the future, and she had to protect it for the sake of all those whose lives might be drastically changed. James could not become regent, she couldn't let him be seduced by Sir Dominic's conspiracy. He had to disappear into anonymity, so that no one in the future ever

223

learned of the existence of Prince James Edward Stuart.

Yet what could she say to convince him? He saw only the good he could do for the present; she—in her sane moments when not gazing into his eyes—saw only the harm he would cause to the future. A shaky sob escaped her. An irreconcilable dichotomy. And every one of those luring words he heard from this damnable conspiracy deafened him to her own pleas, her fears for the history she knew. Inch by inch, he chose the destiny that would tear England apart.

She drew a steadying breath. Now wasn't the time to try to drum some sense into his head. She'd wait until tomorrow. She'd do best to slip up to bed without risking seeing him again.

As she opened the door, the one into the ballroom swung wide and Lord Brockenhurst emerged into the Great Hall. Instinctively, Christy eased hers closed. The viscount cast a surreptitious glance about, then set off toward the corridor which led to the library—and the door he had previously taken outside.

Perhaps if she learned something, James might listen. That thought gave her new hope. The guests' wraps had been placed in the next salon; she remembered seeing the footmen going in and out, earlier. She ducked into the room, selected a warm cloak at random, and set off in pursuit of Brockenhurst.

Chapter Nineteen

As Christy eased her way closer to the library, the sounds of rustling fabric and of something knocking against a table sounded within. The door stood an inch ajar, and she peered through the narrow crack. Lord Brockenhurst dragged a greatcoat and boots from their hiding place behind a chair in the corner and put them on.

Christy waited, barely breathing. Did he need to report his attempt on James's life earlier had been a failure? He opened the French window, and, heart pounding, Christy set off after him.

What had James said, something about these not being the nights to go out, because the spirits wandered abroad between St. Thomas's and Christmas Eve? Great, one more night and she'd have been fine. It amazed her how the most innocent of shrubs took on a ghostly demeanor in the depths of the night.

She huddled into her borrowed cloak and tried to walk as silently as possible. The snow gave off the faintest crunch as she trod on it, barely audible, nothing like the crack of twigs might have been. She should be glad. Freezing air filled her lungs as she crept along the path behind the great Georgian mansion.

Pale moonlight reflected off the clouds, bathing the white landscape in a soft glow. She could just make out Brockenhurst's figure heading by the straightest possible route to a small summerhouse at the end of the rose garden. The ideal place for a meeting. He went inside, and Christy kept low, hugging the hedges. That little building had far too many windows for her comfort. Just to be safe, she would circle around to the side. . . .

Someone was there before her. Christy froze. A diminutive-cloaked figure stood on tiptoe and peered through one of the glass panes.

Now what? Find out who else watched Brockenhurst, she supposed. Possibly James had another friend—or enemy. Christy crept closer, keeping behind anything that hid her from view, until she reached the other side of the mysterious figure.

She took another step, her foot slipped on an icy patch, and she clutched a dead branch to keep from falling. It snapped in her hand, and the person at the window spun about.

"Miss!" Nancy breathed after a moment's stunned silence. "Well, I never!"

"Me neither." Christy steadied herself and joined the girl at the window. "What's going on?" she whispered.

"Meetin' 'er, 'e is. Just as I suspicioned. She kept pretendin' to be all tired-like while we was dancin', but I knew she was up to somethin', I did, the brazen cat. So when she slipped out, so did I."

"Who?" Christy craned her neck to see inside, but lacked the necessary inches.

"Daisy." Nancy said the name with scorn. "Miss Nuttall, I should say. No better than she should be, the way she's all over 'im. I—" She broke off and turned away with a flounce. "Well, if *she* wants to get all cold with that sort of goin's on out 'ere, that's 'er lookout. Miss 'Igh-and-Mighty. But what 'e sees in as tricksy a bit o'game as I never did set eyes on, with nothin' in 'er cockloft and the looks of a three-day-old trout, I don't know. Just because she talks flash and I don't." She stormed away from the window.

Christy blinked. Was that all Brockenhurst was up to? Meeting some maid? Christy hurried after her. "Why doesn't he just have her in his room instead of going through all the cold and discomfort? Sneaking out on a freezing night isn't *my* idea of a romantic interlude."

Nancy sniffed. "And risk bein' seen with someone so far be-

226

neath 'im? 'E's too 'igh in the instep, is my great viscount."

As they neared the back of the house, the merry tune of a fiddle and the laughter from the servants' hall drowned out the more refined strains of the chamber orchestra from the ballroom. On the whole, it sounded like a much more fun party. More like home.

On impulse, Christy asked: "Would it bother anyone if I join you?"

Nancy's eyes widened. "You, miss? Whatever would the major say?"

"What he doesn't know—" She broke off as a dark figure separated itself from the shadows of the house and stepped into their path. Christy caught her breath and drew back.

Nancy kept going. " 'Ere, what're you doin' out in the snow?" she demanded.

"You were not the only one in need of a breath of fresh air." Wickes's deep, disapproving tones sounded, familiar and reassuring.

Christy heaved a sigh of relief. She was getting too jumpy. Must be all the coffee she'd been drinking. Too bad decaf hadn't been invented yet.

"Miss Campbell?" Wickes, incredulous, saw her. "Come in, miss. It's a cold night."

"Thank you. If it's all right? I—I didn't feel comfortable at the ball."

A frown settled on the man's features as he ushered them into the warmth of the kitchens. He had a nice face, Christy realized—squared and dominated by a broad nose, perhaps, but kindness lurked in his pale blue eyes. She doubted he'd gone out for the air. His manner might remain stiff and vastly superior, but he gave all the impression of a worried watchdog hovering over Nancy.

He took the girl's cloak from her. "It will be best if you warm yourself by the fire." For a moment his gaze rested on her.

Nancy glanced at him, caught that troubled expression that flickered across his face, and her whole countenance brightened. Abruptly, Wickes backed away and made a show of ushering Christy through the doorway into the servants' hall.

Far more people than Christy would have expected crammed

227

this spacious apartment. Each of the visitors must have brought a coachman, a groom, perhaps even a footman. Holly and ivy garlands hung everywhere, interspersed with laurel wreaths and huge red bows and clusters of berries. On every face the festive spirit prevailed.

Several couples danced a lively reel while an elderly man played his fiddle with verve. On the other side of the room, several grooms, footmen, maids, and visiting coachmen engaged in a rousing game of blind-man's buff, accompanied by much shrieking and laughter.

The long table, along with its candles and garlands, boasted almost as many plates heaped with tarts, cookies, cakes, and meats as had the supper table upstairs. The delicious odors of cinnamon and ginger mingled in the air with that of spiced wine and ale. Feeling much more at home in these less formal surroundings, Christy retired to a corner to enjoy herself.

Nancy, a mischievous twinkle in her eye, caught Wickes's hand and led him, protesting, to join the dancers. By the time the fiddler stopped for a rest, a smile stretched across the valet's normally wooden face. As they headed to the table for refreshment, Wickes looked down into Nancy's laughing face with a mixture of dawning awareness and horror.

Christy grinned. Poor man, to fall for so lively and undisciplined a girl. She would add much needed enjoyment to his life. If he'd let her, at least. Even as she watched, Wickes handed Nancy a glass of the steaming wine and left her. He took refuge at a small table in the corner, where the butler and Sir Dominic's valet played cards. The girl's gaze followed him, her expression woebegone once more.

A shriek of delight drew Christy's attention to a huge cauldron where a maid bobbed unsuccessfully for an apple. Behind her, a visiting footman, his livery impeccable, maneuvered a very pretty girl beneath the mistletoe. The fiddler, his tankard of home-brewed drained, struck up another tune, and this time most of the revelers broke into song, some even on-key.

In another corner, three giggling maids and four footmen in various liveries sat about a wooden table, with a pewter bowl filled with mounded flour before them. On the top rested what looked like a bullet. By turns, each cut a slice until the bullet fell, and the girl who had been cutting at the time cried out in mock dismay. Holding her arms behind her, she stuck her face into the flour, burrowing about. With a cry of triumph, she straightened, her face covered in white but the bullet in her teeth. One of the footmen handed her a towel, then drew her under the mistletoe. Giggling, she pushed him away and broke into the round dance that encircled the fiddler.

Christy hugged herself. This was a far cry from the stuffy formality that took place upstairs. She much preferred it — except it made her miss her own family all the more.

The set ended, and James escorted his partner from the floor. With her once more ensconced beside her starched-faced mamma, he bowed and took himself off in relief. It wasn't any simpering young miss awaiting his hand for the next dance he unconsciously sought, though, but a very different female. He scanned the ballroom and frowned. Christy still hadn't returned. Now where the devil . . .

He slipped out the door and glanced about the Great Hall, but could gain no clue as to where she might have gone. He should have followed her at once, instead of giving her time to be alone. She was confused, and no wonder. To accept him and the life he offered meant she must deny her own world as she knew it.

A longing came over him for her, to feel her in his arms, even just to see her. Perhaps the card room. . . .

Only St. Ives and an elderly gentleman played piquet, no sign of Christy. She must have gone to her room. He hesitated, but a need too strong to deny drove him up the stairs in search of her.

He knocked on her door, but she didn't respond. He tried the handle, found it unlocked, and looked inside. Empty. As empty as he felt himself, without her.

Slowly, he descended the stairs. Where could she have gotten to? Another room? A quiet one? He began a systematic search, but each chamber he glanced into was dark, cold, closed. Their bits of Christmas finery failed to cheer him.

The laughter from the servants' hall caught his attention as he left the library, the only other room where a fire had burned that night. *Would* she?

Certainty filled him, followed by a rush of irritation. Here he'd been looking all over for her, worrying she'd sought solitude to ease her aching heart, and all the time she'd been enjoying herself in the one place she had no business to be. That was exactly the sort of thing his Christy would do.

He threw open the door, traversed the short corridor, and entered the long, festive chamber. A scene of carefree merriment met his gaze, as most of the occupants cavorted in a round dance about a lively fiddler. In a corner near the door sat his quarry, her contemplative regard resting on the revelers.

His first thought, to ring her neck, appealed to him. He took an unsteady step toward her. "What the devil brought you in here?" he demanded.

She started, then looked up into his face. "Oh, hello, James."

" 'Oh, hello, James,' yourself!" he snapped. "Why did you run out of the ballroom like that?"

Her animated expression closed over. "You didn't need me in there."

The devil, he didn't. He bit back the words before he spoke them aloud.

"Come, we'd better go," she said suddenly. "I think you're putting a damper on things."

He glanced up. Two grooms in a corner watched him, their expressions uncertain. Wickes laid his cards on the table, his features their customary blank mask. Nancy bumped into James's groom, with whom she danced. Laughing, she pulled him on. Kepp stumbled, then continued, studiously ignoring James's presence.

A small hand grasped James's arm, and Christy dragged him from the room. "You don't want to interrupt them," she said.

"*You* were."

She shook her head. "I'm different. Hadn't you noticed?"

He had, all too much so. She broke every rule he knew, yet he shied at contemplating life without her.

"There's something I want to tell you, anyway." She led him to the library. "I thought I had your attacker, but I was wrong."

"You certainly seem cheerful about that fact. Whom did you suspect?"

"Brockenhurst. Remember I told you how he snuck out last night?"

230

He nodded, but what he remembered more was that argument they'd had, then retiring to his lonely bed that night aching for her.

"He snuck out of the ballroom, so I followed him," she said.

Dear God, what would she do next? He clenched his jaw.

"There's a small summer house behind this place," she continued, "and he went out there. He was having a highly improper meeting with some maid here by the name of Nuttall. I couldn't see in the window, but Nancy told me. She's caught onto the fact Brockenhurst is nothing but a king-sized rat, at least."

"The damned loose screw," he muttered.

"What a delightful way of putting it." Christy's infectious grin flashed, only to fade the next moment. "Poor girl. I don't think she ever really wanted to be his mistress, though. But with Wickes being so snobbish about her pickpocket days, you can't blame her for falling for Brockenhurst's rush job."

James stiffened. "It is not considered proper to gossip with the servants, particularly about their amorous indiscretions."

"Oh, come off it, James. Quit being so stuffy. The poor girl had to talk to *someone*."

"Either you have no sensibilities—" he began.

"Oh, to hell with your sensibilities. Do you have to be such an upper-class *snob?* What do you do, advocate the rights of the poor and underprivileged—as long as they stay in their place and remember to bow to you?"

"That is quite enough—"

"Obviously it isn't! They're people, James, not just servants. Have you even noticed what Mr. Wickes is going through right now?"

"Mr. —Do you mean my valet? What do you mean, 'what he's going through?' "

"You *haven't* noticed."

Her tone of angry satisfaction grated on him. "You will kindly explain yourself."

"*He* could, if you'd ask him."

"Christy—" He broke off, trying to keep his temper under control. "I'm in no mood for your games."

"It's not a game. Mr. Wickes is suffering from the same snobbism you are. He's fallen for Nancy, but she's too far beneath

231

him to marry. Why are you looking so surprised? Aren't you glad his class sense is winning out?"

"No, I—" He broke off, trying to gather his startled thoughts. "I'd never thought of him marrying, that is all."

"Well, why not? Where do you think the next generation of valet-lets will come from?"

"The—" He struggled for a moment. His ill-temper faded, and a reluctant chuckle broke from him. "And maid-lets, too, I suppose?"

"Certainly. But *not* pickpocket-lets. Nancy promises me she's reformed, and I don't think Wickes would permit it. Providing she can overcome his snobbery."

"You obviously think he should," he said with considerable feeling. The girl had no concept that she behaved and thought with a complete lack of decorum. Nothing put her to the blush. Yet neither did her manners betray vulgarity—only a completely different approach to life based on honesty rather than appearances. He found it decidedly refreshing—yet also a continual reminder she came from an alien world. How she would hate to be hedged in by conventions she could neither understand nor approve.

And where did that leave them? His gaze rested on her, and visions of a quiet life, of a small country estate and several children rose to his mind. Of Christy at his side, as his wife. . . .

Yet he was a Stuart, with all the incumbent obligations and demands. And he had no guarantee she would even remain in his time. No, the life he envisioned was a hopeless dream. He studied her upturned face, saw the question in her huge blue eyes, and fought the temptation to stroke back her riotous curls. She stood so close, the scent of violets drifted about him, increasing his yearning.

"We'd better go back before we're missed." He moved a safe distance away. Not safe enough, he realized the next moment—not as long as he could see her.

"Are they still dancing?" She hung back, her expression reluctant.

"I thought you made a very apt student." He wouldn't mind leading her through the movements once more. With her, the whole concept of dancing had taken on a new—and very alluring—meaning.

She drew a long breath. "There's a card room, isn't there? Would you teach me to play piquet?" Just a touch of wistfulness colored her voice.

"Of course." It would make one more ability that might help tie her to his world, make her realize she could be happy here with him.

They returned her borrowed cloak to the small salon, then made their way to the drawing room set aside for cards. St. Ives and his elderly companion were no longer alone. At another table, directly before the hearth, Sir Oliver Paignton broke the seal on a new deck while Lord Brockenhurst set glasses of wine before them. Apparently, the viscount had completed his tryst and focused on another of his favorite pastimes. Christy stiffened at James's side.

He gestured her to silence, and ushered her to a table a little distance from the others. After pouring them each wine from the holly-decked decanter, Christy took her seat opposite him. James opened a deck, sorted out the lower pips, and shuffled.

"The key," he said, "lies in developing mastery of a suit."

Christy nodded, her expression intent, and he explained the complexities of scoring. A frown of concentration formed on her lovely brow, but at last she pronounced herself ready to give it a try. He dealt out a sample hand faceup, and explained which cards she should discard and why.

She drew replacements, and he showed her how to arrange her hand. Together they tallied her scores for points, set, and sequence, then did the same for his. He played it out to its end, showing her which cards to use from each hand, and wound up taking the majority of the tricks himself.

A slow smile touched her full lips. "Let's give it a try."

Pleased with her quickness, he shuffled and dealt again, then allowed her time to puzzle out her cards on her own. St. Ives and his partner, James noted, watched them in some amusement. Unlike Sir Oliver and Brockenhurst. They had eyes only for their own game.

Christy fumbled with her discard, he dealt the replacements, then did the same for his own. While she determined her points, his gaze once more strayed to the other table. Brockenhurst shuffled, holding the cards near his body, his fingers flying over the pieces of pasteboard.

James's eyes narrowed. Something didn't seem quite right. Absently, he played his hand, all the time watching that other game. Did Brockenhurst nick the cards, or was he mistaken? The viscount had won the last hand—the last several, in fact, judging from the small pile of vowels lying before him.

Christy's cry of delight recalled his attention to his own game, and he realized either through luck, through an innate talent, or through his inattention, she had won. He gathered the deck, shuffled, and dealt again.

Brockenhurst and Sir Oliver continued to play, and the pile of papers grew steadily before the viscount. He made half-apologetic noises, which Sir Oliver waved aside with impatience and returned to the game with the feverish intensity of the addicted gambler. To Brockenhurst's suggestion they quit, he turned a deaf ear, demanding only that his opponent deal once more.

Sir Oliver, James remembered, had something of a reputation for being a gamester, though not one for having luck. This time, it ran even worse than usual. Or did luck play any part in this? James frowned. He might be letting Christy's suspicions of Brockenhurst prejudice him against the man.

The viscount's nocturnal ramblings had proved innocuous enough—unless, of course, he met someone *besides* the obliging Miss Nuttall. That possibility warranted further consideration. His gaze lingered on the man's overly handsome countenance, his brown hair artistically brushed into the Windswept, the bright hazel eyes with their knowing gleam. Definitely, he didn't trust Brockenhurst any more than did Christy.

Strains of a Christmas carol drifted into the room, replacing those of the chamber orchestra. They finished their hand, and Christy led the way back to the ballroom. There they found the dancing had stopped, and the guests, voices raised in song, gathered about the Yule log which still burned brightly. Christy closed her eyes, her expression somber.

"What is the matter?" James leaned close to speak softly in her ear.

She shook her head, and her lashes glistened with unshed tears. "My family," she said simply.

Longing stirred in him. He had never known a home life that could produce such a warmth of feeling like she seemed to experience. He was jealous, he realized. He would give a great deal for some of the happy childhood memories she must have known.

He touched her shoulder, almost a caress, and she managed a bright smile. When the next carol began, she joined in, although here and there she sang a different word or two. Somehow, it comforted him to know that no matter what else of history might change, Christmas remained, as did its songs.

"Do you have Yule logs?" he asked suddenly.

"Some people do. We always have one."

"And games and mumming?"

She shook her head. "Not really. We have — other traditions. The spirit is the same, though."

He would like to know what her customs were. Yet at this moment he didn't want to ponder on their differences, but on the similarities of this timeless season.

After the next carol, the ball guests trailed into the Great Hall and prepared to take their leave. Christy hung back, as if loathe to let the evening end. Softly her husky voice rose in a carol unfamiliar to him. Something about a silent night and all being calm. He liked it. She continued it with a second verse while he escorted her to her chamber. He bade her good night, and sought his own apartment.

Wickes awaited him, with his night rail already laid out over the bed and the water warm in its pitcher before the blazing fire. James looked about the room made comfortable for him by his devoted valet's hand, and realized how much he took this man's services for granted.

He transferred his gaze to the valet's impassive face. Wickes appeared impeccable, from the top of his receding blond hair to the toes of his polished slippers. As if he had nothing else on his mind except to tend his master's needs.

Deftly, the valet assisted him from his close-fitting coat of emerald velvet. Not a sign of discontent marred his features. If James didn't have Christy's assurances, he would have no clue the man suffered inner turmoil.

Love, that damnedest of all human emotions. If Wickes really cared for Nancy, then why the devil didn't he admit it? Because of her dubious background and uncultured speech? The valet could be as stiff-rumped as the next man, and knew the importance of his position better than most.

Alone at last, he settled in the chair by the fire where he could warm both his tools and his wax. From its soft cloth he unwrapped the figure of Christy, now complete, and studied the rounded face. He hadn't quite captured her laughing expression — nor her soul. Yet the graceful curve of the figure brought her lively movements forcibly to his mind.

He quelled his impulse to go to her. She needed time to accept his altered position, time he could only hope they would have. Abruptly, he returned the carving to its protective cover, unfolded the other chunk of wax, and began a crude rendition of himself.

A knock sounded on his door, and he looked up. If Christy had come . . . Desire surged through him and he rose, setting the wax aside.

"Master James?" Wickes's voice sounded from the hall.

The depth of his disappointment dismayed him. She really had become part of him — and one he couldn't live without.

"Master James?" The valet knocked again.

James let him in. "What is it, Wickes?"

"Your wine, sir." The valet swept past him, carrying a glass on a salver. He set it on the table by the hearth and, with a slight bow, wished his master good night.

James thanked him, then settled once more in his chair. An excellent man, Wickes. This was just what he needed. He took a sip, and rolled the heady liquid in his mouth.

After savoring it for a moment, he swallowed — and choked on the bitter aftertaste. Suddenly suspicious, he held the goblet up to the branch of working candles and examined the ruby contents. Clouds swirled in a liquid that should have been clear, and his mouth and throat burned.

Poison.

Chapter Twenty

Sir Dominic Kaye, wrapped in a dressing gown of deep purple satin, held the ruby wine before his candle, sniffed the contents, then dampened his tongue. A shudder shook his thin frame. "My dear sir, that this should happen, and in my house. I am appalled."

James's brow snapped down, and he straightened from where he perched on the arm of an overstuffed chair. "I wasn't mistaken, then?"

"I wish you had been." The elderly man set down the glass. At that moment, he appeared to need a restorative—though one of a healthier nature. He crossed to a bureau, where a decanter stood on a tray with two glasses. He poured a dose of amber liquid into each, and handed one to James. He sipped it, then sighed as he stared into the fire. "How can I ever apologize?

James waved that aside. "What do you think is in it?"

Sir Dominic hesitated, and the frown marring his brow deepened. "I wish I knew. Not laudanum. I very much fear something deadlier, something that might eat away at your stomach."

That same thought had occurred to James—had continued to do so, in fact, during the whole fifteen minutes he had spent rinsing out his mouth and drinking water.

"That an attempt should be made upon you, and here—!" Sir Dominic raised his haggard face to look at James.

James rose and set down his glass, untouched. His mouth still burned. "Let us question my man, first. Someone must have set it out for him to bring to me."

Yet Wickes, when roused from his slumbers, could shed little light on the subject. Shortly after he had retired to the chamber allotted to him, a footman had knocked on the door with the information that his gentleman required a glass of wine. The young man had brought one with him.

They next awakened the footman, who yawned and knuckled his bleary eyes. "In the kitchens, it was," he announced after a moment's thought. "Already poured and on the salver, with a note saying as how it was for Major Holborn. Thought it might be a cordial, so I took it along to Mr. Wickes."

"Where is the note?" James demanded.

The footman stifled another yawn. "Threw it in the fire. Lucky I chanced on it at all, seeing as how I was the last one through there. Don't know why someone hadn't a-taken it up afore." His bleary gaze focused on the gentlemen before him, and a worried expression crept into his eyes. "It were all right, weren't it?"

Assured no harm had been done, the footman returned to his bed. James and Sir Dominic headed for the main wing of the building. The elderly man leaned on his cane, his shoulders bent.

Not until they reached the Great Hall did Sir Dominic speak. "Someone within this house is trying to kill you." He directed his troubled gaze at James. "We have a traitor in our midst."

"Yes, someone has been indulging in a spot of inefficient assassination. Have you any idea who it might be?"

Sir Dominic shook his head. "None. Each man—I would swear every one of them is completely loyal to you."

"Someone is not." James couldn't keep the dryness from his voice.

Sir Dominic led the way up the dimly lit stairs, his chamber stick clutched in his trembling hand. "Which one?" he muttered, over and over. When they arrived at James's room, they entered together. Sir Dominic crossed to the fire and stared into the crackling flames. "Have you any suspicions?"

"Sir Oliver?" James suggested.

Sir Dominic shook his head. "He is my trusted assistant — and has been for nigh on twenty years."

"He also has a weakness for the gaming tables, and an ill-luck that is the talk of the town. And do not forget, his years in the Home Office have already been rewarded with a knighthood. I have even heard a barony mentioned as a possibility for him. That might well concentrate his loyalties on the current regime."

Sir Dominic, his expression stricken, sank onto a chair as if his legs could no longer hold him. He made no denial. After a moment, he said: "What of Lord Farnham? His estates are grossly encumbered. It is possible, however much we might wish to deny it, he might have been willing to betray our cause for sufficient financial gain."

James inclined his head in acknowledgment. Absently, he tossed another log onto the grate. "Viscount Brockenhurst? He has been slipping out of the house, apparently to meet one of your housemaids in the folly."

"On an icy December evening?" Sir Dominic demanded, incredulous.

"Supposedly he doesn't wish to be detected lowering himself to such a liaison," James explained. "I thought it sounded a bit dodgy, myself."

Sir Dominic clasped his hands together. "You think he is using that maid as an excuse to slip out, in case he's seen?"

"It does seem a possibility. I believe he is also guilty of cheating at cards."

Sir Dominic flinched, as if that revelation pained him. "That is not a reason to want you dead, though." He sank back in the chair, his expression thoughtful. "He was brought into our conspiracy by his father. His dedication might not be as real as that of the others."

"Why does he work with you?"

Sir Dominic actually smiled. "He says Prinny is 'devilish bad *ton*.'"

James studied the lines of strain on the older man's face, and nodded. "He has always mocked my work with the poor. It is possible he fears what I might do, the changes I might bring about, if I possessed more power."

"Power. Yes, you said the attacks on you began back in October." For a long moment he stared into the flames. At last, he looked up. "It was at the end of September, when the discussions intensified over the regency bill, that I revealed it was you who were the Stuart heir."

So one of those men at last learned the identity of the hated Stuart — and set about arranging his death. James drew a deep breath. "We cannot forget St. Ives."

"Your cousin?"

James shook his head. "A year ago, on his father's death, he must have learned I was no blood relation."

"But to kill you? Surely — the ties of childhood —" Sir Dominic broke off, appalled.

"There is no love between us. He is the elder by nearly ten years, and his father lavished attention on me."

"Resentment," Sir Dominic murmured. "Or even jealousy. But why would he wait so many months before making an attempt on you? He knew the truth long before the others."

"Perhaps he bided his time until a sufficient number of men to cloud the issue were presented with a motive."

Sir Dominic nodded. "Or perhaps it didn't really matter to him until your becoming regent became a likelihood. I believe you should have your man spend the night in here. You should not be alone."

"I doubt my enemy wishes to reveal himself. I will do very well if I lock the door."

James escorted Sir Dominic to the corridor, and his host waited until James not only turned the key in its hole, but also removed it. As Sir Dominic's footsteps retreated, James strolled to his washbasin and drank the remaining water.

This changed things. No longer did the attacks on him loom as a personal grudge. His assailant wanted the Stuart heir dead, and it was only coincidental that James Holborn was that heir. It depersonalized the matter somehow, but at the moment, James wasn't certain if that made it any better. More understandable, perhaps, but no, not better.

He climbed into his great, cold bed, and left the curtains back. Lord, what he wouldn't give for the sweet comfort of Christy's arms. She'd come to him if she knew about the wine — but he wanted her there by her own choice, not because he roused her protective instincts. Thoughts of her burned through him until at last, desperate to distract his mind, he concentrated instead on her words.

Torn by uncertainty, he stared into the fire, watching the flames dance along the logs. She swore Prinny's regency, despite his wastrel and profligate ways, would not cause the revolution so much feared by Sir Dominic's cabal. Yet he knew how much good he himself could do as regent, then king. He cared for the welfare of the people, unlike Prinny. He could make all he worked for reality.

Christy claimed Prinny *did* become regent. Yet history could change, the shifting type in his book proved that. And the alteration of events depended on one catalyst. Him. What did he—or didn't he—do?

Or was everything Christy had said and done a lie? Was she truly from the future—which was blatantly impossible—or did a faction who knew him for a Stuart, and opposed him, plant her on him? Did they provide her with a copy of his notes, printed into a book, so she could convince him by pretending to have brought it with her from her own supposed time? Was she the source of that poisoned wine?

Yet he wanted to believe in her, in the love for her that filled him. There had been a magic between them when she shared his bed. How could anything that perfect be a lie?

But if he *did* believe in her, then he had to accept the possibility that the appearance of a Stuart, and one advocating social reform, would cause the very revolution he hoped to prevent.

Restless thoughts jostled against one another, confused and confusing, blending into fragments of memory and dream. Restful sleep evaded him, yet when he opened weary eyes once more, soft light filtered into the room. A world so still and silent greeted him, he knew without looking that snow fell once more. Christmas morning.

A gentle tapping sounded at his door, and he realized it was a repetition of what had awakened him. Wickes's worried voice called to him, and he rose, drew on his dressing gown, and found the key so he could admit his man.

The entire house party gathered for the morning meal, greeting one another with wishes for a merry Christmas. Plates and trays heaped with food lined the sideboard, and the decorated Christmas candles burned bright amid their greenery. The footmen moved with care about their duties, as if they nursed sore heads after their night of revelry.

James checked which dishes the others had sampled, then made his selections from these, filling his plate with slices of rare beef and smoked herring. The eggs he avoided; the chafing dish appeared to have been freshly replaced, and no one had as yet scooped a serving. The butler offered him spiced cider from a large pot, which he deemed safe to accept.

It would be the very devil, wondering if every dish or cup presented to him contained poison. Settling at the table, he regarded his fellow guests. For a moment, all gazes rested on him, then with an excess of politeness, the men looked away.

Did they wonder if he were in a mood to listen to their entreaties? All except one, of course, who must be dismayed to see him still alive.

Christy's tales of warm family gatherings at Christmas stood out in sharp contrast to this motley assortment of political intriguers. Each one of them, using the holiday to advance his plans, and very probably his power. If these men brought a Stuart to the throne, they might well expect numerous favors in return.

Lady Sophia smiled a welcome to him, not a trace of constraint or worry on her gentle brow. Her husband, it seemed, had told her nothing of the night's occurrence.

His gaze met Christy's, where she sat between Lady St. Ives and Lord Farnham. For a long minute she studied his face, until James looked away, not wanting to reveal too much. The sparkle in her magnificent eyes faded, and Christy directed an aimless question to Farnham. That gentleman beamed at her, and murmured something that brought a smile once more to her full lips. Irritation stabbed through James, which he recognized as jealousy.

He ate his beef with savage force, then excused himself from the table. An hour still remained before they were to depart for church, and he wanted to take some more notes for the next chapter of his book.

When the handle on his door turned, he tensed and muttered

curses at himself for leaving it unlocked. His fingers closed about the letter opener that lay on the small writing desk, only to relax as Christy slipped inside. If only she had come last night. . . .

Not passion, though, but worry, marked her expression. She advanced into the room, only to stop two paces from him. "Are you all right? You looked like death warmed over at breakfast."

"Thank you." His lips twitched. "What a delightful description. As you see, I continue tolerably."

"Oh, cut it out, James." She perched on the edge of the desk. "You were looking at everyone around the table as if you had X-ray vision."

"As—what?"

"Like you were looking right through them," she amended.

He leaned back in his chair, his gaze held by the sparkling determination in those bright blue eyes. Such lovely eyes. No, he couldn't believe she worked against him. Not his beloved Christy.

"Well?" she demanded.

He brushed the thick curls from her cheek. "Someone sent a glass of poisoned wine to me last night."

"Someone—" She broke off. Her lips parted, and her complexion paled, her usual becoming color fading to an unnatural pallor. The hand she reached toward his cheek trembled. "You didn't drink it," she managed at last.

"No more than a sip, and I rinsed away all traces."

"Oh, James—" Her voice broke on a sob.

Temptation proved too great. He gathered her into his arms, holding her close. She clung to him, as if she feared he would be dragged from her at any moment. He buried his face in her curls, breathing deeply the scent of violets that clung to her. Dear heaven, he wanted her. . . .

"It's all right," he murmured against her hair. "Christy, it didn't work, and I'm warned, now. I'll take all precautions."

She drew a shuddering breath. "I—I'll stay with you."

She was his for the taking—but for the wrong reason. Hunger for her wrenched his heart, but he shook his head and forced a smile. "You should go, now. You know perfectly well it's shocking for you to be in my room. If anyone saw you,

243

you wouldn't have a shred of reputation left to you."

"What does it matter?" Her voice sounded hollow. "I don't exist in this time."

Only in his heart — and that was one place she didn't want him to keep her — yet. He escorted her to the door, promised he would see her downstairs in a few minutes when they departed for the village church, and shut her out in the hall. If only she would come again. . . .

He turned back to his notes and glanced over the account of the house party. He wrote it just as Christy predicted. But would it stay that way? He had thought all he had to do was get this down on paper, and the possibility of revolution would be avoided. But what if the print in his book altered because he wrote first one account, and then the other? Frustrated, he gathered the pages together and shoved them into the drawer.

Twenty minutes later, the party departed for the small church located less than a mile from Briarly. Sir Dominic and Lady Sophia rode in their carriage, along with Sir Oliver and Margaret. The rest elected to walk through the snow to enjoy the crisp morning air. They passed others, all of whom waved and exchanged Christmas greetings. The peeling of the bells rang clear and loud, summoning them to worship on this joyous morning.

James gave himself over to the pervading spirit. For a little while, at least, he lost himself in the celebration, and raised his rich baritone to join in the anthems and carols that filled the church. Closing his eyes, he listened to the vicar's words of hope, and almost he could forget the difficult decisions awaiting him on the morrow — or the possibility of death which awaited him at every turn.

All too soon, the organ struck the final chords of the closing Christmas hymn, and with regret he returned to his present concerns. With the others, he filed down the aisle, exchanging felicitations with total strangers. It gave him a warm feeling. Christy, though, would be missing her family — and probably blaming him and his muddled affairs for taking her from them during this season.

He glanced back, to where she had been walking with Sir Oliver, and saw the old man alone. In fact, he realized after a few minutes of searching the crowd, he didn't see her anywhere. He turned, his fears rising, and found Sir Dominic watching him.

"Is something wrong?" The elderly gentleman hurried forward.

"Christy. Miss Campbell. Do you know where she is?"

Lady Sophia, who had followed her husband, shook her head. "She was with me a few minutes ago. Then I believe she went toward the carriages."

James set off in pursuit, following the line of motley assorted vehicles. He reached the end without catching so much as a glimpse of her. Had she started back to Briarly? She might have experienced the melancholy which came from spending Christmas so far from those she loved, and sought solitude.

A few of the churchgoers broke away from the milling crowd and headed for their carriages. James circled about the ancient stone building, making one last check before starting the trek back to the manor. Still no sight of her met his searching gaze.

As he reached the front, a piercing scream rent the serenity.

Chapter Twenty-one

The fear for Christy James had held in check broke loose, and he took off at a run, his heart pounding in his chest. Christy. . . . If something had happened to her—

He rounded the corner of the church to see the milling crowd turned in the direction of the carriages. He pushed through, oblivious to everything except reaching the landau with several people gathered about it.

"Gor' blimey, is she dead?" he heard an uncouth voice ask.

Unceremoniously, he thrust a little man aside and reached the carriage's door. A middle-aged gentleman knelt on the step, looking at a crumpled figure within, wrapped in an all too familiar pelisse of brown wool. In his hand, the man held a vinaigrette, though he didn't seem certain what to do with it.

"Christy?" James took it from him and clambered into the vehicle. His fingers found the pulse point in her neck, and relief flooded through him at the gentle beat.

Sir Oliver's head appeared in the doorway. "What—" He broke off. "I'll fetch Lady Sophia." He disappeared.

James checked Christy for obvious injuries, and found none. By the time Lady Sophia and Margaret joined him, he had opened the vinaigrette and held it to Christy's nose.

"How did she get in here?" Margaret chafed Christy's wrist.

"I don't know." He looked out the door. "Sir Dominic, is your barouche ready?"

"Yes, yes, of course." The man looked about, uncertain. "I'll get it."

St. Ives, who stood just outside, strode down the line of vehicles to the Briarly conveyance. James gathered Christy into his arms, then realized he couldn't maneuver them both through the carriage door. Lord Farnham appeared below, and together they eased her inert form outside. James took her once more, and Farnham accompanied them to the now-readied vehicle.

"What happened?" Farnham demanded.

"There's a swelling on the back of her head," he said.

"My God," Farnham breathed. "First you, and now—" He broke off.

James clenched his jaw. "I presume this was in light of a warning to me. Will you be kind enough to spread it about that nothing that happens to Miss Campbell will affect my decisions?"

Farnham gaped at him. "Do you mean you would allow some ruffian—"

"The devil with some ruffian!" James stopped at the Briarly carriage door. "This is the work of a member of our house party, not some mohawk. If I give in to this sort of intimidation, there will be no stopping it."

He glanced around and saw Lord Brockenhurst and Sir Oliver just behind them. "You may be very sure I will find out who did this, and whoever is responsible will regret it very much indeed. But neither this, nor any possible future attack on Miss Campbell, will be allowed to influence my decisions. Is that understood?"

"Oh, quite clearly." St. Ives opened the door. "May I be of assistance to you—Sire?"

James glared at him, then at Brockenhurst who stood nearby. He didn't want any of them to touch her. And for all his bravado, if she were to be held hostage, he very much feared he would acquiesce to any demands to keep her safe. He only hoped these men would not guess as much.

A soft moan escaped her lips, and she stirred in his arms. Farnham pushed past him and climbed into the carriage, then

247

held out impatient arms for her. With reluctance, James released her.

"What — ?" Christy's eyes fluttered open. "Ow!" she added, as Farnham laid her on the seat.

"Who hit you, Christy?" James joined them in the carriage, leaving no room for Margaret, who hesitated just outside.

Christy's long lashes fluttered, her eyes opened, and she winced. It took a moment before her gaze settled on James's face. "You're safe," she murmured.

His lip twitched. "Indeed I am. And what of you?"

"Me?" She shook her head, then grimaced. "I feel like a horse kicked me. A horse!" Her blue eyes widened. "James, that man on horseback — not the one Sir Dominic had watching you, but another. He was lurking among the carriages, and I tried to get a better look at him. Then — someone must have knocked me out."

"And shoved you into a carriage so you wouldn't be seen." The thought of some villain touching her, manhandling her into the landau, set his fists clamping into punishing bunches of fives. When he finally caught up with this curst rum touch, he intended to supply him with a bit of very satisfying home-brewed. And he was not a man who normally took pleasure in violence. For this, he would make an exception.

"Did no one see anything?" Farnham demanded. "That hardly seems possible."

"The line of carriages stood between Miss Campbell and anyone who might have been watching. If some of the coachmen weren't with their vehicles, and her assailant caught her as she began to fall — " Brockenhurst shook his head.

Margaret touched James's arm. "Let us take her back to Briarly. She will be far better once she is settled comfortably in her own chamber."

James glanced at his erstwhile cousin's wife. Her worry-filled gray eyes appeared unnaturally large against the pallor of her complexion. "You look all knocked to flinders. Come." He extended his hand to assist her. "Get in, Margaret."

Farnham jumped down, and ushered the countess inside. James settled beside Christy, his arm still about her. Margaret positioned herself on the facing seat, and Brockenhurst climbed up and settled beside her. Sir Dominic waved the driver on, and the carriage lurched forward.

"You are accompanying us?" James raised a questioning eyebrow at the viscount.

Brockenhurst shrugged. "You need someone to help you assist Miss Campbell down at the other end. Devilish bad *ton* to leave you in the lurch. You are, I believe, a man who understands duty?"

"I am." James watched him with growing distrust.

Brockenhurst nodded, as if to himself. "Yes, duty. More like than not, it proves an unpleasant mistress. It is not often the observance of one's duty can bring power and status. Ah, and so many other rewards. Really, you are quite to be envied."

"Indeed? Yet my sole specific request, not to have this matter broached until *after* Christmas, has not been honored by a single person."

Brockenhurst stiffened. "If I have given offense, sir—"

"Major," James snapped. "Until this matter is settled, I would have you all call me 'Major.' "

Duty. His gaze strayed to Christy, who leaned back against the squabs, her eyes once more closed. What happened when duty strayed so far from desire? To take a royal bride, when Christy filled his heart, was as unthinkable as Christy said.

But why should he marry—just yet, at least? He was only eight-and-thirty, and his own father hadn't wed until he was almost sixty. James could do the same. Then he would have twenty years with his beloved.

Provided she remained in his time. If he lost her . . . no, then it wouldn't matter to him whom he wed. Duty would be all that would carry him on.

As they pulled up before Briarly, Christy roused. Stoutly she refused the assistance of either gentleman from the carriage, and descended on her own. "I'm much better," she assured James, and caught herself as she wobbled.

James steadied her, his hands cupping her upper arms, guiding her up the stairs. Brockenhurst trailed after them. With a murmured excuse, Margaret hurried ahead, anxious to reach her own chamber. The probable date of her confinement loomed barely weeks ahead, James realized. She must feel the strain terribly. The carriage set off down the drive, returning to the church for more passengers.

"What happens now?" Christy asked as they entered the house.

"You rest," James said.

She shook her head—though with care. "Do you think I intend to miss a single minute of Christmas? I'm a lot better, now. I want to stay here, where I can see you."

And where he could see her. He led her to a sheltered alcove, partially hidden by a trailing tapestry, and settled her in a chair. She leaned back, eyes closed, and becoming color once more crept into her cheeks.

The servants, who had walked back from the church, swarmed into the Great Hall. They rearranged tables, brought out bowls of punch and plates heaped with delicacies, lit the decorated Christmas candles, and straightened the bows and berries which were strewn amid the holly, bay, and ivy. A maid hung fresh bunches of mistletoe while a footman placed more logs in the hearth. No winter chill would long linger here.

The house party had barely returned to the festive hall when the first of the visitors arrived. James folded his arms and stood beside Christy like a dog guarding his mistress, while about them, the country gentry mingled with the government officials, exchanging pleasantries and devouring the elaborate collation. This would go on for hours, he realized, with more guests stopping by, until at last the growing dark or the renewed snowfall brought the celebrations to a close.

Christy leaned forward, and he looked down at her at once. Lines of strain marred her features, and pain pinched her brow.

"Are you all right?" he asked quickly.

"Just a headache. What I wouldn't give for some aspirin."

James let the strange word pass. "How about some plum brandy? I believe I saw some a few minutes ago."

He caught a passing footman, who obligingly fetched him a couple of glasses—poured, the lad assured him, from the same decanter from which the other guests drank. The servants, it appeared, had been alerted to James's danger.

He carried the crystal goblets filled with their deep purple liquid to where Christy waited, and he toasted her before taking a sip. The sweet liquid burned down his throat, warming, easing his tension. She managed a half smile in response.

"What do you think of our Christmas?" he asked.

"It makes me homesick." She twirled the stem between her fingers. "If I were at my mom's, we'd be building snowmen and taking presents to friends and decorating more cookies because Matt and the kids would have eaten all of them. Then Jon and Gina would get out their guitars again and we'd sing—" She broke off and shoved her hand toward the side of her gown, but apparently couldn't find what she sought. "Damn, I wish I had some chocolate."

"I am sorry if you have been disappointed in our celebrations."

She shook her head. "It's not that. I'm enjoying your Christmas, but there are things I miss. *My* traditions. I want to string cranberries and popcorn, *in spite* of the fact I always prick my fingers and get salt in the cuts, and get sore from forcing the needle through the hard berries. I want a *tree,* and I didn't get to hang up a stocking for Santa Claus. I didn't even make my annual new decoration this year."

He reached toward her, then allowed his hand to smooth over her unruly hair. "You have happy memories." He could wish the same for himself.

Her lips twitched. "I suppose that's all they'll be, now, unless I can find a way home. At least I can have a tree—once Victoria marries Albert, of course." Her half smile slipped awry. "She hasn't even been born, yet."

Against his better judgment, James asked: "Who is Victoria?"

"She'll be queen after her father William dies. He's king after your Prinny."

"And she's responsible for some of the customs you like?"

Christy nodded. "There's nothing that says I can't do them on my own, of course."

He regarded the impeccable shine of his glossy Hessian boots. "And what if your Victoria never becomes queen?"

Very slowly, Christy turned to look up into his face. "James, do you really *want* to be king? History manages very well without you."

251

"Did you, in your time, know of my existence? As the Stuart heir, I mean?"

"No." She shook her head. "But then I never studied much British history, either. I only know the regency is given to Prince George, with no trouble attached. You weren't mentioned in any of the books I checked."

He paced a few steps away, then back. "History *could* follow a completely different course."

She nodded. "To revolution instead of empire."

"Christy—" He broke off. There it was again, their irreconcilable point of contention. He could forget it—briefly—in the pleasure of her company—and of sharing Christmas with her. But always it would loom up again between them.

Margaret came down the stairs, and James took the excuse to escape Christy. He needed time to think. Assured Margaret did as well as could be expected, he saw the woman into the care of Sir Oliver, who stood in conversation with Lord Farnham. St. Ives glanced in their direction and nodded, as if satisfied his wife stood in no need of him. James remained at her side, his polite smile in position but his thoughts drifting far away.

This Christmas season stood apart, unlike any in his past, unlike any he might experience in the future. No happy recollections lay behind him—but what loomed ahead? What would his Christmases—his entire future—be like, now he knew himself for a royal Stuart? The life he had known, he realized with a sense of anger, had been irrevocably taken from him.

Throughout the remainder of Christmas day, visitors continued to flow through Briarly. James kept Christy constantly in sight, though she shied away from him, avoiding any resumption of the intimacy they had shared earlier. He would win her back, he vowed, convince her she harmed no one by being in his arms, in his bed. With an effort, he wrenched his mind from the conjured image. Right now, he needed to concentrate all his attention and energy on keeping them both alive.

When at last the final guests departed, and only the house party remained, Lady Sophia regarded the scraps of food remaining on the once laden tables. She shook her head. "I believe it might be an excellent idea if we all rested before dinner."

Sir Dominic patted his wife's arm. "A period of quiet will be just the thing. Gentlemen?"

Sir Oliver nodded. "A hand or two of cards, perhaps? Brockenhurst? Saint Ives? Will you join me?"

"That's the ticket," Brockenhurst said. He beamed at the assembled company. "And you" — he hesitated "— Major?"

"Yes, thank you." James glanced toward Christy. She remained in her corner, eyes half closed. Her head must ache terribly.

As if she felt his gaze on her, she looked up, then rose. "May I watch?" she asked.

At least he wouldn't have to worry about where she was — and in what danger she might be. Relieved on that account, he followed the men into a salon, where card tables remained. Christy drew up a chair by the blazing fire and seemed comfortable enough.

Sir Dominic rang for fresh decks, and within minutes Lord Brockenhurst had set up a faro bank. James took a seat, placed his bet on red, and his gaze traveled about the assembled company. One of them wanted him dead.

And Christy had suffered because she tried to protect him.

They played through the deck, and Sir Oliver watched every turn of a card with abject concentration. Not so Sir Dominic, though. Before Brockenhurst could begin once more, the elderly gentleman rose.

"Saint Ives, a hand of piquet."

The earl agreed, and the two men excused themselves and withdrew to another table. James doubted Sir Oliver paid any heed to their departure.

"Come on, man," he urged Brockenhurst. "Turn the cards."

At the end of the second round, Farnham also excused himself. "Not enough of a challenge," he explained, with an apologetic smile. "Major, will you honor me?"

They, too, retired from the faro bank, leaving only Brockenhurst and Sir Oliver. James glanced at Christy as he took his new chair, but she remained by the fire, staring into the depths of the flames. He stifled his impulse to go to her to discover where her mind wandered. Instead, he studied the men at the other table.

Farnham dealt, then followed the direction of James's steady gaze. "Sir Oliver enjoys his game," he said after a moment.

James nodded, then dragged his attention back to his own cards. In Farnham, despite the man's free imbibing over the course of the day, he found a worthy opponent. Still, he found it difficult to concentrate on the pastime he normally enjoyed. Not when betrayal and deceit lurked in the room.

Sir Oliver was addicted to gambling. *Would* he betray James — and Sir Dominic — for money? It was a possibility they could not overlook. And then there was Brockenhurst, smiling so affably at him while he fiddled the cards. Cheating, though, did not make him a traitor to the cause — necessarily. Unless betrayal was a basic part of his nature. Nor could James forget Farnham, who even now demonstrated his cunning, and St. Ives, so bound up in politics he ignored the obvious needs of his wife.

Somewhere within the deep recesses of the house, the gong sounded, announcing time to change for dinner. James saw Christy to her room and into the surprisingly competent hands of Nancy before retiring to his own chamber and the ministrations of Wickes. An evening of merrymaking lay ahead. For once, he dreaded it.

Dinner, to his relief, proved a lively affair. Farnham had polished off a considerable amount of spiced wine and rum punch during the course of the afternoon, and was now well above par and inclined to indulge in scraps of song. In this he was aided by St. Ives, also in his cups, and while the footmen cleared the second course, the two dignified members of the House of Lords edified the company with a racy ditty culled from a musical farce. When the covers at last were cleared, the wassail bowl made its rounds, with each guest sipping from the large goblet.

"A play!" Lord Brockenhurst cried as they rose from the table *en masse.* "We must have a play. Sir Dominic, you must be Roast Beef. I have a fancy for the role of Mince Pie."

St. Ives swept an inebriated bow in the direction of James. "Gentlemen, may I present our Lord of Misrule?"

James tensed, though he accepted the honor with grace. As the party headed, somewhat unsteadily, to the drawing room, Christy caught his arm.

"What did they mean?" she whispered. "I thought they *wanted* you to be regent!"

James guided her forward. "The Lord of Misrule is the traditional master of ceremonies for the Christmas revelries."

She shivered, her distress patent in her lovely eyes. "James, that's exactly what you'll be! A Lord of Misrule, with your kingdom rioting. If you live that long. Please, you've got to listen to me. You heard Saint Ives's tone. He *doesn't* want you to be regent."

James's gaze traveled to his cousin. No, he reminded himself once again, not his cousin. The barrier of his true identity had risen between them, destroying what little fellow feeling they might ever have shared.

And what remained? Hatred? So intense, perhaps, that he would betray the cause he had been raised to uphold? Loneliness crept over him, at this sundering from the life he had known, had thought was his birthright. He had no family, no one to rely on except himself, and the odds stacked heavily against him.

Only Christy stood by him—and found herself in grave danger for her loyalty. He couldn't bear to have her at risk. Yet how could he protect her, let alone himself, when he had no idea from which direction the threat loomed?

Chapter Twenty-two

Boxing Day dawned cold and overcast, with the threat of more snow heavy in the air. It matched James's spirits. If he were the sky, he'd indulge in a rousing good blizzard.

His first impulse, to remain in his chambers, he refused to indulge. He could no longer delay the discussions of his future—and that of all England. He was no coward, but the enormity of the decisions that must be made during the next couple of days could not but weigh heavily upon him. Duty loomed over him like a two-edged sword of Damocles, and the thread by which it hung wore very thin.

Duty. He slowed as he reached the last landing. He had been raised in the certainty that one performed one's duty, however unpleasant. That belief had carried him through more than one horrific campaign. He had believed it the motto of the Holborns.

Well, he wasn't a Holborn, after all. He was a Stuart. And he was being offered an opportunity the likes of which his royal father—a man he had never known—would have given anything to possess. His duty to his name, his duty to England—he could only hope they lay along the same path, despite Christy's fears.

No one, to his relief, occupied the breakfast room. He went to the sideboard, then hesitated—and cursed himself for a cowardly fool. No one would dare poison food which might be consumed by the others. Yet he found himself unwilling to sample a single dish.

The arrival of Farnham, followed closely by St. Ives, both nursing aching heads, solved his problem. If so many of them had yet to eat, surely his enemy would not dare to act. James helped himself to a substantial meal, though he found little enjoyment in the eating of it. The other two finished long before he did.

As he at last exited the breakfast parlor, the butler approached him, bowing with a deference that should have flattered him. "Sir Dominic awaits your pleasure in the library, sir," the man said. "If you are ready?"

"Thank you." He didn't miss the formality of the invitation, nor the fact the man obviously had lain in wait for him. With a sinking sensation in the pit of his stomach, he followed the butler along the familiar route. The man opened the door for him, bowed him inside, then withdrew.

A blazing fire warmed the apartment against the chill without. Someone had drawn back the curtain over the French windows, revealing a snow-covered prospect and a leaden sky. Six chairs stood in a circle before the hearth. Sir Dominic, Lord Farnham, and Viscount Brockenhurst awaited him, and rose at once upon his entrance.

James stepped forward, with the distinct feeling he approached his execution. "Before you ask," he said, "I have as yet come to no decisions."

Sir Dominic nodded. "Sensible, very sensible, sir. Major," he corrected hastily. "Will you be seated?" He gestured to the chair nearest the fire.

In the center of the circle rested a small table, on which stood two decanters and an assortment of glasses. James declined his host's offer of madeira, and took his place. Sir Oliver and St. Ives joined them, murmuring their apologies for their tardy arrival.

Sir Dominic, his expression solemn, nodded. "As I believe we are all aware, time is running short. We may expect the regency bill to be passed at any time, and at this moment there is only one possible candidate of which the members of Parliament are aware."

"And you know where that will lead!" Farnham leaned forward, a gleam in his brown eyes.

"To an excess of execrable taste," Brockenhurst murmured.

Sir Dominic ignored the interruption. "Major, you, who have so long concerned yourself with the interests of the poor, must be aware of the disaster this could mean. The French didn't believe it could happen to them, yet the *sans-culottes* destroyed the very fabric of their society. We cannot let this happen to us."

Brockenhurst paused in the act of opening his snuffbox, and shuddered. "There is only one other alternative. Major, we must beseech you to save England."

"Playing regent will certainly give you increased scope," St. Ives drawled. "Indeed, my dear—Major, your duty must loom clear to you."

"Can one of you not think of a reason why I *shouldn't* declare myself?" James asked.

The others exchanged frowning glances. "None, Major." Farnham picked up a glass, then set it down again. "Only many reasons why you should. Your birthright—and obligation—remains with you, however much you may believe yourself in command of your decisions."

Sir Dominic tapped the head of his cane. "Indeed, once it becomes public knowledge the son of Charles Edward Stuart lives, and is a Protestant, I greatly fear the matter will be taken from your hands. It will surprise me very much if there is not an uprising among the people, a call for you to save them from Prinny's wastrel ways."

James held his host with a steady gaze. "And what if it *doesn't* become public knowledge?"

St. Ives's jaw dropped. "Do you mean—Dear Coz, would you actually deny your Stuart heritage and continue to claim the Holborn name?"

"If it meant the safety of England, yes."

Sir Dominic poured himself a glass of wine with an unsteady hand, and took a revivifying sip. "That, gentlemen, is what we must determine. In which direction lies the best interest of our

258

great country? Though I believe every one of us here, with but one exception" — he bowed toward James " — has already considered that problem."

"In short, then, you merely await my permission to approach the Lords." James's gaze traveled around the circle, resting on each serious face in turn. "Have you spoken with people on the streets? Have you *asked* anyone how they feel about Prinny's regency?"

St. Ives leaned back in his chair, swinging his quizzing glass by its riband. "Have *you* not read the scathing reports in our daily newspapers? Prinny is not popular. Another choice would be hailed as manna from heaven."

"Possibly." James rose. "If you will excuse me, gentlemen? Since you have nothing new to add, I believe what I need most is time for reflection."

Somewhat to his surprise, they allowed him to leave without protest. He closed the door behind him, then paused in the corridor, frowning. One of those men in there spoke less than the truth — in fact, violently opposed the nomination of a Stuart. *But which one?*

He repressed the urge to find Christy. He wanted a long walk outdoors, but he needed to think, not hear her familiar arguments over again. He made his way to the front hall and looked out one of the wide windows. Snow drifted down, silent and thick, wrapping the world in a blanket of white. The serenity of the stillness beckoned.

"Major!" Sir Dominic came up behind him. "Will you join us in a game of cards? I have often noted the efficacy of a logical pastime while attempting to order one's thoughts on other matters."

"Is this perchance Sir Oliver's suggestion?" James pivoted slowly, and fixed the elderly man with his penetrating gaze.

Sir Dominic faltered. "He is very partial to a hand of piquet," he admitted.

"Too partial. He loses a great deal."

"It has never been a problem for him. The Paigntons are well heeled."

"Are they?" James continued to hold his gaze. "Under the

circumstances, it might be advisable to have his finances investi-
gated."

"You cannot think—"

"Can I not? In case you have forgotten, someone in this house
has a penchant for assassination."

For a long minute, Sir Dominic stared in silence at the falling
snow. "It is a subject that has occupied my mind a great deal over
the past thirty-six hours."

"Have you told them, yet? That they are not as unanimous in
their thoughts as they suppose?"

Sir Dominic nodded. "Just now, after you left us."

"And what was their reaction?"

"Dumbfounded." The aging man shook his head, his expression bleak. "Like me, they cannot believe one of our select number could be disloyal."

"Did no one betray himself? Not even by the flicker of an
eye?" He should have been present himself when the announce-
ment was made, to better judge their reactions. "Do they understand the significance?" he pursued. "That violent opposition
exists to their plans—and within their own ranks?"

"They do, but one person does not express the sentiments of
all England. You will see how your arrival upon the political
scene is greeted."

Perhaps he could still judge reactions. James allowed his host
to escort him back to the library, where the gentlemen now sat at
various tables with decks of cards.

As they entered, Sir Oliver laughed heartily at something
Lord Farnham said. "You must not take your encumbered estates so much to heart, my boy. How else can you come about if
not by cards or dice?"

Farnham shook his head. "Your play is too rich for my blood.
Take Brockenhurst for your partner. He has the devil's own
luck."

Financial problems. More causes were betrayed for gold than
any ideological belief. Sir Oliver and Lord Farnham, both living
on insufficient income. And what of Brockenhurst? He'd never
heard if that gentleman suffered monetary difficulties. Or St.
Ives. . . . No, the earl had more than enough blunt. Personal

hatred for a lowly cousin being abruptly elevated to a station far above his own, though, might be a very different matter.

James seated himself across from Sir Dominic, and concentrated on the cards. Yet this occupation in no way assisted his thought processes, and after three hands he excused himself. Before he reached the door, Christy bounced in with her light, dancing step, enveloped in her pelisse, snow clinging to her masses of dark hair.

Lord Farnham's gaze fixed on her. "By Jove!" he murmured, his expression appreciative.

James couldn't blame him. She was a vision, with her eyes bright and her rounded face flushed with the cold.

She smiled on them all. "It's beautiful outside. Why are you all indoors?"

"Lamentable taste," James informed her.

Sir Oliver regarded her with a frown. "Are you not frozen?"

She laughed. "I have antifreeze in my veins. Besides, I couldn't resist making some snow angels. Won't any of you join me in building a fort for a snowball fight?"

Farnham's eyes gleamed. "I will," he said.

Brockenhurst rose. "As will I. This sounds a treat not to be missed."

"It seems there will be four of us, then." James turned to the other two volunteers. "Gentlemen, shall we find appropriate garments?

The remainder of the afternoon passed all too rapidly, filled with a carefree merriment unequaled in James's experience. Christy possessed deadly aim, landing her snowballs with precision, then ducking behind trees and shrubs before he could reciprocate. Brockenhurst, despite his expressed enthusiasm, quickly tired of such childish entertainment, and before long drifted back indoors, taking Farnham with him.

Christy ignored their departure, and began packing the base for a good-sized snowman. James joined her, and together they sculpted a three-tiered creation with creditable results. By the time they finished, dusk crept across the already darkened sky.

"He needs coal for eyes and a carrot for a nose. And sticks for hands." She stood back, eyeing their masterpiece. "Do you think we could find a hat and scarf for him? He looks cold."

She raised her laughing face to his, and he caught his breath. Slowly, the smile faded from her lips and she gazed at him, longing filling her expressive eyes. Lord, this was what he wanted, endless days filled with Christy's love, a small estate outside of London where he could continue his work and set up his nursery. . . .

But duty decreed his children be born of another woman. His every instinct rebelled. Christy should be his wife, not his mistress, and her children—*their* children—should be his legal heirs, not his royal bastards.

"What's wrong?" Christy touched his cheek. Her warm breath huddled in a cloud between them before dissipating.

Only by tremendous effort did he keep from gathering her into his arms. He was as confused as she, wanting her, yet foreseeing only heartache. "I'll send a footman for what we need." He forced himself to stride away, leaving her with her icy companion.

The footmen rounded up the necessary items, and all too soon—or was that not soon enough?—he returned to where Christy waited in the rapidly failing light. She at once set about making the additional improvements to their snowman, then stood back to admire the effect.

"Well?" she demanded.

In spite of his disturbed state of mind, his lips twitched. "Charming."

She drew off her drenched gloves and slid her hand around his arm. "What would you like to do next? I wish it weren't too dark to stay out here."

"I have to reach some decisions, answer some questions in my own mind." He raised her chilled hand to his lips. "You prove too great a distraction."

She returned no reply. She continued to stare at him for a long moment, then turned and led the way into the great house. They found Margaret and Lady Sophia sitting together in the Blue Salon, embroidering, and he left her, silent and solemn, with them. At least he would not have to worry about her safety while he occupied his mind with other matters.

After securing Sir Dominic's promise to keep his other guests safely within doors, James set off for a long tramp over the icy grounds. Early darkness closed about him, but the few stars peeping through the clouds bathed the paths in a faint but sufficient glow.

Here, in the tranquillity of the garden, the threat of an assassin seemed more imagined than real. A very good chance existed he had temporarily eluded his assailants, and that none lurked within Sir Dominic's inner circle. His riding accident might have been caused, as originally conjectured, by poachers. The wine might merely have been bad.

Still, he couldn't quite convince himself. He strode through the leafless remains of the rose garden, down the graveled paths between neatly pruned branches. His thoughts raced in circles, over and over, until it seemed to him they followed a rutted track. He made no progress, no sense out of this morass, out of what he should do. . . .

Before him he glimpsed a glimmer of white: the folly, where according to Christy, Brockenhurst had dallied with that maid. He headed in the other direction.

Here, a gardener had swept the stepping-stones clear of all but the most recent snow; apparently he now followed a well-trodden path. A shrubbery arch loomed ahead, trained from what appeared to be a giant, ancient hawthorn. Darkness spread out on either side, as if walls had been erected to channel a chance passerby into the leafy hold.

They *were* walls, he realized as he drew closer, living walls of branches and leaves. He stepped under the bower and found himself facing another wall, with walkways on either side. A maze. Unhesitatingly, he turned to the left and placed his hand against the scratchy surface. Maybe finding his way through this puzzle would help lead him through his own.

It must be winding him about, he decided after about fifteen minutes. He'd taken only left turns, yet still he hadn't reached the center. He came to another junction of paths and headed left again.

From somewhere all too near came the sound of footsteps crunching over the snow-covered gravel. James froze, every sense alert to danger. Someone had followed him into the maze. He glanced over his shoulder, but could see no likely shelter beyond the darkness and the unpredictability of the paths. His pursuer would be following his tracks, but would catch on to the continual left bearing in a very short time. Then he would undoubtedly quit straining his eyes and proceed with less caution.

A grim smile touched James's lips. He would backtrack, with care, and take that last right fork instead of the left, and wait. . . .

He positioned himself, crouching low, ready to spring. The footsteps approached at an uneven rate. Sometimes they faded from hearing, only to come louder as the winding passage brought the person near. Once, it sounded as if he must be directly opposite the wall beside which James waited. Then a dark shape emerged, little more than a shadow, enveloped in a dark cloak against the blacker shrubs.

James coiled his muscles and sprang, knocking the figure to the ground. He knelt over him, pinning his shoulders to the gravel, and dragged away the hood that covered his face.

Not his. Her. With a sigh half of exasperation, half of relief, he stared into Christy's terrified eyes.

"James." Her voice came out ragged, hoarse. "You scared me."

He shook his head. "You deserve to be beaten! What the devil are you doing out here? I thought Sir Dominic was keeping everyone inside."

"I just needed to see you. James, I —" She broke off.

The yearning in her expressive eyes said more than enough. He brushed the tangled curls from her face, then trailed his finger along her cheek to her lips. Their soft moistness brushed against his flesh in a kiss. The temptation proved too urgent to be ignored.

Slowly, he lowered his head, seeking her mouth. She pulled free of his hold, wrapped her arms about him, and dragged him down to her side with a desperation that sent fire shooting through him, overriding any other thought or consideration. He only knew how much he wanted her, that despite his duty, despite her coming from another time, they belonged together.

The crunch of gravel, right beside them, brought James to his feet in one swift movement. Christy scrambled after him, and he caught her hand. On the other side of the hedge, he realized. Someone else approached — and must have a fairly good idea where they were. He'd moved with amazing stealth until now. This time, he feared, an ambush wouldn't work.

Gesturing Christy to silence, he drew her along the path, away from that junction. If he could leave her where she would be safe, he might be able to lay another trap. He rounded a corner, realized they had taken several jagging turns, and knew himself to be lost within the maze. If their stalker was familiar with the key, that placed them at a severe disadvantage.

"I didn't *mean* to lead anyone to you," she whispered, and her grip tightened on his hand. After a moment, she added: "You haven't been writing anything lately, have you?"

"Why?"

"Well, if you haven't finished the section about the house party, then you should be all right. Shouldn't you?"

He drew a deep breath, and a chill crept along his skin. "I've been making notes. I'm afraid a publisher could easily polish it up after my death."

Her hand clenched on his, and a quaver sounded in her voice. "Oh, God, James, what if that bloodbath I saw in your book is averted only because you're killed?"

They reached the next intersection of paths, and a shadowy figure completely enveloped from head to toe in a dark cloak stepped in front of them. Faint light flickered off the metal tracings on the flintlock pistol he pointed. The slightest click sounded, and fire flashed from the pan as a deafening explosion filled James's ears.

Christy heaved herself against James, knocking him sideways. A cry escaped her, and she crumpled to the ground.

Chapter Twenty-three

Complete numbness gripped Christy, then pain exploded through the side of her head. The snow-covered gravel flew up to slam into her face—only she lay on it, the icy sharpness of the tiny rock digging into her hands and throat. Something heavy dragged over her legs—a boot, as someone stumbled over her.

Her senses whirled, and sound, even awareness, grew hazy, as if caught in an ebb and flow. Grunts, the sickening thud of fists beating into midriffs and jaws, the scrape of heavy shoes finding uncertain footing on loose gravel, all rose and receded as the two men struggled on top of her. She couldn't move, she couldn't help James, she couldn't even drag herself out of his way. . . . Silence closed about her like a muffling cloak of cotton wool, and she floated, weightless. . . .

The pounding of running feet burst into her world, and she lay once more on the icy ground, something sharp digging into her shoulder blade. Branches snapped as someone crashed through them, forging a new path, and she floated once more, spinning in circles, high above the landscape.

She really did rise. Her head lolled back, and with an effort she rotated it until her cheek came to rest on soft fabric, not sharp stone or snow. Strong arms held her. In the distance, men's voices shouted, the crunch of running footsteps came nearer.

James's voice murmured something unintelligible in her ear.

James. She snuggled her aching head against his bulky great-coat, knowing herself safe with him, and consciousness faded away.

The throbbing brought her back to her senses, and in vain she tried to slip once more into oblivion. It didn't work. She lay on something soft, enveloped in warmth. James—

With an effort, she opened her eyes, and blinked into the sunlight streaming through the window. A small room, familiar. . . .

"Christy?" James caught her hand in a sustaining clasp.

"You're all right," she breathed, too weak to manage more. He sat beside her bed; from his appearance, he seemed to have been there for some time.

"Lie still, dear." Mrs. Elinor Runcorn bent over her and touched her aching head. "You received no more than a scalp wound, though you bled a great deal. The major quite feared for your life, even though we assured him you were in no danger."

They had wrapped a cloth about her forehead, Christy realized. That's what felt so strange. She should be glad her wound was minor, she didn't want to subject herself to the doctors of this era. What did they do for blood loss, draw more? Yes, and with leeches or something disgusting like that. . . .

"There, I'll leave you now, dear." Mrs. Runcorn rose and went to the door. "James, don't keep her talking for long. You should try to get some rest, too, you know."

Christy's wandering mind clicked back into gear, and she struggled into a sitting position. For a moment the room spun, then it settled once more right-side up. "What happened?" she demanded.

Gently, he pressed her back down. "Our attacker escaped last night, I'm afraid."

"Last night . . ." The significance of the sunlight at last hit her. Not mere minutes had passed. She must have slept the dark hours, with James at her bedside. His haggard countenance told clearly the worry he'd endured during that time. "Go on," she managed.

He nodded, still clasping her hand between both his own.

"He'd brought only one pistol, which he intended for me. I don't think he'd expected you to be there—at least finding he'd shot the wrong one of us unsettled him. It gave me a moment before he went for a knife in his boot, so I was able to get it away from him. Then he ran. Unfortunately, I tripped, and he disappeared in the maze."

"Then we still don't know who it was."

"I'm afraid not."

Christy sighed. "Have you told the Runcorns about yourself—about being a Stuart?"

He ran his thumb over her fingers, his expression solemn. "I warned them last night, when I brought you here."

"Did they mind?"

He released her hand at last, and paced to the window. "I don't know. It changes nothing, as far as I am concerned, yet still—"

"I don't think it will with them, either," Christy assured him. "They're friends. *Real* friends."

He turned slowly to face her. "Like you?"

For a long minute she gazed into his eyes. He was so vulnerable, so very much alone. It tore at her, making her want to offer comfort, yet she knew his masculine pride would revolt at the thought he had betrayed emotional need.

A knock sounded on the door, and the Reverend Mr. Thaddeus Runcorn's balding head poked around the frame. "James, we need to talk."

"In here?" James gestured toward the chair, and himself perched on the end of Christy's bed. "I believe Christy must be included, under the circumstances."

"Terrible circumstances," Mr. Runcorn agreed. "James, you are no longer safe anywhere, you know that, don't you? Now that you know who you are, those who oppose you must have you dead as quickly as possible."

"That fact has been made abundantly clear to me. There are only the three of you I can trust, and my presence here places you all in danger. I want you to shelter Christy for me." He drew several folded sheets of paper from an inner pocket of his coat. "Take these to my solicitor, will you? This will ensure the orphanage will be taken care of, no matter what happens."

"James—"

"No," he silenced Mr. Runcorn. "I am being practical, you know that."

The elderly man nodded. "What I fear is the orphanage can no longer afford you sufficient sanctuary. It would be far too easy for someone to find a way in here."

"It's true, James." Christy leaned forward. "And there are the kids. We can't risk anything happening to them, *or* the Runcorns."

James's jaw set. "I'll leave under cover of darkness, I promise. If you'll take care of those papers for me, I won't have to emerge again for some time. Will you do that?"

"Of course, James." Mr. Runcorn clasped his hand. "Where will you go?"

"Into hiding, until I make up my mind what to do."

Mr. Runcorn's solemn gaze rested on the major's face. "You have been granted by God the opportunity to do much good for a great many people, James. There are some causes for which it is worth risking all."

James nodded, but he glanced at Christy. "I might also bring much harm to those who would support my claims. I need to know more. This is not a decision to be made lightly."

"You may have little to say to the matter." Mr. Runcorn rose. "Remember, your very existence poses a threat. Your choice may well lie between fleeing the country to live in exile, or claiming the throne. It will not be possible for you to continue as you have before."

James stood also. "I am well aware."

So was Christy—all too aware. No matter which of the two choices he made, the result would be rioting. Only his death would prevent that. The ache in her heart spread, becoming unbearable.

For a long moment, Mr. Runcorn clasped James's shoulder. "Take care. I'll arrange for your escape tonight." On that, he left the room.

"James?" Christy held out her hand to him. "What do you have in mind?"

"I am going to find out how people really feel about Prinny. I have only Sir Dominic's word for how much he is hated. For what I must decide, I cannot have any uncertainties."

"And what if you choose exile? Where would you go?"

A slight smile touched his lips, easing his expression. "My father lived in Rome. Yet I have little taste for anywhere but England."

"And what will you do with your life? Continue your writings?"

He seated himself at her side, and brushed her hair away from her bandage, a sad smile reflecting in his dark eyes. "My duty as a Stuart is to marry a princess and beget more pretenders to the British throne, which will be the fate of my son and his son after him. What a damnable life."

"What if you refuse to play that game?"

"I doubt I will live long enough to make that choice."

"James—"

He took her into his arms, and for a very long while she clung to him, seeking what comfort they could share together.

The door opened, and James released her as Nancy bustled in, bringing Christy's luggage with her. "Good morning, miss, sir." Nancy bobbed an awkward curtsy. The sight of a gentleman in Christy's bedchamber she seemed to take in her stride. "Cor, don't you look—" She broke off, then proceeded with painstaking enunciation. "I'm glad to see you was not 'urt bad, miss."

"Did our leaving like that create a stir?" Christy asked.

Nancy rolled her eyes. "Lor' bless you, miss, if'n that old roast—" Again she broke off, her expression vexed. "Yes, miss. That worried, Sir Dominic was. And their ladyships. Such a to-do, what with the gentlemen and footmen and grooms all runnin' around the garden, bumpin' into each other and findin' not a trace of you."

"Was anyone else missing?" James asked quickly.

"No, sir. All them other guests, they was runnin' about and shoutin', and askin' each other what was a-goin' on."

"Whoever did it must have slipped in among them," Christy said. "Damn, if only you'd managed to mark him in some way, we could have figured out who it was."

"Blame my slow-wittedness," James remarked, his tone dry.

Nancy started to unpack, but Christy stopped her. "Don't bother. I'm leaving this evening."

"No, you're not," James declared.

"I *am*."

"Christy—"

She shook her head. " 'Wither thou goest, I shall go.' You don't think I'm leaving you to fend for yourself, do you? *Someone* has to know what becomes of you."

"No, Christy—"

She pretended to pout. "And I thought you wanted me with you."

"I do, but it won't be safe—"

"Can't you see I'm far too weak to argue with?" She fluttered her lashes at him. "You'll just have to humor me. So don't unpack, Nancy," she added. "And make sure the major has a change of clothes ready, too."

"Will I be goin', miss?"

Christy hesitated. "No, I shouldn't think so. This is going to be dangerous, and I've deprived the Runcorns of you for too long already."

Nancy folded her arms, her expression grim. "What about Mr. Wickes? If *e's* a-goin', so am I."

" 'Whither thou goest,' " James murmured, an ironic twist to his lips. "No, Nancy. This is one time I fear I must leave him behind."

He retired to the window until the maid left, then turned back to face Christy. "Have you considered the fact it will not be easy leaving tonight?"

Christy nodded, refusing to acknowledge the tingling of fear his words caused. "Mr. Runcorn called it 'escaping.' "

"That's exactly what it will be. Until then, we must hope no direct attack will be made on this house, for their sake as well as ours."

"Like holding the fort until the cavalry gets here. Only this time, there isn't going to be any cavalry." She shivered. "I wish this didn't feel so much like the Alamo."

A slight smile eased the tense lines of his face. "One of these

271

days, my dear, I would love to discover what you are talking about."

"It's not important. So," she tried to force a note of cheerfulness into her voice, "do we make a dash for it, guns blazing?"

"I would rather make as quiet an exit as possible. If you don't mind, that is?"

"Oh, I'm all for it. I'd just like to know *how*. The minute you set foot outdoors, someone's going to take a potshot at you. You're a walking target."

"What a delightful way you have of phrasing things. We will have to create a diversion."

"Yes?" She waited with an elaborate air of expectancy.

His deep, enticing chuckle sounded. "Yes, my dear, I am beginning to have a plan. But if you can contain your curiosity for a little while longer, I believe I had best consult with Mr. Runcorn."

He left her chamber, only to return fifteen minutes later with that smugly satisfied smile that drove her up a wall.

"Well?" she demanded.

He shook his head. "You are to rest for the remainder of the day. If you really intend to leave with me, you had better be a great deal stronger."

"I will probably worry myself into a breakdown if you don't tell me what's up," she threatened.

"We are to go in disguise."

She rolled her eyes. "Oh, right. As if they won't be expecting that. No matter what we dress like, we're going to be unmistakable, you know that, don't you?"

"Why should we? We'll be lost in a crowd, after all."

"Lost in a — no, you can't mean to send the boys out with us to give us cover?"

His brow snapped down. "Of course not. I wouldn't so endanger them. Nor is there any need. What do you think the effect will be if at least twenty people come to a meeting here this night?"

"Will they?" she asked, skeptical.

"Mr. Runcorn is even now sending the boys with messages, summoning his friends. He anticipates no difficulty in smug-

272

gling two people out of his house without in any way endangering the other occupants."

"I see. Two more than came will leave. Very good. What about our things? Will we be able to take our valises?"

He nodded. "Most of the people will carry a bandbox or valise of some sort. You and I will leave separately — without luggage, I might add — and meet later."

"Where?" She didn't like the idea of letting him out of her sight at all.

"The Boar's Head. Your escort will take you somewhere else first, where he will hand you over to another of Mr. Runcorn's friends who will take you to a second inn. Eventually, we will both arrive at the same one."

Christy touched his cheek. "What if you — if you *don't* come?"

"I will." He cupped her face between his hands and gently kissed her. "How could I let anything keep me away when you're waiting for me? Now, we must stay in here for the next few hours. Piquet?"

They spent the remainder of the day in Christy's room with a deck of cards. At intervals, James paced the limited space, restless, and Christy couldn't blame him. She didn't like being cooped up, either. Yet they had little alternative at the moment. She would like being shot again a great deal less.

By evening she felt stronger, though her head still ached. When she removed the elaborate bandage, she found her skin just over her eyebrow badly torn and with a tendency to seep. A flesh-colored plastic bandage would be useful at the moment, instead of strips of cloths tied together, but that wasn't one of the options. She put on a new pad and allowed James to fasten it in place with the strips of torn muslin.

"How are we to disguise *this?*" she asked.

He pursed his lips and arranged a cluster of curls, then shook his head. "Where is your bonnet?"

He fetched it from the dresser and set it on her head. The teasing light faded from his eyes, and he regarded her with solemnity.

"Well?" she asked. She peered at the mirror. "Is it all right?"

273

"Charming."

"Then why are you frowning at me like that?"

He shook his head. "Am I? I can't think of a single reason why I should be concerned, can you?"

"None in the least," she agreed. If that could only be the truth. . . .

The sounds of arrival from below signaled the onset—or onslaught, Christy reflected—of their plans. As soon as a fair number of guests arrived, Christy and James made their way downstairs to join in the card games and general discussions taking place.

Nancy, it seemed, had gone out during the day to purchase confections and various foodstuffs with funds provided by James. Men and women, from various walks of life, graced the tiny salon and sitting room, partaking of these delicacies. They squeezed together in close proximity to allow for the others who continued to arrive.

For over an hour, Christy moved among them, spotting several women who were about her general size and build. She might be considered tiny in her own time, but here five-foot-one seemed the norm. And James—no, he had more trouble. Very few gentlemen stood nearly six feet tall. The Stuarts, it seemed, were exceptional in more ways than one.

Mr. Runcorn hailed her, and bustled to her side, dragging in tow a diminutive man barely an inch taller than herself. His clothing seemed to indicate he belonged to the lower classes, though nothing about him hinted at slovenliness.

"My dear, this is Mr. Jordan. He will be only too delighted to deliver you to the first inn."

Christy shook his hand, and Mr. Jordan flushed in acute embarrassment. "If you could be ready in fifteen minutes, miss? Our turn, it will be."

"Already?" Christy glanced about, but couldn't see James. "Where—"

"Upstairs, Miss Campbell." Mr. Runcorn gave her a confident smile. "He is changing into outer garments more suitable to this present endeavor. You, too, have been provided with a cloak which should conceal your gown."

"And our valises? I hate to sound picky, but I don't have any idea how long it'll be before we can come back."

"Your valises have left already."

"Now, that *is* efficient."

A tall man entered the room, garbed in the rough garments of a dock worker, a hat of doubtful heritage pulled low over his face. It took a moment for her to recognize James. She hurried to him and caught his hand.

"You'd best get ready," he said, smiling. "I'm leaving now."

"With whom?"

"Elsie. That tall woman."

Christy clutched his hand, then stood on tiptoe to kiss his cheek. "Be careful."

His lips brushed the top of her curls. "You, also. I will see you at the Boar's Head. Fare well."

Christy stationed herself by the sitting room window and stared out over the front porch steps. James and his Elsie, in company with two others, said their goodbyes to Mr. Runcorn in loud, uncultured voices, then trod down the snow-covered steps. In a very few minutes, the darkness swallowed their retreating figures.

Christy let out a deep breath. Now for her. She donned a bonnet and a cloak whose better days must have been pretty shabby. She wrapped it about her gown, found her obliging Mr. Jordan, and set forth into the icy coldness of the night on what would be the first leg of her journey into hiding.

At the Swan and Drake, Mr. Jordan bought her a cup of gin that could have taken the paint off a wall at thirty paces. After one whiff she set it down, not even bothering to taste it.

"No hurry," her escort assured her. "Sammy won't be along for another ten minutes or so."

Sammy, when he arrived, proved to be a great gawky fellow, with massive biceps and a broken nose, who eked out a meager income in the warehouses that lined the Thames. When he smiled, though, Christy's unease evaporated. She could actually pity anyone who tried to waylay them.

He brought with him another cloak and bonnet, and Christy changed into these. Sammy duly delivered her to the Cat and

275

Fiddle tavern in another street, where a Mr. Withern already awaited her arrival. Again, she changed outer garments. Mr. Runcorn, it appeared, had attended to every detail of James's plan to perfection.

"Where to, this time?" Christy asked as they set forth once more.

"Boar's Head," replied her new escort, the first — and last, as it turned out — words he spoke to her.

The Boar's Head. That meant James. Her heart beating rapidly with nerves, she walked quickly at his side.

They hurried through dark streets, passing others into whose business, at a shrewd guess, it would be best not to inquire too closely. She really wouldn't mind *not* putting her self-defense class to the test. At last they entered a noisy inn, rancid with foul odors and packed with people.

They hesitated in the doorway, scanning the crowd. After a minute, her companion grunted in satisfaction and led her up to a rough character in a frieze coat, with a patch over one eye. A small woman hovered at his side. The man smiled, and with a sense of shock, she recognized James.

He raised the greasy tankard he held in a toast to her. "I told you I'd be here."

With a soft cry, Christy flung herself into his arms. They wrapped about her, holding her close.

" 'Ere you go, love." The woman dragged off her cloak and bonnet and held them out to Christy.

Within a minute, they completed the exchange. Mr. Withern bowed to them and departed with the girl, leaving Christy staring at James, bemused.

"You don't look at all like yourself," she whispered.

A slight smile relieved the tension in his face. "Nor do you. Elsie has found us a room. Shall we go?"

He led her out a back door, down a maze of dark alleys, then up a flight of rickety steps and into a dilapidated building. A chill breeze whistled through the hall.

Christy shivered. "How delightful. Are you sure the local ghosts go home after Christmas Eve?"

A soft chuckle escaped him. "She assures me it will get better, still."

Christy threw him an amused look. "You have no idea how I'm looking forward to it. Lead on."

They climbed three flights to the accompaniment of crying children, two voluble arguments, and a variety of creaks and groans from the stair boards. Finally, they reached a windowless corridor lit only by one smoking, guttering candle. An uneasy quiet gripped the floor, as if a storm were about to descend with a thundering crash at any moment. Christy slipped her hand into James's.

He drew a taper from his pocket and lit it from the one near the steps. This provided sufficient illumination to keep them from tripping over the threadbare patches of what had once passed for a carpet. He unlocked the third door they reached and threw it wide.

Christy stepped inside and repressed a shudder. If possible, the temperature had dropped ten degrees. But that was probably only due to the hole in the windowpane. The snow on the floor beneath it could be mopped up readily enough.

Slowly, she turned about, her gaze touching the wooden chair with the broken leg, the uneven floorboards, and the single bed with its soiled bedspread. Home.

"Well, the surroundings might convince you to make your decision fast," she said, the only positive comment that sprang to her mind.

"You know my options as well as I."

She nodded, her heart sinking. If he remained in England, his only chance for survival lay in publicly declaring himself to be a Stuart, and a pretender to the throne. He had to gain the support—and protection—of the masses. If they didn't rally to his call, he hadn't a chance for survival.

"Hold me." She wrapped her arms about him and buried her face in his disreputable frieze coat.

He smoothed back her hair, and his lips brushed her forehead. "No more doubts, my love?"

"None. My objections before just don't matter anymore. I realized that last night." Between assassins and the possibility of her own time reclaiming her . . . She shuddered and held him tighter. "Let's just live for now. It's probably all we've got — at least together."

For a long moment, he didn't speak. Then: "God help us," he breathed, without the least trace of irreverence.

Chapter Twenty-four

Christy held aside the towel she had used to cover the hole in the glass pane and gazed out onto the filthy alley. She would have expected snow to make everything clean and pristine, lending an air of crisp beauty to any environment. Not here. Soot and a variety of filth she'd rather not contemplate tinged the white to various shades of brown and gray.

She closed her eyes. At least James was safe, if only for the moment. She could be thankful for that. And he had yet to finish the snowdome, too. That meant — she hoped — he could not be murdered, not while his signature wasn't yet in place on the wooden base. A few days, at least, must remain to them in which to share their love. She warmed at the memory of last night, of the two of them together in the too small bed, which had proved more than large enough.

She gazed at his auburn head, bent over the figurine he carved of the horse. The tiny gig with its sled runners stood on the table at his side, complete except for the shafts which would connect it to the animal. How she loved James.

But what if her own time dragged her back? How could she exist without him, centuries away from being able to protect him, possibly never knowing his fate? If he were murdered before it became known he was a Stuart, the history books would have no reason to mention either him or his death. Nor would the poor of England have any reason to riot, nor the factions divide in bloody revolution. . . .

She shivered and reached into her coat pocket for her plastic bag of chocolate chips. Empty. A shaky sigh escaped her.

James looked up from his work. "Is something wrong?"

Managing a joking grimace which she hoped hid her fears, she held the bag upside down and shook it. "I'm all out."

He chuckled. "Poor Christy. How appropriate, though."

"Why?" She crossed to the bed and tried to sit cross-legged on it. With a muttered oath at the tightness of her skirt, she curled her legs under her instead.

"It's the Third day of Christmas. Holy Innocents' Day. Also called Childermass, and known to be the unluckiest day of the year."

"Darn, I suppose that means I won't be able to find anymore." She inhaled the lingering scent from the bag.

Smiling, he shook his head. "For St. John's Day—yesterday—the old almanacs specifically say to beware of eating too much Christmas chocolate." He switched tools and warmed the new knife over the oil lamp.

She groaned and fell back on the blankets. "Maybe it's time I went home. Did you know the first chips won't be made until Nineteen Thirty-Nine?"

"You certainly know a great deal about it."

"It's a subject dear to my heart." She rose, restless, and strode about the room. Her gaze fell on the wax he held. "How much longer?"

"This is the last. The figures are not as refined as I would like, but they should do. What do you think?" He held out the horse to her.

She took it and ran a finger over the clean wax lines. Not refined, perhaps, but—Her heart gave an uncomfortable lurch. It matched her memory of the figure in the snowdome. It only needed casting in silver and enameling. She handed it back, wordless, and returned to the window.

Below, a couple of ragged children threw snowballs at each

280

other. An elderly man sat slumped in a doorway, watching them with the hopelessness of one who had nothing else for which to live. Christy turned away, unable to see such utter dejection, knowing at this moment there was nothing she could do to help the man. "Doesn't anything ever change?" she demanded.

James looked up. "In what way?"

"The poor. There's someone out there, he reminds me of the people who come to the homeless shelter where I work. Hungry, with nowhere to sleep, no one to turn to."

He lowered the delicate knife. "How can a future that offers the wonders you've spoken of still permit social injustice?"

A derisive laugh escaped her. "You think you need to crusade *here!* We need someone to wake up a few overfed congressmen in *my* time."

"Your *own* time." His solemn gaze rested on her.

Her own time. . . . Longing seeped through her, followed almost at once by a bleak emptiness. Her own time, the people she loved, a work worth doing. Everything, in fact, except her beloved James.

"There's a very good chance you'll go back." His voice sounded hollow. "You might only be here for just one reason, to help decide a turning point in history. Once it is settled—" He broke off.

"Or I might be here to stay." But was that realistic? She didn't belong here, while he did. Two worlds, two times, two separate lives.

He set the wax shafts of the gig about the horse and heated his knife once more to seal the join.

Her throat constricted. "No one has ever heard of you in my time. What if—" She broke off, unable to voice the obvious.

His lips twitched into a wry smile. "I have no intention of dying. It will not mean the end of the world, as you know it, if history undergoes a few subtle changes. It might, even, mean no poverty in *your* time, if we eliminate it in mine. Here." He held out the carved figures to her. "It's time to take them to the jeweler. I want you to be able to come to me."

281

But what if it took her away, as well . . . ?

Keeping that thought to herself, she helped him wrap the wax pieces in cloth, then accepted the purse he pressed into her hands.

"I don't like your going alone." He adjusted her bonnet to cover the bandage she still wore, then tied the ribands beneath her chin.

"I'll be all right. I told you, I've taken self-defense. And we can't run the risk of you being seen until you've come to some decisions."

He dropped a gentle kiss on her forehead. "Hurry back."

After ordering him to barricade the door after her, she eased her way down the rickety steps and emerged into the icy alley, only to stop short. All well and good, her assuring him she'd be fine. She should have asked him for a map, to get her to a main street where she could find a hackney.

James's directions, though, proved sufficient, and within twenty minutes she climbed into a closed carriage bound for a jeweler in the City, whom James had never before frequented. She sank back against the cushions and closed her eyes as they jostled through the narrow streets.

The shop, when she stepped inside a half hour later, impressed her favorably. No ostentatious displays met her gaze, only neat showcases filled with quality workmanship. And no other customers.

A thin little man with sandy hair and neat attire emerged from behind a counter and cast a shrewd glance over her, as if he assessed her potential value to him. Apparently she passed muster, for his smile broadened and he greeted her with marked warmth.

Christy brought out the wax figures. "I need these cast."

The jeweler examined each piece, and nodded to himself. With only a little haggling, he agreed to cast the pieces at once. She could return for them the following afternoon, he assured her, and escorted her to the door.

The first hackney she flagged stopped for her. She strode up to it and fixed the jarvey with a determined eye. "I want a confectioners," she said. "Someone who understands chocolate."

The man rubbed his neatly trimmed beard with a considering hand. "Well, now, miss, I thinks I knows just the place. You just climbs in and leaves the rest to me."

Christy did, and a short while later found herself in front of an elegant little shop on Jermyn Street. Within these portals she discovered an array of visual delights to please all but the most finicky of tastes. The quality, though, she feared would be another matter. Still, desperate times called for desperate measures, and at the moment she was desperate. She purchased a selection of what the proprietress assured her were the most excellent chocolates available, and stowed all but one in her reticule.

Barely waiting until she was outside, she bit into her prize and closed her eyes to savor the flavor. The texture might be coarse and grainy, the taste both bitter and sweet at the same time where the bits blended imperfectly with the sugar, but it would do. Oh, how it would do.

So much for the unluckiest day of the year.

The next jarvey she hailed seemed reluctant to carry her to the quarter of town she indicated, but she at last convinced him she did indeed wish to enter the seamier alleys of London. Muttering about the odd ways of the Quality, which she took to mean herself, he set his horse forward. She settled comfortably on the ancient seat and turned her avid attention to another of her chocolates.

In a surprisingly short time, she found herself once more before the disreputable house where they had taken lodgings. She hurried up the broken stairs and tapped on their door.

James dragged it open. "Where have you been?" he demanded, drawing her inside.

"You should have checked to see who had come. What if it had been Sir Dominic—or worse, your cousin?—instead of me?"

"I saw you from the window. What took you so long?"

Guiltily, she drew forth her purchase.

283

He stared at it for a moment, then chuckled and shook his head. He drew her close. "I should have known."

"Well, of course you should. You didn't think I could survive without it, did you?" She studied his lined face. "What's wrong?"

His chin jutted forward. "I'm going out tonight."

"Oh?" She folded her arms before her. "Where are *we* going?"

"To places I have no intention of taking you."

"Sounds like fun."

"Christy—"

"Haven't you learned *yet* you can't dictate to me? If you go, I go, and that's final. Now, where *are* we going?"

He ran his fingers through his dark auburn hair, then nodded as if coming to a decision. "All right, it might not be a bad idea to have someone to watch my back. I intend to visit a few inns and gin houses."

"Is this what the British call a 'pub crawl?' I always thought that was a very evocative term."

He turned a pained look on her. "I don't intend to drink. I want to talk to people."

"But—" She broke off.

"I have to, Christy." He placed his hands on her shoulders, his thumbs caressing her throat. "I *must* know what the people think of Prinny, about social reform."

"And revolution." She gazed into his dark eyes and read the determination in their depths. Nothing she could say would change his mind, and she wasn't fool enough to embark on useless argument.

When the early darkness shrouded London in safe anonymity, they donned their disreputable borrowed clothes and set forth for the nearest gin house. As they walked through the doorway, Christy clung to James's arm, looking about the dingy interior in a mixture of fascination and revulsion. She wouldn't want to meet any of these people in a dark alley—and the neighborhood consisted of nothing else. Men in the meanest garments, women whose dresses and lewd behavior left no

284

doubt as to their calling or inclinations, even ragged children mingled in the smoky fug of the room. She had the distinct feeling at least three different men in their vicinity had already sized up the potential worth of their wallets and planned approaches.

James ordered gin. A rough man with a cauliflower ear and broken nose started at the sound of his voice, cast an appraising eye at him, then backed away. Christy's mouth went dry. She waved away the drink James held out to her, and he smiled.

"It's not the best, but I doubt it would kill you."

"I think it would put me under the table, and one of us had better be alert."

"I think I stood in more danger at Briarly."

Christy glanced about the room, then drew closer to him. "You're sure about that?"

James cast her a considering look, then addressed a comment to the man with the cauliflower ear. He received a grunt in response. Hardly encouraging.

He tried another opening, only to be cut off by the murmur of disapproval coming from the door. The crowd separated, giving wide birth to a young clergyman who strode in with Holy zeal, Bible in hand. He claimed a stool and stood on it, addressing the assembled company with resounding voice. Some listened, most raised their own voices and continued their various conversations.

James waited for an opening, then turned once more to the man who determinedly ignored him. "Some of us try to alter the government, not the people."

The man snorted into his empty gin.

James handed him Christy's untouched glass, and for the first time since his initial assessment, the man cast him a suspicious glance.

"If the government is to be reformed to help people," James said, "we have to know what's needed."

"None of them nosy redbreasts to interfere with a man's gainful employment," his companion declared.

285

Another man standing nearby laughed, a harsh, grating sound.

"What do you think of Prince George being made regent?" James pursued.

"Won't 'ave no effect on me," the first responded, and the second man agreed.

James's hand tightened on his glass. "What if a Stuart returned to the throne instead of a German George?"

The first man guffawed. "What difference would it make to the likes of us?"

The other spat on the floor. "Me granddad died at Culloden Moor. Them Stuarts have caused enough trouble. We don't want none of them back in England."

"If someone with your interests at heart, someone who would look after your concerns—"

The man pressed his face close to James's and exhaled a gusty mixture of garlic and onion. "*I* looks after meself. Me and Bessy, 'ere." He pulled aside his heavy frieze coat to reveal the handle of a horse pistol. "Them royals can go do what they like," he said and added an obscene suggestion as to what that probably was. "Long as they don't go tryin' to makes us fight for 'em. 'Cause we won't do it."

"James." Christy tugged at his arm and gestured toward the door with her head.

After a moment he nodded, and led the way out. "They don't care." His voice sounded dull.

She leaned her cheek against him. "Why should they? They've got their own world here, and it has nothing to do with yours."

"I could change that!"

She looked up into his drawn face. "Do you really think they want you to?"

About them, out of the darkness, drunken voices rose in a Christmas carol. Other sounds emitted from darkened doorways, but James stopped Christy from investigating.

"But I saw a woman—" she protested.

"Where else is she to take a man?" he demanded.

286

Christy fell silent and kept her eyes straight ahead after that.

They visited two more gin houses and a public house, where the denizens reiterated the comments voiced by their brethren in varying degrees of profanity and hostility. In the last, the Stuart name provoked a brawl, from which James barely extricated Christy before the watch arrived.

They returned to their mean lodging in silence. Christy bolted the door behind them, and James sank onto a chair and lowered his head into his hands. She touched his shoulder, but he didn't seem to notice. After a moment, she left him to think while she prepared for bed.

By the time she returned, he hadn't moved, except now he stared out the window at the snow which had once more begun to fall. From below, voices drifted up with snatches of carols as the nightlife of London went about its varied business still in a festive spirit.

"James?" Christy caressed his arm, and repressed a shiver at the chill temperature of the room.

"Go to bed," he said, his voice hollow.

She hesitated, then did as he asked. He needed time. She fell asleep in the narrow bed, still waiting for him to join her.

Sunlight, filtering through her makeshift curtain, fell across her face and awakened her at last. She rolled onto her side and indulged in a luxurious stretch—There was too much room. She sat bolt upright, her eyes flying open. James. . . .

The room stood empty. He hadn't come to bed. . . . Dear God, when had he gone out? She threw aside the bedclothes, dragged on her gown, then stopped, having no idea where to search for him. She could only wait.

A partly stale roll served as her breakfast, along with several of the so-called chocolates she had purchased the day before. Still, James didn't return. She paced the inadequate chamber, cursing herself for a fool for falling asleep and leaving him alone. Of course he'd go out to ask more questions. He was a fighter. A Stuart.

She couldn't just stay here, doing nothing. In another minute she'd start screaming in frustration—or was that in fear? If he'd gone back to those gin houses alone, started another fight over the Stuart name. . . .

The assassins might find their job done for them.

She ran her hands through her hair, her fists clenching in the thick curls. If he'd been killed or hurt, where would he be? She didn't know enough about London at this time. She didn't even know whom she could ask —

Mr. Runcorn.

She sank down on the chair before the table James used as a desk. Grabbing a sheet of paper and one of the awkward quills, she dashed off a note to him, asking him to meet her at the Boar's Head. She splattered ink every other word, but it remained legible enough to do its job. She folded it, then went outside and found a youth willing to carry the message for her, for a promise of a shilling up front and two more when he returned with an answer.

She paced the length of the winding alley, then back again. James couldn't be dead. He hadn't finished the snowdome yet. He had to be somewhere, possibly in a hospital, possibly in some dark, evil-smelling alley, bleeding. . . .

Almost half an hour of worry passed before the boy returned with Mr. Runcorn's promise to meet her as soon as they could both get to the inn. Christy hurried along the now-familiar twisting route until she reached a street where she flagged a hackney. In a very little while, she entered the Boar's Head.

Mr. Runcorn sat in the inglenook, a mug before him, staring into the fire. An absurd desire to cry welled in her at sight of his familiar ruff of silvery hair and rosy complexion. She wended her way through the tables, bumping into chairs in her hurry.

He looked up, then rose to greet her, catching her hands as she reached his side. "James —?" His strained gaze sought hers.

"I don't know. He went out last night, while I was asleep, and he hasn't come back. I don't know how to go about finding him." She related the tale of their evening's expedition, and their disturbing gleanings of public opinion.

Mr. Runcorn's jaw tightened, but the hand he laid on her shoulder was gentle. "There is nothing you can do, my dear, and there is always a chance he may return at any time. Go back to your lodgings and wait. I will send a message to you the moment I learn anything."

Numerous arguments sprang to Christy's mind, only to be rejected. She could do little to help, and as Mr. Runcorn said, he might return to his temporary home. In the meantime, she would cling to the fact he had yet to complete the snowdome.

With that thought in mind, she went next to the jeweler in the City to pick up the newly cast figurines. They were indeed ready, and she ran her finger over the couple, arms entwined, locked forever in the skating steps of the country dance. How she would love to join James in it again. At least she would have this memory to last her through the long years, to remind her. . . .

"Are you all right, miss?" The shop's proprietor eyed her with concern.

Christy sought in her reticule for a tissue and found instead one of James's large handkerchiefs. She wiped her eyes and managed a falsely bright smile for the man. "Yes. How much do I owe you?"

She paid him, then also purchased a piece of ivory to be whittled into snowflakes for the scene. For a very small additional sum, the proprietor offered to go ahead and enamel the pieces and place them inside the glass ball filled with water as she described, and even attach the wooden base. After a moment's rapid reflection, Christy agreed. James's signature would not yet be in place. He would—he *must*—remain safe until then.

After handing over the ivory, she went out into the street. *Yesterday* was the unluckiest day, she reminded herself. Today was the Twenty-Ninth, St. Thomas of Canterbury's Day. Of course, St. Thomas hadn't been all that lucky, either.

Tears again filled her eyes, and she blinked them away, angry with herself. What did James call it, behaving like a watering pot? An apt expression. Instead of doing anything so patently useless, she had better get home. He might be there. . . .

She hailed a hackney, gave the direction, told the jarvey not to argue, and climbed in. Apparently, her distracted manner worked, for without a single remonstration they set forth through the streets.

Blindly, she stared out the window. What more could she do? She had turned the search over to immensely capable hands, she had—

A chill crept through her, numbing in its awful intensity. She had met with Mr. Runcorn, and been so upset she had done nothing to conceal or confuse her movements after that. If the clergyman had been followed, he had led James's enemies directly to her. And she even now led them to the one place James believed to be safe.

Chapter Twenty-five

Panicking, Christy swung about in her seat to lean out the window and search the faces of the people behind her. Did one of them follow her? She called to the jarvey to slow, which produced a surge of traffic passing them. No one lingered, matching his pace to hers.

She couldn't take chances. Calling to the driver once more, she ordered him to take several quick turns, which he did. She held her breath, biting her lip, scanning the passersby for anyone familiar, anyone suspicious. . . .

Her heart stopped, then resumed with a lurch. That frieze-coated figure on the chestnut, with his hat pulled so low over his face she couldn't see his features. . . .

No, he rode by them without so much as a glance at her hackney. She slumped back against the squabs, trembling with reaction. Apparently, no one followed her.

Still, she had the driver stop, and she got out of the carriage. After paying him off, she hurried to the corner, turned right, then right again. She found herself on a busy thoroughfare, and ducked into the first shop she reached.

The proprietor looked up, startled. A quick glance informed her she had entered an establishment specializing in gentlemen's hats.

"Just looking." She offered him her most engaging smile.

After a moment, the man bowed to her and returned his attention to the brim he steamed. Christy pretended to browse, all the while searching the street for signs of pursuit. No one. Still . . .

"Do you have another entrance?" she asked.

He looked up in surprise. "Yes, miss. It lets out onto naught but an alleyway, though."

"Fine. Where is it?"

His dubious gaze rested on her.

"Please. There's—there's a man—" She cast a glance out the window, then batted her lashes at the man in her best impersonation of a helpless female in distress.

Enlightenment—and anger—flashed across the man's face. "Certainly, miss. And if anyone comes in here, he'll have me to reckon with." Squaring his shoulders, he escorted her through a curtained opening into a supply room, and bowed her out the door.

She thanked him, then set off she knew not where. When she reached another large street, she flagged down a hackney and had it take her to Jermyn Street. There she changed to another vehicle, and, at last convinced no one could have kept track of her, she returned to their dingy lodgings.

She mounted the creaking stairs with dragging steps, tired both from her exertion and the strain of worry. Without James waiting for her . . . How could she face that bleak, freezing little room?

Unless, of course, he had returned.

Clinging to that hope drove her up the last flight. She ran down the hall, anxious, yet dreading to find the room empty as she most likely would. She reached the door, and her hand hesitated on the handle as she gathered her courage to face disappointment.

It turned beneath her fingers, and she jumped, heart pounding, as if it had shocked her. The door swung open.

A gruesome face towered above her. She shrank back, a strangled cry catching in her throat; then relief flooded the man's expression, and her fear evaporated.

292

"James?" She barely got out his name as he caught her in his arms. Half laughing, half crying, she clung to him. "I've been so scared! What happened?" She extricated one hand, and brushed a gentle finger over the ugly purple and red bruise that covered his left eye and cheek.

"Another brawl." He drew her inside and bolted the door once more.

"Thank heavens it wasn't worse." She released him, though with reluctance, and stepped back to view the damage. "You need an ice pack." Gently she probed the broken, swollen skin. "In my time, we call that a shiner."

"In mine, we call it having one's daylights darkened."

She giggled, mostly in relieved tension. "How appropriate. What does the other guy look like?"

His lips twitched into a rueful smile. "A lot worse."

She shook her head. "Men. Your knuckles are all bruised, too, aren't they? I'm glad I'm having the jeweler finish the snowdome. You'd never be able to paint with the enamels. Where did you spend the night?"

The lines of tension returned to his face. "In the streets. I think I was followed."

"You were—How?"

He strode to the window and drew aside the towel that covered the hole. Chill wind whipped inside, but he didn't appear to notice. For a long minute, he stared into the narrow alley.

"If I was, I seem to have lost him," he said at last. He looked back at her. "I don't know where I picked him up. Perhaps they anticipated my haunting the gin houses. It might have been sheer bad luck. Or I might have been wrong and spent a damned uncomfortable night for nothing. But it was a chance I couldn't take. I started the fight—"

"You started it?" She sank down on the edge of the bed. "Dear, gentle James?"

At her shocked tone, he smiled. "It seemed the best way to occupy the man I thought followed me. I couldn't get any information out of him—he kept denying anyone set him after me." He brushed a hand over his bruised knuckles, reminis-

293

cently. "He might have been telling the truth, but I didn't think it advisable to take him at his word. The fight gave me an excellent opportunity to give him a leveler."

"A—level, as in horizontal?" She shivered. "At least you're safe. A black eye is a reasonable exchange for your life. Why didn't you come back at once, as soon as you'd laid him out?"

"He might not have been alone. I ducked through a few alleys, then found a shelter. I'd meant only to stay for a half hour or so, but I fell asleep." He crossed to her and took her hands. "Now, what have you been about?"

"I—" Memory of her earlier fright flooded back. "Oh, James, I nearly ruined everything! I was so worried, I sent for Mr. Runcorn."

"The devil you did. He came here?"

"No, the Boar's Head. I had that much sense, at least. But not much more. I wasn't careful when I left. It's all right," she hurried on as his jaw tensed. "When I left the jeweler's, I realized how stupid I'd been, and I went to the most ridiculous lengths to shake pursuit. I don't think anyone followed me, though. But we'll have to let the Runcorns know you're all right."

With that, he agreed. He strode to the table, and for the first time she noted the papers scattered across the surface. He had been working on his book. . . .

Quickly he scribbled a note to his friend, then Christy carried it down to the alley where she found another boy more than willing to run the errand. When she returned to the room, James once more sat at the table, writing. She waited until he paused, then interrupted him.

"Have you come to any decisions?" she asked.

Slowly, he swiveled his gaze to rest on her, his expression closed. "I don't want to inflict internal war on this country when Napoleon remains a threat. But I have only your word, *your* version of history, to indicate I might cause a revolution. That could alter. The world you know could change—and for the better. There is every reason to believe it could all be done peacefully."

294

She drew a shaky breath. "Then why did I come back through time, if not to influence your decision?"

He regarded her, all sparkle gone from his dark eyes. "To torment me."

She hugged herself. "The people don't seem to care who rules."

"I could make life better for them! They *do* care about that."

"So maybe you *do* bring about social equality." Christy stood and paced to the broken window. "Maybe it's the rich who riot in the streets, demanding back their privileged status."

He waved that aside. "I would take nothing from anyone, only make it fashionable to provide for the lower classes, see to their comfort and education."

"You'd be the first person in recorded history to manage it."

"Maybe I am." He held her gaze for several seconds, then returned his attention to his book.

She watched him in silence until she couldn't stand it a moment longer. She *had* to know if he recorded one of the versions she had read, or a different one entirely. History, as she knew it, might very well hang on the end of his pen.

Silently she moved up behind him and read over his shoulder. The house party. She released the breath she held in a ragged sigh. The government officials out to further their own ends during the Christmas season.

And what did they do now? Search for their recalcitrant pretender to the throne? Accuse one another of attempting to assassinate him? She would dearly love to see into what confusion she and James had thrown them by running away like that. Almost, she could pity Sir Dominic. The elderly man had devoted the greater portion of his life to the Stuart cause. Too bad he hadn't been more careful in his choice of confederates.

James's quill scratched on, his fingers clutching it with an awkward determination. His swollen and bloodied knuckles didn't stop him from continuing his work. Christy curled into a corner with a copy of *The Castle of Otranto,* which someone—probably the considerate Mrs. Runcorn—had slipped into her valise.

James still worked when hunger at last drove Christy to a nearby inn. She brought back a couple of meat pies, the ingredients of which she made a point of not inquiring about. James grunted his acknowledgment, absently took a bite, and went on with his writing.

He worked with a feverish intensity that defied interruption. At this rate, he would be finished very soon, probably before New Year's Eve, only two days away.

New Year's Eve. . . .

Christy swallowed, but it didn't relieve the sudden dryness of her throat. New Year's Eve. What more appropriate time for her return to her own world, if that was to be her fate? The snowdome would be finished, James's book would be complete . . . and for good or ill, his decision would probably be made. Unless someone killed him in the next couple of days.

She watched him in silence, her heart aching. She could burn the book, then he'd have to live long enough to write another. Or would he die anyway, and history merely change, his book disappear? Then it wouldn't exist in her own time, with its shifting type and terrifying versions. She would never hear of him, never try to learn more about him, never come back through time, never know him or experience his love.

She wouldn't exchange so much as one moment with him to remove all the suffering she would know if he died.

At last, the late hour and the guttering candles forced James to lay down his pen. He joined her in the narrow bed, and for a little while Christy lost herself in the wonders of his love. For this hour and more, time—that terrible barrier—ceased to hold any meaning.

Finally, as his breathing slowed and deepened into sleep, she clung to him, and her fears rushed back like a wave returning to the shore. Possibly only one more full day remained to them, one day in which to ensure the safety of England, in which to experience a lifetime of love. Then he might be killed. Or she might be dragged back to her own time, and nearly two

296

hundred years might separate them forever.

She must have drifted off to sleep at last, for she awoke to the feel of his arms about her. She snuggled close, burying her face in the curling hair of his chest, and tried to memorize the smells that were so uniquely him. "Is it morning?" she murmured, praying it was not.

"Almost. I didn't mean to wake you."

"Fine with me." That meant a few more minutes to share with him, a few more memories to treasure. . . .

No, she wouldn't go maudlin and spoil what little time they might have left. "I suppose today is another saint's day?" she asked, hitting on what seemed to be a nondepressing topic.

"As a matter of fact, it isn't." His lips brushed her hair. "Yesterday was devoted to wassailing, and today is devoted to seeking cures for excesses."

She nodded in approval, and her cheek rubbed against his chest. "Sounds good to me."

"Are you never serious?" A touch of amusement crept into his voice, then faded at once. "Dear God, Christy, how am I to face the future without you?"

She froze, then tilted her head back to stare up into his face, still shrouded in the darkness of early morning. "You sound as if you knew, for certain . . ."

"Not for certain, but don't you feel it, too? Everything—at least your part—is drawing to a close. My dear love, I'd give anything to keep you with me."

"I'm staying. If there's any possible way—"

"The choice may not be yours." He caressed her arm. "I deposited a considerable sum for you with the Bank of England yesterday morning, before I came back here. They were rather uncertain about the complicated arrangements I made, but I fixed it so you can collect it in your own time. With the accumulated interest, you will be extremely wealthy."

She tried to swallow the constriction in her throat, but it had too firm a hold. "James—"

He kissed her forehead, then her eyes. "My book is finished."

"Is it?" She struggled up in the bed and reached for her coat where it lay at the foot. She shivered as the icy air caressed her bare skin, and she dragged the chill nylon of the coat over them as she searched the pocket. From it, she drew forth the printed copy of *Life in London*.

"Well?" He took it from her and flipped to the last section, which had been blank when she showed it to him before. Now, blurring words appeared on each of the pages.

"You still haven't made your decision," she said. "It can all be changed."

He studied the lines with care. "I can't make out the words with any clarity. I think there are more than just two versions here, though."

"Which means—"

"We've discussed it as a possibility, and this may confirm it. Perhaps that is why you came back to me. To set my regency on the proper path. Your warning to me just might prevent the revolution which the Stuart name otherwise might have started."

She blinked. "You mean—we really *are* changing history, and for the *better*? Eliminating poverty here, so in my time—" The possibilities staggered her. A world, in her own time, where no social injustice would be tolerated, perhaps where the environment hadn't been trashed and polluted. Dear God, what a Christmas present that would be for the whole planet.

And perhaps she could stay with James. She could tell him about the problems of the future, and he could demand legislation from Parliament that would control industrialization and encourage conservation. Everything would be all right, they could remain together. . . . A hope she hardly dared acknowledge dawned in her.

They breakfasted in a different inn, to avoid any possible pursuit. James spoke little, concentrating instead on his plate and tankard. Christy refrained from conversation, knowing too many matters still lay unsettled, uncertain. Being with him, being able to see him, was enough. Neither of them, she noted, seemed eager to bring the meal to a close.

At last, James stood. "To the jeweler's?"

"Are you coming with me?" She hesitated. "Are you sure you should?"

"I cannot remain in hiding forever. No," he held up his hand, stopping her from speaking. "I've done with this slinking about, skulking in dark alleys. I wish to consult with Mr. Runcorn, and I will do so at his home, in the light of day."

One glance at his determined, bruised face warned her argument would be to no avail. With a muttered comment about pigheaded obstinacy, which he appeared to ignore, she wended her way through the tables and out into the overcast day.

A hackney set them down before the jeweler's in the City, and Christy, nerves on edge, led the way inside. No dangerous figures awaited them; apparently, she had not been followed the day before. She let out a shaky breath and approached the proprietor.

He beamed at her. "Miss Campbell. I have it ready for you." He disappeared into his back room, only to emerge a minute later holding the finished snowdome before him.

A sense of helplessness settled over her, as if her threads of control slipped away, leaving her unable to struggle against the flow of events. She reached out, her hand trembling, and for one frightening moment time swirled about her. Her heart jerked painfully, and the room settled once more.

James took the ball from the jeweler and weighed it consideringly in his hands. "What do you think?" he asked Christy.

"It—it's exactly as I re—" She broke off. "It's everything I imagined it would be." Her gaze rested on it in a mixture of longing and loathing. It brought her back to James, and the conviction grew in her it would take her from him, as well.

James cast her a sharp glance. "It's missing only one thing." He turned to the jeweler. "Do you have a pen?"

"No!" Christy breathed.

James ignored her. The jeweler handed him a quill and an ink stand, and James signed the bottom with a flourish, adding the date.

The jeweler smiled. "Only two more days of the year. We

299

have it finished just in time."

"You have done an excellent job." James paid him, above the agreed-upon price, then took Christy's arm and led her toward the door.

"*Two* more days." Christy's fingers tightened on his arm, stopping him. "Couldn't you have waited to sign it until midnight, tomorrow night?"

James shook his head. "What if something *does* still happen to me? I couldn't take any chances on never having known you." He held the ball out to her.

"No!" She drew back. "I don't want to touch it."

"We don't know you'll be taken from me," he said softly.

"I keep hoping, but—no, I don't want to risk it. Just seeing it—" She shook her head. "It *will* take me home. James—"

"I thought that was what you wanted, to be with your family, the people you love."

"I love *you!*"

"And the choice between times is tearing you apart." He gazed at her for a long moment. Abruptly, he stepped outside.

Christy followed, and ran into his back as he stopped short. She looked around his shoulder, and caught her breath on a cry of alarm.

The elegant, dapper figure of Sir Dominic stood directly in their path. He inclined his head toward Christy. "Thank you for leading me to the shop, my dear. I knew it would be only a matter of time before you came back. Sir." He awarded James a bow of deference. "I believe we have much still to decide."

"Such as whether I am to become regent, or be forced into exile like my father—or be killed?"

"At the moment, I believe the most important decision concerns your safety. You would not seem to have fared well since I saw you last." His frowning gaze rested on James's bruised face. "I believe it will be best if I accompany you while you collect your valises, and escort you back to Briarly."

"If you think—" James broke off.

Three men, who had been standing a short distance away, came to stand at Sir Dominic's back. One glance at their grim expressions proved sufficient to warn Christy of the danger of refusing. She slid her hand into James's.

"This is an invitation, of course." An apologetic smile just touched Sir Dominic's lips. "I cannot permit you to come to further harm. You must see that."

"And how do you hope to ensure that? With the assistance of your friends here?"

Sir Dominic shook his head. "My other guests have all left my home. You—and Miss Campbell, of course—will be quite safe."

"Christy?" James raised a questioning eyebrow.

She hesitated. "I suppose you *will* be safer there. And how can we refuse such a gracious invitation?"

Sir Dominic's smile slipped awry. "Believe me, my dear, it pains me to be reduced to such measures. If you will enter my carriage?" He gestured toward the street, and a town coach drew up before them.

One of Sir Dominic's henchmen stepped forward and opened the door. James bowed Christy inside, then followed. Sir Dominic took the forward seat.

"What, are your watchdogs not accompanying us?" James regarded their host with a set smile.

Sir Dominic shook his head. "There is no need. They will follow in another carriage. Where shall I tell my driver to take us?"

"Golden Lane."

Sir Dominic's eyebrows rose. "Do you mean you have remained in hiding at the orphanage? Remarkable."

"We have not. I wish to assure the good reverend of my safety. Under the circumstances, I do not believe a message would prove sufficient."

Sir Dominic smiled. "Perhaps not." He called his orders to the driver, then leaned back once more.

Christy clenched her hands in her lap. This whole setup bothered her, but she supposed Sir Dominic was right. James would be safer at Briarly now that none of the other guests remained. They would certainly be more comfortable, too.

They'd escape the everlasting cold of that room and feel warm once more. Still, she'd be sorry to leave it; it was the nearest thing to being an idyll she would ever share with James.

St. Luke's Parish hadn't changed much in the few days they'd been absent. The snow might be a bit thicker—and dirtier—but in this desperately poor quarter of London, few candles or laurel wreaths decorated the windows and doors to mark the joyous season.

They turned off Golden Lane, and the carriage pulled up before the orphanage. James jumped down at once and extended his hand to help her. Sir Dominic descended more slowly.

Nancy opened the door to them, and so far forgot herself as to embrace Christy. "That worried, we've been, miss. And Major." She clasped his hand and sniffed. "There, I'm forgetting me trainin', and won't Wickes be fit to bust his buttons."

"Mr. Wickes?" Christy asked, smiling.

Nancy nodded, her smile coy as faint color crept into her cheeks. "Down in the kitchens, 'e is, fixin' things up."

"Wickes? Here?" James looked from Nancy to Christy. "I'll be devilish glad to see him myself."

"I'll just go tell 'im you're 'ere, and 'e'll fix you up somethin' for your face, 'e will. I—" She broke off as Sir Dominic left his coachman and came up the steps. "Sir." She bobbed him a curtsy, but her gaze, rife with suspicion, rested on him.

"It's all right, Nancy." James gestured for her to go. She cast him a dubious look, and hurried off.

Soft, hurrying steps sounded on the stairs, and Elinor Runcorn appeared, leaning over the banister to catch a glimpse of the hall. "It *is* you!" she exclaimed, and ran down the remaining flight. "You're safe!" She embraced Christy, then turned to James. "I—" She broke off, staring at his bruised face in horror.

"A slight difference of opinion, that is all," he assured her. "This is Sir Dominic Kaye."

Mrs. Runcorn stiffened, and acknowledged the introduction with reserve. "Will you not come into the sitting room?

My husband will be here at any moment, I make no doubt." She escorted them into the front apartment.

James followed her. "Nancy tells me Wickes is here, and has gone to fetch him."

"Yes, he has spent a great deal of time with us over the last couple of days. We are very grateful to you, James, for sending him."

James's eyebrows rose a fraction. "Did I?" he murmured, and cast Christy an amused glance. Aloud, he said: "He likes to make himself useful. I have long felt you stood in need of a manservant."

"Indeed, sir." Wickes's chilled tones sounded from the doorway. James turned, and a shudder passed over the valet's normally imperturbable expression. "If you will be seated, sir?"

"I am pleased to see you have carried out my instructions so well." James settled in the large chair before the blazing hearth.

Wickes didn't bat an eye. "I endeavor to give satisfaction, sir."

"Yes, your presence here has made it quite unnecessary for me to worry about the Runcorns," James went on, smoothly.

"Indeed, sir."

Christy bit back her smile. Under that polished exterior, she would swear the ever so proper gentleman's gentleman actually blushed in embarrassment at having been caught out in his subterfuge. At least he had made good use of the time gained by those tactics. Nancy's manners and speech showed the influence of his presence and teaching.

Wickes probed the inflamed skin and muttered to himself, and Christy settled on the sofa opposite James to watch. Sir Dominic took a chair near the fire, and laid his cane on the floor at his side.

"Wickes is the greatest treasure." Elinor Runcorn seated herself beside Christy and spoke softly. "He has taken over so many of the organizational tasks from dear Thaddeus, and he is a positive genius with the boys. I don't know how we shall get on without him, now."

Christy glanced at the valet. He should stay at the orphanage, where he could do so much good, but he would never willingly leave James. And if James were forced into exile, Nancy, too, would find herself torn between conflicting loyalties. What an awful mess it would be for all of them.

Mr. Runcorn pushed wide the door of the sitting room. "Nancy says—" he began, then broke off as James turned in his chair to face him. For a long moment, the clergyman stood in silence, staring at his old friend. "Have just your questions triggered violence?" he asked at last.

"Upon occasion," James admitted, not elaborating.

Mr. Runcorn nodded, his expression sad. "I, too, have spoken with a number of people. I have discovered a general anger among them toward our prince and his people, but also an indifference toward doing anything about it. You see, James, the poor might not like things the way they are, but they have had no influence for so long, they are willing to accept what fate throws at them with nothing more violent than grumblings."

Sir Dominic waved that aside. "It is because they have no hope. Once the major is regent, all of England will rally to his call."

Christy cast a worried glance at James. His expression remained blank, unreadable. What went on in his mind?

James winced at something his man smeared near his eye. "Do you not fear that if I step forward to claim the throne, the country will be divided with hotheaded factions out for blood on either side?"

"Only if you claimed it directly. By being declared regent first, you will be eased into the position. The people will be prepared."

Christy swallowed. That made sense. Perhaps history really could be changed, and in a variety of different directions. James might be able to make a better England, a better world, eliminate poverty. . . .

A violent banging on the front door interrupted her thoughts. Nancy's footsteps ran along the hall to answer the furious summons, and the creaking hinges barely preceded a man's frantic voice demanding to be shown to Mr. Runcorn upon the instant.

James stiffened. "Saint Ives," he said, and met Christy's dismayed gaze.

The sitting-room door burst open, and that exquisite dandy paused on the threshold, hat askew, greatcoat imperfectly buttoned. His gaze fastened on James, and he took an unsteady step forward. "There you are!" he breathed. "Thank God!"

James's lip twitched. "I am, of course, delighted to see you as well, Cousin."

"And Sir Dominic." The earl dragged his beaver from his sandy brown hair and cast it on a table. "What the devil did you mean, James, by disappearing from Briarly like that?"

"Since one of my fellow houseguests appeared intent on killing me, it seemed the safest course of action."

"Safe for you, perhaps. Good God, man, had you no thought for others? That you could so heartlessly endanger the life of an innocent woman—"

"I kept Christy safe," James snapped.

"Not her." The earl ran an unsteady hand through his disordered locks.

"Whom, then? I endangered no one"—his gaze strayed to Christy "—at least, no one who was not willing."

"And what of my wife, and the child she carries?"

"Margaret?" James's brow furrowed. "Explain yourself."

From his inner coat pocket, St. Ives dragged a folded piece of paper and held it out with a trembling hand. "This. She found it a little while ago in her evening reticule—the one she carried last night. It never left her wrist, and both she and her woman swear the note wasn't there when she left our house."

James took it, and his scowl deepened as he scanned the sheet. He crumpled it, and for a very long minute he stared in thunderous anger at the fire.

"James?" Christy ventured at last.

He looked up. "Hell and the devil confound it." He spoke so

305

softly she could barely hear, but murder lurked in the depths of his voice.

"What—?" She reached out, just touching his hand.

"It says Margaret could have been abducted last night, instead of this message being given to her. And she will be—and killed—if I do not present myself at a certain warehouse on the docks alone at noon, New Year's Eve. Tomorrow."

Chapter Twenty-six

White-faced, St. Ives regarded James, his habitual sneer replaced by an expression of pleading. Fear—real fear for the safety of his wife and unborn child—lurked in his blue eyes.

James raised his angry gaze to Sir Dominic's stricken face. "Is this the fate of the Stuarts?" he demanded. "By God, it would have been Christy, not Margaret, if she hadn't gone into hiding with me. Is this what I can expect? Those I love threatened?" He shook his head, and an icy note crept into his voice. "I'll not have it."

"Then you will keep this meeting?" St. Ives leaned forward, intent, as if desperate to see the confirmation in the major's face.

"You cannot!" Sir Dominic exclaimed.

Christy sank on the floor at his side, anguish welling up within her until it could not be contained. "James, you can't. Please."

"It would be to walk into a trap," Mr. Runcorn agreed.

"Am I to let Margaret be killed? And who would they take next? Elinor?" He glanced toward Mrs. Runcorn, and his anger glinted in his eyes. "No, I've done with this. The matter must be settled, and now."

Christy's fingers tightened on his arm. "You can't just let them murder you."

"Murder me?" A slight smile just touched his lips. "No, that would not be my first choice. I have something else in mind."

"You'll renounce any claims to the throne?" Christy sat back on her heels, hoping, watching the intensity of his expression.

"That would solve nothing. I remain who I am. My only option is to come forward, this minute, and force Parliament to acknowledge me. Then you will all be placed under protection, until their decision is made."

Christy swallowed. "And what if they refuse you? For the rest of your life, you'll be a threat to the regime."

A muscle in his cheek twitched. "Then I go into exile, like my father before me."

"You would give up all for which you have worked?" St. Ives demanded.

"Not in the least. I would continue my writings, my demands for social reform. But my position would be better, far better." He leaned forward, his dark eyes flashing. "The government would be forced to make concessions to me, to prevent me from following in the bloody footsteps of my father. Whether I am made regent or not, the people of this country will benefit."

Christy caught his hands. "There's a good chance people will be killed. You've seen the effect of the Stuart name."

"I have, but my options are somewhat limited. I appear to have the choice between claiming my heritage or allowing myself to be murdered." He rose. "It seems my decision is made, Sir Dominic. What now?"

The elderly man picked up his cane and came to his feet. "We will collect your things and return to Briarly. First, though, with your permission, I will send messages to various members of Parliament to attend us there this afternoon. By this evening, I promise you, England will know a Stuart has come forward to claim the regency he so rightly deserves."

St. Ives's fingers whitened on the back of the chair. "And what of my wife?"

"Give Margaret my love," James said, "and my apologies for the fright she has undergone. Keep her safe for tonight. By tomorrow morning, our villain will know how I have responded to his threats."

"Thank you." The earl grasped his hand, and a shadow of his former sneer returned to play about his mouth. "Fare you well – Sire." With a bow directed at the assembled company, he took his leave.

Christy shivered as the door closed behind him. "And what if that was all an act, and *he* was your enemy?"

"Then undoubtedly there will be an attempt on my life some time within the next couple of hours."

Christy swallowed. "Let's get out of here before he comes up with any bright ideas."

Wickes cleared his throat. "Sir, will you be wanting your rooms in Clarges Street vacated?"

"It will be best," Sir Dominic said. "My home is entirely at your disposal until more suitable arrangements can be made."

James inclined his head. "Well, Wickes, do you come with me or stay here with the Runcorns?"

The valet stiffened, his expression pained. "If I have failed to give you satisfaction –"

"Get off your high horse, man. If I am not offered the regency – which is more than likely – I will be forced into exile. To live among foreigners, whom I know perfectly well you despise."

"Doubtless, sir, the services of a superior gentleman's gentleman will be invaluable to you in that case."

James gave a short laugh. "Are you quite certain you wouldn't rather remain here? The Runcorns would welcome you as their man of affairs."

A long moment passed before the man answered. "It would not be right to leave you, sir."

Yet he was torn. Christy could see it in his not-quite impassive expression. "And what of Nancy?" she asked.

Wickes made a show of gathering the medicines he had brought into the room. "I could hardly bring myself to answer for that young person, miss."

"And leave miss to the likes of you?" Nancy pushed her way into the room, her color heightened. Obviously, she had been eavesdropping. Her gaze rested for a challenging moment on Wickes, then moved on to Mrs. Runcorn. "Lor', missus, I 'ates to leave you and the reverend, but—"

Elinor Runcorn nodded. "Their need for you is undoubtedly greater than ours. Go, now, and collect their things. The major will not be safe until he is within the walls of Briarly."

James nodded. "Let us return to the lodging to collect my book. Thaddeus," he turned to Mr. Runcorn. "I believe I will be somewhat occupied over the next several days. Will you see to the publication, for me?" He cast a humorous glance at Christy, "There should be no difficulty about it."

"Of course, James. Is there anything else?"

"No, I will contact you as soon as matters are settled." He grasped the man's hand. "Take care."

Once more, they entered Sir Dominic's town carriage. James gave the coachman the disreputable direction of their lodging, and they set forth. James had made his decision. Christy inched closer to him and clung to his hand, trying to block from her mind her fears for the consequences to her own time. If it came to a choice between his life, though, and preserving history as she knew it to have occurred, she willingly would sacrifice the future to keep him safe here and now.

They drew up in the familiar alley and climbed down. James tucked the snowdome securely in his arm and started up the rickety stairs. For a long moment, Sir Dominic looked about, his expression appalled, then with obvious reluctance he followed them up to their dingy corridor.

James inserted the key in the lock, but the door swung inward without his turning it. Christy caught her breath as it creaked wide, revealing the squalid furnishings, their few possessions—and the raven-haired gentleman seated directly before them on the room's rickety chair. A flintlock and one of a pair of dueling pistols lay crossed in his lap, the other he held in his hand, pointed directly at James's heart.

Christy froze. If they tried to escape, James would be shot. At that range, the man couldn't miss. . . .

James straightened his shoulders and stepped into the room. "Good morning, Farnham."

"Major Stuart." Farnham awarded him a mocking bow without rising. "Ah, Miss Campbell, not so close, if you do not mind?" He gestured her away from James. "And Sir Dominic. I see you, also, have located our friend. I must commend you on your methods. The major appears to be a master at hiding himself."

"Not quite good enough, it seems." James set the snowdome on the table. "You must forgive me if I do not offer you refreshment. The amenities of this establishment are few. Now, what may I do for you?"

Farnham's mouth thinned. "You will oblige me by *not* becoming regent."

James inclined his head. "Exile is an acceptable alternative. I will still be able to do much good."

"I fear that cannot be permitted." Farnham gathered the two pistols in his left hand and rose. The third never wavered. "I cannot risk letting the Stuart heir escape me again. Until now, you have proved singularly difficult to kill."

"*Why?*" Sir Dominic demanded, his tone bewildered. "Farnham, *you*, of all men . . ."

"You see, whether he wishes it or not, by birth he is a pretender to the throne, and so he will remain as long as he lives. You and your fellow Jacobites have worked far too long and hard, hiding him, educating him, preparing him for this moment. You will never permit him to retire into obscurity. You will drag us once more into civil war."

"But you are one of us!" Sir Dominic took an uncertain step toward him.

Farnham backed up until he leaned against the door, then gestured for the elderly man to join James and Christy on the opposite side of the narrow room. "It shouldn't be that diffi-

311

cult for you to understand. My grandfather died at Culloden, fighting for his Stuart prince, and my father died preventing an assassination attempt against him after his exile. My family has sacrificed enough."

He straightened, and the light of pure hatred flickered in his eyes. "There will be no more Stuarts to wreak havoc on England." Slowly, deliberately, he raised the pistol to James's head.

With an anguished cry, Christy lunged forward, pulling up her skirt. She spun about, and delivered a perfect self-defense class version of a karate snap kick to Farnham's midriff. An explosion of smoke and noise erupted from the pistol as Sir Dominic threw himself against James. As the two men fell on the bed, the ball grazed Sir Dominic, then shattered what remained of the window. Acrid smoke filled the air, gagging Christy.

With a sweep of his arm, Farnham hit Christy in the throat and swept her aside. She staggered and caught her balance, only to find herself staring at the other dueling pistol. He clutched the flintlock in his left hand.

"Back against the wall." His voice rasped in his throat.

Christy glanced behind her. Sir Dominic had fallen to his knees, clutching his lower arm. Blood seeped through his fingers. James drew himself up slowly to stand tense, hunched up. Christy started toward him, but with the slightest shake of his head, he turned her aside.

Farnham's gaze never wavered. He advanced one step toward them, and Christy shrank back. "I believe we will do better without you, Miss Campbell." He swiveled the barrel until it pointed once more directly at her. "I am truly sorry, my dear, your company is quite charming, but we must all make sacrifices for the good of England." With slow deliberation, he drew back the hammer.

In a fluid movement, James released the knife he had drawn from his boot. With a strangled cry, Farnham fell backward to the floor. After a moment, his left hand crept to just below his right collarbone and pulled the knife free.

He collapsed, eyes closed, and lay there unmoving.

Sir Dominic let out a ragged sigh. "It is over, then."

"Is it?" Christy clutched the bedpost for support.

James dragged his gaze from Farnham and looked at the elderly man. "How badly are you hurt?" He helped Sir Dominic off with his blood-soaked coat. Tearing back the sleeve of the fine lawn shirt, he exposed a nasty gash. "Christy, have we something to make a bandage? Just to hold you over," he added to Sir Dominic. "You'll need a doctor."

Sir Dominic made no protest. He sank onto the chair, his face white and drawn.

Christy found a couple of rumpled neckcloths and handed them over. James appeared competent—probably from vast experience with his regiment—so she left him to deal with Sir Dominic's gaping wound.

Was it over? She looked from one to the other of them: Sir Dominic, so pale and drawn; James, so tense; and Farnham, who appeared to have lost consciousness. One of them had better tend him, as well, unless they wanted him to bleed to death. Shaky, cringing at the prospect of so much blood, she found another of James's rumpled neckcloths.

"I'll take care of him." James left Sir Dominic to lie on the narrow bed. "Shoulders are the merry devil, to bind."

Christy nodded, relieved, and turned away. It really was over. They had found their assassin, James had made his decision—but where would it lead? From her pocket, she drew the small leather-bound volume of *Life in London*.

The last forty pages blurred and scrambled, though in slow motion. She gripped the book, scanning the fragmenting contents. The tale of bloodshed stood out clearly, faded momentarily into the account of the house party, then shifted back to the horrors of revolution. Both versions readable, with no other alternates. Two possibilities only. But which. . . .

For several seconds, the deadly version remained in heart-wrenching clarity before it blurred once more. It returned all too soon, and stayed this time for nearly five seconds before the shifting began again. The next time, it remained for ten.

"James—" The agonized cry broke from her.

"What?" He looked up quickly from where he worked over Farnham's inert form. He dropped the shirt with which he'd been about to bind the man's arm.

"Look at this." Trembling, she held the book out to him.

James took it from her, then swore long and fluently. "It's taking form. I'm causing a revolution. My blood is cursed. If this"—he waved the volume before Christy—"if this is what it means to be a pretender to a throne, I'll have none of it."

"Sir—" Sir Dominic dragged himself onto his elbow.

"My few supporters in constant danger?" He spun to face the elderly man. "Is that what you want?"

Sir Dominic tried to stand, but fell back, too weak. "You owe it to England," he gasped.

"What do I owe? Bloodshed? Revolution? More bitter memories of hopeless causes like my father brought? I'd be a Lord of Misrule, in reality. There will always be those who will fight the Stuart name. I'll not sacrifice the lives of those I love—nor will I sacrifice the *country* I love—to such carnage."

Christy leaned against the table and stared into the snowdome. To her, those sentiments made James a truer ruler to his people than any crown he might wear.

James straightened, his eyes blazing. "I'll choose a powerful pen over an impotent—and explosive—crown any day."

Christy shivered. "But what if you can't—"

Movement, glimpsed out of the corner of her eye, focused her attention on Farnham. He half sprawled, half sat on the floor, the deadly gleam in his eyes directed at James. In his good hand he held the major's blood-tinged knife. He drew it back, taking careful aim.

Christy screamed, and grasped the first object she encountered and heaved it at him.

She reeled, dizzy, as the snowdome hurtled through the air, its ivory flakes swirling. . . . The room swirled, as if she spun, not the ball. . . .

James clutched his chest, falling, and blood welled between

314

his fingers. Only she saw it from a great distance. Farnham caught the snowdome in a reflex action, clutching it to him as he collapsed once more, his energy spent. The world spun, blurred, receding from Christy's vision.

"James!" she screamed, but the sound echoed, hollow in the complete silence that engulfed her. She'd inverted the snowdome. . . .

She reached for him, but he was no longer there. A chill wind whipped about her, and she fell. . . .

Christy knelt on her hands and knees in snow. She shivered with a cold that surpassed the merely physical. So very cold. . . .

She sat back, trembling, and gazed about her. Several children skated on a frozen pond. She blinked. They wore jeans and sweatshirts, or down jackets like hers. The flakes fell thick and fast, covering the street and the cars parked by the curb. Somewhere, from a building behind her, a radio blared an acid rock version of a Christmas carol. Her own time, back in the park where she started.

Her gaze dropped to the ground before her, where shattered shards of glass protruded from the snow. With a hand that shook, she picked up the wooden base and turned it over. James's signature. . . .

Anguish washed through her. With a trembling hand, she picked up the enameled figurine of the horse which had lain beneath it. The others . . .

Desperate, she brushed the flakes aside, collecting the fragments of glass. She uncovered first the gig, then the renditions of James and herself, still locked in the embrace of their eternal country dance. She clutched them to her, too numb to move.

"Are you all right?" A young male voice sounded just above her.

She looked up into the face of a teen punk, his expression all concern.

315

"Got to watch your step, it's a bit slippery." He held out his hand, and when Christy took it, he pulled her to her feet. "Here," he added, and scooped up the purse that lodged at a rakish angle in the snow.

She stammered her thanks as she took it. With a wave, he took off at a run to join a couple of other youths who waited a few yards away.

Christy stared blankly at the bag she now held. It *was* hers. But how—?

She made her way to a bench and sank down on the snowy surface. Her purse. The figurines. They shouldn't still be here, not after so many weeks. . . .

Unless no time had passed. . . . Her trembling increased.

She swallowed, and the cold, hard edges of the figurines bit into her palms as her hands tightened on them. No time had passed. Had none of it been real? Could she have dreamed the whole thing? And James—dear, beloved James—had he been no more than a phantom of her longings?

She closed her eyes, too confused to make sense of this. Her heart ached, unable to tell the difference between illusion and truth.

After several long minutes, she dragged herself to her feet. She couldn't sit here, mourning a love—a man—who existed only in her dreams. The icy wind whipped about her, chilling her to her soul, plastering against her legs her snow-dampened skirt . . . her snow-dampened *Regency* skirt! She stared at the rose muslin with its single flounce hanging about her booted ankles.

It *had* been real. All of it. And James. . . . She dragged his book from her pocket and opened it to the last few chapters. The print remained solid, unshifting, the tale the one of the house party.

Not one of revolution. And not so much as a mention of a Stuart met her rapidly scanning gaze. Had he escaped Sir Dominic and gone to live in exile? She closed her eyes, and the vision rose before her of him clutching his chest, falling. . . .

He had died. The realization struck her like a physical blow.

There, in that dingy lodging, without her, he had died.

James. . . . An aching void opened deep within her, an emptiness which she knew would never be filled, would never heal. She had lost him forever.

She looked down at the figures in her hands. All she had left of him. . . . She clutched them to her, and stared into nothingness, numb and empty and drained. . . .

"Christy?" A deep, familiar voice sounded behind her.

She spun about, incredulous. For one long, disbelieving moment she stared at the disheveled figure, then flung herself into his arms. "James . . ." she breathed, his name no more than a whisper on her lips.

"Careful." A shaky laugh escaped him. "I have a small cut there."

"I thought you were dead . . ." She clung to him, half laughing, half sobbing. He was here, alive, not torn from her. . . .

His mouth found hers, and he kissed her with a thoroughness that took her breath away. His lips brushed her cheek, her eyes, then returned to her mouth with the fierceness of desperation. Joy and disbelief ran rampant in her, until she had to draw back, to actually *see* it was really him.

"How—how did you get here?" she managed at last.

"The same way you did." He smoothed back her hair, then kissed her once more. "When you disappeared like that, the others were too startled to react. I realized what had happened—and that my disappearing as completely would be the only way to prevent revolution. Sir Dominic and his cabal—" He shook his head. "They never would have given up until the country ran with blood."

"So you inverted the ball." And gave up his way of life, everything he had known.

His arms tightened about her. "It seemed the only chance to avert the revolution. I'd have tried it at once, but I had to bandage that slice Farnham gave me, first."

"Farnham. He—he caught the snowdome," she said, recalling the whirling scene. "What happened to him?"

317

"He's dead." James's jaw set. "Sir Dominic, though, will be all right—if he recovers from the shock of seeing us both vanish."

A tremulous laugh set Christy's shoulders shaking. "He must have, by now." Her gaze fell on his strained face. "Come, you're cold and hurt. Oh, James, let's get back to my hotel."

"Where?" For the first time he looked about, at the people, the cars on the street. An expression of wonder entered his dark eyes, and he shook his head. "I've left my own time," he said, as if the reality of it just struck him. "My God, what have I done?"

She sobered. "Sacrificed your birthright to save England."

"Have I?" For several long seconds, he stared at her in silence. Then his lips curved in a slow smile. "In that case, I've freed my descendants from the curse of being pretenders to a throne. I can continue my work—" He broke off. "We shall have to visit the Bank of England to see how well I provided for us—and the poor of this time."

"We're bound to be filthy rich. We'll be able to fund all sorts of shelters and programs. My brother—" she broke off as laughter again welled within her. "James, do you realize no time at all has passed while I've been gone? It's only the beginning of December, still. That means we can be there for my brother's wedding."

A warm glow suffused his entire face. "And what of ours?"

For a moment, her heart stopped. "I'm not a European princess."

"Good. The few I've met have been dead bores."

To be his wife. . . . Happiness surged through her, driving out the last traces of pain, and she snuggled her head against his shoulder.

"I suppose I'll have to establish a new identity." He rubbed his chin on the top of her curls, and a contemplative gleam lit his eyes. "I believe the poor won't begrudge us a little of all that money so I can buy whatever papers are necessary. Surely such things must be obtainable in this time?"

She nodded, bemused and relieved. James, in any era, appeared extremely capable.

His lips brushed hers. "Let's go. I have a burning desire to obtain a marriage license." He caught her hand, and saw the enameled figurines she still gripped. "The snowdome. Never mind, my love, I'll put another together for you."

"Don't you dare!" She tucked the pieces into her purse. "What if it took me away from you, again? We'll put them in a display case, where they'll—where *we'll*—be safe."

"An excellent suggestion." He led her forward, only to stop in his tracks as he stared at a Christmas banner which hung from a lamp post beside the path. "Decorations all over the streets, just like you said." The last remnants of tension faded from his expression, and he grinned down at her, as delighted as any of the Runcorns' boys. "Two Christmases in one year. Come, my love, I've got years of traditions to catch up on. Show me what Christmas is like in *our* time."

ELEGANCE AND CHARM WITH ZEBRA'S REGENCY ROMANCES

A LOGICAL LADY   (3277, $3.95)
by Janice Bennett

When Mr. Frederick Ashfield arrived at Halliford Castle after two years on the continent, Elizabeth could not keep her heart from fluttering uncontrollably. But things were in a dreadful state. Frederick had come straight from the Grange, his ancestral home, where he argued with his cousin, Viscount St. Vincent. After his sudden departure, the Viscount had been found murdered.

After an attempt on his life Frederick knew what must be done: he must risk his very life, and Lizzie's dearest hopes, to trap a deadly killer!

AN UNQUESTIONABLE LADY   (3151, $3.95)
by Rosina Pyatt

Too proud to apply for financial assistance, Miss Claudia Tallon was desperate enough to answer the advertisement. But why would any man of wealth and position need to advertise for a wife? Then she saw his name and understood why. *Giles Veryland.* No decent lady would dream of associating with such a rake.

This was to be a marriage of convenience—Giles convenience. Claudia was hardly in a position to expect a love match, and Giles could not be bothered. The two were thus eminently suited to one another, if only they could stop arguing long enough to find out!

FOREVER IN TIME   (3129, $3.95)
by Janice Bennett

Erika Von Hamel had been living on a tiny British island for two years when the stranger Gilbert Randall was up on her shore after a boating accident. Erika had little patience for his game of pretending that the year was 1812 and he was somehow lost in time. But she found him examining in detail her models of the Napoleonic battles, and she wanted to believe that he really was from Regency England—a romantic hero that she thought only existed in romance books . . .

Gilbert Randall was quite sure the outcome of the war depended on information he was carrying—but he was no longer there to deliver it. He must get back to his own time to insure that history would not be irrevocably altered. And that meant he must take Erika with him, although he shuddered to think of the havoc she would cause in Regency England—and in his own heart!

Available wherever paperbacks are sold, or order direct from the Publisher. Send cover price plus 50¢ per copy for mailing and handling to Zebra Books, Dept. 3581, 475 Park Avenue South, New York, N.Y. 10016. Residents of New York, New Jersey and Pennsylvania must include sales tax. DO NOT SEND CASH.